Book VI

GAMADIN

The

WILD StraiN

Tom Kirkbride

WIGTON

Publishing

Also by Tom Kirkbride

Gamadin Book Series

> Book I - *Gamadin: Word of Honor*
> Book II - *Gamadin: Mons*
> Book III - *Gamadin: Distant Suns*
> Book IV - *Gamadin:* Gazz
> Book V - *Gamadin: Core*
> Book VI - *Gamadin: The Wild Strain*

Gamadin Short Stories

> *Stinky's Island*
> *Surfing Roots*
> *Apollos' Flags*

Gamadin Titles in the Works

> *Lakewood* (A Prequil)
> Book VII - *Gamadin: Mamua*

Copyright Notice

Published by Wigton Publishing Company
32857 Fox Lane, Cottage Grove, OR 97424

1st Paperback Ed. Copyright ©2018 by Tom Kirkbride

Gamadin, Harlowe Pylott, Mowgi, robobs, ceffyls, dakadudes, swampdaks, Gamacoin, characters, names and related indicia are trademarks of ©Tom Kirkbride.

For ordering information or special discounts for bulk purchases, please contact:

Wigton Publishing Company, 32857 Fox Lane,
Cottage Grove, OR 97424 (541) 246-4135

Design and composition by Tom Kirkbride.

Kirkbride, Tom (Thomas K.)
  Gamadin. Book 6, The Wild Strain / Tom Kirkbride. -- 1st Paperback Edition

  ISBN: 978-0-9883633-3-5

1. Extraterrestrial beings--Fiction. 2. Space warfare--Fiction. 3. Surfers--California--Fiction. 4. Science fiction. 5. Fantasy fiction. I. Title.

Printed in USA

10 09 08 10 9 8 7 6 5 4 3 2 1
1st Paperback Printed Edition

For my wife, Nancy...
            aka "The General."

and

For the Bros of Lakewood
who were gracious enough
to lend me their names,
their monikers, and their
personas for this book . . .

Thank you.

You are all true Wild Strains!

TK

Who were the Gamadin?

Many, many thousands of years ago, when Hitt and Gibb were the cultural elite centers of the Omni quadrant, the Gamadin ruled the cosmos -- not in an authoritarian way, but as a protective force against the spreading Death of evil empires and their acts of conquest and domination. A wise and very ancient group of planets from the galactic core formed an alliance to create the most powerful police force the galaxy had ever seen. This force would be independent of any one state or planet. They were called "Gamadin."

Translated from the ancient scrolls of Amerloi, Gamadin means: "From the center, for all that is good." The sole mission of the Gamadin was to defend the freedom and happiness of peaceful planets everywhere, regardless of origin or wealth. It was said that a single Gamadin ship was so powerful, it could destroy an empire.

Unfortunately, after many centuries of peace, the Gamadin had performed their job too well. Few saw reason for such a powerful presence in their own backyard when the Death of war and the aggressive empire building were remnants of an ancient past. So what was left of the brave Gamadin simply withered away and was lost, never to be heard from again.

However, the ancient scrolls of Amerloi foretold of its resurrection:

"For it is written that one day the coming Death will lift its evil head and awaken the fearsome Gamadin of the galactic core. And the wrath of the Gamadin will be felt again throughout the stars, and lo, while some people trembled in despair, still more rejoiced; for the wrath of the Gamadin will cleanse the stars for all; and return peace to the heavens . . . ."

"The Dragon has always believed that the earth is His, and of course, he's mistaken."

The Watchman
December 22, 2014

"The bankers and their enforcers, Governments, do not play 'nice' by ANY means!"

Sovereign Economist
October 24, 2014

"There is always a power behind the throne…either wanting to sit in it directly, or win it in secret."

The Watchman
June 5, 2015

CODE IS LAW

The
Wild Strain

"All of humanity was created to be slaves.

Our species is not alone in that. There are many slave species out there in the vastness of universe.
Even our paranoid power elite will now admit to trillions of trillions of planets...so you can bet your ass we have more slave species cousins out there.

We may well be different, if not unique, in that we are the slaves abandoned, the strain run wild. Lost to the vagaries of universe by a whim of universe, we humans are the self-modifying genetic wild child in the galactic garden of created species. We are as universe wished us to be. Specifically universe arranged to have us isolated, and left to mature on our own.

Unique among slave species? Perhaps.
Extremely rare? Almost certainly.
Extremely valuable due to our rarity? Also, almost certainly.

They, the master species, are gone. What remains, are the remains. Ruins, and all our questions, about humans, universe, our creators, and what the hell to do next?

My thought is to say, screw it! Human we are made, and human shall we be.
And we have an attitude!

So watch out cousins, here comes the wild strain!"

Excerpt: *Two Tribes, Alta Report*
by Clif High
April, 2017
Halfpasthuman.com

1

Return to Nod

"CODE IS LAW, Captain," Ian Wizzixs said to Harlowe Pylott, as he handed him the blue card. The two were standing beside a large open hatch, which offered an unobstructed view of the planet Nod. After a harrowing journey to the galactic core to repair their ship, Millawanda, she was now fixed. She was better than new, better than the day she was first launched 17,000 years ago! She had so many upgrades that Harlowe figured it would take a lifetime to understand them all, and even then, he and his crew would only be scratching the surface of what the repair facility at Orixy, Millie's origin, had done to her. The first blow-your-socks-off moment came when the massive saucer left Orixy for home and went to light-speed. In their eagerness to get home, Harlowe ordered Maa Dev to put the pedal-to-the-metal, not realizing that their new propulsion upgrades went far beyond her normal 2000 times hyper-light cruising speed. Instead of racing through space like she once did, Millawanda now folded space like an accordion, increasing her speed exponentially. What had previously taken months to travel 35,000 light-years to the galactic core, she now made in mere days. So, on their voyage back to Earth, and with much less flight time to consider, Ian and the two Nodian crewmen, Cheesa and Maa Dev, had requested a slight course change back to Nod.

Harlowe studied the card between his fingers. On one side was a round gold coin with a capital G in the center surrounded by stars. On the back was a holographic image of Molly and Rhud lying in the sun. Mowgi, in full dragon mode, was flying in the sky, while the ceffyls grazed in the background, and Pigpo walked into a small pond. "What's it do?"

"Use it like a debit card. I thought it might come in handy when you get home."

Harlowe read the name on the front. "Gamacoin, huh? Cool."

"Chee gave me the idea. On Nod, the resistance used a kind of digital money that the authorities couldn't trace. They passed a card like this between themselves and used it to buy food, clothes, you name it, just like cash. Anything money could buy, this could buy. She says the swampdaks were unable to trace it. I tweaked it a little bit. There were some flaws in the code but it's cool now."

"No jail breaks?" Harlowe asked, referring to hacking the code.

"None. It's law."

Harlowe smiled with an added wink of appreciation. "Thanks. Is this the only one?"

"Nah, I made a whole slew of them."

He put it in his shirt pocket and asked, "Have you checked your list, Captain Wizzixs?" Harlowe addressed his science officer that way because in a few moments he would be taking *44*, a much smaller version of *Millawanda* to the planet's surface. The Earth-like planet was Cheesa and Maa Dev's home, but they had no plans to stay beyond their mission. They were both Gamadin now, and as proud and honored members of galactic enforcers, they were returning to Nod to clean up the unfinished business they had left behind months ago.

Harlowe had originally nixed the idea outright when Ian first proposed the idea to him in his cabin. "No way, Mr. Wizzixs. It's too dangerous. Wait until we have a little R & R on Earth, and we'll come back here and drain the swampdaks the Gamadin way." "Swampdaks" was the crew's new moniker for the corrupt groups of monarchs, dictators, political leaders, and or whatever governing bodies sought to control everybody and everything. They all had one thing in common: power! So they were swampdaks to the Gamadin.

Ian sat casually on the edge of Harlowe's desk. Only two other people were allowed to take that kind of liberty without finding themselves body slammed against a bulkhead. One was his First Officer and second in command, Matt Riverstone, and the other was his science officer and soul mate, Leucadia Mars. He smiled knowingly saying, "I told them you would say that but…"

Harlowe interrupted: "But what? They want to do it themselves because Nod is their home and their problem?"

"You talked to Cheesa!"

Harlowe grinned, displaying his well-rehearsed all-knowing guru smirk. "No. Because that's what I would want to do if Earth were overrun by swampdaks."

"Thankfully President Delmonte and Tinker are running things now."

Harlowe could think of no two people better to run the United States government back home than his mom, now First Lady of the United States and her husband, President Pete Delmonte. "Ain't that the truth?"

Ian's blue Gamadin eyes stayed firm in his support for Cheesa and Maa Dev. Harlowe had said no, but by looking at him and knowing him since they were small kids growing up in Lakewood, California, Ian knew it wasn't an "absolute" no, just a "first no." There was some wiggle room there, if he had made a good enough case. However, when it came to his crew, there was no one who had more confidence in his crew to get the job done than Harlowe. "They're ready, Dog," Ian said with a strong hint that they wanted this mission.

Harlowe took a breath, mulling over the idea of allowing part of his crew to leave without the support of the mothership and the rest of the crew. This wasn't a slam-dunk. If things went south, and they usually did, calling for help would take some time, even with their new propulsion system.

"How long until I have to make a decision?" Harlowe finally asked.

"Two hours."

"We've come that far already?"

Ian chuckled. "Yeah, we're really bookin'. Folding space is a game changer. We'll be home before Christmas."

Harlowe leaned back in his chair in amazement. He knew they were going fast, but not that fast. "I'll say. I can see the White House now. Tinker will have it all decorated in Marine Corps green and red."

"No doubt." Ian changed the subject. "Didn't Dodger have a birthday last month?"

Harlowe thought a moment. Unable to remember dates while they were in space, he tapped a holographic screen above his desk for a calendar. "He did. Wow, the little dork is ten now."

"He's going to want his own uniform, too," Ian noted.

"That's a given. We'll put some special hash marks on his collar."

"Surfboards."

"Perfect! He'd like that." Harlowe kept shaking his head in disbelief. "It seems like yesterday I was smelling his stinky diapers. And now he's ten. Sheessssh."

"There's not many ten-year-olds with his kind of courage. Without him on Gazz, we'd still be there sailing the high seas with the Tails."

Harlowe went serious, as though the fear of God suddenly struck him. "If you ever tell Tinker about that trip, I mean what really happened, I'll take you back there, and you'll be scrubbing decks with the Tails for the rest of your days on the *Millie*."

Ian raised his right hand, making a pledge. "Your secret is golden, Dog. What goes on with the Gamadin stays with the Gamadin."

Harlowe sighed and relaxed. "Good answer, Wiz."

Ian slid off the desk and headed back to the bridge. "Let me know when you've made your decision."

Ian had activated the cabin door when Harlowe called to him. "Wiz..."

Ian looked back. "Yo..."

"Permission granted."

"Come again?"

"Set course for Nod. You got three weeks to clean things up, and then I want you home for Christmas. Deal?"

Ian left with a satisfied grin and a thumbs up. "Deal!"

Nod's blue oceans, swirling cloud systems, and brown and green soft sandy landmasses were incredibly Earth-like. If the continents were shaped a little this way and that, one could easily believe it was Earth they were looking down upon through the hatchway.

Ian returned a confidant wink. "Aye, list is complete. Don't worry, we'll find out who's been naughty down there, starting with Imperator Muuk."

Harlowe gave him a soft fist on the chin. "You the man, Captain Wizzixs. Get 'er done."

From the top of *44's* ramp, a female's voice called down. "Your ship is ready, Captain."

Ian saw Cheesa smiling down at them. He gave her a pride-filled nod and a hand signal. "Be right there, Chee."

"You have a fine crew," Harlowe praised, his self-assured blue eyes leaving little doubt of how proud he was for Ian. He put the card in his pocket. "So what's the second thing?"

"Something for Dodger's birthday. You'll love it as much as he will. Guaranteed. When the robobs have finished it at Dodger's Place, you can make sure the kinks are ironed out."

"I'll do that."

When it came to his ship or his crew, Harlowe never liked being out of the loop on anything. But he also knew what Ian had conjured up was, for all practical purposes, all in fun. So he let the confidentiality between his science officer and his brother slide. It was their thing, their little secret together. Let them have their amusement, he figured. He trusted Ian, as he did all his crew. Besides, it was good for morale. And after being gone for so long, everyone needed a diversion unrelated to Gamadin life. When they finally touched down on Earth, his crew would go their own way for a while and do the things they had been hankering to do for months when they got home. Riverstone wanted to go to a movie, drive a real car, eat in a real restaurant, and go to a Dodger game. Simon had another sci-fi script about their journey he would hawk to Saul, his Hollywood movie agent, starring himself, of course, as Julian Starr in *To the Galactic Core and Back*. It was another mega hit, he boasted. Leucadia was eager to see what Jewels had done with the new additions to her Newport Beach house, and hoped the Mars financial empire had held up in her long absence. Jefferson Braxton, her handpicked, handsome attorney, who handled their family's affairs for twenty-one years, had been managing the trillion-dollar empire in her absence. "We've only been gone two months," Harlowe told her. "It was nearly three months, Pylott," she corrected him. "Three, huh? Well, still, Mr. Braxton's a smart dude. Your Dreamliner will still be there," he kidded. "Don't worry about Jewels, either. He's got great taste. When you see Riverstone and him playing the ponies, everything will be cool, Babe, just like we never left."

Harlowe sighed heavily. Consoling her was a wasted effort. She was going to worry every waking moment until they put down, regardless. That was just the way it was going to be, and there was no use trying to fight it. As for him, he had only two wants: to see his mom first, kiss and hug her; then to fly to an isolated surfing spot in the south Pacific with Dodger. He also thought about how his mother, Tinker, was doing married to the President of the United States, and how Dodger was doing living in the White House. For a ten-year-old surfer dude, being stuck in a big white house so far away from the California beaches would be tough. Harlowe chuckled inside. Yeah, rough life Dodger, being around all those cool Secret Service guys and badass U.S. Marine guards. He bet the bank California was an afterthought.

"Captain..." Ian's voice called to Harlowe. "Permission to disembark."

Ian was already at the top of the ramp looking down at Harlowe, waiting for a salute to carry on. "Aye. Permission granted, Captain Wizzixs. Safe trip. See you in three weeks. No excuses," Harlowe saluted, acknowledging his request.

Ian returned the salute. "Aye, Captain, count on it."

"Get out of here, then, Captain."

Ian gave one more thumbs up, and then the hatchway close behind him. Harlowe wrinkled away the sting he felt in his nose. With an added lump in his throat, he watched 44 slide through the open gap in the hull and float down toward the planet. Two seconds later, the small saucer blinked away and was gone from sight. Harlowe waited for the hatch to close before he ordered, "Set a course for home, Mr. Platter."

Monday's deep voice replied happily, *"Aye, aye, Captain. Home it is!"*

2
Saturn is MIA

Millawanda Bridge

"WHERE'S SATURN?" RIVERSTONE wondered aloud, as he stood up from the center command chair and surveyed the vastness of space through the giant forward windows of Millawanda's bridge. They had just dropped out of hyper-light a billion miles out from the sun, expecting to see the gas giant planet and all it's glorious rings floating like a huge beach ball out the port side window. But oddly, Saturn was gone.

Riverstone turned to Monday, who was at his system's station studying main readouts on the overhead holograph. "What gives, Mr. Platter?"

Monday eyed Riverstone like he was joking. "Saturn's missing?"

"Yeah, she's MIA."

Monday checked the navigation array. "The planet should be right off our sunrise bow." During their training days on Mars, there was no left side or right side because *Millawanda* was a perfect circle. Points on a compass were meaningless to them. The sun, however, on Mars, where they were marooned during their training, always came up on the same side of the ship and set on the other side. So for the rookie crew, who had no experience with port and starboard terminology, the left side of the ship became the "sunrise" side and the right "sunset." And it's been that way ever since. Problem solved. Monday pointed to the left. "Right over…" But it wasn't there. "It's missing all right."

Harlowe came through his cabin door off the bridge and immediately felt the unease. "Problem, Mr. Riverstone?" Even though they were childhood friends, once a crewman stepped on the bridge, ship protocol became law, no matter what. First names and monikers were dropped for the appropriate mister or miss or Ms. title.

"No Saturn, Captain," Riverstone answered.

Harlowe came to the center command chair, as Riverstone slid off to the right to his normal First Officer's seat. He studied the upper holographic screen, where the orbits of the planets circled the Sun. "Where is it then?"

Monday quickly scanned the solar system and found it far out of position. "There, Captain," he said, pointing up at the screen, "She's at two o'clock."

"And she should be here with us at six, Captain," Riverstone added.

"We better get Lu up here ASAP. Where is she?" Harlowe asked.

"It's dinner time. She's down at poolside, feeding the animals with Rerun and Mr. Prigg," Monday replied.

Harlowe looked up, wondering why half his crew had to be on their pet's mealtime when a couple of robobs could do the same task. "Okay, call her up here." He held up his hand. "But be sure and ask nicely, Mr. Platter."

Monday smiled, understanding the caution. "Understood, Captain."

A moment later, Leucadia's holograph appeared on the bridge. She was dressed in a kind of tight-fitting coverall, holding a slab of beef for one of the white tigers. Before she spoke, she tossed it to Rhud who devoured it like an hors d'oeuvre. "Problem, Pylott?" Harlowe glared at her instantly for neglecting bridge protocol. Sometimes he wondered if she did it just to tease him. She gritted her teeth with a rascally grin. "Sorry…ah, Captain. Problem, Sir?"

"We dropped out of hyper-light and—"

She didn't let him finish. "Wow, already? That was fast. Shall I tell Jewels to put our double-doubles on hold?"

Harlowe looked away briefly, sighed, then ordered, "Get up here immediately, Ms. Mars."

"I don't understand. If it's not the double-doubles—"

Now it was Harlowe's turn to cut her off. "Get up here now! We dropped out of hyper-light and Saturn's not where she's supposed to be."

Leucadia's tone changed to one of concern. "Where is she?"

"A third of the way around her orbit."

"How can that be?"

"I don't know. Riverstone doesn't know, Platter doesn't know, and if I asked Mowgi, I'm pretty sure he wouldn't know either. That's why I want your hind end up here, and pronto, so you can figure it out. Now move, lady! Captain out!" And with that, Leucadia's image vanished in a blink. Harlowe turned to Riverstone and Platter, shaking his head. Riverstone opened his mouth to make a comment, when Harlowe pointed a hot finger at his nose. "Don't say it. Not one word, or you're walking home from here."

Riverstone glanced over at Monday, trading snarky expressions. "Not a word, Captain."

Two seconds later, Leucadia stepped off the bridge blinker. "This fast enough for you, Captain?" And knowing she wasn't in a proper uniform for the bridge she added, "I would have dressed, Captain, but I knew you were in a hurry."

"Just find the answer, Ms. Lu, and we'll be happy, and you can go back to feeding the animals," Harlowe said.

"Yes, Sir. Right away Sir," Leucadia replied in her most sarcastic tone. She then looked up at the main screen and asked Monday, "The planets are in their present positions now, Mr. Platter?"

"That's correct, Ms. Lu," Monday answered.

After a quick reflection she came back with, "Wow, that's incredible."

"Why?" Harlowe asked.

"They're all out of whack."

"All? Not just Saturn?" Harlowe asked. "Explain."

Leucadia waved her right hand across the screen. "The planets are all out of sync."

Harlowe, Riverstone, and Monday were all confused.

"Hold on," Leucadia said, as she went to her science station and then came back to the main holo screen to continue her inquires. "Millie," she said to the screen, "position the planets in their orbits where they were the day we left Earth." Instantly, the holo screen placed *Millawanda* in yellow, indicating where she was when they dropped off Dodger before leaving for the galactic core. Sure enough, Saturn was now, not exactly, but pretty close to where she should have been at just past six on the clock.

"Close but no cigar," Riverstone quipped.

"Stay with me, Mr. Riverstone," Leucadia urged, as she directed the screen, "Millie, position the planets forward two months and twenty-one days from that second point in time." She turned to Harlowe. "That's how long we were gone. Eighty-three days and a few hours." As directed, the screen added in red the third planetary position. And there she was. Saturn was now in the exact position she was supposed to be, right off their sunrise bow.

"So why is she way over there," Riverstone asked, pointing at the screen. "and not here?"

"More importantly, why are all the other planets messed up, too?" Harlowe asked.

"Because we've been gone longer than eighty-three days, gentlemen," Leucadia concluded.

Riverstone and Monday's mouths dropped open large enough for a gerbid to pass through. Harlowe asked the all-important question of the day. "So how long is longer?"

Leucadia returned to the screen. "Millie, calculate the time it takes Saturn to travel from the first yellow point to her present location. In Earth time by years and days, if you please."

The screen read: **11 years, 73 days.**

3
What IS That?

Arecibo Observatory
Puerto Rico

THE ARECIBO OBSERVATORY, constructed in the early 1960s and located in a large karst sinkhole in the hilly region of Puerto Rico, is one of the largest radio telescopes on the planet. Its 980-foot wide dish was originally developed to detect incoming ballistic missiles in the 1950s, but with Earth orbiting satellites doing the job, Arecibo turned its attention to more peaceful projects. Nowadays, one of its primary purposes is to assist the SETI project in searching for intelligent life in the universe. On this day, it was pointed along the elliptic in the Canis Minor region, when Astro Engineer Marcee Newton, who had only come on duty five minutes ago, heard the contact alert buzzer go off. The diagnostics had barely completed its run before she poured her first cup of morning joe. *What's up with that?* Thinking it was a minor hiccup from the 900-ton receiver platform when the azimuth arm finished its rotation, she finished pouring her coffee, added a healthy swig of half and half, and walked unhurriedly back to the receiver station to reset the arm. She was

11

about to do another complete F9 boot-up and clear the entire system of readouts when a long thin line on the computer screen coming out of the Procyon star group caught her attention.

"My, oh my, what IS that?" Marcee asked herself, believing it was starting to be one of those days when everything that can go wrong, does go wrong. She backed off the F9 and set her coffee aside to check the gravitation scale on another screen. "Oh my God!" It was off the scale. How is that possible? She tapped the intercom and called, "Mike, I need you in the SETI control room."

"What? Marcee, I can't find my cup anywhere!" Astro Engineer Mike Farrah shouted back over the intercom. From the slamming of cabinet doors and clinking of glass she heard, Farrah was having trouble locating his favorite coffee mug, Hazel, again. Whenever he came back from his weekend, the cleaning crew had always put it somewhere he couldn't find it. *"Christ, why can't Silvia just leave Hazel on its hook?"* Until Farrah had his first jolt of caffeine, he was a bear to be around.

"Mike!" Marcee called again.

"WHAT?"

"GET UP HERE NOW, DAMMIT!"

The slamming doors continued, along with a string of four-letter words, before Farrah shouted back, *"I want my cup, Marcee! Have you seen it?"*

"Forget your damn cup, Mike, SETI has a hit!"

The slamming suddenly stopped, followed by footsteps and a door opening and closing. A moment later Farrah entered the SETI control room, tying his long blond hair back into ponytail. "You sure it's not an azimuth hiccup?" he asked her, as his eyes went straight to the computer screen.

Marcee pointed at the thin green line coming out of Procyon. "You tell me."

Farrah studied the line. "It's gotta be some kind of malfunction. Nothing moves that fast."

Marcee pulled his arm toward the gravitron station. "I thought that, too, until I saw this. The object's gravity waves are off the charts."

Farrah looked over the screen and added a few tweaks of his own to confirm the reading. "Wow, it checks out. And unless we find some bug in the system, it's a live one, all right. What's its location?"

"A billion miles out."

"Saturn's orbit. That means these readings are two and half-hours old. Something traveling that fast could be anywhere by now," Farrah calculated. "Do we have a course direction yet?"

Marcee pulled a sheet of paper from the printout bin and handed it to Farrah. ""We do. It's Earth. Direct line."

"Holy crap!"

"Who do we contact on this one?" Marcee asked. "What's the protocol on a light-speed Unidentified coming to pay us a visit?"

Farrah stared at Marcee with an answer. "Whatever it is, it's not a breaking news item. It's military."

"Why military, Mike? They could be friendly travelers. The military will shoot first and ask questions later."

Farrah kept shaking his head. "It's not for us to decide, Marcee. Sure, they could be the Jetsons coming here on vacation, or they could be one of Julian Starr's space creatures come to eat us all alive, or something in between. We just don't know. Look at the gravity waves that thing is putting out. This is way beyond our pay grade. You want to be responsible if this thing turns out to be a full assault on our planet?"

Marcee fell silent. Mike was right. They lacked enough information to give any kind of intellectual answer on who or what this object was. The Unidentified could very well be innocent aliens dropping by to say hello. And even if that were the case, how would the world see them? Judging from the past, probably not so well. She recalled from her history class in college, Orson Wells' radio play of *War of the Worlds* in the 1930s. Back then there was all kinds of hysteria when listeners of the broadcast thought there was a real live alien invasion of Earth from outer space. And that was only a radio play. What would happen to the planet when it was the real thing? Were she and Mike qualified to make that decision for the entire planet? The answer was clear.

"No," was Marcee's response.

4
Full Dark

Cruising Into the Inner Planets

AFTER THE SHOCK of time loss sunk in, Riverstone tried to disguise his fear by asking Harlowe a silly question. "Does this mean you just slipped from number one son in the Pylott family to number two?"

Harlowe was as stunned as everyone else and went to Leucadia, genuinely disturbed by the revelation. "Does it?"

Her insanely beautiful green eyes came to Harlowe with a mixture of sympathy, reality, and amusement as she replied, "I think so."

"Wow," Riverstone quipped, "one quick trip to the galactic core, and you're the baby of the family."

Harlowe found no humor in his observation at all. He quickly turned to Monday and ordered him, "Tap into an Earth broadcast, Mr. Platter, and find us today's date." Despite the fact that it takes a little more than an hour for an Earth broadcast to reach *Millawanda*, it didn't matter. An hour this way or that was unimportant when they were talking missing years.

"Aye, Captain," and after a few quick probes, Monday had an answer no one wanted to hear. "Every broadcast is the same. The year is 2020.

14

Do you want the month and the day, too?" Monday asked the bridge.

Harlowe sat down in Leucadia's command chair. It was the nearest place he found without falling on the floor. "No...I've heard enough."

Riverstone had more sarcasm to announce. "Our parents are going to be real happy with us. Where have you been for the last eleven years? You don't write, you don't call. Oh, sorry about that, Mom. We had to go to the center of the galaxy to fix our ride. Mail delivery is a little slow, you know..."

"All right, all right," Harlowe cut in, with an edge to his voice, "we get it."

"Do you, Captain? ELEVEN YEARS! Eleven years have passed!" He glared at everyone on the bridge, including Prigg. "Are you kidding me? Eleven years! Oh, my God! No one is going to know who Rerun is. And Saul...his agent. How has he survived without his number one client?"

Simon just caught the last of Riverstone's rant as he stepped off the blinker. "What about Saul? What happened to him? Is he okay?" Simon looked at the dire faces around the bridge and knew something bad had happened. "He's dead, isn't he? Saul's dead."

Leucadia went to Simon, as he walked hesitantly forward and held him by the shoulders. He looked past her at Harlowe's troubled silence, and she said to him, "When we came out of hyper-light, we discovered Earth is eleven years out of sync with us."

Leucadia's words had no real meaning, until Harlowe's eyes met his and the gravity of the moment was clear. This was no joke. "Listen, to Lu, Mr. Bolt."

Simon's focus traveled down to Leucadia. "What...eleven what?" he kept asking.

Riverstone, in his usual cavalier manner, replied straight out, "Years, brah. Eleven years have passed since we left Earth, so we don't know if Saul is alive or not. That's not the point. The point is eleven frickin' years have gone by without us tagging along, pard!"

Simon went to Harlowe again for confirmation. "Captain?"

Harlowe walked over to his crewman. "Appears so, Mr. Bolt." He pointed up at the overhead screen. "We expected to see Saturn as six o'clock, but now she's up there at two. Lu figured out the problem, and

Mr. Platter confirmed it just before you stepped off the blinker."

As Simon came to Monday, he got another silent validation that what everyone was saying was right. "Wow, eleven years, huh?"

Leucadia turned back around to Harlowe, with another eye-opener. "That means Digger and your mom are no longer in the White House."

"How do you know that?" Riverstone asked.

"Because U.S. Presidents are only allowed to serve two terms, unless Congress passed a Constitutional amendment canceling the 22nd Amendment. Digger, I mean President Delmonte, if he was elected to two terms, is no longer President," Leucadia explained.

Queasiness came over Riverstone at the possibility of another swampdak President like Sandborne, who tried to kill their parents in his effort to get his hands on the most powerful weapon in the galaxy... *Millawanda*. His mind was so distracted, he couldn't think of the man's name who was next in line to be President. "That attorney of yours. Jim what's his name?"

"Jefferson Braxton?"

"Yeah, wasn't he in line to take Delmonte's place after he left office?"

"Yes, that was the plan. But eleven years is a lot of time, Matthew. In politics eleven years is forever. Before we left, I put Jeff in charge of Mars Corporation. We should contact him as soon as possible to get up to speed on the current state of our country's affairs."

Harlowe agreed. "Aye."

"Captain," Monday said cautiously. "I have some info on Mars Corporation. The reports say under the Civil Asset Forfeiture laws of the United States, all of Ms. Lu's property and Corporate assets were seized by the government."

Leucadia suddenly lost her casualness and became instantly hostile. "They what? Under what grounds?"

"Tax evasion and drug trafficking, Ma'am."

"Are you serious?"

"Those were the headlines, Ms. Lu, right after President Delmonte was impeached for treasonous acts of misappropriating government funds and selling secrets to the Russians and Chinese," Monday stated.

"Digger would never betray his country!" she fumed. "What about Braxton? He would have fought it. He was the President's personal lawyer."

Monday kept reading. "There was no trial, Ms. Lu. The government just took it."

"No trial without due process? How can that be? I thought we were a nation of laws."

That made Riverstone as angry as Leucadia. "My dad will have something to say about this." To Harlowe he said, "The question is, what are we going to do about it?"

Harlowe didn't have an answer for that, but asked Monday, "How long ago was Delmonte impeached?"

"Six years, Captain. Halfway through his second term, he was found guilty by the House of Representatives and impeached for high crimes and misdemeanors."

"Where is he now?" Riverstone asked.

"A federal prison in Colorado," Monday replied.

"What about my mom and Dodger? Anything on them?" Harlowe asked, hoping for some good news in all this muck.

It took more time than Monday wanted, but he found what Harlowe deSired. "Here it is, Captain. It seems both your mom and Dodger were nowhere to be found. The government has been looking for them for years, and they still haven't found them."

Leucadia had been looking over a second screen next to him, when she suddenly covered her mouth and began to lose her balance. Luckily, Monday caught her, as he looked over her screen. "It's Braxton. The Mars corporate jet went down somewhere over the China Sea just after leaving Hong Kong. No survivors or the plane were ever found, Captain."

Harlowe went to Leucadia and gathered her in his arms. She looked up, her bright green eyes full of tears. "This is ugly, Harlowe. It's wrong. All wrong. We were never into drugs, and we always paid our taxes."

Harlowe dabbed her eyes with his sleeve. "I know, Babe, we'll figure it out."

"My dad will have some answers," Riverstone said. "He was well connected in California. I would like to start there if that's okay, Captain."

Simon added, "Saul, too, Skipper. He's Hollywood. Talk about connections, he's got a ton in New York, Washington, London, and Tel Aviv."

Harlowe kissed Leucadia on the forehead. "You okay?"

Harlowe's shoulder was the strength she needed to get her composure back. "No, but I'm all right. I wasn't expecting Jeff to…" She started crying again, but Jewels came out of nowhere with a hanky for her and glass of Blue Stuff. "Thank you, Jewels."

"We need to fix this, Captain," Riverstone said.

Harlowe didn't have the luxury of feeling blue. About two seconds was all the time he had for a good sulk before his mind began to calculate. "We will. But we're not going in with guns blazing until we find our parents and make sure they're okay first. For now we go in dark and gather the info we need to get ourselves straight on the present. Understood?"

"Aye, Captain," Riverstone agreed for everyone.

Back to Monday, Harlowe asked, "Where is General Branch? Is he still at the Pentagon?"

Monday's eyes went wide and his teeth clenched. "No Sir. He's in the cell with President Delmonte. They're roomies, Captain."

Harlowe stared at the tiny specks of light against the blackness of space. In the time it took *Millawanda* to drop out of hyperspace, until now, she had had traveled past the orbit of Jupiter and the asteroid belt, and was now approaching Mars. His concentration was totally on the tiny blue speck of reflected light dead ahead. "Good. We won't have to look for him then."

Leucadia eased under his arm and handed him the half-empty glass of Blue Stuff. "You have a plan, don't you, Pylott?" she asked so softly that only he could hear. "I can see it in your eyes."

Harlowe remained silent. There was no point in discussing anything at the moment. His way had always been to keep his cards close to his chest until the time was right. And now, when everyone was in a what-do-we-do-next tizzy, they all had to stay calm, and keep everything at arm's length. Leucadia didn't expect immediate action either. She knew the way he worked. The crew knew it, too. They all knew it, and they all had that confidence a plan was already in motion. Finally, he took the glass of Blue Stuff, downed it, and returned the glass to Jewels. Harlowe sat down in his center seat and gave the order, "Full dark, Mr. Platter."

"Aye, Captain, full dark."

"Mr. Riverstone. Mr. Bolt. If you would take your stations, please."

"Aye, Captain," they said together. Simon obediently walked to his weapons station, and Riverstone took his chair at the right hand of his captain.

"Mr. Prigg."

"Yes, Your Majesty."

"Set course for Lu's Place," Harlowe ordered.

"Aye, Your Majesty."

"Lu's Place, Captain?" Riverstone asked.

"We need some quiet time."

As *Millawanda* altered her course for Mars, she went dark. Not a satellite listening device, not a single radar installation or telescope on Earth was able to see or detect the 54th Century ship of the stars. They were so completely and utterly invisible to the planet that no Earthly technology could detect them.

Harlowe rubbed the pocket containing the blue card Ian had given him, as he leaned over to Leucadia. "It's not the homecoming we planned, is it, Babe?"

She reached over and squeezed his hand, her tears still lingering. She was steady as a rock, though, competent like always, ready for payback. "It never is, Pylott."

5

Hokey-Pokey

Vatican Advanced Technology Telescope (VATT)
Mt. Graham, Arizona

IT WAS SUNSET on Mount Graham, high in the remote Pinaleño Mountains in southeastern Arizona. The riot of blood colors was at their zenith; reds, oranges, and yellows raging war against the dark purples, indigos, and bruised colored strata of the coming night. It was then that the chime of Father Mike's email notification sounded on his iPhone. Father Mike, as everyone knew him, a lanky, easy-going, grey-haired priest, was the head research astronomer for the Vatican Advanced Binocular twin 8.4-meter telescope. In one hour and twenty-four minutes he would be opening the observatory's outer doors to peer deep into the heavens. His first search would take him to the constellation Orion, his favorite. The urgent email from a colleague and close friend, Deborah Peele, PhD, director of operations at the Mopro Radio Telescope in the outback of Coonabarabran, New South Wales, Australia, changed those plans. The email read: OPEN ENCRYPTED FILE NOW!!!!! Followed by five explanation points.

Father Mike's chest stiffened. The good father was a calm man and not prone to visible displays of excitement. He was, after all, a man of God. He was well aware, however, that Deborah Peele was his opposite. Calm under pressure would hardly describe her personality. She was outwardly passionate, and would call at any hour, day or night, for his opinion. The Comet Peele she discovered in 2018 brought her world fame. Their two collaborations were extraordinary. The first was the discovery of an Earth-like planet around Proxima Centauri called Proxima b. It was 4.2 light-years from Earth, and with the VATT, they were able to determine Proxima b had many Earth-like qualities. Their second partnership on gravitational waves was completed last year. That one changed physics history when it was announced the first direct detection of gravitational waves — ripples that stretch and compress space itself—verifying Einstein's fundamental link between space and time. She hit the roof on that one, and rightfully so, he felt. Even so, she had never written him an email with such urgency before. This was completely out of character for her.

After deciphering the 26-symbol blockchain coded phrase, Father Mike opened the email and read the contents:

Fr. Mike, Discovered Object first detected at 0231 AEST, Canis Minor Constellation, RA 7h, 51s, DEC +2° 15' 29.98", AZM +129 09' 13.43". Traveling .7832 speed of light. Absurd, I know. The radio charts say otherwise. See support doc attachments. Object is indeed moving beyond all comprehension on direct path to 4th planet, RA 3h, 60'0 5", DEC 17° 28' 51.34". AZM +50 58' 37.61". At current rate of speed Object will arrive at said planet 33 minutes into your first run. Can you verify with Pope Scope?   DP

Father Mike's glasses nearly fell from his nose as he fumbled to readjust them on his face. He grabbed his hands to calm his shakes. If true, if Deborah's sighting was real, if an object could travel at three-quarters light-speed, what did this all mean? It was unnatural, that was certain. No natural object could do that. Given the Vatican's concern over the validation of Christ our Lord, after all these centuries of searching the heavens for His return, could this be the pivotal moment humanity had been waiting for? But what if this proved false? What if they discovered Jesus was not the true Son of God? Was he able to distinguish the eyes of the Lord for something else, something unholy, perhaps? Several reports of astronauts sighting "angels" over the planet were thought to be proof that God indeed did exist. There were also the many planets discovered by astronomers where the angels Michael and Gabriel were seen orbiting those planets. That is all the proof you need, Father, he told himself. It is but a mere formality for you to confirm Deborah's discovery. You would only be confirming the Church's being and all its glory. Go forth, Father Mike, he urged with confidence. Go forth and show the world that our Church is the one true Church of God. Go forth and welcome His return!

Father Mike took a moment to pray for strength before he called a meeting of his staff. He informed them of a change in plans. "By order of the Pontiff himself," he told them, "We will be making a special photographic run of Mars tonight." "Why now," they asked him. "By this time next week, Mars will be in a much better position to be photographed." "It is not I who has ordered the change," he said, "but the Pontiff, himself. His commands must go unquestioned. And when our run is complete, you will be dismissed until further notice." The stunned looks that came his way were expected. "There is nothing to worry about," Father Mike said with a compassionate smile. "Think of it as a paid vacation. No one is being fired or let go. This is only temporary. So have some fun and enjoy your time off."

Father Mike clapped his hands. "Now we must hurry. We only have a small window before Mars disappears below the horizon."

The worried frowns evaporated as everyone left the room to tend to their respective duties.

Shortly after the run, Father Mike followed everyone out the door, making sure no one had stayed behind, like Elizabeth Miramontes, who refused to leave until her desk was clear of Observatory business.

"Betty, why are you still here?" Father Mike asked.

"I'm not finished, Father."

"It will keep."

"I will not come back to a messy desk, Father. Just go ahead and do your work. I'll be all right," Ms. Miramontes insisted.

Father Mike picked up her purse and handed it to her. "Absolutely not. You're going home, and that's final. Do you want to hear from the Holy Father?"

Ms. Miramontes eyes flew open. "It's that important?"

Father Mike placed a warm arm around Ms. Miramontes, as he walked with her to the door leading to the parking lot. "Everything His Holiness asks of us is important, Betty."

"Yes, of course, Father. I understand. You'll be okay here by yourself?"

"Yes, Betty, I'll be fine. Thank you." As she went to her little red Honda Accord, he said in parting, "Be careful. I want you back in one piece."

"Yes, Father. Good evening."

He waved to her from inside the doorway, as she drove away, and then locked the door behind him. On his way to the processing lab, he stopped by the refrigerator and picked up a Reed's ginger ale. All the suspense made him thirsty. As the night's run on Mars began, he was the only one allowed to sit at the viewing station. The VATT's double 8.4-meter lens saw everything in stereo with amazing clarity. The LBT (or Large Binocular Telescope) was one of the world's most advanced optical telescopes of its kind. Its mirrors combine to make it the second largest optical telescope in North America. Even though Mars may have looked striking through the viewing lens, his eyes were unable to see anything tangible. Deimos and Phobos, Mars' moons, hung like tiny specks of reflected dust against the dark backdrop of space. They were the only two things he saw, other than Mars itself. During the entire observation time, nothing passed by Mars that wasn't normal. For a brief instant, he thought something did blink behind the backside of Mars. Maybe it was something, maybe it wasn't. It happened so fast there was no way his eyes could have distinguished anything so distant. Fortunately, the Large Binocular Cameras (LBC's) were rolling at the time. If there was something there, the two wide-field cameras mounted on the prime focus swing arms with four EEV42-90 CCDs (2048 x 4608 pixels, 13.5 microns x 13.5 microns per pixel) would capture it.

When the super dense OLED computer blinked on, the first images proved negative. It wasn't until Father Mike rolled to the point on his time sheet where he saw the tiny speck of blue light blink by that he knew he had something. "BINGO!" he cried out. "There you are!" The blue speck shot across the planet's surface and disappeared behind the backside. It was real. Deborah Peele was right. She had indeed found an unnatural object coming from outer space on a direct path toward the inner planets, and from the looks of it, the object had landed on Mars. But why Mars? Why had it chosen a lifeless planet when Earth, a beautiful blue planet of fluffy white clouds, oceans, mountains, and forested valleys full of human life was so near?

He made five stills of the object, and with the blackness of space as a background, he put the digital images through the special enhancement software and waited five seconds for the program to do its thing. The first image boost was all it took. There it was, big as life. A flat, saucer-shaped object that was not actually blue in the upgrade photos, but golden, with an aura of blue light surrounding it. Father Mike sat back in his chair, mesmerized by what was on his screen. According to the spectral readouts at the bottom of his screen, it was made of an unknown material, as was the power wavelengths that it projected. Therefore, the only conclusion possible was that it had originated from a place other than Earth.

"Wow…" His Holiness, the Cardinals, the Bishops, the Fathers at Castel Gandolfo, and especially Father Ricardo Espinosi of the Holy See, will all celebrate this day, he mused, delighted. He rose from his chair and danced, arms swinging, hopping up and down, foot tapping, and singing, *"You put your right foot in, You take your right foot out, You put your right foot in, And you shake it all about, You do the hokey- pokey, And you turn yourself around, That's what it's all about!"*

And when he was out of breath from the 10,000 foot altitude, he flopped back down in front of his computer and fired a three-word encrypted email back to Deborah Peale in Coonabarabran that read: CONGRATULATIONS! OBSERVATIONS CONFIRMED! Fr. M. Attachments.

6

OOHRAH!

Lu's Place
Planet Mars

"YOU ALL LOOK so handsome," Leucadia complimented Harlowe, as he laid the keyboard in the back of the Grannywagon next to Vivaldi's violin, two Mozart flutes, and Neil Young's Martin guitar. It was time to pay their respects to the General, he told her earlier. He kissed her and promised they would be back before dark. She had been invited to go along, but she knew it was their private time together with the man who made them who they were. . .Gamadin. . .and she graciously declined.

Harlowe stepped around to ride shotgun and climbed in. Monday, Riverstone, and Simon were already in the back seat. They were all dressed in their dark Gamadin blues, reserved for special occasions. He tapped the dash and gave the order, "To the *Mons*, Jewels." The robob with the bright bowtie and erudite lift of his triangular head pressed his round flat foot to the floor, and off they went in the gold and blue Granny, as the crew affectionately called their wheelless car. Ian and Riverstone had designed it around his grandmother's 1962 Chevy Nomad station wagon.

They bolted from the entrance of Lu's Place, a little half-acre oasis of life Riverstone discovered when the lot of them nearly died in their trek across *Valles Marineras*. Reaching a top speed of 300 miles per hour in just seconds, the Granny blew out from under *Millawanda*'s protective force field and headed on a westerly course toward *Olympus Mons*, a thousand miles away. During the three-hour drive, they reminisced about the time General Gunn dropped them off at the rim of the two hundred mile diameter *Schiaparelli* impact crater 1800 miles east of Lu's Place, nearly killing them all. It was their final test, a kind of graduation that gave them the right to call themselves Gamadin. Gunn had left them without transportation and with barely a tenth of the rations they needed to even make it halfway back to their home base at the edge of the Mons. They survived only through a whole lot of luck, tenacity, guts, and relying on the know-how the General's hardcore training had taught them. But if Riverstone had never stumbled onto the entrance to Lu's Place in a driving sandstorm, Mars would have been their graveyard, and *Millawanda* would still be parked at the edge of the giant extinct volcano's rim.

"Dog, tell us again how you duked it out with Gunn," Simon urged. "We love that story."

The entire back seat thought it was a great idea. "Yeah, Dog, tell us again," Riverstone prodded, touching Harlowe's shoulder from the back seat. "Were you shaking in your SIBA when you saw that ugly puss of his waiting for you behind the force field?"

"We have a three-hour trip ahead of us, Captain," Monday said. "Ya gotta tell it."

Harlowe detested old wounds. The fight with Gunn ran deep. After leaving their little sanctuary, they were well rested, but they still had two thousand miles to go with only four power cells left among them. They nearly made it, too, and were within a hundred miles from the *Mons* escarpment when the killer sandstorm hit. The afternoon temperature suddenly dropped below minus one hundred sixty-five degrees Fahrenheit, and, with one power cell left, they had no place to hide from the storm on the open flats. Harlowe wanted them all to go on. For him, it was all of them or nothing. The thought of leaving anyone behind never occurred to him. But even Simon knew Harlowe was their only hope. Together they didn't have a chance, but Harlowe, the toughest and most skilled fighter among them did. Riverstone put it to him bluntly that day. "Deal with Gunn, and come back with the Granny to pick us up. I'm hungry." He tried protesting, but Ian stepped between them before the storm got any closer. He had always listened to Wiz, even more than Riverstone. Ian placed the last of his half-used power cell in Harlowe's SIBA claw. "You need this to stay alive, Wiz." Ian closed Harlowe's claw around the cell as he pushed it back. "We'll share what we have left, Dog. Get 'er done." Ian then shoved him toward the *Mons*, looming high above the Amazonis Plains, to do what they all believed he could do...save them.

The Granny raced through the Ius Chasma of the Valles, as Harlowe began the blow-by-blow, fight-to-death combat with General Gunn. He left out nothing. Every gory detail was recounted like it all happened yesterday, and for all of them, it was yesterday. Weaving through the *Noctis Labyrinthus* maze of jagged, steep gorges and dead end canyons, he narrated his climb up the 15,000 foot south face of the *Mon's* escarpment wall, and by the time he reached the ship and its lifesaving atmosphere behind the great force field, he was on his hands and knees, out of power, out of oxygen, out of everything to keep him alive, except his resolve. His had already stiffened from the minus 150-degree temperature. He felt nothing but numbness in his limbs. Mars was sucking the life from him as he pressed on, inch by measly inch, scratching, crawling, not even close to the barrier. He was still 2000 feet short of his goal when he realized he was dead unless... he reached for his pistol. He fought wildly against the urge to fall asleep. Somehow he attached the piton to his pistol and fired the explosive head at a target he could barely see, reeling out a life saving line. Unable to determine if he hit anything, he shut his eyes and hit the rewind. To this day he never knew if he hit anything or not, but when he came to, miraculously, he found himself on the other side of the barrier, growing warmer, breathing oxygen, as his whole body grew stronger by the second.

Jewels navigated through the gorges with expert precision, popping out of the two-mile deep ravines, as Tharsis Mons, another extinct Martian volcano, came into view, pointing the way to their goal. The first thing Harlowe remembered was waking up from the intense cold and seeing the soft golden underbelly of *Millawanda*'s hull. He knew then that he was alive. Initially, Gunn himself, was nowhere in sight, but it didn't take a rocket scientist to know the General was watching his every move. His SIBA was useless so he ditched it just as a fast moving shadow caught his eye trolling through the equipment scattered on the ground. Wearing only his underwear, he faced Gunn who stood rigid at the muster line, waiting for him. "You made it, soldier. Congratulations," he remembered him saying.

The banter continued. "No thanks to you, Sir," Harlowe said, pointing his pistol at the General's gut.

"Are you going to use that?" Gunn asked.

"It's over, General. Millie is ours now."

"Think you're good enough to take care of her?"

"I do, and good enough to walk in your boots, General."

Gunn tried on old trick, pretending to unbuckle his belt, but with blinding speed he caught his pistol and drew. Harlowe was ready and blasted the sidearm from the Gunn's hand.

"An old trick, General."

Fists flew after that, with the General catching Harlowe on the jaw, laying him out flat. "A little slow, Dog. Tired? Want to rest awhile before we play?"

Harlowe touched his chin with the guys looking on, mesmerized by his account. There were still times his jaw felt the shock of that blow. With tuned Gamadin reflexes, Harlowe leaped up, and returning the volley with two pulverizing blows of his own, and smashed the old soldier backwards on his backside. "Not that tired, Sir."

The battle for *Millawanda* went on for hours. Back and forth, trading punches, tumbling, smashing each other across one side of the sanctuary to the other until Harlowe finally got the lethal hit that ended the fight for good. The General's final words were: "You can do it, son. With what you already know, you'll lead the greatest fighting unit the world . . . no, the galaxy has ever seen, soldier. The madness has come. It is time to face it and destroy it everywhere you find it. To survive the madness you must become evil. You must rumble in its own yard. Until you feel its breath on your face, you will have no understanding of its power. It will always be with you. The madness will suck the life from you if you lack sufficient evil in you to combat it. That must change in all of you. Kindness is no ally, soldier. Evil is! It must be with you every moment of the battle. Recognize it. Know it. Feed on it. For without it, I promise you the madness will destroy all that you love. It will prey on your weakness and kill you, your family, and our planet. Do I make myself clear, soldier?"

"Sir, yes, Sir!" Harlowe shouted back.

"Do you understand me, Dog?"

"Sir, yes, Sir!"

"Do you?"

"Sir, yes, Sir!"

As broken and defeated as he was, Gunn rose up and cried out, "DO YOU?"

Harlowe replied, screaming at the top of his lungs, screaming so loud he thought he might awaken the Martian ancient dead. "SIR! I UNDERSTAND. I WILL DESTROY THE MADNESS EVERYWHERE IT EXISTS…SIRRRRRRRR!"

Jewels brought the Grannywagon to a slow stop in front of Olympus Mons, the solar system's largest mountain, rising 134,000 feet off the *Amazonis Plain*, just as Harlowe finished his chronicle. With eyes wet and his nose stinging, Harlowe cleared the lump in his throat. "That's pretty much it. His final words were, 'Take command, Captain, the Gamadin ship is yours.' You guys know the rest. I found you buried in a ditch, saved you toadheads, and now here we are."

"Yeah, here we are," Monday repeated, acting uneasy about going on.

Riverstone had no such feelings. He leaned forward, staring at Harlowe's eyes. "You're not getting all misty-eyed again, are you, Dog?"

"No way," Harlowe replied, defensively.

It was Simon's turn this time. "I think he is. He's tearing up, gents. What do you know, our Captain really does have a heart."

Monday, always the loyal soldier, tried to stifle his laugh, but couldn't hold it for long, and turned away.

Harlowe flashed them a pinky finger, saving his very best for another time. "I should have left you toads out there to suck sand for another week."

"Dog," Riverstone continued. "Gunn was a droid. He wasn't real. He died back on Earth before we got here. The dude wasn't human."

Harlowe looked up at the three-mile high escarpments, still saddened by the fact he had taken down his mentor. "Yeah...well...call him what you want, but his soul kept us alive."

Jewels shifted the throttle to vertical, and the Granny began floating upward alongside the three-mile high face of the volcanic rim.

Riverstone, never one for lack of opinion, went on: "If it was anyone's soul, it was *Millawanda*'s. She made us Gamadin. Not Gunn. If anyone's to blame for us being who we are, who we've become, it's her, putzhead! It's her fault that we're..."

And then, with Riverstone leading the charge Simon, and Monday cried out, "THE MOST BADASS SOLDIERS THE GALAXY HAS EVER SEEN! OOHRAH!"

Jewels drove to the 86,000-foot level of the giant caldron, where the memorial was located. Nothing had changed. The cavernous blast hole, carved out by a Gamadin rifle shot during their training days on the *Mons*, was untouched. Just inside the opening, the General's motionless body was still there, dressed perfectly in his Marine Corps dressed blues, his three stars polished and bright on his collar, the twelve rows of service ribbons on his chest, and the beautiful light blue ribbon around his neck, holding his Medal of Honor over his heart. He seemed so peaceful sitting in his special lounge chair, looking out at the sunrise, with his wife Mary in his heart.

Jewels expanded the Granny's force field wide enough to allow them to move around the memorial without their SIBAs. When it was safe, and the air was warm and comfortable enough for them to breathe, they piled out of the Granny and unpacked their musical instruments. They set up their chairs in a half circle around the entrance and laid their instruments in the chairs. Riverstone faced the General. "Good day, Sir, still ugly as ever."

"Go ahead, touch him, Rerun," Harlowe urged.

Simon shook his head. "Not me."

"Even God would have second thoughts," Monday joked.

Next they lined up in front of the opening and came to stick-straight attention. Drawing their sidearms, they fired three volleys in the air, re-holstered their weapons and saluted crisply. "Sir, WE THE GAMADIN SALUTE YOU!"

After that, Harlowe switched on the power to his keyboard, Simon picked up the guitar, Monday the violin and Riverstone his flute. Simon tapped the face of his guitar three times and said, "Let the concert begin, Gamadin!" They played all the General's classical favorites for over an hour, performing works by Handel, Bach, Pachelbel, Haydn, Telemann, and the French composer, Saint-Saens. For the grand finale, they played a special medley of Vivaldi's, *Le Quattro Stagioni*, the *Four Seasons* concertos to close the concert. To end the service, they put away their instruments, stepped to the line before the General, saluted, and remained that way, as Simon took two crisp steps forward and sang all three verses of the *Marine Corps Hymn* so beautifully, it brought tears to everyone's eyes, including Riverstone's. Snapping their arms at their sides, and clicking their heels together, they shouted, "OOHRAH!"

As they were packing up, Harlowe gave one last farewell salute to Gunn. "*Semper Fi*, General!" He then returned to the Granny and gestured for Jewels to drive on. No one said a word the entire ride back to Lu's Place. From here on out they were back on the clock.

7
Father Espinosi

Vatican Observatory
Castel Gandolfo, Rome

ESCORTED BY A dozen heavily armed Swiss Guards, a Vatican
intelligence courier entered Father Ricardo Espinosi's chambers just
after midnight and handed the sleepy-eyed priest a "For Eyes Only"
packet addressed to him from Father Mike at Mt. Graham, Arizona. The
courier, along with his Swiss escort, had made the fourteen-hour flight
back to Rome in a 787 Vatican jet from Tucson International Airport.

Father Espinosi touched the deep red wax seal of His Holiness'
impression with the black ribbon of secrecy running through it. "No
one has touched this?" he asked the courier.

The courier bowed. "Only you, Father. I witnessed the good Father
authenticate the envelope with my own eyes."

After blessing the courier for his divine duty to God and Church,
Father Espinosi dismissed him. When everyone had gone and the door
to his chamber was bolted shut, Father Espinosi walked to his desk, his

hands shaking. The packet was no surprise. He had been expecting it. As Director of the Vatican Observatory and President of the Vatican Observatory Foundation, he was responsible for all research connections between meteorites, the evolution of solar system bodies, and the origins and structure of possible extraterrestrial contact from outer space. Ever since Pope Leo XIII's issuance of a *"Motu Propio"*, a personal decree that in 1891 re-established the Vatican Observatory and the telescope at Castel Gandolfo, Italy had been vigilant in its search for celestial callers traveling to Earth. Father Espinosi stared uneasily at the envelope. If Father Mike had indeed discovered an off-world vessel headed toward Earth, how would the world see it? More importantly, how would the Church see it? Might they be a race of beings who could change their way of life, their culture…or even their religious beliefs?

Father Espinosi opened the packet and began reviewing the material. He gave a cursory glance at Father Mike's cover letter, going directly to the astronomical photograph of the alien vessel itself. Father Espinosi clutched his chest. It was indeed an alien contact. The vessel, flat and golden, blue in its aura, was exactly how Father Mike had described it in his scrambled communiqué. He believed in his heart that the ship was indeed the Second Coming. Theories deep in the Church, however, believed the Creators placed man on Earth as slaves, and that the Church, the true savior of man, was given the sole authority to control humanity by these same Creators.

But what if this ship was the "Master Race" returning to reclaim their property? Was it not the Church's role to continue? That thought alone shook Father Espinosi's soul. What would happen to the Church then? Would he, the Vatican, and all that the Church stood for all these centuries cease to exist? What was the bigger threat to humankind: the Second Coming or the destruction of all God's children on Earth?

He stared at the ship and asked himself the all-important question… what was the purpose of this ship coming to Earth? Was it as master or benevolent traveler?

The Church would undoubtedly discover that answer, and more. Did the Church have the power to meet such a threat to their existence?

He lifted his phone and immediately called for a special meeting with the Holy Father. The Pontiff's secretary said His Holiness was unavailable until after his morning prayer. Father Espinosi empathized with his Holiness and told the secretary he could wait, but the fate of mankind and the Church itself might not. He bowed respectfully and said, "It's your decision."

His Holiness was awakened immediately.

8

Salad Plate

Colorado Springs, Colorado

IT WAS PITCH dark, just after 2 a.m., when U.S. Marine Sergeant Max Enihoo and his girlfriend, Air Force Lieutenant Arlene Chapman, were riding up Rock Creek Canyon Road on his air-cooled, Harley-Davidson Iron 883, heading back to Peterson AFB. They saw a large disk-shaped object flying overhead, going from a southeasterly direction toward the west. The skies were crystal clear, and the stars were bright. The moon had already disappeared over the Rockies three hours ago, so there was nothing disturbing their sighting of the object as it came silently overhead. Max slowed his Iron to a stop in the middle of the two-lane country road, as they both tried to decipher what it was they were actually seeing. Arlene estimated the object was no more than a thousand feet above them.

"One of ours?" Max asked, removing his helmet.

Arlene unbuckled her chinstrap and removed her helmet. She wanted nothing to obstruct her view. "I don't think so, Maxi." Maxi was Arlene's pet name for Max. They had been seeing each other under the radar for three months, ignoring the military policy of improper fraternization of an officer and an enlisted soldier, a long-standing punishable offense. Depending on the weather, their normal meet-ups were somewhere off base, usually along Rock Creek Canyon Road, where Arlene could securely park her red Mustang in the trees during their trysts. If it was snowing or raining too heavily, Max would leave his Harley at his cousin's house south of the city and Arlene would pick him up in her car, while he walked along the road somewhere. It was not an elaborate strategy, but one that, so far, had worked for them. They figured as long as they stayed away from the normal military haunts, they were safe. Occasionally, they would see each other on base, but a casual salute and maybe a quick wink was all the affection they dared display.

As the object came directly overhead Max exclaimed, "That's the biggest salad plate I've ever seen!"

Arlene kept studying it, trying to figure out how it fit in the Air Force's arsenal of flying aircraft. She had a level three clearance and would have been privy to something this large. She saw no markings of any kind on the gold-colored hull. "That's not ours, Maxi, I'm sure of it."

Max looked down at her, the soft bluish glow from the saucer's lighted perimeter rim highlighting her beautiful high cheekbones, intelligent eyes, and blond hair. "Then whose salad plate is it?" Max asked her directly, his six-foot-six inch, two hundred eighty-pound, black muscular frame towering over her.

She kinked her five-nine, hundred and thirty-five pound, solid statuesque body up at him and replied honestly, as she tried to come to some sort of logical explanation, "I don't know, Maxi."

"Rusky?"

"No."

"Chicom?"

"No. None of that. I don't even know what's keeping it up."

"Yeah, how is it doing that? I don't hear a thing."

The object continued on a short way, as Max removed his cell from his leather jacket and snapped a shot of it. Then, as if it were camera shy, it took off over the mountain ridgeline and disappeared in a wink.

Arlene wrapped Max in her arms. Stunned, she gathered her wits, and stated unequivocally, "I can guarantee you there is nothing from this planet that can do that."

9

Put Down

Nevada, U.S.A.
38° 56' 47.7312" N
117° 45' 43.3872" W

HARLOWE, LEUCADIA, AND Mowgi stepped off the blinker together at ground level near the perimeter edge of the force field. Passing through the barrier, they tasted the fresh air of Earth for the first time in what seemed like an eternity. Harlowe had put aside his Gamadin uniform for his SoCal garb of blue denims, blue t-shirt, and a dark blue hoodie. His Wilson Kaos sneakers were black with stylish light blue trim. It was the most extravagant color on him. Leucadia, on the other hand, had a different objective in mind. Even though the government had taken all that she owned, when she entered a room she wanted people to know she was still a force to be reckoned with. She wore a charcoal grey Armani pinstriped suit, crisp white shirt, black tie, under a black sable fur and wool cape. Her small, gold buckled cordovan leather purse matched her Christian Louboutin high heels that showed off her sculptured tan ankles to a tee. As far as Harlowe was concerned, there was no one more formidable in a high-level business meeting than she was.

Harlowe spread his arms as he looked out across the desert valley below them. The pink and yellow sunrise was just now coming over the distant mountain range to the east. "So beautiful, Lu. Blue sky, yellow sun, fresh air. We've been 35,000 light-years to the center of our galaxy and back, and there's still is nothing like Earth anywhere."

But the world for Harlowe was not all sunshine and clear skies. He was heartbroken. Inside, his guts were boiling. In the short time between coming out of hyper-light travel and discovering they were eleven years out of sync with Earth, his crew had read all the news accounts. President Delmonte had been impeached. Jefferson Braxton's jet had crashed in the South China Sea killing all aboard, and the election of the new President, Nootzy Shame, resulted in a sudden global depression and an arms race between American, Chinese, and Russian military forces toward a possible thermonuclear war. By Presidential decree, nearly all of President Delmonte's work to rebuild the United States was overturned, putting millions out of work. The planet was in trouble. It was clear that the powers in charge had no interest in settling their differences peacefully. The bigger question was why? Why had those in charge chosen such a path when it was obvious President Delmonte's policies were working? Who was at the center of this madness? And why, oh why, would they want to destroy our beautiful world, Harlowe kept asking himself. Nothing made sense.

"It's not going to end well, is it?" Leucadia asked, knowing beneath Harlowe's poised and self-confident posture lay a troubled young man.

Harlowe stared at her imposing figure with satisfaction. He recalled when he first attended a meeting with her on the island of Malta. They had flown all night with little sleep, in the Mars Corporate Dreamliner. The world's top oil executives from Russia, Dubai, Kuwait, Great Britain, and Norway were in attendance. They had all come to take on the new head of the Mars Corporation, the beautiful blonde-haired heiress, in a bidding war for oil rights in the Gulf of Mexico. The execs figured her for a young, inexperienced pushover. She would also be tired from her trip from the eight-hour jet lag. It was a perfect setup to combine their power and overwhelm her with whatever offer she submitted. But not ten minutes into the meeting, they discovered that not only had she come prepared, she had spent the previous two weeks studying the daily mud samples from the Gulf oil rigs. She even dove to the bottom of the Gulf in a diving pod to survey the sea floor and its inhabitants. She talked to every oilman on the exploratory platforms, who, after seeing her elegant form, were eager to tell her everything she wanted to know. And Harlowe had been with her every step of the way. Before she walked into that board meeting, she knew exactly what she wanted and the amount of money she was willing to pay for it. The oil representatives never stood a chance. When she presented her bid at five times what they were willing to pay, the meeting was over before the coffee was served.

Harlowe laughed, remembering how angry the executives were at being stomped on by the beautiful American socialite in an Armani suit.

That's my girl!

"I don't know how it's going to end, Babe," Harlowe said straight out. "It's our home we're taking on."

She took his arm and held his hand as she rested her head on his powerful shoulder. "You're Gamadin. You'll figure it out, Hon."

Harlowe pressed his lips tight. The road ahead was never easy. Maybe, if he had a plan, he could see a little daylight at the end of the tunnel. But right now, at this particular moment, he felt like he was staring down a galactic-size black hole. "You'll have them drooling in their boxer shorts, Babe," he said slowly, genuinely awed by her air of confidence.

Leucadia took hold of his loose hoodie and pulled him to her, kissing him and saying, "Thanks, handsome." She then added a piece of caution, "I guess telling you to stay out of trouble is like arguing with the sun."

Harlowe squished his face against hers. "It's in my DNA."

After kissing her again, he came back to the desert valley. There was no ocean anywhere in sight. A beachfront putdown like that on Orixy or #2 would have been cool. Considering what they had been through the last couple of months, he guessed being grateful they had made it back at all from the galactic core was in order. A landscape of arid sand, prickly beavertail cactus, mesquite trees, and dark green and brown yucca trees would not make his top ten list. Miles across the valley lay a small range of craggy mountains, while on the sunrise side of the ship, not far from *Millawanda*'s perimeter, was a large pool of water fed by an underground spring. Pigpo will love munching on the tall grass, he thought. Even though their put down site was nothing to write home about, it was what they needed; a location far away from prying human eyes.

"Where are we?" Harlowe asked.

"A small park," she replied, and began pointing out the different directions. "North is that way. Vegas is that way, 200 miles. California is over the ridge behind us." She pointed across the desert valley toward the mountain range to finish the tour. "And that way is New York."

"That's where you're going first?" Harlowe asked.

"I'm meeting Jewels there," Leucadia replied.

"How is the old war horse anyway?"

Leucadia's face turned solemn. "I'm worried, Harlowe. He didn't sound healthy. I think the past eleven years since we've been gone have taken a toll."

"Yeah, our family and friends could be the same way. The sooner we get them back here to Millie, the better."

"Broken hearts are tough to mend, Pylott."

He pulled her close. "Listen, we're going to make Humpty Dumpty whole again. There's just no other choice."

She looked him in the eye. "Keep working on that plan?"

"Count on it."

As he was particularly good at, Riverstone interrupted their private moment together, stepping through the barrier, looking like someone dressed for a 1960s tie-dye, hippie convention. He had on a patchwork of bright yellows, a red striped shirt, and an orange ball cap. His green-laced Nike SB Flom Dunk high tops were the most conservative accessories of his getup. His new hairdo, a close buzz around his head leaving the top long, only added to his amusement.

"Say, brah," Riverstone said, sliding his way through the force field. "What a fine day to start changing the planet. And…whoa!" he exclaimed, catching Leucadia's stunning outfit. "Lu! Look at you, girl! Aren't we stylin'? Ralph Lauren or Calvin Klein?"

"Armani," Leucadia corrected.

"So hot! You goin' to see our new President or something?"

"Not the first stop, but she's on my list."

"Who's the homey next to you?" Riverstone asked, eyeing Harlowe like he was an afterthought.

Harlowe couldn't help but laugh at Riverstone's garb. "Who dressed you this morning . . . Lady Gaga?"

"Somethin' Rerun and I put together. We looked up the new styles, and this is the latest, Dog. You'll be amazed at what they're wearing these days. Eleven years is mega lifetimes in the fashion world, pard."

Speaking of Simon, he stepped through the barrier next. "Where's our ride?" he asked, walking up to the three of them. He froze when he saw Leucadia. "Wow, you should be going with us, Lu. We'd have a ten figure movie deal, with no questions asked."

Leucadia took his arm and kissed him on the cheek. "You'll do just fine, handsome."

Simon looked over at Riverstone. "I don't mean to be too pushy, but I have a meet-up with Saul at Spagos for lunch."

"He's still in showbiz?" Harlowe asked, surprised.

Simon snickered. "Well, sort of. He had to take a few pills when he heard my voice on the phone."

"No doubt," Harlowe chuckled.

"Shocked the bejeezus out of him. I thought he was having a heart attack. He's still in business, but not like the good old days with Captain Starr. That lasted about ten seconds before he wanted to know if I had a script ready."

"Of course you do," Leucadia said.

"Daaah...I told him, you bet your Rolls Royce I do." He laughed again. "He said he had to trade in his Rolls for a cheap Cadillac. Pissed him off to no end."

"Sounds like a first-world problem," Harlowe muttered.

Riverstone surveyed their surroundings. "Millie going to be okay here, Dog?"

"Look behind you," Harlowe replied, nodding back at the force field.

Riverstone and Simon nearly lost it. "Where did she go?" Simon asked, aghast at *Millawanda*'s sudden disappearance.

"She's still there. A little light bending and she's a goner," Harlowe replied.

Riverstone stuck his head through the barrier, leaving his body outside. It made him look like the Headless Horseman gone mod. "Yep, beautiful as ever," he confirmed, pulling his head out.

"Here comes our transportation now," Leucadia announced, as she faced the two vehicles driving up. One was a long, dark blue limo with gold and silver trim, followed by Harlowe's ride, the familiar Grannywagon. The Granny was the only vehicle that had to be customized to make it street legal. It needed four wheels, taillights, headlights, bumpers, rearview mirrors, and current California license plates for both cars, so the Highway Patrol wouldn't be pulling them over every mile or two. Both cars were also capable of flight, and floated above the ground for appearance.

Before getting into their transports, Riverstone asked, "Are Platter and Prigg okay with holding down the fort?"

Harlowe tapped Riverstone confidently on the shoulder. "We're covered."

"Are you going with Dog in the Granny, Lu?" Simon asked.

Harlowe pointed up at a white platform floating down. "She's taking the high road." The translucent platform was a recent addition to the ship's stable of terrestrial transports that Harlowe brought back from Orixy. He thought it would be cool to have a airborne platform like Ali Baba's flying carpet, only the Orixy platform was waaaay cooler and much, much, faster than any rug.

Harlowe helped Leucadia step up onto the platform with her high heels. "Stay low, stay safe."

She winked back. "Aye, aye, Captain."

Mowgi yipped, wanting to go. "Sorry, Mowg," Harlowe said to the undog. "You're with me."

"See you in New York, Pylott," Leucadia said, as she dialed into the control sequence.

"Are you bad?" Riverstone asked, meaning did she have protection with her.

She tapped her purse, then leaned over and kissed him on the cheek. "Very bad, Matthew."

Harlowe mouthed the words, Love you, just before she hit the go and whisked away across the open desert at incredible speed.

"Captain Starr could use one of those," Simon quipped.

Harlowe went along, acting like a mother hen telling them to be careful and not to trust anyone. "Did you each get one of Wiz's money cards?"

Riverstone and Simon patted their pockets. "Aye, Captain, right here," Simon replied.

"What are you going to do first?" Harlowe asked them.

Riverstone didn't hesitate. "Order a stack of double-doubles and fries, animal-style, from In-N-Out."

"Save me some will ya?" Harlowe requested.

Riverstone winked. "Maybe one."

Harlowe put his arms around him and squeezed. He didn't know why he felt so worried. He just did. They were Gamadin, after all. He let go, and Riverstone climbed in without another word between them. Harlowe went to the girlbob driver next, reached in, and tapped her shoulder. "Good to go, Alice." The limo sped off in a gust of wind, taking a hard right turn south and was immediately out of sight. Harlowe looked down at Mowgi, his big yellow eyes full of tears, like he lost his best friends. Harlowe reached down and picked him up. They both needed support. "I know big guy." He carried him to the Grannywagon, but didn't get in. Together they sat on the fender looking across the valley for a long while, thinking, just thinking. There was no rush. The wind blew cold from the north, as he strained to see that tiny speck of light inside the tunnel. And still there was nothing, not one flicker of hope on how to begin. He looked down at his feet, and there it was, the beginning without light. That one step yet to be taken to start the journey. It was all that he needed. *Take it, dude. If you don't, we all die and the world with us.*

He turned to Jewels, waiting patiently for him, without complaint. He sighed, stepped in, and from in the shotgun seat, gave the command, "Just go!" The Granny took off, accelerating to top speed in a southeasterly direction, never touching the ground.

10
The Hunks

1037 hours, Pacific Time
Barstow, California

THE BIG, RED-TRIMMED white In-N-Out restaurant was already packed, and it was still an hour and a half before lunchtime. Amanda Littman, shoulder length jet black hair, wearing a thigh-length, "TALK DERBY TO ME" yellow tee over black leggings, stood in the order line holding her two-year old daughter, Claire, ready to eat the wrapper off a burger if it came to that. She was tired, hungry, and the smell of fresh-made fries was driving her crazy. She had driven from Las Vegas early this morning and had two and a half more hours to go before reaching her parents' house in Camarillo for a relaxing weekend by the pool. Little Claire had been eating Goldfish crackers since she woke up an hour out of Vegas, and, like her mother, was starving for real food. But the two tall hunks at the front of the order line were taking forever. She had watched them order a dozen double-doubles with everything, ten orders of fries, and three shakes of each flavor to go. Enough for an entire baseball team, she figured. The hunk she dubbed the "movie star" reminded her of an old-time actor from long ago, that her parents said was the hottest sci-fi actor of his day.

The movie star tried to pay with fresh hundred dollar bills, but the auto-teller wouldn't accept the cash. A real person, probably the manager, she thought, came to the register with a big smile and asked them what the problem was.

A heavy-set lady standing behind her interrupted her concentration with a compliment. "Your daughter is so cute."

Amanda forced a smile. The tiny-mouthed woman, who outweighed her by double, had sickly, white skin, inset eyes, crooked teeth, and kept brushing her bright, red hair with purple and green ends out of her eyes like she was swatting a fly from her face. Her entire look was greasy and unkempt. Amanda wanted no part of her. Besides, she was too hungry to socialize, and Claire was getting heavy in her arms. She really wanted to put her down. But something told her the crowded restaurant was not the place to let her roam unattended. "Thank you," she replied to the woman, and turned Claire away from the too friendly stranger.

While the movie star hunk spoke with the manager, his friend talked to his watch like some government agent on TV might do.

"Look. This is cold hard cash. I'll even pay double for everything," the movie star said.

"It doesn't matter," the manager said politely. "We can't take paper money anymore even if we wanted." The manager wasn't trying to be difficult. Everyone knows, Amanda thought, that unless you're from another planet or something, the governments around the world had outlawed paper money several years ago.

His friend interrupted the conversation. "It's okay, Rerun, give him your card."

"Card?" the movie star asked his friend.

His friend patted his shoulder. "You know, the one Dog gave us, brah."

"We take all money cards, Sir," the manager informed the hunks.

The movie star patted his pockets like he had misplaced his card. "Hold on. I thought I had it."

"That's ok," Riverstone said, "I'll call Alice and have her bring you another one."

The manager placed the bags aside as he motioned for the next person in line to come forward. The line would move faster now. But Amanda didn't care. The hunks were so gorgeous, she could watch them all day, forget food! They looked like professional athletes. They were tall, well mannered and poised, with broad shoulders and pecs as thick as her upper thighs.

"How old is your daughter?" the woman asked. Her putrid breath was sickening as she came closer to Claire.

Amanda returned a please-leave-us-alone look. "Not now."

"Is she two and a half?" the woman pestered.

The more the woman talked about Claire the more uncomfortable Amanda became with her standing so close to her daughter. "No, she's two. Now if you'll excuse me. I don't feel like talking."

"Oh, she looks older. She really does have beautiful blue eyes and soft hair. Very nice," the woman cooed, stroking Claire's hair in a disturbing way.

Amanda pushed her hand away. "Don't, or I'll call the manager." She wanted to smack the woman with her purse, but held herself in check, hoping she would have her food shortly and be gone. She did the next best thing and turned Claire away from the seedy mess.

Then a strange thing happened, and she forgot all about the menace behind her, as it did everyone else in the restaurant. A five-foot tall, gold-colored droid with blond hair swaying from behind its lampshade head came strutting through the glass door all lady-like on its cylindrical legs and disk shaped feet. The stunned patrons quickly moved aside to let the robot through, as it went straight to the two heartthrobs and handed the movie star a plastic card it had in its four-digit hand. Amanda glimpsed the card with the same disbelief as she did the robot. It was the normal size, but it was a made of a pretty blue translucent material. What made it particularly fascinating were the two magnificent three-dimensional, blue-eyed tigers pictured within the card. Amanda could feel their glistening white fur as though she touched them. The card's incredibility didn't end there. The tigers actually moved, rubbing affectionately up against a beautiful young woman with long blond hair dressed in a designer blue jumpsuit. The final stunner before the card turned away was the big-eared dragon that swooped down behind them in a photobomb.

That was crazy cool, she gasped.

The movie star took the card from the robot and said, "Thank you, Alice. Would you be a dear?" he asked, pointing at the white bags on the counter. Alice dutifully picked up the sacks of food and left the way she came.

The hunk gave the card to the manager, who thanked them with a sigh and a smile, passed the card through the reader, which was confirmed immediately, and asked, "Will that be all, Sir?" as he returned the card.

The movie star looked back at the line of hungry patrons and pointed. "They have all been waiting so patiently. Would you put their meals on our tab, as well?"

"Absolutely, Sir. Would you like a receipt?"

The other hunk took one of the two shakes still on the counter and replied, "No, we trust you, brah." With shakes in hand, the two hunks, who towered a foot over everyone, headed out the restaurant to a clapping crowd of thank yous. The woman behind her didn't clap at all. She continued eyeing Claire like she was on the menu.

As the movie star passed her by, Amanda asked him, displaying her prettiest smile, "Would you take a picture with us?"

"Sure," he replied and bent way down to take the picture. He smelled as good as he looked, and although she didn't recognize his cologne, it was such a wonderfully fresh, manly scent that she took a breath before she snapped her selfie.

"Did anyone ever tell you, you look like a famous movie star?" She giggled, putting her cell phone back in her purse.

"They used to," he grinned.

"He was super hot in my parents' day. He would be much older now," Amanda said.

"No doubt," the movie star said with a wink. Claire reached out to him, and they touched fingers. He then went on to more thank yous from the line, going through the glass door to join his friend. She sighed, sad she would never see either hunk again.

* * *

Amanda's order number flashed on the wall screen. Holding Claire by the hand, she picked up her free #1 combo lunch and went directly to the service counter for catsup and a few extra napkins. "Up we go, young lady," she said to Claire, lifting her onto a nearby bench. She turned to the catsup dispenser, and in that moment, a woman's voice said, "Say good-bye to Mommy, Claire."

A sickening jolt of acid shot welled up in her throat, as she helplessly watched the obese woman, who had been behind her the whole time in the order line, snatched Claire off the bench and head for the exit door.

It all happened so fast that Amanda froze for an instant before her motherly instincts kicked in. She dropped everything, leaving her purse and food behind, never thinking for a moment about anything but Claire.

"No—" Amanda tried to scream but a heavy boot came from nowhere and tripped her, slamming her to the floor. She tried desperately to get up. But before she could lift herself off the floor, a massive, smelly man with a dark beard, sunglasses, baseball cap, and ratty old overcoat, smacked her back down with his boot.

"Let me go. That woman has my child!" she cried out.

From under his coat, the man pulled a revolver and put it to her head in front of everyone else, who instinctively scrambled away from them.

Amanda smacked the gun from her head. She would risk it all to save Claire. Now hysterical, she screamed over and over, "Don't take my daughter!"

Like she was being hit by a pile driver, the beast's boot hit her square again. "Say another word, and you'll never see you little dear alive again," he growled, returning the weapon to her head.

She felt nothing, not even the acid drool she spit out her mouth, fighting, struggling not giving up. What else could she do? She had to protect Claire. If she didn't break free, she knew Claire was lost forever. So she fought on with every ounce her hundred and twenty-one pounds could muster.

"Damn you, lady!" the beast roared, raising his gun to give the final blow that would silence her for good.

No one in the restaurant bothered to help her. It wasn't their fight, and the monster was big and brutal and pointing a loaded weapon at anyone who tried to stop him.

Amanda felt the rush of air as the giant hand raised, waiting for it to come crashing down, she closed her eyes, knowing the butt of weapon would crush her skull the instant it hit.

But the blow never came.

With her eyes still shut, something snapped, followed by a sudden expulsion of air. The beastly man shuddered over her, then let go as she felt his stench fall away from her. When she opened her eyes again, he was lying on the tile floor, still as stone, his head twisted to the side in an unnatural position, his sunglasses cockeyed on his face, exposing his frozen eyes that stared at nothing. When she looked up, the movie star hunk, his face full of worry, reached down for her, and carefully, but ever so strongly, lifted her to her feet as if she was a mere toy in his hands, and told her, "It's okay now."

Amanda knew nothing but flight. She blew open the glass doors screaming, "CLAIRE! CLAIRE!" Before she had gone but a few steps, the other tall hunk met her coming out the door. He had a happy Claire in his arms, bringing her back to her. She grabbed her child, thanking God she was safe in her arms, crying uncontrollably, shaking from fear of it all, still horrified, still shocked that she had become a victim of such evil.

Moments later, her breath returning, her composure settling, allowing her to see through her tears, her mouth opened in shock at the scene across the parking lot. The woman who had taken Claire sat on the pavement motionless against the front wheel of an oversized Mercedes Sprinter van. Her rainbow head was slumped over, her chin resting on her chest, as one leg stuck straight out and the other uncomfortably bent under her. Her mouth lay open. Her eyes were half closed. Whether she was alive or dead, it was difficult to tell, but she was still like the beast inside the restaurant. Two other male bodies were motionless. They were even more grotesque and vile than her attacker. One had been slammed through the front windshield, his legs sticking out over the hood of the van, while the second male rested high on the roof of the van, his body unmoving like the others, face up, arms dangling over the side, obviously broken in several places.

But most gratifying of all was the sight of five children sitting in the open doorway of the van. Three were close to Claire's age, a fourth was a boy slightly older, and another girl with dark curly hair was at least ten. The droid, Alice, was handing out fries, hamburgers, and drinks to each of them. They touched her long thin arms and giggled, thinking she was way cool.

A warm arm came around Amanda shoulders. She didn't jerk away. His cologne announced his presence. She knew he was the movie star. "You okay?" he asked.

Amanda wiped her eyes with her free hand, took a long breath, and pulled him by his shirt to her, kissing him on the cheek. "Thank you."

She found it difficult to talk. There was nothing much more to say other than the gratitude her eyes gave him.

"It's kinda what we do," he said.

"Save people?"

He nodded with pursed lips. "Yeah."

She recalled her father's favorite hero from long ago. "Like Captain Starr from the old movies?"

His head reared back and laughed. "Yeah. Like him."

"You're better." She looked at Claire. "Right, honey. He's our hero."

"Hero, Mommy," Claire cackled sweetly.

His friend called to him. "Gotta go, brah!"

"Take care now," he pointed at Claire. "And take care of my girl."

* * *

A beautiful midnight-blue limousine pulled up. Alice was already at the wheel. As he was walking toward the vehicle, she called to him. "Your name! I don't know our hero's name."

He smiled, giving her a small wave goodbye. "Captain Starr!"

He stepped into the limo with the other hunk. Alice then drove away a moment before a horde police units arrived with flashing lights and Sirens. A dozen officers with weapons drawn surrounded the Sprinter van.

"It okay, officers!" the manager cried out, waving his hands. He turned to Amanda and handed over her purse and her #1 combo in a white bag. "You left this in the restaurant, miss." She thanked him, as they watched the police check over the bodies and seal off the area with yellow tape.

"That didn't end well for them, did it?" the manager said a little later.

"No, not at all," Amanda replied. Checking her purse to make sure nothing was missing, she found a translucent blue card with a gold G-coin on one side and a 3D image of the odd looking animals on the other. It was the card the hunks had used to buy their meals. Attached to the card was a note: *A gift for Claire. Enjoy! Captain Starr.*

11

Quatloo

LeBeau Park, Nevada

IT WAS LATE afternoon when Park Ranger Frank Duggie retrieved his LTL Acorn, 12MP, trail camera. It was his last camera pick up of the week, and it was strapped to a Yucca tree, where he had left it five days ago. He opened the back, removed the one-gigabyte memory card, and put in fresh batteries and a new memory card. After rechecking the camera's settings, he reattached it to the tree and switched it on again.

The dry Nevada desert was so rugged, he had to leave his 4x4 Ranger truck parked off the trail and hike four miles into the wilderness for a spot isolated enough for Joyce Moon, his boss, affectionately called "Moony," even to her face. She was a stickler for getting the best remote shots of wildlife in LeBeau Park. He held the memory card up to the sky and smiled, feeling lucky. "One quatloo for two captures," he said aloud, placing his bet. (A "quatloo" was a form of money used by disembodied beings in the original Star Trek Series called The Providers.) It was Frank's camera game, one he liked to play with himself out in the sticks. The bet was under or over, depending on the number of animal hits the trail camera picked up. There was never much, mostly kangaroo mice, and during the summer, rattlesnakes were the rage. Now and then in the winter he might catch a desert antelope or two, an elk if he was lucky. One time he even caught a whole herd of elk. He lost a ton of quatloos that day, betting on the under instead of the over. Humans counted, too, double if there ever was such a creature. In the three years of capturing trail shots in LeBeau Park, not one time had a camera picked up the two-legged animal. "That's why no one cares about the friggin' place, Moony," he told her from a safe, 100 mile distance to the Ranger Station in Gabbs. He discovered early in his ten-year career, that talking to himself kept him sane on the long treks. Until he returned home to Hawthorne, the military town of underground ammo dumps, mothballed military equipment, and beer, and downed his first cold one with his wife, Kitty, at El Capitan's Saloon, the Providers was his only form of entertainment. Because his remote route of replacing twelve memory cards took so long, he often camped under the stars rather than make the 300-mile round trip each way to the Park. Not so bad, really, he thought. He was thankful he had a job. Most of his friends had lost their jobs during the depression. And he was thankful he wasn't stuck behind a desk listening to Moony complaining about the recent UFO sightings. Yes, he was quite thankful.

He laughed as he sang, "Woo, woo, woo, woo," to the heavens and removed his laptop and a Milky Way bar from his daypack. It was routine practice to check the week's capture before leaving the area in case the camera had a malfunction like the time he forgot to reset the lens to the infinite setting and lost an entire week of captures. The close-ups were great but anything farther than three feet away was a blur.

Smug and confident, anticipating a pocketful of quatloos on his over bet this time, Frank bit into his candy bar, pressed the "on" button, and inserted the memory card in the side slot. He waited for the short bootup to finish before hitting the return. The display blinked once, and the list of captures flowed onto the screen like a cascading waterfall. He had never seen so many files on one card…ever! He sat up, dropped his candy bar on his daypack and watched the file dates flicker down the screen. According to the dates, they had all happened this morning, too.

My God, he was going to need a U-Haul to carry all his quatloos back to Hawthorne, he calculated.

The first files had no content. Just a pretty landscape shot of this morning's pink sunrise. Fifty-two seconds later, according to the time stamp, something flashed by the lens. He paused the video, backed it up five seconds, and played it again. Whatever was out there was too fuzzy to see clearly. Without conclusive proof, his fortune was in doubt. There were still plenty of files to go, so his over bet was still intact.

He continued tapping through the files, touching the screen with a sensor pen. His memory card had enough capacity for a month of recording with plenty of memory to spare. Most of the files he found were no longer than a minute. If he looked at each one, he would be sitting here until the sun went down. No way was he hiking back to his vehicle in the dark. The thought of tripping over a rock and hitting his head, or twisting an ankle, or worse, stepping on a rattlesnake…well, there weren't enough quatloos on the planet for that, especially when the nearest cell tower was a hundred miles in any direction. So he skipped through the list and found the largest file, an eighteen-minute behemoth. It was the longest capture any of his trail cameras had ever recorded. If he found nothing in this capture, he was packing up his quatloos and heading for El Capitan's early!

Frank hit the "play" arrow. The scene was the usual view of the oasis looking east toward the distant ridgeline of sawtooth mountains. The elk liked to eat the grass and drink the cool water of the nearby spring on their way north to Montana and Idaho for the summer. The oasis was a perfect place to capture the big ten pointers at this time of year.

Suddenly, a loud "ARRRRRG!" nearly blew out the speakers in his tablet. He slapped the stop on the video and stared at the screen in disbelief. "What in the Sam bull pucky was that?"

He slid the sound to its lowest setting before replaying the file again. The roar vibrated his tablet again, even on the low setting. Moments later another deep and powerful growl made the hairs on his neck stand up. Thick branches snapped off screen of something heavy walking toward the camera from the left, behind the camera. Possibly a second beast, he thought.

No quatloos for you, Frank, the Provider warned, unless we see the animal. "Not so fast, guy," he said to the screen, "They're out there. I'll be two up, and you'll owe me plenty this time, pal."

Suddenly, the camera began to shake and heave like an earthquake had rocked the valley floor. A split second later a herd of elk stampeded across the flats like they were running for their lives. Frank couldn't believe his eyes, when a massive winged creature swooped down out of the sky and snatched a 1000-pound buck on the fly like it weighed nothing at all. It was the most amazing kill he had ever seen. He stopped the video and looked up, wondering if his eyes were playing tricks on him. His first thought was someone had scammed one of his trail cameras. It was Moony! It had to be. But neither she, nor anyone else, had any idea where he had placed them.

He stared at the screen again and was stunned to see there was still seventeen minutes twenty seconds of video left of the file! What could possibly be more shocking than the first thirty seconds, he wondered? And what kind of creature alive today could lift a half-ton ten-point bull elk off the ground like that and fly away?

He hesitated before touching play again. The thunderous hooves of the elk running down the valley and then...

WHAM!

The bull elk that had been captured earlier by the flying beast dropped from the sky and hit the ground not twenty feet from the camera. If that wasn't enough to scare the pants off him, what happened next certainly was, as two massive white tigers pounced on the carcass and tore off huge hunks of meat from the body. The winged creature then flapped down from above and wildly joined in the feast. The creature, dragon, or whatever it was, then glared straight at the camera, it's crazed yellow eyes and twisting parabolic ears, focusing right at the lens like it knew it was being photographed. After that it made the most god-awful scream Frank had ever heard in his life. Not in his wildest nightmare, had he ever heard anything so wildly wicked.

Frank slammed his laptop shut. He couldn't take another second. Not without at least five cold ones and an equal number of tequila chasers lined up in front of him. He stuffed his pack with everything he had and headed back to his vehicle as fast as his legs could carry him. He had only gone a short distance when his greatest fear came true. He stepped in a hole and fell flat on his face. The only thing that saved him from being stabbed to death by a beavertail cactus was his canvas daypack that he held out in front of him as he tumbled. Even then, a couple of sharp barbs nicked his forehead, causing blood to trickle down the side of his face. He turned around, still on the ground, to see what caused his fall. His eyes nearly came out of their sockets at the sight of the sixteen-inch paw print in the sand, along with a dozen more prints all around him.

"Holy crap!" he yelled.

A yipping sound brought his attention to a dog-like creature sitting next to a bloodied rack of ten-point antlers. It was all that was left of the bull elk.

Frank scrambled to his feet and ran and didn't look back. He ran with one eye on the trail in front of him and one eye on the sky above his head. He didn't want to think about anything following him or being the next kill of the winged creature. My God, he would only be a tiny snack for those beasts!

The tall-eared little creature with yellow eyes and strange purple fur followed him all the way back to his vehicle, like he was some kind of protective escort. Frank opened the door of his truck, tossed his daypack in the back seat, and turned to the mutt before getting in.

"Thanks, I owe ya," he said to the mutt. As scared and trembling as he was there was something about the mutt that tugged at his heart. It was tough to describe. Maybe it was simply the fact that he was someone to share his fear with, but whatever the reason, he was afraid the mutt wasn't long for this earth. "Can I offer you a ride?" The mutt just sat there at the side of the road, his maw open, his green tongue out, panting slightly, the fast pace of the run back to the truck not bothering him in the least. "No? Well, see ya around then." Frank nodded back up the trail. "Be careful out there. The dragon will eat you."

The mutt yipped twice like he had no fear of anything.

Frank got in, started his truck, and drove on down the road, his back end fish-tailing as his tires spun, reaching for all the traction they could grab. Looking back in his rearview mirror, the mutt was still sitting there, but now two white cats, larger than his truck, had joined him. There wasn't enough beer at El Capitan to calm his shakes or enough quatloos on the planet to pay him ever to return to LeBeau Park, Nevada ever again!

12

Timmer

Air Force Space Command,
Peterson Air Force Base
Colorado Springs, Colorado

IT WAS 0417 Mountain Time when the USAF super secret X-17 scramjet touched down at Peterson Air Force Base, Space Command in the Rocky Mountain state of Colorado. Captain Robert Searle stood in the chilly, pre-dawn morning with two Marine guards and waited in the darkness for the numberless stealth aircraft with no running lights to complete its 180-degree turn at the end of the tarmac before he strode toward the aircraft. A thin ladder deployed down the side to meet him at the same time the pilot's cockpit opened. Searle spritely climbed the ladder to the cockpit, and after the exchange of ID's, passwords, and security clearances were positively confirmed, the pilot handed Searle a large TOP SECRET envelope that read: For Eyes Only: Airman First Class T. Lane, and beneath his name, General R. Van Dyke. Searle returned to the tarmac and sprinted for his jeep, as the Mach 7 aircraft roared to life. Within moments, the scramjet was airborne, disappearing into the black ether, never to be seen again.

Searle made a cursory scan of the envelope from the Arecibo Observatory in Puerto Rico, while a tall, black Marine, built like a brick house, stood guard. The soldier held his SCAR 17 cocked and ready, with his finger on the trigger, as he continued to scan the airfield with his Gen V night optics, looking for any hostile threats.

Arecibo was critical to Air Force Space Command in its search for extra-terrestrial intelligence (SETI) and messaging to extra-terrestrial intelligence (METI) in order to answer the question "Are we alone in the Universe?" A few years ago a couple of Earth-grazing fireballs became wake-up calls for the governments of the world to protect the planet when a house-size meteor in 2012 passed over Spain traveling three hundred miles in the atmosphere, followed two years later by a slow-moving Christmas Eve fireball over North Africa. The last thing anyone wanted was a meteor like the estimated three-mile wide "Dino Killer" space rock that killed off the dinosaurs 65 million years ago, or the more recent comet in 12,800 B.C. that caused an extinction level event that fried the big mammals like the mammoths, sabor-tooth tigers, giant sloths, and the entire advanced human civilizations of Atlantis, North America, and Europe when it struck the Earth without warning, raising the ocean levels four-hundred feet in days when it melted the glaciers of the Ice Age. Even a lesser meteor rock of two miles could wipe out the human race again if it hit the planet with even a glancing blow. So, for the last twenty years, radio telescopes, like Arecibo, had altered their mission to search out any signs of asteroids or comets, big or small, with an orbital path bringing them near the planet. Several times since Searle's arrival at Space Command three years ago earth grazers had flown close to Earth, even inside the Moon's orbit, but none were ever serious enough to cause this heightened concern.

A chill cascaded through the Captain's body, as he took a moment to think things through.

Normal protocol for such a TOP SECRET communications had always been through the highly secure, encrypted military Internet network. But delivery by scramjet to an enlisted men like Airman Lane didn't meet the smell test. That was the game changer, and it scared the pants off Searle to think of its ramifications. Regardless, Airman

First Class T. Lane's was the top name on the packet. His duty then was not to question why a lowly enlisted airman was the first to receive the packet, his duty was to deliver this packet safely to the recipients on the envelope, regardless of rank or station, even if it meant fighting through an invading army of Chicom regulars to do it.

Searle nodded for the Marine to climb in his jeep. "You're staying with us...ah..." Searle didn't remember the Marine's name. He had come highly recommended, though, that much he knew.

"First Sergeant Max Enihoo, Captain."

"Climb in, Sarge. You're with us for the duration," Searle said.

"Yes, Sir."

* * *

Airman First Class Lane's living quarters, which the base commander General Van Dyke affectionately called "the Bunker," would hardly be categorized as military housing. The customized doublewide shipping container was located on a remote hillside with tall firs and an awesome view of the snowcapped Rockies. The Airman's shelter was as far away from Command Headquarters as the General would allow and still be within the thirty-minute window of driving time to the base. It took a four-wheel drive jeep twenty-nine minutes of switchbacks and rut road driving just to get there on a good day. During the winter months, the limit was blown out of the saddle. The snow was so deep that Airman Lane often had to be picked up by helicopter to get him to work. Fortunately, it was late spring, and the road was drivable. Even at that, Corporal Katich's skilled driving in the dark couldn't make the limit up the steep incline. With an hour until sunup, the stars were still bright and abundant. They even saw a meteor wink across the sky in front of them.

"Wow! Did you see that, Captain? That was a bright one," Katich exclaimed.

"Yeah, it's common up here, Corporal. The thin air and no city lights make them easy to see," Searle explained.

Enihoo in the back seat chimed in with a tale of his own. "My girlfriend and I saw a UFO last night, Sir." Searle traded snarky looks with Katich as Enihoo went on about his sighting. "It had blue light around its rim and traveled all the way across the sky. It was the coolest thing we've ever seen."

"I thought meteors only lasted a split second, Captain?" Katich asked.

"That's right," Searle confirmed, "ninety-nine out of a hundred flash by in a wink. I've never seen a blue one, though. Are you sure it was blue, Sarge?"

"Well, the body of the saucer was gold, but its rim was definitely blue, like the sky, Sir."

"I think the Sergeant and his lady were having a little Rocky Mountain high, if you get my drift," Katich quipped.

Enihoo wasn't about to be humiliated by an Airman half his size. "No, we were both sober as a judge, I swear. We were coming back from the City, and we saw it up on Rocky Ridge Road."

"Oooh, lovers lane," Katich giggled.

Enihoo grabbed the Corporal's shoulder, pressing him down in his seat hard. "We saw it clear, dude, and it was blue and golden."

Katich gritted his teeth, feeling the pressure. "You bet, First Sergeant, I believe you."

Searle thought anything was possible, but "Depending on the elements of the meteor, its ejecta may throw out bright white or yellow particles so it appeared like it was gold."

"It wasn't a meteor. It was a UFO," Enihoo insisted.

Searle thought the Marine might have been watching too much sci-fi. "It had to be a meteor. It's the only explanation, Sergeant."

Enihoo didn't care what the two Airmen believed. He and his girlfriend saw what they saw, and it was a UFO. "It seemed mighty close to me, and it went right between those high peaks over there to the west, Sir."

"That smell," Katich announced, suddenly changing the subject from UFO's to an illegal crop. "Someone's growing pot up here, Captain."

The Milky Way was high and bright overhead. The late May temperature in the mountain passageway above Space Command was unusually cool for this time of year, making the aroma of Airman Lane's cannabis patch particularly pungent from a quarter mile away.

"Wildflowers, Corporal," Searle said somberly.

"I don't think so. That's a grow going on out here. I'm certain," Katich stated, not quite understanding Searle's intent.

Searle leaned over and glared at the Corporal unblinkingly. "Wildflowers, Airman," he repeated with earnest. "And nothing but wildflowers, gentlemen," he added with an unmistakable emphasis on the word "wildflowers."

The Corporal suddenly got it as Enihoo laughed, understanding Searle's meaning a mile back. "Yes, Sir, wildflowers," Katich replied, "I smell the wonder fragrance of Rocky Mountain wildflowers, Sir, definitely."

Searle pointed at the Bunker ahead. "Excellent, you're an Airman of fine taste, Corporal Katich. Park in front of the door, avoiding the wildflower patch to the right, if you please."

"Yes, Sir."

Even before knocking on Airman Lane's door, they heard the loud groans of lovemaking echoed throughout the narrow valley the instant Katich switched off the engine.

Enihoo exclaimed upon hearing the grunts and groans coming from within the bunker, "My God! That woman's in trouble in there, Sir!"

Enihoo unlatched the door to rescue the woman when Searle reached back and grabbed the Marine's sleeve. "Freeze! I don't hear a thing." Enihoo met Searle's fixated eyes, and for the second time this morning, the Captain's silent suggestion became clear. Enihoo backed off. He glanced at Katich next. "Do you hear anything from inside Timmer's bunker, Corporal?"

"Not a thing, Sir. Silent as a morgue in there," Katich confirmed as the loud screams continued unabated.

Like a switch turned on in his head, Enihoo mouth turned to a wide grin. "Did you say Airman Timmer?"

"That's right, this is Timmer's bunker," Searle confirmed.

Airman Timmer was legend at Space Command, and from the sudden change of expression on Enihoo's face, the grunts and groans now made perfect sense.

Enihoo sat back. "Yes, Sir, all quiet."

Searle took the TOP SECRET envelope with him as he went to the door and knocked. He rapped a number of times, but the sounds inside were so loud, no amount of pounding could disturb the occupants inside. Searle turned back to the jeep and asked Enihoo, "Could you get Airman Lane's attention for me, First Sergeant?"

"Yes, Sir, gladly." Enihoo pointed his SCAR-17 skyward and fired two rounds, waking the dead for miles around.

"Thank you, Sergeant."

The ear-shattering reports did the trick. The screams and moans stopped, and moments later, a disheveled and exhausted young blond-haired, six-foot-one, athletic, baby blue-eyed airman cracked open the door and angrily chewed the Captain out for disturbing his privacy. "Robby? Man, what are you doing here?" Timmer was Timmer. He didn't give a rat's patootie who was at the door or what rank that person had on his lapel. When he was entertaining, no one was sacred. He proceeded to blow a lungful of cannabis smoke into the Captain's face. "Can't you hear I'm busy?" he fumed.

Without flinching, Captain Searle unholstered his Colt 1911 and touched the end of the barrel to the young man's nose. "Do that again and you'll be swallowing a 45 for breakfast, Airman. I don't care who's pet donkey you are."

This wasn't the first time Searle had interrupted one of Timmer's peccadillos. It seemed common occurrence these days. He learned a long time ago that show-and-tell made a much better impression than trying to explain himself to this hedonistic moron. Timmer, as the General called him, was treated like the son he never had. Say what you will about his lifestyle, Timmer was the best astrophysics analyst at Space Command. To General Van Dyke, there was no one on the planet he trusted more for astronomic answers. The nineteen-year old, Airman First Class Timothy Lane may have lacked the science degrees from MIT, Cornell, or Stanford, like others on the General's staff, but what Timmer lacked in elite degrees he more than made up for in results and hard work. Completely self-taught in astrophysical analytics, he barely completed his two-year associate science degree at Long Beach City College in Long Beach, California before joining the Air Force. It was either that or spend the next five years in federal prison for hacking into the Air Force's super-secret military satellite array to spy on the nude sunbathers in the Greek islands, the French Rivera, and Blacks Beach in LaJolla. His sizzling photos paid big on the Internet before they caught him red-handed selling his wares to porn sites on the dark web. Luckily, it was General Van Dyke who saw his potential. He snapped him up when he blew away all the Ivy League graduates with his handwritten paper on: The Real Earth Threats of Aliens, Near Earth-Grazers, and Other Space Anomalies. When the General, an MIT graduate in astronomy himself, read the manuscript, he wasted no time in transferring Timmer to his staff at Space Command…no questions asked. Timmer may have been a handful for the military establishment; he had been brought up for court-martial six times for his misconduct and indiscretions, but he beat them all. Everyone on the base, officers and enlisted alike, knew to treat him with kid gloves, or they would find themselves staring down the cold blue eyes of General Van Dyke and doing midnight guard duty for a month. It didn't matter what rank they were. Space Command was General Van Dyke's kingdom. You screw with the Timmer, you screw with the King. It was a shot across the bow that no one, not even full bird colonels, were willing to challenge.

Timmer turned away, leaving the door open for Searle to enter. "Make it quick, Robby, I still have a couple of hours with Darlin' left in me," he said with all sincerity.

There were no power lines to the Bunker. The first time Searle approached Timmer's refuge, he expected to see the third world fortification of a survivalist. Having seen the Airman's office, filled with a mountain of TOP SECRET file folders, discarded sandwich wrappers, mixed with adult travel magazines of South Sea island living on a wide desk, the top of which had never seen the light of day since the dawn of the Roman Empire, he figured his home would be even worse. The Airman's sanctuary, however, was not at all what he expected. He was blown away by his perfect grow of "wildflowers" surrounding the corrugated silver and black trim storage bins. Inside was like walking into an Architectural Digest model home. The one bedroom doublewide structure was spotlessly clean and full of wall art he made himself, expensive deep leather sofas, custom wood chairs, and a kitchen any topflight chef would envy. And all of it powered completely off the grid. The metal walls and ceilings were lined with thick, four-inch hard insulation under the drywall and metal walls. It retained heat or cold like a seven hundred dollar Yeti cooler. The window openings, of which there were many, were cut out with a blowtorch and installed with triple glazed windows. A nearby thermal spring fed hot water to a system of radiant pipes in the floor, keeping the two-room shelter toasty warm with enough residual heat left over for an endless supply of hot water. A snow-fed mountain stream farther up the valley served all his water needs year-round, including the swamp cooler that kept the Bunker pleasantly cool all summer long without air conditioning. Twenty south-facing, 240 watt, solar panels on the roof ran all his pumps and lighting throughout and were connected to an array of Rolls-Serrat battery packs inside a small container room behind the Bunker. And if the sun didn't supply enough energy during extended winter nights, a 10,000-kilowatt diesel generator, with enough fuel to run 24/7 for a month, had its own room beside the batteries. Searle recalled mocking Timmer once about his off-the-grid lifestyle. To which Timmer simply smiled and ask how many times the power went out at his house last winter. Twelve he thought. Maybe more. How did that work out for you? Chilly was Searle's answer. So why is your office so disorganized, butthead, when the Bunker is so clean. Another smile preceded his sardonic reply: I work there, buttbreath, I live here.

"Who is this, Timmer? A friend?" a girl asked leaning against the doorway to the bedroom. She was barely dressed, wearing one of Timmer's t-shirts that read: "Want to Play Doctor?" The shirt barely covered her essentials, causing Searle's heart to sputter. Besides being well endowed, she was tall with long dark hair, smooth skin, and dark eyes that would melt an arctic iceberg. On a scale of ten, ten being best he had ever seen, he put Timmer's houseguest at a twelve. He didn't recall ever seeing him with the same girl twice. It was like a continuous *Sports Illustrated* swimsuit parade breezing through the Bunker. Where Timmer found these babes, God only knew. It certainly wasn't Space Command. He had never seen him with a skank, either. The moron certainly had taste; he would give him that.

"A pain in my backside, Darlin'," Timmer replied. He then turned to Searle and pointed at the envelope he had at his side. "Is that for me?"

Searle stood motionless, gawking at Darlin'. A finger snap brought him back from forgetting why he had come to the Bunker in the first place. "Robby," Timmer asked again, "is that for me?"

Searle blinked and handed the envelope over. "Yeah."

Timmer glanced at the cover. "Top Secret, huh? And check that out. My name's at the top. Have I been promoted?"

"In your dreams, suckwad. It was delivered by scramjet from Arecibo an hour ago."

Timmer nodded, "No joke," and began opening the envelope as the girl slid across the room and snaked her arms around his waist. It made Searle sweat watching her rub against his bare chest. Her eyes glanced his way as she said to him, "You have pretty eyes. Are you an officer?"

Searle tried to stay cool under the interrogation while Timmer continued scanning the contents of the envelope.

"Answer her, Robby. Darlin' won't bite," Timmer said.

"Yes, ma'am, I'm an officer," Searle replied.

"Are you single?" Darlin' asked.

"Yes, ma'am."

"Want to meet some flight attendant friends of mine? We fly into Colorado Springs often."

"Not now, ma'am."

"Do you ski?"

"Yes, ma'am."

"Are you hot on the slopes?"

Timmer continued reading through the material but was able to multi-task with some info on the Captain. "He's good, Darlin'. Skis nothing but black diamonds. Isn't that right, Robby?"

"I like to go fast."

Darlin's mouth dropped open impressed. She was about to continue the interrogation when Timmer interrupted the flow. "Whoa!" he exclaimed in alarm. "Stop talking," he ordered. He read on for a moment longer before coming to life. "We gotta go! We gotta go," he kept repeating as he began re-stuffing the papers back in the envelope with no regard to order. "This is beyond serious."

"What is it?" Darlin' asked.

Timmer took her in his arms and said with sadness. "I have to go, Darlin'. If I tell you what it is," he nodded at Searle, "he would have to kill you." Timmer wasn't kidding.

"Shall I have breakfast ready?" she asked.

"No, I'm not coming back for a while. Someone will be by to pick you up." He handed the envelope back to Searle and began putting on the clothes that had been discarded in the earlier getting acquainted phase of the evening. He found his sneakers behind the sofa and his t-shirt draped over a lampshade. Nothing was military. After finding only what he needed, he headed for the front door saying to Darlin', "Just tell them where you need to go, and they'll take care of you." He was almost clear when he poked his head back inside with a rascally smile full of bright white teeth and a glint in his eye and added, "Leave your cell number on the coffee table. We're not finished here."

Then out the door he went without touching the porch steps. Katich had the engine running hot. Timmer climbed into the back seat with Enihoo, yelling, "Move, move, move!" The jeep spun around like a donut, reversing course, and headed down the valley with Darlin', all legs and puppy-dog eyes, waving goodbye inside the doorway.

"JESUS H., Timmer!" Katich gasped. "You leaving that behind?"

Timmer leaned forward, doing his best to keep his head from hitting the roof of the jeep on the rough road while he dressed. "Duty calls, Corporal. Now get to the General's house like your life depends on it."

Katich looked at Searle for confirmation. "General Van Dyke?"

Timmer cut off the silent communication in a hurry. "Don't look at him, Corporal, look at me. I'm giving the orders from here on out, so do as I say. Get our butts to the General's place, and I mean rapido!"

Katich was about to balk when Searle surprisingly sided with Timmer. "You heard him, Corporal, that's a direct order!"

"Yes, Sir!"

As the jeep spit dirt behind it, Timmer kept muttering words of disbelief about the UFO. Enihoo, sitting beside him, unintentionally caught the word and said, "I saw one last night, Timmer."

That got Timmer's attention. "What did you see, Sargeant?"

"A UFO. I heard you say UFO. My girlfriend and I...well, we saw one last night going low and slow between the mountains."

Searle turned around, shaking his head. "He says it was blue meteor. That's not possible."

Timmer turned to Enihoo. "It was blue?"

"It wasn't a meteor."

Searle interrupted again. "There's no such thing—"

Timmer cut off Searle. "Don't listen to him. Robby wouldn't know a UFO if it parked in his front yard. Now tell me again, what color was it?"

"It was blue, Timmer, I swear," Enihoo stated, never veering from his story.

Timmer's eyes flew open. "STOP THE JEEP!"

Katich stepped on the brakes, bringing the jeep to a jaw-biting, sliding stop.

No one understood why Timmer was in such a panic.

"What's your clearance, Corporal?" Timmer demanded to know.

Katich looked back, confused. He had never been asked that question before. "I...I...don't know."

"OUT!" Timmer barked. Katich opened the door, stunned by the directness of the order. "Get out of the jeep, Corporal!" Timmer ordered again, as he pushed Searle aside and took over the wheel.

"It's five miles back to base," Katich balked, looking on in dismay.

Without one word of explanation, Timmer slammed the jeep door shut and hit the accelerator, leaving Katich behind in the middle of a dark, moonless dirt road. "Tell me about that UFO, Sergeant, and don't leave out a single detail."

13

Bunk House Burgers

Cañon City, Colorado

BY MID-MORNING HARLOWE'S stomach found the burger marquee too gut-wrenching to pass up as Jewels drove him and Mowgi slowly through town. Every sense of smell, sight, and taste focused like a *Millawanda* target array on the "Bunk House Burgers" street sign up ahead. "They had better have thick chocolate shakes and fries to go along with the burger," he said to Mowgi, panting next to him. They were starving. They hadn't had a bite since leaving the ship. So, while waiting for nightfall, picking up something to eat was a good way to kill some time.

Cañon City, Colorado was like every city they had driven through from Nevada. The streets of the town were in high disrepair. Cracks in the pavement were everywhere. If it weren't for the fact that the Granny never touch the pavement, it would have been slow going. Businesses were in no better condition. If they were still in business, they were run down, and only open for a few hours during the day. Even large cities like Salt Lake City, Provo, and American Fork, going East on I-70 and on to Grand Junction and Gunnison, Colorado, that were once thriving commercial and industrial centers of the West, were now practically ghost towns. Twice he tried stopping for lunch, but roving gangs of thugs kept him from finding someplace peaceful to eat. He didn't have the time to play policeman. His priorities lay elsewhere. Besides, he had plenty of nutrient meals in the Granny, if it came to that. He would never go hungry, but there was nothing like real food to satisfy his craving for a thick burger and fries. This town seemed peaceful enough to grab a quick bite without finding trouble.

They hummed past a Walmart, and incredibly, there were few cars parked in the massive lot. There seemed to be more armed guards patrolling the outside of the giant store than there were people inside shopping. An O'Reilly Auto Parts store came up next. It looked like it had been closed for some time. Its windows were broken, and the building exterior was marred with vile drawings and bullet holes. A Subway, Burger King, and a McDonalds were next. The fast-food chains that he thought never in a million years would ever close, had all suffered the same fate as the auto parts store. They were boarded up and never coming back.

Pulling into the Bunk House parking lot, a beggar met Harlowe and Mowgi getting out of the car. "Spare anything to eat, son?" The man in his thirties with a straggly beard, torn clothes, tattered shoes, and baseball cap stared at Mowgi like he was his next meal. A sudden anxiety came over Harlowe as he scanned up and down the empty streets. Come to think of it, in his trek across the west he saw no dogs or cats roaming anywhere. Even large animals like horses, sheep, and cows were missing from the pastures they drove by. It was like the planet Osset, he reminded himself, when he and Monday searched for the lost city of Lamille. In their trek across the planet, they found a once thriving civilization that had fallen into a great despair because Cornicen and its revenue collectors called Tappers had pillaged the hopes and aspirations of the people there.

Had the system really broken down that fast? Had Earth now become another Osset?

"Hold on, mister," Harlowe replied, sympathetic to the man's plight. "I'll get you something." He would buy him enough food to get him through the next day. That was the least he could do. He bent down to

Mowgi and told him to stay put while he went inside and ordered. The undog's yellow eyes glanced over at the beggar like he was saying to him, I'm not responsible for him being stupid. Harlowe patted him between his parabolics. "I won't be long."

But just to be safe, Harlowe warned the beggar, "I'm coming right back with food so don't mess the dog or your day won't end well."

The beggar saluted him and said, "Roger that, governor."

Harlowe figured his warning had fallen on deaf ears, but at least he tried. "Your funeral, pal," he mumbled to himself as he walked away.

* * *

The mouth-watering aroma of grilled hamburger meat and boiling French fries slapped Harlowe square in the face right when he entered the Bunk House Burger eatery. There was not a soul in the place, but he didn't care. His eyes closed as his senses breathed in every molecule of grease.

"Whoa…" was all he could say as he drooled over the menu, thinking he would order the entire list of entrées, side orders, and appetizers, that is, if there was any food left. To his dismay, three-quarters of the menu was crossed out.

"Can I help you?" the man asked from behind the counter.

Harlowe came out of his stupor to reply to the man. "Yeah, but why all the cross outs?" he asked, pointing up at the menu.

"Regulations, cut backs, restricted produce, you name it. That's all we have. You wouldn't believe the magic we have to do to make that much," the man complained.

"That bad, huh?"

The man looked like he wanted to break a dish over the counter. "If it wasn't for Nootzy's Hoods, we would have closed up just like the corporate guys down the street."

"Nootzy's Hoods. Who are they?"

"You've never heard of Nootzy's Hoods? Where have you been kid, on some off-world planet?"

"On a number of them, actually," Harlowe admitted truthfully. "Nootzy? That's the President now, right?"

"That's right. Seriously boy, you've really been out of touch, haven't ya?"

Harlowe just shrugged. There was no point in trying to explain something that wouldn't have any meaning to the man when he was so hungry he could eat the kitchen rag the guy had in his hand.

"So what can I get you, son?" the man asked.

Harlowe pointed at the menu board. "Five of those big Bunk House Cheese Burgers for a start."

"Don't take this wrong, son, but can you afford that much meat? Those burgers are pretty pricey. Ninety new dollars each."

Harlowe had spoken to Riverstone earlier about what to expect when buying anything. The dollar is history, Dog, he said. Rerun pulled out a wad of Franklins, and they just laughed at him. Use Wiz's card, he told him, it works.

Harlowe pulled out the blue G-coin card and showed to the man. "This good enough?"

"If it goes through, it is."

Harlowe handed the man his card. "Give it a shot. Add three orders of fries and three chocolate shakes to the bill, if you would, please."

"Are you guvment, kid?" the man asked suspicious.

"No, just hungry."

"No one orders like that unless they're guvment."

"How do the Hoods pay for it?" Harlowe wondered.

"They have a special card like you. It comes out of everyone's hide, you know."

"It always does." Harlowe pointed at the G-card in the man's hand. "Add another ten Bunk Houses to the bill and keep the change. That comes out of a bankers hide, and that's all you have to know."

The man squinted disapprovingly. He didn't believe a word Harlowe told him until he ran his card and it came back good as gold. "My apologies for doubting you, son. It passed with flying colors. Came back with five out of five green stars, too. I've never seen a money card score that high. If you ain't guvment , you must be connected."

Harlowe pointed at the man's nose in jest. "If I told you, I'd have to hurt you."

The man laughed uproariously. "I'll keep that in mind. Your order will be right up, son."

14

Dutch

JUST PASSED 1100 Base Commander, General Richard "Dutch" Van Dyke, chewing on a fat, Montecristo Grand cigar, blew through the high security doors of Space Command, Base Operations Headquarters like he owned the place . . . which he did . . . every square inch of it. He removed his cap, folded it crisply, and tucked it in his right-rear pocket, exposing his close cut, flame red hair as he barked loud enough for everyone in the large room to hear, "Who in here has TOP SECRET (TS) clearance?"

Command Chief Master Sergeant Steven McDonald was taken by surprise. The old man wasn't due at Operations for another hour. After a delayed leap to attention, CMSgt. McDonald shouted out, "Space Commanding General in the Building! Atten hut!"

The giant operations room, full of blazingly fast quantum computers, massive overhead display screens that covered three-quarters of the total

71

wall space, and over two hundred space systems personnel that included radar specialists, recon analysts, astrophysicists, and communication operators, came to full attention, as the world stopped and became so quiet one could hear an ant fart. A bird colonel, two captains, and a third of the computer specialists raised their hands.

Van Dyke glared in the colonel's direction as he doused his Cuban in the nearest receptacle. Not even four-star generals were allowed to smoke in the controlled Operations environment. "That's it, Colonel Morgan?" Van Dyke asked.

The Colonel saluted crisply. "Yes Sir, General, that's it for the night shift. We have twenty more with TS clearance personnel coming at oh, eleven-hundred, Sir."

Van Dyke turned to Searle and Timmer who came with him. "Captain. Got your pen ready?"

"Yes, Sir," Searle replied, grabbing his pen from his front left pocket.

"Confer with the Colonel. Get the names of all TS personnel on the base, and get them to operations pronto. We need to fill these computer consoles within the hour."

"Yes, Sir."

While Searle was getting his TS list together, the General turned back to the room. "How many have Secret clearance?" Eight more hands raised. "All right, you airmen now have TS clearance. Is that understood?"

"Yes, Sir!" came the collective shout.

The General waved his hand over the room. "The rest of you clear out. You are dismissed until further notice. Do not leave the base, see your girlfriends or wives, or make a quick trip to Costco for gas. We may need you at a later time. That is all." As the operations personnel without the proper security clearance filed out the main doorway, Van Dyke ordered out the side of his mouth, "Stay with me, Timmer."

"Yes, Sir, like Gorilla glue," Timmer replied.

The General rolled his eyes. On their way to the high-security situation room, off the main operations center, the General had a change of plan as they went by Searle and the Colonel. "Delay that order, Searle. I need you here." He glanced to his right. "Colonel you get those TS personnel over here on the double."

"Sir?"

Van Dyke could see the Colonel was uneasy doing the work of a lower grade officer, but this wasn't the time to worry about bruised egos. His steel blue eyes blew a hole through the Colonel's forehead. "Do it, Colonel."

"Yes, Sir!"

When the Colonel left, Van Dyke went to Searle as they entered the situation room, and Timmer closed the door. "When's Vice Commander Wirstlin due back from his fishing trip?"

"Tomorrow, Sir," Searle replied.

"Hell, the whole damn planet may be swarming with ETs by then."

"Yes, Sir."

"Find out where Hatchet is and get his butt back here. No one knows Misty, Gambit, Magnum, and Maxwell," the military's super secret space satellite system, "like he does."

"I'm on it, Sir."

Searle was headed out the door when the General stopped him again. "Hold on, Captain, I'm not done with you yet. Contact General Mike Jackson at NORAD and General Gilman at ADCOM. Give them a heads up on what's coming down here."

"Yes, Sir."

"Tell them to keep everyone dark until we get a handle of what these ETs are up to."

"What about the Pentagon, Sir?" Searle asked.

Van Dyke's face went hard. "Especially the Pentagon! Dark as ink, Captain. Too many ass wipes back there, and with Drgastin being the President's number one butt kisser, no one's to be trusted except for the people I, and I alone, designate as solid. Understood, Searle?"

"Not even the President, General?"

Searle thought the General would bite through a 16d nail with the mention of her name. "That goes triple for that witch."

Searle was well aware of the bad blood between General Van Dyke and President for Life, Nootzy Shame. Twice she had threatened him with demotion for refusing to send SAC jet fighters from Peterson AFB to quell rioters in the Denver suburbs of Stapleton and Montbello. "We don't fire on our own, Madame President," he told her straight out, defying every threat she used against him. He figured one day he would end up in a cell at the Administrative Maximum Facility (ADX) in Florence, Colorado next to former President Delmonte and General Ivan Branch. They were heroes in his book, especially General Branch, who had been a mentor of his when he was a green lieutenant just out of the Naval War College.

"Yes, Sir."

The General glanced at Timmer. "Anything else, Timmer?"

The Airman faced Searle and rifled off a few requests. "Have someone pick up Darlin'. She needs to be at the airport by thirteen hundred hours. And while you're going by the mess hall, order us up some eggs over easy, crispy bacon, hash browns, none of that mushy crap, make that crispy, too." He pointed at Van Dyke. "Apple juice good for you, General?"

"Cranberry."

Back to Searle, Timmer went on. "Add cranberry and a two-gallon pot of Arabica coffee."

Searle's eyes narrowed, fighting off an effort to punch Timmer in the face. "Got a particular brand in mind, Airman?" he asked with an obvious cynical bite to his question.

"Glad you asked. Pleasant Hill Farms, restaurant blend. Chief Sergeant Miller always keeps a stash. If he denies having any, check out his personal freezer. It's there, trust me."

Searle glared at Van Dyke disgusted. "Just do it, Captain."

Searle bit his lower lip. "Yes, Sir."

Van Dyke turned his attention to the packet of Top Secret docs long enough for Searle to extend his long middle finger at Timmer. Timmer grinned back with an added wink. Searle turned and headed out the door when Timmer added, "Make sure that bacon is crispy, Searle."

Searle hesitated, shivered, then continued on to carry out his mission.

"He's a good officer, Timmer," Van Dyke commented, watching Searle through the office windows, taking charge, pulling a female officer aside, giving her orders like he was five levels above her rank. She gave him that look of who-do-you-think-you-are, Captain? That didn't concern Searle. He had orders. He pointed back at the situation room where Van Dyke's riveting eyes shot right through her. In slack-jawed fear, she faced Searle again like she was demoted to basic airman. He proceeded to give her his list of demands and continued to his next task without a second thought.

Timmer nodded in agreement. "He's damn good, General. Best man on your staff. You should make him a bird colonel when this is over."

"I'd lose him to General Gilman if I did. How 'bout major? Will that work?"

"Done, but we keep it to ourselves. I don't want him getting a fat head," Timmer quipped.

Van Dyke chuckled, then went totally sober, tapping the packet of Top Secret papers. "What do we have, Timmer. Is this the real deal?"

Timmer's face had already drained of any humor. He was total business from here on out. "More real than you can believe, General. The existence of Earth may depend on what we decide here today."

It seemed like a god-awful eternity before Van Dyke said straight out, "Tell us what you have son. I'll make that decision."

"Of course, General," Timmer acknowledged, as he began emptying the contents of the packet onto the dark, rosewood conference table that could easily seat thirty people comfortably even in the overstuffed, Corinthian leather captain's chairs surrounding it.

There was a black clipped, inch stack of papers with all kinds of mathematical formulations and calculations that looked like something Einstein or Hawking might have drawn up. Timmer just tossed it aside like it was package stuffing.

"Don't you need that?" Van Dyke asked.

Timmer pointed at his head. "I got it, General." He went right to the white, foot-wide square sheet of folded paper, and kept unfolding it until the document was four feet wide along each side. "This is astronomical photo taken by Arecibo." He checked the series of world time clocks on the wall. "Taken nine hours ago and change."

Arecibo has four radar transmitters that send megahertz wavelengths out into space. The observatory's most effective range bounce back was to Saturn's orbit. That takes 2.6 hours for the bounce back to reach the deep parabolic reflector and its 900-ton platform receiver suspended 150 m (492 ft) above the dish by eighteen cables running from three reinforced concrete towers. Van Dyke knew all this and much, much more. As an MIT graduate in astrophysics, extragalactic astrophysics, and with emphasis on gravitational wave detection, it was completely unnecessary for Timmer to explain to the General how to read an astronomical photographic document. He could read them in his sleep. Timmer's function was to add observation, conjecture, and theory to the solution. Cut to the damn chase, as the General often put it, and visualized for his commander where to focus his attention. The recent Arecibo star map, three maps in all, had over a million tiny black specks of various sizes of magnitude spread out on a giant white background. It was up to Timmer to muscle through the morass and spit out in plain English quickly and decisively why the General was wasting his time staring at a bunch of frickin' dots!

Timmer tossed the top page onto the floor, shuffling to the second document. He took a second longer, glanced over the last sheet and tossed it with the first. "Here! This is all we need."

Van Dyke pointed at the floor. "Out of all that, we only need this?"

Timmer traced his finger along the planetary elliptic plane. "It starts right there, General. See that long thin line?"

"Yeah, so? I see those Earthgrazers all the time."

"That's not an Earthgrazer, General." He pointed to another line. Only this one was less than an eighth of an inch long. "This is a grazer. It's nothing compared to the first line. That's our ET, General. Right there. Arecibo got lucky and caught it right when it blinked onto the scene."

"That line is over an A.U. long! (astronomical unit) What goes that fast?"

"ET, General."

"Holy mother…"

Timmer continued: "At that point ET was heading through Canis Minor, breezing by Procyon there on its way along the elliptic to that point there. It stayed put there for twenty minutes. Why, I don't know, but then headed in and stopped here," he said, stabbing the point on the document with his index finger.

Van Dyke bent down and read the plate. "Why that's—"

"Correct, Sir, Mars!"

Van Dyke appeared confused. "Why Mars? It's a dead planet. Nothing there but dust, sand storms, and leftover NASA junk."

Timmer shook his head. He didn't have an answer for that one either. "They're still there, though."

"How do you know? With their transport speed, they could be anywhere by now."

Timmer retrieved the first sheet from the floor and returned it to the table, smoothing it out as he searched what he was looking for at the bottom of the page. "This was taken two hours after the last page. No sign of them leaving, yet Sir. Plus...," He reached to the floor and picked out a stack of papers and proceeded to peel through several pages. "These are the gravitational specs. Not one instance of abnormality."

Van Dyke checked the sheet himself. "So you think they're still there, huh?"

"I know they are." Timmer hesitated. "Correction. Let me rephrase that, General. At the time of this printout they were."

"Back to my question: Why Mars?" the General asked, hoping for any answer the made sense.

"I don't know, Sir, but I've never seen a more powerful gravity signature than this. It's off the charts." He thumbed through two more pages and turned the docs around for Van Dyke. "Here, Sir, tell me what you see."

At a single glance, Van Dyke's breathing stopped.

15

Officer Cox

Lakewood, California

RIVERSTONE'S GUT TURNED queasy the instant Alice drove
the Gamadin limousine off the Interstate 605 Freeway onto Del Amo
Boulevard. In was a bright, cloudless noonday, too, a perfect day to be
alive and back in Lakewood, riding through his old stomping grounds.
It looks the same, he thought, preferring his robob's company as he
rode shotgun rather than riding alone with all that empty space in the
back. They had dropped Simon off earlier at Saul's, his movie agent, on
Wilshire Boulevard. The plan was to meet later for dinner at Spago's, a
Hollywood hotspot for the in-crowd, according to Rerun. They both
wanted to spend a week at their respective hangouts, but everyone's off-
the-clock time was limited until their business planet-side was done.

As the limo motored west between the spring growth of sycamores
that bordered each side of the wide avenue, Riverstone found it difficult
to visualize a whole generation of his friends growing up without him.
All his sisters, even Joni, the baby of the family, were five years older
than him now. He kept shaking his head at the thought of his little sister
bossing him around. How can that be? He had to laugh. Not because

there was humor in it, but what else could he do? Time passing that swiftly was a Sci-fi Channel thing, not his reality.

Geez!

Cruising in from the outer planets, there were moments he wanted to break his Stradivarius violin over his night table. It wasn't fair. Time had played a cruel trick on them. Eleven years gone! It was only a few months for him, but eleven years as far as his family was concerned. Eleven years his dad, and especially his mom, must have agonized over never hearing a word from their galactic son. No phone calls. No text messages. Not even a Gama-gram or interstellar conference call. Nothing at all to let them know if he was alive or dead . . . for ELEVEN YEARS!

After a string of well-deserved lyrics of rage, he turned to laughter again to hide his frustration. His parents knew where Fate had taken them. They had gotten used to the fact that he would be gone for weeks at a time, flying around the galaxy, saving damsels in distress. At least that's what he told his dad, anyway. Evan Riverstone never believed his son for a second, nor would his dad have believed the real stories either. Their training on Mars, *Mons* diving off a 15,000-foot cliff, his captivity on Erati, his falling in love with an alien female, Ela, the forever love of his life, or the saving of an entire planet from a gamma-ray burst...twice! Even he had a hard time believing half of what the hand of Fate had already dealt them.

Regardless, the Riverstones were proud of their son, proud of his higher calling. Proud like they had a son who joined the military to serve his country. But it was much more than that, of course. He and his Gamadin crewmates served not only the Earth, they served the galaxy. He chuckled again, recalling how his parents conjured up little white lies for his sisters, their neighbors like Mrs. Knaub, and his friends from school who wanted to know why he didn't graduate from high school with them. Even his grandparents: Nany and Papaw, on his mom's side, and Grindad and Mary, his second wife, on his dad's side, thought he was a special forces soldier, off fighting bad guys overseas. All of which was true, but not necessarily on this planet.

Thinking of his grandparents made his nose hurt, hoping they were all still alive. To never see his Grindad's joy again when he ran into his arms was almost too much to bear. He sucked in a huge lungful of hope, as the limo passed over the Del Amo underpass, taking his mind away from the memory. The tunnel beneath the boulevard was where he and Harlowe took down Avitia and his two goons, Tatoo-arm and Angel Hat. The Avitia gang had entered Lakewood to seize the territory for their drug empire. But not that day, Riverstone smiled. That day they ran into a couple of Lakewood protectors who made Avitia and his two brain-deads scrub the graffiti off the walls. He sighed. It was also the day Rachel entered his life.

Such a long time ago, he thought, not eleven years, either, but a lifetime ago.

Riverstone pointed at the street sign up ahead. "Turn left on Woodruff, Alice." Alice tilted her head slightly. She didn't talk but her small gestures were quite clear. This isn't the way to your house, dude. "I know," Riverstone responded, eyeing a police officer parked along the side of a service street. He gave the limo a scrutinizing eye as they drove by. It was the third black and white patrol car he had spotted since leaving the freeway. "I wanna go by Lakewood High. It's sorta on the way," he told Alice.

Alice flicked her blond hair back. Whatever...

The McDonalds came up first on the left. It was where he and Harlowe ate a lot before the first In-N-Out came to Lakewood. The Golden Arches looked empty and dirty. My God, it was closed! How can that be? The parking lot was littered with plastic cups and discarded wrappers. At least it was spick-and-span when Harlowe made the college jocks clean the entire lot after disrespecting their dates. On the same side of the street the limo passed Del Valle Park and the Marine Corps "Skyknight" jet fighter still flying high on its pedestal, but the once flawless fuselage was now marred by graffiti along its beautiful silver body. Even the bus stop where he and Wiz found Harlowe stretched out on the bench was crisscrossed with black and red paint. When they were here, Lakewood was clean. No one painted their city or they paid for it just like the homeboys who tried to kill Harlowe had. The bullet only grazed his head. He caught them on foot, running flat out through Mae Boyer Park. They didn't know Lakewood streets like he did. Their car hit a lamppost when Harlowe cut them off, smashed the driver's window, and yanked the three of them out of the car. When he and Wiz found him, he was resting on the bus bench, waiting for them to pick him up to go surfing. The homeboys were already laid out on the streets where Harlowe beat the ever-loving snot out of each one. His scraped knuckles were his only injuries.

Pointing again, Riverstone told Alice, "Turn right here, Babe." The limo went half a block on Centraila when a patrol car turned on its flashing lights behind them. Alice dutifully pulled over to the curb and stopped. Riverstone knew Alice was innocent of any wrongdoing. Her programming would never allow it to break the traffic laws unless a Gamadin told her otherwise. The Officer walked stiffly up to Riverstone's side of the limousine, as he lowered the window. "Afternoon, Officer, ah…" Riverstone read the nameplate. "Kenneth Cox."

"Your plates say you're from out of town?" Officer Cox began.

Riverstone looked over at the school, stunned by the run-down grounds, dead grass, cracked windows, more graffiti everywhere along the walls, and the high, black-barred metal fencing around the entire school. It looked more like a prison, not a school.

"Yes Sir, I used to go to school here. What happened to it?" Riverstone asked.

"No money. Simple as that. Your auto-driver have a license?" Officer Cox asked with an unpleasantness to his tone.

Riverstone grinned like his hand was caught in a cookie jar. "License?"

Officer Cox pointed at Alice. "Is she some kind of joke?"

"No. What's the problem?"

"That hair is ridiculous."

Riverstone glanced at Alice. "She just permed it this morning."

Office Cox stiffened, placing his hand on his hips. "Are you being a wise-ass, son?"

"No, Sir."

"This vehicle registration in order?"

"Yes, Sir. Up to date."

"The droid's license," Officer Cox stated again. He seemed to be getting less patient by the second.

Riverstone turned to Alice. "Alice, do you have a license?"

"That's its name, Alice?"

"Yes, Sir."

"The license."

"Yes, Sir." Back to Alice, Riverstone mouthed, not really saying anything, "You got one, right?"

Alice reached over, opened the glove box, and removed a card with her picture on it, handing it to Riverstone.

"Here you go, Officer."

"I've never seen a droid do that," Officer Cox said.

"She's the newest model. She has a lot of extra features."

Officer Cox stared at the license, scrutinizing every square inch, turning the card around, reading the back, raising it to the air, and tapping it against the windowsill of the limo. "Seems authentic."

"It is, Officer," Riverstone assured him.

"We'll see about that. I'll be right back."

When the Officer Cox went back to his patrol car, Riverstone called the ship. "Hey, need a little help here."

Monday answered. *"Got you covered, Mr. Riverstone. How are you and Mr. Bolt doing? Any changes?"*

Riverstone scanned the high school again and replied, "Too many changes, Squid. Lakewood's not like it used to be. It's a dump."

"Lakewood isn't the only place that's run down. Dog checked in and reported entire neighborhoods across the nation are suffering big time."

"Why? I thought President Delmonte had everything firing on all cylinders."

"Yeah, he did, until he was removed from office. The new administration took over and—"

"I'm sorry to interrupt you, Sir," Officer Cox said upon returning. His total demeanor had suddenly shifted to Officer Friendly for whatever reason.

"No problem, Officer, I was talking to a friend. Is everything in order?"

"Yes, Sir, absolutely. If I would have known you were a personal representative of President for Life Shame... Well, I'm sorry, I would have never pulled you over."

Riverstone quickly figured out what Monday had done for him by giving him one of the highest profiles imaginable. Without skipping a beat, and making Simon proud, he stepped up to the plate and continued his performance. "I totally understand, Officer Cox. Alice and I were trying to keep a low profile is all, if you get my drift."

Officer Cox smiled defensively. "Oh, yes Sir, I completely understand. Undercover are we?"

"That's right. Hush-hush. So is there anything else, Officer?"

"No, no, you're free to go. And I'm so sorry for any delay."

Riverstone held up his hand, smiling wide. "Oh, think nothing of it. No harm, no foul, you know."

"Yes, Sir. Can I escort you to your destination?" Officer Cox asked, trying desperately to make amends.

"No. We'll just be on our way."

Officer Cox bent down and pointed at Alice. "Her hair is lovely."

"Her hair? Oh yes, her hair. Well, thank you."

Alice nodded, appreciating the compliment.

Riverstone motioned for Alice to drive on.

As Alice began to pull away, Officer Cox said, "Good day, Mr. Riverstone, have a nicer one."

Riverstone hesitated with his counter, finding it odd how the officer mentioned "nicer," instead of nice. Was it a slip of the tongue, or something deeper that had to do with the state of the country? He shrugged it off and waved. "TTFN!" and added in the same breath, "Toad…"

16

Nootzy's Hoods

Cañon City, Colorado

HARLOWE LEFT THE Bunk House chewing on a fry he snagged from one of the five bags of burgers, shakes, and fries he had in tow. He hadn't taken two steps out the door when three carloads of dark clothed thugs pulled into the parking lot. From the government plates on the front of their black SUVs and the way they arrogantly exited their vehicles, Harlowe figured they were no doubt part of Nootzy's Hoods that the Bunk House owner described earlier. Harlowe wanted no part of what they were selling, so he nodded politely at the bunch and tried to walk by the first group of Hoods peacefully.

"Yo, waa, wait a second, son," the driver of the first vehicle said, stepping in front of him. "Where do you think you're going with all that food?" He was a good six inches shorter than Harlowe but he was big and brutish, about his same weight, and wore a 45 Glock on his hip like the rest of his horde did.

Two other hoods began looking over the Granny and oohed and aahed menacingly.

Harlowe nodded toward Mowgi who was alone, sitting next to the

Granny where he left him. The beggar, however, was running terrified down the street. Obviously, he and the undog had a couple of words before he ran away.

"I'm taking some of it to my friend over there," Harlowe replied, and started to go around the big guy. "Now if you'll excuse me."

The driver's heavy hand stopped Harlowe before he could take a step. "Where does a boy like you get enough new dollars to purchase that much food?"

Three more Hoods surrounded Harlowe while the others in the squad of vehicles went inside, figuring the driver and his group had the situation under control.

"Not to mention that cool ride and the droid driver," the Hood added.

"I have a rich mother," Harlowe explained.

The Hood to Harlowe's right reached for his bags. "I think we should take these bags as evidence of a crime."

A third Hood added, "I believe I saw him leave the Bunk House without paying, Dolt."

Harlowe pulled the bags away and stared at the driver, grinning. "Your name is Dolt?"

"That's right, punk. You find that amusing?"

"I do. The name certainly fits." Harlowe looked around at the others and quietly transferred all the bags to left hand. "Wait 'til I tell my girlfriend I beat up a family of Dolts today. She'll think that's the funniest thing she's ever heard."

Dolt saw zero humor in Harlowe's comment. He reached for his sidearm to pistol-whip the young punk where he stood. But before he could hit him, his Glock was ripped from his hand and all three of his associates were laid out flat on the ground, out cold, right before his eyes.

Harlowe kept the pistol pointed at Dolt's gut. "Now I want you to wave at all the other dolts inside, and let them know we're all having a friendly little chat out here." The way Dolt's SUV was situated, no one on the inside could see the unconscious bodies lying on the ground. Dolt raised his hand like he was told and waved. "That's it. Nice big smile, buttbreath," Harlowe said, jabbing the barrel harder into Dolt's side. The Hoods inside waved back, and Harlowe put his arm around Dolt's shoulders like they were pals. With his food bags in the other hand, he waved back, and said to Dolt, "Now be a good little thug, and hand me your government money card."

"That's my only card," Dolt said, afraid he was going to lose it for good.

"You should have thought of that when you started picking on an innocent teenager."

"You're not so innocent. Not the way you handle yourself. Who are you, anyway?"

"Someone you don't ever want to screw with again."

Dolt glared up at Harlowe. "I'll find you, kid. I'll bring an army after you, and then we will see who's lying face down on the ground."

"Get in the car," Harlowe ordered. Dolt followed directions, and when he sat down in the driver's seat, Harlowe handed his Glock back. "Careful. It's loaded," he said with a smile.

Harlowe had his back to Dolt walking away, when the pistol exploded behind him. Dolt screamed, grabbing what was left of his bloody hand. Harlowe had neglected to warn him that he crushed the end of the barrel before handing it back to him.

* * *

Harlowe found the beggar walking across the Walmart parking lot and handed him a burger. "I'm not hungry," the beggar snapped. "I don't want to eat. I want to go."

"You need something," Harlowe said with concern.

"What is it?" the beggar said, nodding disgustingly at the undog.

"I told you to leave him alone."

"I thought he was going to eat me."

"He will eat you if you try and hurt him. That's a fact," Harlowe warned.

"But I didn't do a thing. I just tried to pet him, that's all."

That was a lie and Harlowe knew it. But like his dad always said, arguing with stupid is a waste of good energy. Harlowe set the bag of food on the ground and tossed the beggar Dolt's money card. "Consider this your lucky day, pard," and returned to the Granny to finish eating the Bunk House burgers. When Jewels tried to leave the parking lot, Dolt and his gang of Hoods came storming into the lot, screeching and sliding to a stop in front of the Granny. Sixteen Hoods blasted out of their SUVs with weapons drawn, and pointed them right at Harlowe. Dolt came limping out of the back seat of his car, holding a red stained kitchen towel wrapped around his right hand.

Harlowe stuck his head out the sunroof to confront the Hoods. "Dolt, you moron, you don't want to do this." Harlowe was never one to mince words when he was outnumbered sixteen to one.

Spitting hot mucus as he spoke, Dolt fumed, "Get out of the car, turd. I'm going to shoot off both your hands, and as you're squealing for mercy, I'm going to grind up your dog for hamburger meat and eat him in front of your stupid face."

Harlowe had enough talk. He drew the pistol Jewels had handed to him and blew away every Hood, shooting each one between the eyes, missing no one, except Dolt. Harlowe kept him alive.

Dolt stared in disbelief at the bodies around him. Every Hood was dead. Their heads were all crackling and smoking from the sizzling projectiles that had pierced between their eyes. Harlowe handed his pistol back to Jewels and took his shake. "This is just the beginning, Dolt. I would take up another line of work if I were you."

"The government will get you, punk. There's nowhere you can hide from us."

Harlowe took the final slurp of his shake, sucking it dry with a loud hiss. He tossed the empty cup in a nearby trash can and said, "I'm afraid you're right, Dolt. Until next time then."

"What's your name, punk?" Dolt asked as Harlowe was handing Mowgi his last bag of fries.

"Harlowe Pylott," he replied, and sat back down and tapped the back of Jewels' seat to drive on.

17

Cellblock 23

Time Unknown
United States Supermax Penitentiary
Administrative Maximum Facility (ADX)
Florence, Colorado

GENERAL IVAN BRANCH sat inside his cell at the supermax penitentiary in Florence, Colorado, where he had been since the fall of President Peter Delmonte five years ago. Before that time, he had been the Chairman of the Joint Chiefs of Staff during both the Sandborne and Delmonte administrations. That was then. Today he was deemed one of the most dangerous criminals in the U.S. Federal penal system. After a short, three-hour court-martial trial, he was found guilty of treason and brought to the supermax, underground holding cell, where he was to remain for the rest of his life with no possibility of appeal, parole, or early release for good behavior. The government of the United States had effectively thrown away the key to Lower Level 3, Cellblock 23. He was not allowed any visitors, not even counsel for his alleged crime against the State.

The only contact he had was the camera located out of reach above his cell door that constantly monitored his life. The cell accommodations included a wall ledge for a single bed with a thin mattress, no sheets, a thin blanket, and one pillow. Branch's sickly thin, 6-foot-4-inch frame stuck a foot beyond the end of the bed. During lights-out, he had learned to curl up in a fetal position to keep his size 14's from becoming painfully stiff from the cold. A one-piece stainless steel sink/toilet was also provided. His routine always began at 0500, when a 60-watt bulb turned on in the ceiling and a tray of tepid oatmeal, stale toast, and an eight ounce cup of weak coffee was passed through a flap-door opening in the cell wall. The door to the cell was a solid grey, four-inch thick, reinforced concrete slab with a slit for food and a small view port that could only be opened from the outside. At precisely the same time every day a buzzer sounded, and his cell door opened. He affectionately called this period of the day his "nooner" for lack of a better term, because being three stories underground, he never saw the light of day or spoke to any guard or another inmate…ever. His nooner lasted one-hour, and not one second longer. During that time, he could walk up and down the 30-yard hallway inside his cellblock corridor and do whatever he wanted in the way of exercise. Once a week was shower-Saturday. It was the highlight of his existence. He was granted a five-minute lukewarm, never hot, shower that day. Whether it was Saturday, or not, it didn't matter. It was like his nooner. They were both automatic, all done without a single human being present. If he missed returning to his cell by one second, his nooner was canceled for three days. A second infraction canceled his Show-Saturday. A third infraction meant no nooners or Shower-Saturdays for an entire month. Needless to say, Branch was always prompt and returned to his cell a good two minutes early to avoid missing a single luxury of his feeble existence. At exactly 1900 hours, dinner was served, usually, with some small variation of a mystery meat sandwich on white bread, stale potato chips, pasta salad, sometimes coleslaw, an eight-ounce watered down apple juice, and occasionally a sugar cookie for dessert. Water from the sink was allowed freely. That was pretty much it. At 2100 hours the ceiling light would go out until it was 0500, and his routine would begin again.

After returning from his nooner this day, and his cell door closed with a clank, Branch thought he had finally succumbed to his imprisonment and isolation when he saw a rather tall, taller than he was, human being standing at the back of his cell in front of his toilet.

"Who…" he gasped. Unable to converse with anyone for years, Branch found it difficult to talk.

Harlowe understood his difficulty. "It's me, General. Harlowe Pylott."

Branch panicked and looked up at the camera in fear. "They'll know…"

"It's okay," Harlowe said calmly. "The camera has been fixed. They can't see anything but you going to your bed and lying down."

Branch pointed at the toilet. "May I pee? I go a lot these days."

"Of course." Harlowe stepped aside and gave the General his privacy.

After he was done, he turned back to Harlowe and asked, "Are you real? I mean where have you been? We thought you died when you didn't come back." Branch's voice was unsteady but clear enough to understand. At times he began to cry and wiped his eyes. "Sorry… It's just…"

Harlowe patted him on the back and guided him to sit on his bunk. "It's alright, General. I've come to take you away."

Branch glanced at Harlowe skeptically. "You seem real."

"I am."

Branch studied him closer with his glasses. "But you haven't changed. You're still…"

"Young?"

"Yes, young."

"Long story, General, but you have to believe me, I'm Harlowe."

"Your ship?"

"Better than ever."

"So much has happened. We… the President… we were…we were brought down…deceived by…so many, Harlowe. The world turned on us. They didn't want change. They accused the President and me of treason. So much happened," he kept repeating, "we were all alone against them."

"Who, General? Who took you down?" Harlowe asked.

Branch looked away. It wasn't the wall he was staring at but the past. It was flying by him, coming to life as it broke his heart to think about what had happened to his country. "I'm so sorry, Harlowe. We let them take it away from us."

"Not your fault, General. We're here to make it right again."

"You? As powerful as you are, you can't defeat them, Harlowe. They're too deep, dark, and everywhere."

"Tell me, General. Who are they?"

Branch began to cough. He wasn't well. It sounded like his lungs were about to collapse inside him. Harlowe handed him a small flask of blue liquid. Branch took one sip and closed his eyes. After tasting nothing but foulness for five years, the sweetness of the Blue Stuff filled his head with an explosion of euphoria. "Thank you, son," he breathed with relief. "Thank you."

"Who are they, General?" Harlowe asked again.

The General raised his head. His eyes were much clearer than even a half minute ago. "The Cartel. They are known by many names. Zmaji mostly. Very secret."

"The Zmaji. Who are they?"

"We don't know. The President...we tried to understand them. But they had infiltrated the highest offices, politicians at all levels, and the banks..." He took Harlowe's hand with the flask and drank again before he continued. "Yes, it was the banks, the very old and established banks that have controlled the world for centuries. They framed me first..." Branch stared at Harlowe hard. "You don't think I committed treason do you, Harlowe?"

"No, General, I know you would never betray our country, or the President."

"He only wanted the best for our America, Harlowe. You know that don't you?"

Harlowe faced the wall. "I do, General."

Branch grabbed Harlowe by the arm and wouldn't let him go. "Don't go, son, there is so much more to tell you."

Harlowe patted his hand to comfort him. "I'm not going anywhere without you, Sir. Can you hold on for a little longer, I need to see the President next. I'm taking you both away tonight."

"But how?"

"Leave that to me, General. Just follow what I say and we'll make it," Harlowe assured him.

Harlowe pulled out a small device from his pocket, while Branch looked on, wondering what Harlowe was up to. After manipulating a lighted yellow actuator with his thumb, Harlowe pressed the device, and a blue light the size of a doorway projected onto the concrete wall. The instant the light touched the wall, a subtle crackling began, like someone pouring milk over a bowl of Rice Krispies. A moment after that, an opening that led into the adjacent cellblock appeared. Harlowe stepped over a small pile of white dust and looked in. The cell was empty.

"Where's the President, General? He was supposed to be in the cell next to you," Harlowe said alarmed.

Branch kept staring at the portal, wondering how the concrete had dissolved so easily. "That is incredible," he said, staring at the device in Harlowe's hand.

"The President. Where he is?" Harlowe repeated.

"I don't know, son. We tap on the wall using Morse code. He said he wasn't feeling well. They might have taken him to the infirmary," Branch figured.

It made sense. The prison guards would have taken him there if he were sick. He tapped the side of his neck and spoke to someone unseen. "Mr. Platter. Do you have a lock on me?"

"Yes, Captain," a husky voice replied. It sounded like it came out of thin air.

"Find President Delmonte. He's been moved from his cell. The General says he was ill, and they might have moved him to the prison infirmary."

"Checking, Captain." Several seconds went by before Monday's voice replied, *"Got him. He's not in the sickbay. He's in an isolation room of some kind. I think they're going to let him rot there, Captain."*

Harlowe's face suddenly turned red. "Is he still alive?"

"Yes, but extremely weak. He's almost gone, Captain, his vital signs barely show up on the screen."

"Understood. Give me the fastest path to him, Mr. Platter. While I'm finding the President, bring Millie here. We can't waste a second getting him into a medical unit."

"Aye, on our way, Captain."

"Tell me when you are in position, Mr. Platter."

"Thirty seconds and counting, Captain."

Harlowe went to Branch and stood him up.

"Here, Captain, Millie's in position," Monday confirmed.

Harlowe put his arms around the old soldier and gave the order, "Now, Mr. Platter." A blue light shot down through the ceiling and engulfed them both. A split second after that, a bright yellow light struck the entire federal compound. The flicker of light penetrated every square inch of the penitentiary, rendering every living being within a mile radius unconscious. When the veil dissipated, Harlowe guided the General to a small disk beside his toilet. "Step on that, General. A robob will meet you and guide you to a medical room, where you will be attended to."

"A robob? My Mr. Ed? I miss him."

Harlowe smiled. Mr. Ed was the name the General gave to his own personnel robob Harlowe had given him to protect him from anyone poisoning him, or trying to assassinate him. Sadly, Mr. Ed was unable to protect the General from a trial and being put into a prison far from the Pentagon. That he hadn't planned on. No one had.

"Yes, Mr. Ed will meet you, Sir."

Branch stepped on the disk but stepped back off again like he had forgotten something. "May I pee first?" he asked, politely.

Harlowe smiled and gave the General his privacy again. "Sure, General. Mr. Ed will wait."

18

Dodge

Aztec, New Mexico

A LANKY, BROAD shouldered, young man in ragged, dust-covered denims jeans, worn hiking shoes, his head covered by a hooded, dark blue sweat shirt, walked into Kare Drug Store off Llano and Main, found the antibiotics he needed, and tried to pay for them at the checkout counter using a cash card.

"I'm sorry. Your card was rejected, Sir," the pretty girl at the counter said, regretfully.

"My mother is pretty sick. Do you mind running it through again?" he asked.

His voice was respectful and well-mannered, and when he pulled back his hood revealing his wavy dark hair, stunning blue eyes, ruggedly handsome and tanned face, the girl tried to catch her breath. His unshaven dark beard only added to his towering six-foot-three studliness. "Ohhh my." She forced herself to breathe and asked, "Where did you come from?"

"A ways," he replied, nodding toward the desert.

"We don't get many like you this way."

He had little concern for small talk. "Can you run it again, please?" he asked again.

She ran the card through, with the same result. Her sad eyes told him the bad news. He reached for the card, and she pulled it back. "We're supposed to keep the rejected cards."

He looked around the store. "Is there something I could do to pay for it? Clean up around the store? Pickup outside? I'll do anything."

"You don't look like one of those street people."

"I'm not. I just need the medicine for my mom," he pleaded, his voice becoming more desperate. He pulled out a hunk of metallic rock the size of a golf ball and laid it on the counter. "Would you trade this for the medicine?"

Her eyes went round. "Is that. . .?"

"Yeah, it's silver."

"That is worth a lot more than the drugs."

"An even exchange then."

She shook her head. "I can't. I wish I could, but I can't." She picked up the rock to give it back. "Oh my, it's heavy."

"Yes, it's real."

Putting the rock in his hand, she offered, "Look, let me pay for it."

The young man became uneasy. "No… I can't let you do that. Come on, let me work for it."

The girl put the bag of drugs in front of him. "I'll lend you the money." The young man pushed back the bag, but she took his hand, feeling his strength. It was considerable. "Are you good for it?" she asked.

"Yeah…"

"That's it, then. It's only a loan. Okay?" She forced the bag back. "Take it. Get your mom well, and when she's okay, take me to lunch. That's my payment. Deal?"

The young man reached for the bag with a counteroffer. "Make it dinner."

She smiled with a glint of joy. "Even better."

"It's a date then, ah…" He read the name tag on her blouse. "Ann." He gave her one good look before he turned away and walked out.

He pushed open the glass door, and she called after him. "I don't know your name."

He waved goodbye, and as the door closed, shouted back, "Dodge!"

A short time later, when the store was about to close, a group of fifteen male and female teenagers from the nearby city of Farmington arrived in pickups and cars and entered the drugstore. Ann greeted the hooded teens with her usual friendly smile. Her heart leaped, though, when two large bodies stood by the front door as the others began ransacking the shelves and stuffing candy bars, snacks, and anything they could easily carry into their backpacks. Ann came out from behind the counter and confronted the mob. "Stop that! I'll call the police!"

A female jumped behind the counter and ripped out the phone. "I don't think so, missy."

Two other teens grabbed her from behind. "Let me go!" Ann whipped around and slapped the closest teen in the face, knocking him down onto the floor. She kneed the second one in the groin, and he cried out doubling over in agonizing pain. The first teen staggered to get back up. Ann was about to kick him again when she was rushed by two big females twice her size. They slapped her when she tried to escape and tore the buttons on her blouse.

Someone cried out, "Tear her uniform off, Batrice!"

The first teen had payback in his eyes and pushed aside one of the others to get a shot at Ann's face. He cocked his fist to hit her when the tall young man in the hoodie he earlier saw leaving the drugstore, came through the front door. "I forgot something," he said to Ann.

The huskies guarding the door tried to stop him, but were easily pushed aside. The first recovered fast and threw a punch at the handsome face. But Dodge slapped his fist away and knocked both huskies across the aisle, slamming them against the knickknack racks.

"Leave Dodge, it's not your fight," Ann pleaded.

The female heavy yanked Ann's arm. "Shut up! No one's talkin' to you."

A husky from the door had gathered his composure and pulled a knife. "Give me the word, Billy, and I'll take out his Adam's apple," he growled, as he brought the blade of his knife close to Dodge's throat.

"Hold on, now." Dodge seized the husky's wrist, holding the blade fast. The guy tried pulling his hand away, but it was like being squeezed in a vise. The harder he tried to pull away, the harder Dodge squeezed, until the pain was so great, tears began to roll down the guard's face. "I'll make you a deal."

"No deals, big man!" Billy growled, pulling out a long blade of his own from the top of his boot.

The husky fell to the floor, his face twisted and misshapen, pleading for relief. "Do somethin' Billy, before he breaks my arm."

The second husky charged Dodge, thinking he would blind-side him from behind. Like he had eyes in the back of his head, Dodge's fist found the guard's jaw. His head snapped back, his jaw pivoting sideways unnaturally as his legs flew out from under him. He spasmed once before he went completely still.

Dodge continued with his offer. "When you let my friend go and clean up your mess, I promise you'll be able to leave here without medical assistance."

The mob laughed.

Billy's expression went from amusement to stone cold homicidal in an instant. He pointed his blade at Ann's throat and hissed, "We don't like your offer, maaan," and drove the knife home.

But in that split second, between the six inches Billy's blade had to travel to reach Ann's neck, a punishing blow tore the blade from the teen's hand with the force of a sledgehammer. The blade went flying, harmlessly skidding across the tile floor.

Billy had no idea what happened next. He went down hard, his face broken in three places. The female's arms holding Ann cracked as her forearms snapped in two. The others saw what happened to their friends and tried to escape, but couldn't. Arms, legs, and rib cages were crushed or broken. The total annihilation of the mob was over in less than a minute, except for a girl and a boy. Dodge found them huddled together at the back of the store and brought them to the front where Ann was looking over the bodies in utter shock.

"You going to kill us, too?" the boy asked.

Dodge bent down and pointed at Ann. "See her?" They nodded. "She owns you. You follow all her orders and make sure everything that was taken is put back all nice and neat where it belongs. If this place isn't spotless…well…"

"Yes Sir, yes Sir, we get it," the girl said, "Don't we, Connor?"

"Yeah, we get it. Whatever she tells us to do, we do," the boy said, nodding.

"All right. I'm going to leave now. But if I hear you disobeyed one thing she asks to you to do, I will hunt you down. Is that clear?"

"Yes Sir."

Dodge wasn't finished with their life's lesson. "Consider this a wakeup call. If I ever hear you're a part of something like this again, trust me, as I stand here with tears in my eyes, it will not end well for you." Dodge's cold hard eyes did not flinch, move, or blink.

"Yes Sir."

Dodge sent the two on their way to clean up. He then turned to Ann, who was trembling and in tears. He put his arms around her and said, "You were incredibly brave."

She looked in his eyes, not letting go, suddenly realizing something was missing. "You're not even shaking."

"Inside I'm terrified," he admitted.

"No you're not." She held his hands. "You're calm, like this never happened. How?"

Dodge knew there was no answer she would accept. No logical one anyway. Even a short version was off the charts crazy unbelievable. His father, a double Medal of Honor recipient, his mother a widow and remarried to a former President of the United States, and a galactic warrior brother who fought bad guys across light-years around the galaxy, might be a little hard to digest when they just met. Mostly, though, it was the genes he was born with. "My mom and dad are both former Marines."

Her cute little button nose wrinkled up as she smiled. "Both Marines?"

Dodge snickered. "I didn't get away with a whole lot growing up. My brother forgot to take out the trash once and was thrown through a window for his slip-up."

"Oh my. Your dad was tough."

Dodge chuckled. "No. That was my mom."

They laughed again, and then Ann reviewed the scattered bodies on the floor. Some were moaning, some crying, but mostly they were still. "They need medical help, Dodge."

"I can't stay, Ann."

"The police will want to talk to you," she said. "You're a hero, Dodge."

The way he looked at her, she knew heroics didn't matter to him. He wasn't from Aztec or Farmington or anywhere close. He seemed anxious, like he needed to leave.

"Are we still on for dinner?" Ann asked. "I mean, you've more than paid back the store. As far as I'm concerned, your loan is paid in full."

"Nothing doing. A deal is a deal," Dodge replied.

They embraced one last time and he was gone moments before the flashing lights, Sirens, and ambulances filled the parking lot.

19

Good Guys & Cookies

Space Command Headquarters
Peterson, AFB, Colorado

TIMMER BROUGHT THE satellite prints in from the astro-photo lab and laid them on the situation room table for General Van Dyke and the other three-star generals, Irwin Wirstlin and Brent Gilman, both out of Cheyenne Mountain, Strategic Air Command (SAC), and handpicked by Dutch himself. The Generals and their abbreviated staff of two each, were air lifted to Petersen AFB by two of the world's fastest military helicopters, twin rotor, CH-47F Chinooks. General Wirstlin was the hardest to find. He had to be plucked out of the Arkansas River trout fishing. Most generals, especially the three-star types, like to brag of their exploits. Generals Wirstlin and Gilman were no different. Wirstlin claimed he had a ten-pound rainbow on the hook when the Chinook crew found him. No one believed him, least of all Dutch, who always joked the biggest fish Hatchet (that was Wirstlin's high school nickname because no one chopped down opponents on the football field like he did) ever caught was a fillet he bought at Safeway. General Gilman, (Faceman, the moniker printed on the cockpit of the personal F-21 fighter he flew on the weekends) was on the third hole that morning. It was a long par five that doglegged to the right. He barked at the crew that he was about to sink a double birdie when their Chinook blew his ball into the nearby lake when it landed on the green.

Dutch greeted them both in the situation room, shaking hands, hugging, and patting each other like the old friends they were during their Air Force Academy days. "Welcome to Space Command you lying sacks of bat guano," Van Dyke cried out, as the two generals and their staff entered the situation room. Before their string of complaints hit his ears, Van Dyke stuck a Cuban Montecristo in each of their mouths and asked: "Would you rather harass a fish, play golf, or catch an ET?"

General Gilman pulled the cigar from his mouth and grinned at Timmer. "Depends. If ET looks like one of your boy's castaways, I'm all in." Apparently, Airman Lane's reputation ranged all the way to SAC.

"We're trying to find the ETs, Faceman, not scare them with that ugly puss of yours."

Gilman grinned, his movie good looks having only improved with age. "You always were a smooth talker, Dutch."

Wirstlin was more to the point. "Damn, Dutch, a real live one, huh?"

"Appears so, Hatchet," Van Dyke replied, calmly.

After Timmer gave the Generals and their staffs the Cliff Notes version to bring them up to speed, he slid the fresh stack of astro-photos from the lab in front of them.

"That's Mars," General Gilman responded, recognizing the topography immediately. "How old are they?"

"Taken two days ago, Sir," Timmer replied. "Best I could do. It's taken forty-eight hours to download the entire file."

General Wirstlin studied the photo right down to the number of pixels per inch. With grave concern, he asked, "That's a Harmonia image." He looked at Timmer like he was going to arrest him for treason. "No one knows about that satellite, except—"

Dutch pulled him aside. "Except me, Hatchet," he said, taking Wirstlin's arm to cool his jets.

"I know Timmer's your guy, Dutch, but good God, man, the President doesn't even know about Harmonia," Wirstlin fumed.

"We're going to keep it that way, too, Irwin."

Wirstlin came back, "You can't keep ET from her for long. She has eyes that look right up your poop shoot, Dutch."

"We need to put Washington off long enough to figure out if they're friend or foe."

"Doesn't matter to her," Wirstlin countered. "She couldn't care less if they're friendlies or not. When she finds out, she's going to kill them. She can't afford to lose her power. I was in there at the White House when she took down Branch and Delmonte. We're on her short list, Dutch. You know that. So is Faceman."

"That's why you're here and not Drgastin. He'd lose a boatload of virgins in a kiddie pool if he got hold of this intel."

Wirstlin chewed the end of his Montecristo. "No joke."

Van Dyke stared at the table of top-secret intel. He thought long and hard that if this was the real deal, as Timmer insisted it was, then the military's top brass needed to figure out something quickly. Nootzy Shame had already purged the military of the best and brightest. Ever since General Branch was taken down, there were very few left in the officer corps who could be trusted. Admiral Meads from the Navy was the only other high-ranking officer not present whom he trusted. Assassination wasn't beneath her, as a mounting list of bodies proved. The three of them, including Huey, their nickname for Admiral Meads, had so far kept their heads. But with war with the Chicoms and the Russians on the horizon, she could not afford to take out her best generals just yet. She needed them as much as the country needed them. The last thing Van Dyke wanted was Shame to have enough power to take over the planet. If somehow she got her hands on an alien technology that gave her that kind of power, she would use it in a heartbeat to eliminate those on her blacklist and anyone else who got in her way. Van Dyke sighed heavily, praying they would discover what the aliens wanted first. "Lets hope they're good guys, Hatchet, and they've brought cookies."

Wirstlin approved. "Amen, Dutch."

General Van Dyke turned back to the table. "Carry on, Timmer, start your show."

"Yes, Sir." Timmer started with a large photo he projected onto the wall screen. "We know ET stopped on Mars," the Airman began, "and that they landed here," he said pointing at what looked like a long tear in the sandy-colored Martian surface.

"*Valles Marineras?*" Gilman asked. "How did you find them there?"

"Gravity waves, Sir. As soon as I saw ET put down somewhere on Mars, I tweaked Maven's ion mass spectrometer to look for any anomalies on the planet's surface."

Wirstlin was impressed. "You did that, and you're only an Airman?"

"Yes, Sir. No biggy. Thirty minutes and a little reprograming and we had them."

"You found ET in thirty minutes on a planet a fifth the size of Earth?" Gilman was impressed.

"Yes, Sir. They were sitting there all casual like." Timmer switched to another slide. It was a clear shot of a golden saucer-shaped object parked on the floor the solar system's longest and deepest canyon. "It makes sense. It's the lowest part of the planet where there's the greatest air pressure."

"They built something there?" Van Dyke asked.

"No, Sir, not built, vacationed." Timmer brought up another photo of what looked like some Southern California beach scene. The Generals were stunned to see water running into a clear pool that was surrounded by an oasis of yellow palm trees. "At least that what it looks like to me," he said, pointing at the colorful surfboards along the shoreline.

Wirstlin stared at the overhead in disbelief. "Those are surfboards?"

"Yes, Sir, that's exactly what they are." Timmer displayed another photo. "Looky there, Generals. They're surfing on the waterfalls. Can you believe it?"

"They look human, too," Van Dyke said.

Gilman pointed to another human shape. "And that one's getting a massage by a droid with dark hair. That's got to be a joke."

"That's a pretty human thing to do, General," Timmer said.

"Rough life," Wirstlin quipped.

Van Dyke looked across the table at everyone. "This is nuts. Everything we've ever known or thought about ETs has just gone out the window." The General glared at Timmer. "If this is some kind of joke, son, I'll have you cleaning toilets so far north—"

"No, Sir, General. There's nothing fake about these photos. They're all real, every detail."

Gilman ordered Timmer to go back to the photo of ET's ship. "How big is that saucer, son?"

"Huge, General, a little over 1500 feet in diameter. Think of six Nimitz-size aircraft carriers fitting inside her hull with room to spare."

"How close to light-speed can she get with that kind of size?" Van Dyke asked.

Timmer looked across the table knowing no one had truly grasped the alien ship's flight specifications. "Way beyond light-speed, General. My guess, a thousand times faster than light, probably more, a lot more."

That calculation was too far fetched for Wirstlin to swallow. "Thousands of times the speed of light, huh?"

Timmer looked at the General with all the seriousness he could muster. "The power signature registered by Maven is off the charts. It took less than a nanosecond to fry its magnetometer. The ship can produce more energy in a second than Earth has produced in all mankind's history. And that's a fact that includes every atom, hydrogen, cobalt bomb ever made."

"Wow..." was Gilman's only response.

Van Dyke spread his hands out across the table, as he leaned forward with a hard stare. "Are we agreed then that Shame can't get near these ETs for one second?"

"Agreed," Wirstlin concurred.

"All in," Gilman added without hesitation.

Van Dyke asked Timmer the hard question. "So why is ET here?"

"I don't know, General. But I do know they've left Mars."

Timmer's statement shocked everyone in the room.

"They have?" someone in the Generals' staff blurted out.

"How do you know that?" Wirstlin asked.

"Because we have an eyewitness who saw the saucer two days ago flying over Colorado," Timmer replied.

"You're sure?" Van Dyke asked.

"He's a Marine with impeccable stats, Sir. He described ET's ship right down to the smallest detail."

"Where is he?" Wirstlin asked.

"Who is he?" Gilman asked.

"Sergeant Max Enihoo, Sir. He's been standing outside operations all morning, eating everything in sight. He's not here with us now because he doesn't have the clearance to enter Space Command."

"SERGEANT ENIHOO!" General Van Dyke shouted, shaking the entire Operations headquarters with his thunderous voice. It goes without saying when a four-star general commands a soldier to stand front and center, even God helps to locate that soldier. "I just gave him Top Secret clearance. Now get that Marine in here ASAP!"

A hard stare from Van Dyke sent a major looking for Enihoo. "Yes, Sir!"

Enihoo marched through the open door and stood at attention like a six-foot-seven rod of black chromium steel. "Sergeant Enihoo reporting as ordered, Sir!"

"Holy-moly," Wirstlin groaned, "that's not a Marine, that's a one man killing machine. How much do you weigh, son?"

"Three twenty-five, General!" Enihoo replied.

"There's not an ounce of fat on him, Hatchet," Gilman added. "You're fortunate you didn't run into him on the football field."

"I'm a U.S. Marine, Sir, fat and quitting are not in our lexicon," Enihoo boasted.

Gilman pointed with enthusiasm. "I LIKE THIS GUY! I sure am happy he works for us and not the Chicoms."

"At ease, Enihoo," Van Dyke said, cutting off the banter. "You stand any stiffer and you'll start breaking glass around here."

"YesSir, General." Enihoo put his hands behind him and spread his legs. Even at ease, the soldier's mouth was the only part of him that moved. Everything else on his body remained rigid.

"Airman Lane says you saw something the other night," Van Dyke began.

"Yes, Sir, I saw an Unidentified."

"Go on, Marine, describe what you saw," Gilman urged.

"Sir, it was round and gold and had this blue ring around it," Enihoo said.

Wirstlin leaned over to Van Dyke. "He's dead on, Dutch."

Van Dyke continued with the questioning. "Which direction was it traveling, Sergeant?"

"West, General."

"You're sure?"

"Yes, Sir. My gal and I saw it head straight across the Rockies."

Gilman turned to Van Dyke. "Damn, Dutch, ET went right over your house, and you didn't see it?"

Van Dyke grunted his dissatisfaction. "Apparently the world's best tracking radars didn't see it either."

"It was silent as a cat, General. It made no noise except for the wind. That kicked up a little as it flew by."

"How fast was it going, Sergeant?" Wirstlin asked.

Enihoo appeared perplexed. "I don't exactly know, General." The Sergeant raised his hand and cupped it in the shape of a plane. "It just traveled along all cool like. You know, like one of your big bombers coming in for a landing. Then as it approached the Rockies it just blinked away."

Gilman snapped his fingers. "Like that?"

"Exactly, Sir. That fast."

Van Dyke felt the silence in the room. There were no more questions they could discuss in front of the Sergeant for security reasons. He dismissed Enihoo and thanked him for his observation with some added instructions. "You're not to discuss what you saw with anyone. You're to stay in area. We may need you later. Who's your girlfriend? We may need her statement, as well."

Enihoo tried to speak. "Ah, ah... You see, Sir. . ."

"Cat got your tongue, Sergeant?" Gilman asked.

Timmer saw the problem immediately, having been down that road more than once himself. He leaned down to Van Dyke and whispered in his ear. Van Dyke nodded shaking his head. "I get it. I get it." He looked up at Enihoo and said, "Tell her to keep her mouth shut, Sergeant."

Enihoo clicked his heels together and saluted. "She will, Sir," and then he left the room. When the door of the situation room closed again, General Gilman stated, "SAC had no reports of a radar contact over Peterson either, Dutch. Something that size could not have gone undetected."

Timmer spoke next. "Excuse me, General, we have stealth bombers with radar signatures the size of a bee. Are we to believe a vessel that can travel across space faster than light can't hide itself from our radars?"

"Good point, Timmer," Van Dyke said to his boy. He then addressed the room. "All right, we have an ET out there that's landed and can't be seen by radar."

Timmer interrupted. "Sorry, Sir, I would add that it can't be seen by any visual means, either."

"No satellites."

"Probably not, General."

Wirstlin jabbed a hot finger at the wall of ground surveillance displays. "We can photograph the butt hairs on a field mouse from three hundred miles up, and we can't find a ship the size of six aircraft carriers? That's absurd!"

"There's a way, General," Timmer said, coming back to the table of Mars photos. "The same way we found ET on Mars. Gravity waves." Van Dyke motioned for Timmer to continue.

"How do we do that? We don't have any Harmonias circling Earth we can tweak," Wirstlin pointed out.

Timmer was on a roll. "I have a gravity wave spectrometer at my house."

"You do? A gravity wave meter? What are you doing with that?" Wirstlin asked, concerned there may have been a breach of Top Secret security.

"I made it, General."

"You made a gravity wave detector?"

Van Dyke had Timmer's back. "If he said he made one, trust me, he did." The General went to Timmer. "What's your plan then? Fly you and your wave machine up in a 91?" (The 91 was military lingo for the Air Force's new, super secret, super stealth, scramjet, the SR-91, used for high altitude reconnaissance.)

"That bird is still experimental at Area 7," Gilman informed the room.

Timmer broke in. "No, Sir, I don't need the 91. One of your Chinooks is cool." Before any of the Generals could object, the Airman drove his point home. "Look, Generals, ISS has a grav anomaly detector for tracking magma movements under the Earth's crust. They installed it last year when they thought Yellowstone was going to blow. It will be over the Western states in six hours," he checked his watch, "twenty-two minutes, right along ET's path. We don't have much time to set up. If ET stayed on that course, I can find it."

"And if you don't," Gilman asked.

"ISS will. How loud do you think its alert will sound when ET trips its grav meter? It will blow it off the scale."

"Alerting every SAC station this side of the Mississippi, including Cheyenne Mountain," Gilman stated.

"All the way to Shame's desk," Van Dyke groaned.

"You think you can find it before the ISS, son?" Gilman asked.

"I know I can," Timmer replied confidently.

"They're going to want to know why an Airman is taking a Chinook for a joyride," Gilman said.

Van Dyke stepped in. "I'm the commanding general of Space Command. They don't need to know squat." He turned to Timmer. "Get what you need, Lane."

"You'll need backup," Wirstlin offered. "Take a squad of Delta Force with you."

"No thanks, Sir, the fewer the better."

Van Dyke's eyes narrowed. "You take someone with a gun, Airman, that's an order."

"I'll take Enihoo, Sir. Nothing spooks him."

"And Searle," Van Dyke insisted.

Timmer's shoulders dropped. "Searle, Sir?"

"That's an order."

"May I ask why, Sir?"

Van Dyke pointed at the four stars on his shoulder. "No. Now get your gear and your squad in the air before that space station beats you to it."

Timmer tossed whatever he had in his hand on the table, "Yes, Sir," and headed for the door.

A staff officer opened the door for the Airman, as Van Dyke called after him, "God speed, son."

"Thank you, Sir, we'll find ET for ya," he said with a thumbs up and then double timed out the building shouting for Enihoo

20

The Little Secret

Situation Room
Space Command Headquarters
Peterson, AFB, Coloarado

THE STAFF STARTED to restack the photos to begin the process of putting them back in their top secret tubes and file envelopes, but before they got very far, General Van Dyke motioned for them to stop and leave the room. He appeared pretty down, like he wanted to be alone, so Hatchet and Faceman thought they were included in the dismissal. They started out the door with their staff, when Van Dyke told them to hold on. "Did someone give you two Generals permission to leave?"

Wirstlin came back with Gilman behind him. "There's more, Dutch?"

Van Dyke looked at them both, as the door sealed behind them. "This ET thing ain't over by a long shot."

Wirstlin asked, "You believe your boy will find them?"

That wasn't Van Dyke's worry. "Oh, he'll find them. It's not him I'm worried about. It's the planet."

Gilman's eyes exploded. "The planet? What about the good old

U.S.A.? You know as well as I do, Dutch, we've been at Defcon I for two months straight, ever since Nootzy sabotaged the Chicoms oil rigs off in the East China Sea. They were mighty upset about that, and to be truthful, I don't blame them. It's not our water. That's why it's called the China Sea."

"She did the same thing to the Rusky's pipeline across Iran," Wirstlin added. "Does that woman have a single brain cell in her head?"

"She's not running things, and we all know it," Van Dyke said. "She's a puppet on a string, and we're under her. If we're going to stop this war, we have to get ET on board with us to stop it. We have to take out the powers that are running this country and the world. The privileged masters who brought us Shame, that banker cohort of hers, Tucker, from Alabama, General Drgastin, Ayala of Mexico, and Chancellor Milberg of Germany. We have to take them all out, if this planet has any chance of surviving. The power behind the throne is not about to stand by and let ET take over their world."

Both Gilman and Wirstlin grew angry at the thought. Wirstlin gave his opinion. "I hear ya, Dutch, but look what happened to Delmonte and Branch when they upset the apple cart. He was the best President this country ever had, and they still took him down and threw away the key."

"Yeah, every officer with a lick of sense knows it was a setup from the get go. The last general on Earth to commit treason is Ivan Branch," Gilman fumed.

Van Dyke filled them in on a little secret. "Well, listen up. The scuttlebutt has it both Delmonte and Branch escaped ADX last night."

Wirstlin jaw dropped. "You're certain?"

"That's the intel from General Lander. He said everyone was blacked out, and when they came to, the only people who were missing were Delmonte and Branch."

"How did they pull that off? That place is escape proof," Gilman wondered.

"They had help for sure. But I don't know who. No one knows, not even Langley. So put that together with ET, and no telling what's going on when they turn Shame loose. She's got the football (The name given to the briefcase that contains the nuclear launch codes the President takes wherever he or she goes.). The powers behind her will turn this planet into a firestorm rather than give up their power," Van Dyke explained. "That's what worries me gentlemen."

"What power do we have to stop it? We haven't a clue as to who our puppet masters are, do we?"

Van Dyke's sad eyes displayed little hope, but, at the same time, there was a spark of determination in the way he removed a fresh Montecristo from his lapel pocket. "No, but until they drag our cold dead bodies from this room, we follow that Marine's motto."

"Enihoo is his name," Gilman offered.

Van Dyke bit the end off the cigar and struck a match off the table to light up. "Yeah, we don't quit!"

21

Going Surfing

Millawanda
LeBeau Park, Nevada

WHEN LEUCADIA ENTERED the medical room, the robobs were busy working on President Delmonte where he was, lying next to General Branch. She burst into tears the moment she saw the two men with their pallid faces and what was left of their starved, frail bodies. Branch was in much better condition than the President. As she read their body scans on the wall displays, Harlowe spoke to General Branch. "Do you know what happened to my mom, General?"

Branch's mind drifted in and out of lucidity. It was like he was thinking inside a room full of fog trying to see out. "Your mom? Tinker?"

"Yes Sir, Tinker. Do you know what happened to her?"

"Have I peed yet?"

"Yes, Sir, you just went."

Branch's lips moved as he tried to sit up. "No…not, not sure." He looked at Harlowe with pathetic eyes. "I think… She left D.C. Went somewhere… I… I…"

Harlowe eased him back down. "Don't talk now, Sir. You need rest."

"She left D.C." Branch kept repeating, as a robob medic touched him with a blue crystalline ball and his eyes closed.

Leucadia came to Harlowe's side, putting her arms around him. "Did he say anything?" she asked, her green eyes well aware she needed to be strong for Harlowe.

Harlowe scanned the wall readouts with her. Branch was already showing progress. A flask of Blue Stuff and a couple of double-doubles, and he would be good as new. Delmonte, on the other hand, was less than fifty-fifty. He had not seen a body scan this bad since Quay when he brought her in an enviro-bag from a lifeless moon. She had survived, but she was physically much stronger than the President. Her will to live had saved her. Would his resolve carry him through? He had to live and tell him where his mom and brother were.

"Not much," Harlowe replied. "She left D.C. That's all he said." He squeezed her, bringing her closer, feeling her warmth, the soothing scent of strength and courage he could always count on to lift him up in time of crisis. "Delmonte. Did he say anything?"

Her eyes went to his. On her tiptoes she kissed him. "Tinker," she told him. "That was all he mumbled."

They walked out of the med room together. She nudged him to go on without her. "I'll let you know if there is any change, Pylott." The boyz with a "z" they thought of themselves collectively, all call him 'Dog' in their private moments or when they were off the clock. Leucadia never aspired to being one of the boyz. Her endearment for him had always been his surname. Why exactly, she didn't know. It wasn't particularly imaginative or loving to call him what his coaches addressed him by. But maybe that was it. When they were first dating, she heard Coach Ford, his football coach, yell across the field during a game, "Stop playing kissy face with Riverstone, Pylott, and kick some butt out there! We need a touchdown to win this, not a field goal." Harlowe shouted back, "YES, SIR, COACH! TOUCHDOWN!"

She grinned with pride as he walked away, remembering that day, thinking would he ever say "yes sir" to her? She giggled. "Never in a million years."

He waved at her as he strolled away down the blue-carpeted corridor.

"Later, Babe."

"Where are you going?" she asked as he continued on.

"Surfing."

He stepped on a nearby blinker and winked away. "Of course, that's where you always go when you need to think," she said to the empty corridor, and then she returned to the med room.

* * *

Harlowe walked out of his cabin onto the bridge wearing his ragged and faded purple, No Fear swim trunks and an old, pink, orange, and brown *Endless Summer* t-shirt with the words, "In Search of the Perfect Wave," written across the bottom. He slung his towel over his right shoulder and acknowledged Monday sitting in the center command chair. He was out of uniform for being on the bridge, and normally, he would be dressed in the uniform of the day, but since he was just passing through on his way to Dodger's Place, no rules were broken.

"Captain," Monday said, returning a salute. He was the only crewman on duty.

"Tinkerville moving along okay?" Harlowe asked, stopping at the edge of the blinker in his bare feet.

"On schedule, Captain."

"Anything Bigbob needs?"

"Got 'er covered. She'll be up and running by the end of the week."

"Cool. InZeeOut?"

"Ready now," he replied and added, "Going for a swim, are we?"

"Surfing."

Monday smiled. "Wiz's new creation?"

"I'm going to give it a test drive."

Monday waved him on. "Have fun, Captain."

Harlowe waved back and blinked away.

22

Me-N-Ed's

Me-N-Ed's Pizza Parlor
Paramount Blvd.
Long Beach, California

*N*O ONE WAS home at his parent's house when Riverstone pulled up in the limo. It was lunchtime, and Mrs. Knaub, his parent's neighbor to the south, and who had lived there for as long as he could remember anything, met him at the sidewalk when no one answered the door.

"Can I help you, young man?" she asked, scrutinizing him up and down like he was some kind of door-to-door salesman. As old as she was, silverish blue hair, round frameless glasses, maybe five feet tall, she patrolled the neighborhood like she was Wonder Woman. Mitzy Knaub knew everything that went on this section of Autry Avenue, between Del Amo and Arbor streets.

"Hi, Mrs. Knaub, it's me, Matthew," Riverstone said, looking down a foot and a half above her.

Mrs. Knaub adjusted her glasses as she gazed up at the towering young man. Her mouth dropped open in disbelief. "My, oh my, that is you. Where have you been, Matthew? And look how much you growwwwwwn!" she said, leaning back.

"I've been working out, Mrs. Knaub."

"And handsome, too. You used to be such a disheveled boy. You and that…that Pylott kid," she said like he had left a sour taste in her mouth. "Always in trouble. Whatever became of him? Is he in jail?"

Riverstone stifled a giggle. "No, ma'am. He's doing okay."

Mrs. Knaub caught sight of Riverstone's limo. "Well, looky here. So beautiful. Is that yours, Matthew?"

"Yes, ma'am. That Pylott kid and I own it."

"You do?"

"We own a few things, Mrs. Knaub." Riverstone looked over at her house. "How is Mr. Knaub doing? He's usually putzing around the garden this time of day."

Her eyes fell. "Fred passed away five years ago this April. Bad ticker. I always warned him about his smoking and his sweets. He never listened to me. I think it was those Twinkies that got him."

A twinge of sadness went through him. Mr. Knaub was a kind and gentle man and always treated him like a second son. There wasn't an evil bone in his body. "I'm so sorry to hear that, Mrs. Knaub."

She turned toward a garden that was overgrown with weeds and had nothing growing in it. "He went peacefully."

"My parents, Mrs. Knaub, do you know where they are?" Riverstone asked. He didn't have a lot of time if he was going to meet up with Rerun at Spago's.

June pointed at Del Amo Boulevard. "Something about going for pizza for little Molly's birthday."

"Molly?"

"Yes, Silve's littlest one. She'll be two today."

A one-knot breeze could have blown Riverstone over. "My little sister, Silve, has a baby girl?"

"And two boys. They're a handful. Like you and that Pylott kid were."

Riverstone had to step up his schedule. Visiting his parents was taking longer than he expected. He thanked Mrs. Knaub and gave her a big hug, telling her he would try and come by more often. He jumped into his limo and told Alice to go west on Del Amo. If they were going for pizza, there was only one place they could have gone.

There were many pizza parlors in Lakewood, some good, some not so good, but only one Me-N-Ed's. Harlowe, Wiz, and he had been going there since the days Buster and his dad, they were the coaches then, brought the whole team here to celebrate their Little League victories. Riverstone thought they would go broke, because he didn't recall losing a game. The thought of an extra large pepperoni with extra cheese, and that special oregano, garlic, and tomato sauce, spread over a crispy outer crust caused him to shake all over in anticipation of that massively large slice of heaven.

"Hurry, Alice, I can smell it from here," Riverstone urged.

Alice made record time, passing cleanly through every traffic signal at Clark, Lakewood Boulevard, and Downey to do it. She even had the green left light at Paramount waiting for them. Of course, Alice had synchronized every light from her dash, but Riverstone would never reveal her secret.

When they were almost to Carson Street, he saw it; the Me-N-Ed's Pizza Parlor sign, situated right between Family Billiards and the Thai Corner Restaurant. The big red and yellow marquee was looking rather worn. It needed restoration. The building, too, was in no better shape. Across the street was McDonalds. Like the one on Woodruff, it was also closed. Another sign of the times, he thought. He sighed, thankful that his favorite pizza hangout was still open. So many victories celebrated, so many pizza slices eaten. But the fights… Ugh! Sometimes it got pretty ugly in the parking lot behind the restaurant. He gritted his teeth. How he and Harlowe survived it all was a miracle. The odds were never in their favor. Maybe Mrs. Knaub was right. Maybe they were a couple of hooligans.

He directed Alice to park behind the restaurant. The limo took up three spaces but there was plenty of room, which he found odd for a lunchtime crowd. He got out and joked with Alice asking her if she wanted an Energizer Bunny to play with. She glared at him in her usual indifferent way and shooed him off to go do his thing.

Riverstone waved, "Okay, suit yourself," and went through the back door and thunk! He hit his head on the top of the metal door, forgetting he was six inches taller than the last time he was here. "Son of va . . . "

He rubbed the pain away, catching a bit of blood on his fingertips that he cleaned on a damp rag the busboy left on the table. It stung for only a moment. The instant he saw his parents any discomfort he had was gone. His family were the only ones in the restaurant. They sat around the long wood table under the "Ye Old Pizza Parlor" sign with all his sisters and the grandchildren, all seven of them. His dad was pulling one of the boys out from under the table when they locked eyes. His sisters thought he looked familiar. Their husbands and a boyfriend didn't know him at all. But his mother recognized him instantly. She burst out crying uncontrollably, screaming "Matthew," as she ran into his open arms.

"Hi, Mom," he said, holding her, never wanting to let her go, her feet dangling in the air. Her fragrance, the shampoo rinse in her hair, her warmth, it was her. If he were blind he would know who it was. Tears fell down the side of his face mixing with hers. "You're okay. My boy is okay," she cried.

"Yeah, mom, I'm okay."

Evan Riverstone, Riverstone's father, put his arms around them both. "Welcome home, son."

Riverstone grabbed his father's head with his large hand and brought them all together. "I love you all so much."

It was a good twenty minutes of introductions, reintroductions, and I-can't-believe-it-yous, and where have you been all this time, before Riverstone could take his first bite of pizza. Evan and his mom knew where Fate had taken him, but they were the only ones. His sisters only knew his work took him across the globe, and it was confidential. They called him their secret agent brother. He asked his dad why they were the only patrons in the restaurant. "There used to be such crowd here, dad."

Evan's face turned grim. "Lakewood's changed, son. It's not the same. We would move but we've been told to stay put or our family, your sisters, and their families would suffer."

Riverstone leaned over and talked softly. "Because of Harlowe and me?"

"I don't know. It might be. When Delmonte fell from power, everything changed. The government became oppressive almost overnight. People in Delmonte's cabinet went missing. The White House lawyer, Braxton, his plane went down somewhere in the Pacific, I believe. Everyone knows Shame was behind it. Her gangs are everywhere. Nootzy's Hoods they call them. It's bad, son, really bad."

His mom tugged on his arm. "Are you here long, Matthew?"

"A few days." Riverstone wanted to tell them more, but under the circumstances, it was best they didn't know much. "Do you still have the force field device?" he asked.

Evan nodded. "Yes. It still works too. Why? Are you expecting trouble."

This time he whispered in his ear. "Stock up on everything."

"When?" Evan asked.

"Start today. You'll know when the robob we left with you activates itself. That's when you get everyone back to the—"

The front door to Me-N-Ed's suddenly blew open and in strode a dozen thugs wearing black boots and heavy leather jackets. They looked like the gangs of goons from an old television show Sons of Anarchy.

Evan glanced at his watch. "I didn't realize the time. We have to go, Matt."

"These toads are why everyone stays away?" Riverstone asked.

"At this time of day, yes. We've overstayed by ten minutes."

Riverstone's sisters were already gathering their kids. "Take everyone out the back door and get in the blue limo outside," he directed.

"What about you?" his mom asked.

He looked at them both. "I'm staying."

"No, son, it's not your fight," Evan said.

"It's always our fight, Pops. That's what we do. Now go. Make sure everyone stays inside the limo. I'll meet you outside when I'm done."

Riverstone's mom wanted to stay and fight beside her son, but his dad knew better. She would be in her son's way when the rumble hit the fan.

Evan and his mom were barely out the door when the first heavy thug came to the table. "This is our table, boy," he told Riverstone, who was now sitting all alone by himself.

Riverstone grabbed a slice and began chowing down. "I'm not done yet."

The thug tried to slap the slice from his hand, but Riverstone was too fast. The thug found nothing but air, making him look silly in front of his peers.

Riverstone raised one finger. "Strike one."

The thug's face turned beet-red and he tried again, and missed.

"Strike two. You only get one more, butthead," Riverstone warned. He placed his slice of pie calmly on the table and stood, towering over the thug.

A second thug behind them said, "He's a big one, Jesse, you think you can handle him?"

"Shut up, Morgan." The thug faced Riverstone. "Do you know who we are, boy? We're Nootzy's Hoods. We're the law around here."

"No you're not. But I would worry more about strike three if I were you," Riverstone warned him.

There were guffaws in the background, as the second thug became impatient. "Come on, Jesse, take care of this moron. We're starving."

Jesse drew his Gen 9 Glock and pointed it at Riverstone forehead. "Still want the table, boy?"

Riverstone ripped the weapon from the thug's grip so fast Jesse didn't realize he was looking down the barrel of his own weapon. Riverstone then proceeded to break the Glock into hunks of worthless polymer and bent steel before a crowd of stunned eyes. "Strike three, buttheads." Riverstone's fist hit Jesse first. The thug's head snapped backwards, his boots jutting straight out as he landed flat, knocked out cold before he hit the ground.

Riverstone had eleven more outs to go before the game was over. When he came out the back door of Me-N-Ed's, he was carrying three boxes of ex-large pizzas to the limo. "Compliments of Nootzy's Hoods," Riverstone said to the surprised faces inside. On the way home several ambulances passed them by going in the opposite direction. Riverstone's mom rolled her eyes as his dad patted him on the back, "Welcome home, Matt."

23

Through the Eyes of God

Vatican Underground Research Center
Rome, Italy

AN ESCORT OF Swiss Guards took Father Espinosi from Castel Gandolfo to a hidden elevator next to the Sistine Chapel entrance. One guard stepped into the elevator with him, inserted a special key, and down they went, ten stories deep, to a vast underground research center. The facility held five acres of computers banks, communication networks, and ultra-sensitive links to listening systems across the globe, including the National Security Agency (NSA), Central Intelligence Agency (CIA), Secret Intelligence Service, (SIS), Military Intelligence Section 6 (MI6), and scores of other snooper agencies, large and small. Father Espinosi always said if anything important happened on the planet, "the eyes of God" saw it first. When they arrived at row 11, cubicle E7, Father Espinosi asked the young technician, "You have something you wish to show me, my son?"

The young technician sat behind three computer screens arranged side-by-side on the cubicle wall above his desk. He was in his mid-twenties and wore a white smock and a security I.D. on his left pocket. He was short, five-foot-five, dark hair, and had an inch-wide red birthmark along the right side of his neck. "I think so Father. I picked up a Daily Mail article this morning. It has reports of two unusual incidents in America. The first is twelve government officials hospitalized in restaurant brawl in Long Beach, California."

"And this concerns us because…?" Father Espinosi inquired.

"Ordinarily it wouldn't, Father. But according to this news article from the local paper, The Press-Telegram, it was a single young man who assaulted the officials, without using a firearm."

"One young man?"

"Yes, Father. A teenager. According to your directive we are to look out for any abnormal individuals with unusual abilities."

"Yes, that is correct."

The tech brought up a surveillance video on his screen. "This is the camera footage from the restaurant. Watch as the blue limousine parks, and the young man gets out of the car," the tech pointed at the screen and zoomed in on the driver. "That is an android, Father, driving the car."

"Yes, an auto driver," Father Espinosi pointed out.

"The android appears to communicate with the young man by waving him away. That is quite unlike any auto driver I know of, Father."

"Fast forward to the young man and the agents, my son."

The tech touched play as the scene continued to play out showing the young man walking into the restaurant and hitting his head on the overhead door. The tech then changed to the inside camera where the young man wiped his bloody head with a cloth before meeting his friends. Fast-forwarding again, the tech stopped where the government officials entered the restaurant. When the young man's family leaves by the back door, presumably for their safety, the young man stays behind and confronts the officials, taking them all down in an incredible display of brute force.

"Not one official escaped, Father."

The tech let that sink in, while Father Espinosi stared at the bodies, scattered unconsciously over tables, chairs, and on the floor. As if that wasn't enough, the tech added, "There's more, Father. A similar altercation with American officials happened in Colorado."

"By the same young man?"

"No Father, by another young man. Watch. This was taken at a Walmart parking lot. Sixteen agents surrounded this young man who proceeded to melt their vehicles and stunned them all except for one agent."

"One agent?"

"Yes, Father. My guess is that he was spared to warn others about who he was…an alien, Father."

The young technician had even more for the Father. "I crossed-referenced the limousine from the first video and found this." The computer tech turned to the left display and brought up another video of a fast-food restaurant in Barstow, California, where the same dark blue limousine parked at the back of the lot and two young men got out and walked toward the restaurant in a hurry. "The scene has changed, but the abnormalities continue, Father. First notice the limousine, it is the same. The android driver is also the same."

"Yes, yes, I see that, and the young man on the right is the same young man. What is the time difference between the videos?" Father Espinosi asked.

"Two hours and four minutes," the tech replied. "It's a three-hour drive through the Los Angeles freeways with no traffic. On that day there was heavy traffic, and the limousine made it from Los Angeles to Long Beach in an hour. No normal car can go that distance in that amount of time, Father, I assure you."

"Yes, I believe you, son. Who is the second man? Can you identify him and where is he now?"

"Hold on, Father, I will image his face."

The Vatican quantum computers analyzed a hundred million faces a second. Five seconds later, the tech found a match. Father Espinosi's face went slack. "I know him. I've seen all of his movies."

"Simon Bolt is an American actor?" the tech asked.

"Yes, a very popular one, until he disappeared many years ago."

"Apparently, he has returned, Father."

Father Espinosi nodded. "Yes, apparently so. It seems he has not aged at all."

"Another abnormality, Father."

"Indeed." The Father flicked his index finger, with the heavy golden ring signifying his high authority in the Church, at the screen on the right. "Continue with your video, my son."

The video of a child abduction played out. When the kidnapers tried to leave the parking lot with the toddler, two very tall, physical men confronted the kidnapers and saved the child, along with half a dozen more children inside the kidnappers' van. At very end, the tech zoomed in on a very grateful mother wiping the sweaty brow of the actor, Simon Bolt. The young tech turned to Father Espinosi and said, "After that she placed the soiled handkerchief in her purse, Father."

Father Espinosi held up his hand. "I've seen enough, my son." Walking back, the good father said to the Swiss Guard, "Call our representatives in America. Tell them I want that mother's handkerchief and the table rag the young man used to clean his bloody head. I also want whatever scraps of blood they find off the top door panel. I want them to scour that parking lot in Colorado for that cup the alien discarded in that trash can, and bring them all to me immediately. They are to handle all items with the utmost care against contamination. Is that understood?"

"Yes, Father."

"Spare no expense. Do whatever is necessary to find that evidence. They cannot fail! God, the True Father, needs those articles."

"Yes, Father."

24

Do it, Betty

Dodger's Place
Millawanda

HARLOWE SAT ON his surfboard at far end of the beautiful, clear pool inside *Millawanda*. The crew called it Dodger's Place, after his brother, who discovered the giant room one day while exploring the immense ship. To this day, and as much as each crewman had wandered about the Gamadin warbird, there were still many places left unexplored, because Millie was enormous. But Dodger's Place was special. It was the one place everyone enjoyed together, even the animals grazed among the lush tropical trees and grasses surrounding the pool. The cliff, where he and Riverstone often dove, stuck high above everything else, rising a hundred feet off the water, and still it was far below the yellow, artificial sun that traveled across the green, artificial sky. There was nothing Earthly about the plant life inside the natatorium, either. The specimens had been gathered from all parts of the galaxy. Their blue, green, and yellow fronds shaded the riot of brightly colored flowers that waved in the subtle breeze that blew constantly across the water. It was a magical canvas that reminded Leucadia of the opening color scene in the Wizard of Oz, as Dorothy danced along the Yellow Brick Road. At the opposite end of the pool, Pigpo, Simon's hippo/pig pet waded in over his head. His nostrils often poked just above the waterline, as he spied on his friends, Delamo and Josie, the majestic horned ceffyls Harlowe brought back from his journey to the galactic core. The horse-like creatures bore twin, seven-foot horns that curved back over their heads as they grazed on the tall grasses nearby. Rounding out the idyllic scene, Mowgi and Rhud lay spread-eagle on the warm white sand at the pool's edge. Close by, Molly, who was much more dignified and feminine than either the undog or her sleeping sibling, sat head up, Sphinx-like and royal, the queen that she was, keeping a protective eye on Harlowe, as he waited for the yellow light to turn blue.

* * *

For the last forty-two hours, Harlowe tried to keep himself occupied. He tried workouts with Quincy, relieving Monday on the bridge, swabbing the deck, or hanging out at the pool, whatever it took to keep himself busy while he waited anxiously for any word from the medical room that Delmonte was going to make it and be able to tell him where his mother, Tinker, and his brother Dodger, were hiding.

A blue light flashed. Harlowe sat up and called out, "Do it, Betty!" A half second later a loud Vaaroom! reverberated throughout the jungle. Birds scattered, Pigpo ducked underwater, the startled ceffyls raised their heads, Mowgi took flight, and Rhud bolted upright from a dead sleep. His blue eyes stretched wide with shock and disorientation, searching for whatever danger was upon them. Once the threat was determined to be nonexistent, he roared his displeasure. The undog added an even louder demonstration with a screech the likes of which made the big cat's roar seem like a purr.

At the far end of the pool, a bulge of water rose up and headed straight for Harlowe. Growing taller, the glassy swell formed a perfect tube the whole width of the pool. Harlowe swung his board around, paddled, and easily caught the wave. He shot right and rose high on the three-foot crest before gliding down its glassy face. He cut back again, switched feet, right foot forward this time, back up the face and down again two more times before shooting the tube and getting covered by its folding crest to end the ride. He rolled his board over and popped to the surface, apologizing to the animals for disturbing their peace.

He was twenty minutes into more "Do it, Bettys," when Jewels stepped to the side of the pool with a dry towel and pointed up.

"Leucadia?" Harlowe asked his robob servant, wading ashore with his board.

Jewels nodded his blue rimmed head yes. Harlowe quickly traded the board for the towel and double-timed to the nearest blinker.

* * *

Harlowe stepped into the med room, his curly dark hair still dripping, and waited for Leucadia to tell him the news.

Leucadia knew what he wanted and told him directly. "Mine."

Harlowe stared, perplexed, at her bright green eyes full of concern. "Mine?" he asked.

Leucadia took him by the arm and walked him outside the med room. "I thought he was saying 'mind.' But that just didn't make sense. Mind what? Unless he was saying "mine." I think he's saying 'mine,' Pylott."

"Why would that make sense?" Harlowe asked.

"I can't be certain, but the only mine I'm aware of is Peter's father's old silver mine in New Mexico."

Harlowe kissed her. "That's it!" He bolted down the corridor, yelling at the top of his voice, "MOWGI!"

She wanted to wish him good luck, but he had already blinked away. She knew where he was headed, though. In her mind, she followed his every step. From a nearby blinker, he ran straight into the utility room where Jewels, now in the driver's seat, had begun lowering the Grannywagon from the hull of the saucer. The car would drop down from the open hatchway and speed away, as Harlowe changed with his "bad" gear behind him. In Gamadin speak "bad" meant he was fully loaded with enough weapons, ammo, thader bombs, and robob cylinders to fight an army of Fhaal storm troopers.

Leucadia smiled lovingly at the thought of Mowgi in the back seat watching him strip off his faded swim trunks, then fully naked, putting on his Gamadin denims, stretching his shirt over his bare chest, shoving his long muscular arms through the sleeves, as Jewels accelerated the Grannywagon through the force field to half the speed of sound across the Nevada desert, east toward New Mexico.

25

Mama Bear

0317 hours, EST
Secret War Room
Underground Bunker, deep inside Virginia Foothills
26 miles from the White House

ACCOMPANIED BY AN entourage of fully armed Secret Service agents and her staff, President for Life, Nootzy Shame, stepped off the subterranean elevator and marched into the Presidential War Room, loaded for bear. Tall and heavyset, a former professional wrestler in her youth, at fifty-three, Nootzy was the kid sister of the former President of the United States John Sandborne, who committed suicide twelve years ago rather than face impeachment. She was classless. Her disheveled appearance, bleach blonde hair, no makeup, rosy fat cheeks, odor of cheap perfume screamed "I don't give a crap!" She was the most powerful woman on the planet. Her beady, often bloodshot eyes, caused from lack of sleep, and her Makers Mark whiskey breath, turned politicians to weak-kneed dribbling yes-men before her, and military generals to stone if they disagreed with her. "What the hell's going on, gentlemen?"

her deep voice roared. "I have the NSA, CIA, and MI6 calling me up at all hours of the night, scaring the pants off every member of my staff that we're about to be invaded by aliens! If the Ruskies and the Chicoms aren't breathing down my neck, now it's ETs. What in God's name is going on, gentlemen? Is this true?"

Four-star General Steven "Sledge" Drgastin met her inside the massive underground bunker, five hundred feet below the Virginia Hills. Behind him, a battery of giant screens surrounded the War Room with the live video feeds streaming in from around the globe. "No invasion determined yet, Madame President," Drgastin said, facing her. "So far it's a single ship."

"How do we know it's alien?" Shame asked.

A graphic of the solar system appeared on the center screen as Drgastin answered the question. "Arecibo tracked it entering our solar system. It disappeared for a time, until one hour later, when our Mars satellite picked it up again parked at the bottom of *Valles Marineris*. Earth has no space vehicle that can even approach one percent of that speed, Madame President."

Shame trolled to the center situation table, pondering the ramifications of an alien contact. "Are they friend or foe? Have they tried to communicate with anyone?"

"We don't know. From the intel we have so far, there has been no contact, Ma'am."

"Who else knows about this ET?" Shame asked.

"The Vatican, Ma'am," responded Drgastin.

Shame's face twisted into a sour frown. "Of course, they have eyes all over this planet looking for the Second Coming. How old is this intel, General?"

"Three days, Ma'am."

"THREE DAYS!" Books and top-secret papers went flying off the table. "And I'm just now hearing about this? What th . . . "

"Arecibo said they sent the intel by top-secret Air Force courier the moment they confirmed the sighting was extraterrestrial, Madame President," Drgastin defended.

"Where?"

"To Space Command at Peterson. Where they send all space related intel, Ma'am."

Shame's broad shoulders rolled toward Drgastin, her knuckles cracking under her weight as she leaned into him. "You mean to tell me that rat general Van Dyke has been sitting on this intel for three days?"

"Appears so, Madame President."

"I should have sacked him and that Admiral—"

"Meads, Ma'am."

"Yeah, Meads. I should have taken those two out when I had the chance. Where is that incompetent now?" Shame asked.

"Intel says he's on a highly sensitive flight to the South Atlantic."

Shame went to the screen where a real-time graphic of all United States naval ships at sea in the Atlantic was displayed. The USS *Eisenhower* carrier group, in particular, caught her attention. She pointed at the screen. "Who's in command of that flotilla?"

"Admiral Meads, Ma'am."

"That's just great. Two buttheads in one. They're cookin' up something, General, and it's smells alien."

"Yes, Ma'am."

"Have that battle group return to Norfolk immediately. Contact the XO, and put Van Dyke and Admiral Meads in the brig."

"What reason do I give the XO, Madame President?" Drgastin asked.

"Treason, sedition, withholding top-secret intel from the President of the United States. Hell, tell them it's for an unpaid traffic ticket. I don't give a rat's bee-hind. Just do it!"

"Yes, Ma'am."

Shame turned to her staff of shaking brown-noses. "Someone bring me a bottle for God's sake!" she roared.

Elbows and butts bumped into each other, scrambling to fulfill the President's order, as a junior officer entered the room and handed Shame a communiqué. She ripped open the sealed envelope, her hands shaking with anger, secretly wishing she were tearing off the heads of Van Dyke and Meads. She poured three fingers of Maker's down her throat and slapped the memo with the back of her hand. "Well, hot damn, finally a bit of good news. Our boys have finally found that broad."

"Madame President?" Drgastin asked, wondering what had brought such an evil grin to her thin red lips.

"Delmonte's wife, General. They found her and that snot-nosed kid of hers in New Mexico."

"That is good news, Ma'am. You've been searching for her too long."

"Way too long, General. Finally some payback for my brother's murder."

"Will the team have orders to shoot on sight, Ma'am?"

Shame's eyes narrowed, growing red and vicious, as she calculated her revenge. There was never any intent of ever giving Tinker Delmonte any trial. She looked up at the displays, while several scenes played out above her. One showed a child kidnapping at a burger restaurant, another was government agents beaten up by a young man, another with more of her special agents being gunned down in a Walmart parking lot, and a fourth video, even more bizarre, of a herd of elk running scared across a desert with two horse-like beasts, taller and faster than any Earthly horses, galloping beside the herd with their riders. But Shame didn't care about any of it. She had in her hand exactly what she wanted; the woman responsible for brother's death. She would get her revenge, regardless of any alien contact, a couple of treasonous generals, or a Second Coming. "I don't care about her kid, but I want her alive. I want to put an end to her miserable life myself," she fumed, stewing in her juice of hate.

26

Huey

Aircraft Carrier, USS Ronald Reagan, Battle Group
Mid-Atlantic
Lat. 43.70, Long. -123.04

THREE DAYS OUT of Newport News, the nuclear-powered supercarrier, USS *Ronald Reagan*, CVN-76, the cornerstone of the Carrier Strike Group Five, was cruising due south at 30.9 knots in driving gale-force winds and a river of rain. After a much-needed retrofit and six months in dry dock, the aging supercarrier was now the belle of the ball, and was headed around the Horn, through the Straits of Magellan, on her way to Yokosuka Naval Base, Japan, her home port. Rear Admiral Joseph "Huey" Meads, Commander of CSG-5, stood on the bridge, gnashing his teeth, keeping a close eye on the overhead radar screen of the approaching F/A-18 jet aircraft.

"Let's light her up, Captain," Admiral Meads ordered.

Captain Colleen Stewart came from a long line of Naval captains, four generations back to World War II. Statuesque, a hachidan level blackbelt, tops in her class at the Naval Academy, she wore a white

132

commander's uniform like no one else in the fleet, but try to pull some sexual pass her way, or whistle at her long legs, she would straighten your attitude but quick, and do it herself. She was tough, she was smart, she was everything her male counterparts were, and more. Admiral Meads had handpicked her himself.

"OOD. Bring the Gipper into the wind, please," Captain Stewart ordered. "We have a bird out there looking for shelter."

"Aye, Captain, Gipper into the wind," repeated the Officer On Deck, First Lieutenant Rodney O'Brien.

Stewart came to Admiral Meads' side to speak privately. "That jet is going to make one hellava mess of my pretty ship if this weather doesn't break, Admiral. Who in their right mind gave that bird permission, anyway? They should have their head examined."

"I did," Meads admitted.

Stewart blinked, her dark eyes holding their composure, despite the misstep. "Sorry, Admiral."

"Final approach, Captain," radar specialist Whitley announced. "She's thirty seconds out and coming in blind."

Alarmed, Stewart was about to wave off the F/A-18 when Meads held her arm. "He'll make it."

"He can't see the ship through that mess out there, Admiral," Stewart warned.

Meads confidently looked her in the eye. "He'll make it." He then made an inquiry to the Chief Petty Officer on duty, "Arresting gear up, Mr. Bailey?"

"Aye, Admiral, all gear up."

"Don't let the bow drift, Mr. Goff. Keep that mark steady," O'Brien ordered.

"Yes, Sir, mark steady as she goes, OOD," Goff replied.

"On my signal, goose that throttle helm," O'Brien said, then he added, "Give me a countdown Mr. Whitley."

Whitley continued the countdown. "Aye, OOD. Nineteen, eighteen, seventeen…"

At the fifteen-second mark, O'Brien called out, "Now helm. Throttle five second burst." He tapped the seaman's shoulder. "Hold her steady, Mr. Goff."

"Holding her steady, OOD."

Right when it looked like there could be nothing out there, the running lights of the F/A-18 dropped out of nowhere and hit the arresting gear dead center, stretching the landing cables to their max. The aircraft lurched forward like it would never stop, then suddenly came to a dead stop just before going over the side of the ship.

Stewart turned back to Meads in eye-popping awe. "I don't believe it. I've never seen anyone make a landing like that and live."

Meads kept shaking his head, laughing, as he rose from his command chair to leave the bridge. "That's Dutch for yah. Always making a show of it. Stay with me, Captain."

Stewart looked at her OOD and stayed with the Admiral. "Outstanding job, Mr. O'Brien."

O'Brien saluted, "Thank you, Captain," then went the command chair.

Stewart saluted her bridge crew. "OOD you have the bridge. Continue the Gipper on course, one-eight-zero."

"Aye, Captain, one-eight-zero," O'Brien, replied.

"The Admiral and Captain have left the bridge!" Petty Officer Whitley announced.

Admiral Meads stepped lively down the catwalk with Captain Stewart practically in his shadow. Neither spoke a word. Stewart was about to ask about the F/A-18 pilot when Meads turned to her with a finger to his lips. He pointed silently toward the door of his quarters as if to say, wait until we're inside. She had never seen the Admiral act in such a manner. Once inside the wood paneled cabin of brass, soft leather furniture, and decanters of Wild Turkey, Russian Vodka, and 18-year old Glenlivet, Meads began removing his uniform and changing into his camouflage utilities.

"Going somewhere, Admiral?" Stewart asked.

"Bring that pilot up to my quarters, ASAP, Colleen. Don't talk to anyone. Just bring him here," Meads instructed.

"Aye, Sir. Can you tell me what his is all about?" Stewart inquired, concerned over Meads' sudden change of behavior.

Fully dressed in what she considered an officer's submarine uniform, he reached down and lifted a small duffle bag and a flat, bronze disk, about the size of a large pizza dish, from behind his desk chair. "I suspect you'll be receiving an order soon from the President. I want you to follow her orders to the letter. I don't want you involved in what is about to happen."

"If you're in some kind of trouble, Admiral, I'll—"

"No, you stay out of it. In case this all goes south, I don't want your career in jeopardy. That's a direct order Colleen. Understood?"

"Yes, Sir, but—"

Meads pointed at the door. "This is the way it has to be. Now scoot. Get that pilot off the flight deck and bring him here. And for God's sake, don't let him pull rank on you to take him to the Chief's Mess first."

"Yes, Admiral."

Leaving his cabin, Stewart glanced back at the Admiral's forlorn look of impending doom. For an instant, their eyes met, giving her the distinct feeling she would never see him again.

As Admiral Meads warned, by the time Captain Stewart made it to the flight deck, the soaking wet, F/A-18, pilot had already made his way to the Chief's Mess. The Duty Officer on deck said the pilot was starving, and he knew where the best grub in town was. The officer tried to stop him, but the pilot pointed to the four stars on his flight suit and said, "Son, I can go anywhere I want on this boat without an escort." The officer agreed. "Yes Sir, you can."

"That was ten minutes ago, Captain," the Officer informed her.

"Did you see the name on that flight suit, Lieutenant?"

"Yes, Ma'am, R. "Dutch" Van Dyke. That was most incredible landing I've ever seen, Captain."

"Thank you, Lieutenant, yes it was."

Stewart took off for the Chief's Mess, and was met on the catwalk by a seaman from communications, who handed her a sealed envelope. "For your eyes only, Captain."

She dismissed the seaman and opened the envelope.

"By order of the President for Life of the United States, Nootzy Shame, Carrier Strike Group Five is to set course for Norfolk Naval Shipyard immediately. General Richard Van Dyke and Admiral Joseph Meads as of this moment are relieved of

their respective commands. You will arrest and detain in ship's brig until relieved by official government authorities upon docking at Norfolk Naval Shipyard.

PFL, N. Shame."

Stewart stared at the communiqué in utter shock. She slowly lifted the ship's phone. It felt like a lead weight in her hand as Admiral Meads' orders spoke clearly in her head: "...follow the orders to the letter." It was the most difficult order of her career. She pressed the receiver and asked for the brig duty officer. "Have two fully armed Marines meet me at Chief's Mess, if you please, Sergeant."

She hung up and walked slowly up the catwalks to the Mess. It was the loneliest walk of her life. Two Marine guards, holding short-barrel carbines across their chests, were already there, standing in front of the mess hall door.

"Anyone in or out, Marine?" Stewart asked.

"Yes Ma'am. A man in a wet flight suit with a sack of food, Ma'am," the Marine replied.

"You let him pass you?"

"Yes, Ma'am. He pointed at his four-stars. So yes, I let him go, Ma'am."

Stewart didn't blame the Marines. Under the circumstances, she would have done the same thing if four stars were flashed in her face. The Marines followed her to Admiral Meads' cabin, and she knocked on the door. No one answered, nor was there any sounds coming from inside the cabin.

She knocked again. "Admiral we have orders to arrest you and General Van Dyke. Admiral? Please answer the door."

No one came to the door.

She tried the doorknob, and to her surprise, the door was unlocked. She announced herself as she opened the door and went in. "Admiral. I apologize for the—" She stopped, suddenly realizing the cabin was empty. Both Meads and Van Dyke were gone. The Marines searched the head, the closets, and anywhere else a person could hide.

"Nothing, Ma'am," the Marines reported.

The small duffle and the golden disk were gone as well.

27

The Wild Strain

Hospital De Santis
Genzano de Roma, Italy

THE ALIEN BLOOD, sweat, and saliva samples the Church agents collected in California and Colorado for Father Espinosi were flown into Rome at 7:23 a.m. A top-secret *Secola Vaticana* courier received the packet of samples and delivered them personally to Father Espinosi, interrupting his morning prayer. The packet was then sent on by the same courier to De Santis Hospital to be analyzed. One hour, thirty-seven minutes later, Father Espinosi received a phone call that the tests were complete. Trembling with excitement, Father Espinosi raced his Mercedes GLC Blue Tech like a Formula One driver, winding his way through Genzano traffic. He arrived at the De Santis Hospital, five miles away, and made a beeline to the laboratory.

"That was fast, Father," Doctor Donmica Rendalli said to Father Espinosi, who was quite out of breath. "I just hung up the phone with you."

Stopping in front of the doctor, Father Espinosi bent over, and with hands on his knees, taking deep breaths while holding back his white cassock. "We need your findings, Doctor. Please."

Rendalli helped Father Espinosi to stand, rubbing his back as they walked to his lab. "I understand, Father."

"Have you told anyone, Doctor?"

"No, you asked me not to tell anyone."

"Yes, it is very important that no one knows of your findings, Doctor."

"You can rely on my discretion, Father."

On the way to the lab, they passed a couple of orderlies discussing lunch and a nurse pushing a tray of daily medicine for patients. Priests walking in the corridors with doctors were common, so no one paid any attention to the two entering Doctor Rendalli's third-floor lab.

Rendalli calmly went to his computer station and brought up the test results showing several graphs of the DNA specimens he was asked to analyze. "What were you looking for in these samples, Father?" Rendalli enquired.

"Are the samples human?" Father Espinosi asked directly.

"Oh, yes, they are human. Were you thinking they were some animal other than human?"

Father Espinosi stared at the screens. He understood the blood type O, glucose level, disease check negative, antibody patterns, pH and cholesterol levels, cardiac enzymes, all seemed quite normal. The Father had mixed feelings. On one hand he was relieved the results were normal, yet the recent actions he had observed of the three young men were not human. After so many years of searching for other forms of life coming to Earth, he was not mistaken. There was something about them that cried out they were, indeed, the Masters returning to Earth. But what was it? What was he missing?

Father Espinosi pointed at the screen. "You found nothing usual, Doctor?"

"No, nothing usual, Father." Rendalli thought briefly before going on. "The blood samples were devoid of any and all disease or infections."

"Is that unusual, Doctor?"

"Yes, quite unusual. That and the fact the blood sample was highly oxygenated beyond what our instruments could measure." Rendalli then asked, "Do you know if the sample was contaminated during transport, Father?"

"Great care was taken, Doctor, but the sample was taken from an archeological site. It's highly possible they could have been tainted there," Father Espinosi replied, fudging the truth to retain his secrecy. (He would attend confession later.)

"That would make sense, then," Rendalli said. He changed the screen to a black and white, microscopic photo of the blood sample. "But this electron microscopic picture of one of the samples makes no sense at all, Father. There were small devices in all the samples."

Father Espinosi lifted his glasses to see the display close up. "Small devices?"

Rendalli took a pencil from the desk and began pointing at tiny apparatuses floating between the blood cells. "They are a marvel of engineering, Father, and so small. Do you know their purpose, Father?"

"No, Doctor. It is a mystery to me, as well," Father Espinosi replied. "What purpose would they serve?" Rendalli crossed his arms in front of him as he stared at the screen. It appeared he was troubled by his speculation. Father Espinosi, however, wanted to know everything about the samples. "Please, Doctor, feel free to speculate."

Rendalli sighed, appreciating the Father's acceptance that whatever his deduction, it would not leave the lab. "I've read about experiments where nanodevices are able to function at a molecular level in the blood stream. I believe this is what we are seeing here."

"Machines, Doctor? How is that possible?" Father Espinosi asked. He was as stunned as Rendalli.

Rendalli grinned, his face changing from anxious to child-like excitement, as he leaned forward and marveled at the screen. "The implications are beyond amazing, Father. Devices like this might include plaque removal and cardiac repair by simply programming them to search out a particular place in the body where the repair is needed. A soldier's wounds could be mended in the field by a single injection of these encoded nanobots. Amazing. Simply amazing, Father. Where did you get these samples again?"

"Well, I was sworn to secrecy, Doctor. I'm sure you understand."

"Of course, Father. I understand this must be very sensitive material."

"It is, Doctor. Is that all you can tell me about the samples?" Father Espinosi asked.

The Doctor looked pensively at the screen. "You said these samples are from young men?"

"Yes, three young men."

"Three?" Rendalli questioned as he displayed the structure of a double-helix molecule turning around on the screen. The matrix was composed of tiny gold molecules, but scattered throughout the helix were bright blue and red ones. "I thought it was from a single source, because they seemed alike in their structure." He spoke to the display, telling it to enhance the three samples and compared them side-by-side. "But you're right, Father. They are very close, yet slightly different. I see that now." He touched the screen in several places. "Here, here, and here are slightly off. They are from the same biological family, however, that I'm sure."

"Brothers?"

Rendalli chuckled. "More like triplets. You see these red molecules here? I've only seen this once in medical school. If my memory serves, the DNA I'm thinking of was taken from an animal somewhere in the high deserts of South America. It lived where there were no trees, no water, seemingly very little to live on in the high altitudes. Ecuador? Maybe Peru," he tried guessing. But he failed to remember the exact country the animal originated. "Anyway, they discovered this dog-like predator had survived on practically nothing. Researchers found that odd, until they analyzed the hair samples of an Amazon dog that was now extinct and compared it to the DNA of this high desert dog. Remarkably, the two species were alike." Rendalli touched the screen with his finger. "It was the red strains of DNA that were common. Somehow, some way, the desert dog broke away from the pack, and against all odds, survived in the harsh environment. It became bigger, stronger, and smarter, living where no animal that size should have existed. As it began to thrive, the species returned to the Amazon and is now the most feared predator of the jungle. The researchers named the red atoms of the helix "the Wild Strain.""

Father Espinosi quickly gathered up all of Rendalli's materials. "Thank you, Doctor." On a nearby desk were the leftover sample packets.

"Are these all the items I gave you?"

"Yes, Father, the samples and the lab results are all there," Rendalli replied, surprised by the sudden change of inquiry. "Are you taking them? There are still more tests I can run on the other samples, Father."

With everything cradled securely under his arms, Father Espinosi walked out of the lab without one word of thanks.

Rendalli waved goodbye at closed lab door. "You're welcome, Father."

* * *

News programs the following day reported an early morning fire at the De Santis Hospital in Genzano de Roma. Apparently, an experiment in the third floor research laboratory caused a chemical reaction to ignite inside the lab. Computers, expensive lab equipment, and furniture were completely destroyed. Estimated damage was over two million Euros. The quick response of the Genzano de Roma firefighters was credited for isolating the fire only to the third floor science lab, saving the hospital and its many patients from the deadly fumes.

28

An Angel

LeBeau Park, Nevada

THE USAF CHINOOK put down at the entrance to a long desert valley and left Airman Lane, Captain Searle, and Marine Sergeant Enihoo behind with their gear. The Chinook's orders were to leave the area immediately and not to return until Captain Searle called for their extraction. For two entire days the Chinook had widened its search pattern, with nothing showing up on Timmer's gravity wave device. Searle was minutes away from calling off the search when Timmer got a hit, halfway across Nevada.

Assuming it was probably nothing more than a false positive, Searle asked Timmer, "Are you sure that device of yours works? We're a long way from nothing out here to go searching for false hits."

Timmer had enough of Searle's bellyaching. "What do you expect? ET to land in Times Square?"

Searle spit in the sand. "I would tell him it's a lot better there than this Godforsaken place."

"How do you know ET's a he?" Enihoo asked. "Could be a she, Captain."

Searle looked out across the dry parchment of land, disgusted with the uncomfortable heat. "Good point, Sergeant. Whatever he, she, or it is, I hope we can tell the difference. On this planet it's hard to tell sometimes."

Timmer waved to the Chinook pilot they were clear. The helicopter revved it's whirling blades, kicking up great amount of gritty sand before it rose and peeled away, flying due west, where it would put down at Hawthorne Army Depot and wait for Searle's call.

That was seven miles back. With forty-pound packs on their backs, the trio trekked along a dry creekbed that meandered its way through the valley. So far Timmer's gravity device had led them on what Searle called a snipe hunt. They saw a craggy range of mountains on the right and a similar one on the left and nothing anyone with a sane mind could remotely call an ET spaceship.

"Did anyone bother to check the weather around here?" Enihoo asked, sniffing the air.

Searle kinked his head skyward, squinting into the sunset. There wasn't a cloud in the sky. "Why?"

Timmer concentrated on his device and wanted no part of the conversation.

"Because I smell rain," Enihoo replied.

Searle gazed far behind them to the south. On the horizon he caught sight of a line of black clouds maliciously striking the earth with repeated bolts of white hot flashes, still too far away to hear. Whether the evil was coming their way on not, was impossible to tell. At this point, there was little to worry about. Searle's "expert" assessment was, "If it stays there, we're cool." And so they continued trekking up the valley until they came to a large pool of fresh water, surrounded by lush reeds and plant life that fed off the spring. A small grove of cottonwoods sat off to the left. Their leaves glittering in the soft breeze added some refreshing moisture to the air, as opposed to the dusty dryness of the desert.

"Finally a place with some charm," Searle commented. "I vote we set up camp here for the night."

Before anyone got a chance to vote, Timmer blurted out, "Oh, oh, I've got something," and then promptly tripped in a hole. Fortunately for him, Enihoo caught him before he fell and broke his wave device. The big Marine pulled him back from embarrassment. "Going somewhere, Airman Lane?"

"Thanks, Maxi," Timmer said gratefully. "I could have damaged my device."

"Oh wow, we'd have to return to base then, huh, stud?" Searle gibed.

Timmer put his device to his side and faced Searle directly. "Do me a favor, Captain Butthead…"

Enihoo interrupted the confrontation, standing over the hole Timmer had tripped over, pointing down. "Hey, look at this. Tell me that's not what I think it is."

Searle and Timmer stared at the massive paw print, uncertain if it was real. The size 12-boot impression Timmer left behind inside the print looked small in comparison.

"Mountain lion, Sirs?" Enihoo speculated first.

Timmer and Searle both shook their heads. "No way. Too big for that," Timmer said.

"Way to bi—" Enihoo nearly choked on the Timmer's carefree approach. "What do you mean, too big? What would fit that paw print then?"

"Something we don't want to meet," Searle said, casually. He spied a small clearing under the grove of cottonwoods, and asked, "How's that for a bivouac, ladies?"

"Works for me," Timmer replied.

Enihoo, who was twice their size, held them up. "Hold on, boys," he said, drawing their attention. "You don't mean to tell me you're actually serious about staying here?" Pointing at the paw print emphatically, Enihoo continued his rant. "What if that thing comes back for a drink?"

Timmer smiled at Enihoo, nodding at the Sergeant's weapons. "That's why we brought you, Maxi. You're fully armed with two Baretta's 9 mils., an HK417 7.62, 2 K-bars, and a pocket knife. I feel pretty safe, don't you, Robby?" Timmer asked Searle.

"Safe as a baby in the womb," Searle replied. "Honor, courage, commitment. Never quit. *Semper Fi*, oohrah, right?"

"Right," Timmer concurred, as he guided Searle toward the cottonwoods. He was tired, too. Early sack time meant early start in the morning to follow up on his wave contact.

Searle assumed the slight shove was a vote in his favor, and gladly went along. Enihoo glared at the two airmen, who were leaving him behind. "If I would have known about beasts this big, I would have brought my 50 cal."

Timmer yawned, following Searle's lead. "Coming Sergeant?"

* * *

A low vibrating hum stirred Enihoo from his sleep. Thoughts of the print's owner's returning to the pond had kept him awake all night. He was groggy and tired, and all he wanted was a couple of hours of good shuteye, and he would be good to go. Like he did on every mission, one hand was always touching his assault rifle next to him. But after scratching his nose, his hand went back to a handful of soft fur. A sudden flash of light lit up the night, taking his mind off his HK for a split second. Lightning, he figured, and began counting the seconds on his black Luminox carbon GMT watch. The orange glowing second hand ticked off twenty-one seconds before the rolling thunder reached his ears. Five seconds to the mile equaled four miles and small change, he calculated. A lot closer than before, but no worries yet, he told himself. A second flash bolted him upright in his bag when the light revealed a massive hippo-like creature lumbering out of the nearby pond. He thought he was dreaming when a third flash revealed the creature's pig-face staring right at him like he was its next meal.

Slowly, Enihoo reached over for his rifle again. Now something rough began licking his arm.

"JAEZZUS H. KEEEYRIST!" he cried out, and bolted from his bag to the nearest tree.

Another flash exposed the biggest cat God had ever created, and it was resting peacefully right beside his sleeping bag.

Enihoo's outcry awakened Timmer and Searle, who were wondering what the Sergeant's freaking problem was.

"Don't move…" Enihoo said in a hushed voice.

The next flash washed the whole valley in light. Not quite two seconds after that, the sky exploded around them. Timmer saw the beast first. "HOLY MOTHER OF—" In nothing but grey t-shirts and white jockey shorts, Timmer and Searle scrambled across the clearing, headed

for Enihoo's tree. The beast, for its part, yawned, watching the comedy act with indifference, as its bright blue eyes blinked in the night between flashes.

"How come it didn't eat us?" Enihoo asked.

"Maybe it's waiting for breakfast," Searle said.

"You know what this means?" Timmer asked.

"Yeah, it's lying on my rifle," Enihoo cracked.

"We're near ET," said Timmer as he studied the cat. Both Searle and Enihoo glared at Timmer like he was nuts. "That cat is not from here, dudes. Look at those eyes. I'd bet the farm it belongs to them."

Searle agreed. "Timmer's right. It could have eaten us in our sleep, if it wanted."

Enihoo removed his K-bar from his ankle sheath. "Maybe it wants to play with us first. You know, like house cats do when they catch something. They play with it awhile before they eat it."

Timmer didn't think so. "Put the knife away, Maxi," and pointed at the cat's incisors that were twice the size of his blade. "It would bite your arm off and swallow it with your K-bar." He stepped out from behind the tree and began to approach it carefully. "Here kitty, kitty."

"Don't be stupid, Lane," Searle said. No way was he going anywhere but behind the tree. "Get back here. That's an order, Airman."

Timmer was halfway to the beast when a bolt of lightening flashed overhead, splitting open the heavens. The next thing they knew a river of water was pouring down upon them. The cat bolted and the hippo-like creature belly flopped back into the pond, creating a wave that swept across their bags and all their gear. Searle and Enihoo scrambled to rescue anything they could, as Timmer watched with regret as the giant white cat leap away into the night. Suddenly, there was nowhere to escape the deluge. The dry riverbed was filling fast and taking with it everything that wasn't nailed down, including humans. Searle, now fighting off calf-deep water, leaped for low tree branch, but it broke under his weight. He fell into a swirling mass and felt his forearm crack when it struck a sharp rock. Twisting in blinding pain, Searle disappeared beneath the inky blackness. Enihoo dove after him. Unable to see anything, he somehow grabbed a leg and pulled him up. Timmer fell backwards, his foot caught between a rock crag, and his ankle snapped when he couldn't break it loose. The water was rising, choking him, his nostrils sucking in black liquid like he was being water-boarded. From out of nowhere, someone snagged his loose wrist and pulled him free of the rock. He looked up at his rescuer and couldn't believe the vision he held in his eyes. She was the most beautiful angel he had ever imagined. She shouted above the roar of water, "Put your arm around my shoulders!"

Heaving him up, she lifted him onto the back of a giant steed that had two great horns growing of its head. The angel, wearing hardly any clothes, a t-shirt and panties at best, was soaking wet from head to toe. With Timmer secured, she leaped onto the horned animal's back, and urged it forward, "Go, Delamo!" she yelled, holding on to Timmer and bounding through the water into the inky darkness.

"My guys… Can't leave them!" Timmer cried out, lifting his head, flopping up and down as they rode, seeing her green eyes, thinking he was already in heaven. "My guys, my guys!" he exclaimed with each gasping breath.

She pushed his head down. "Don't talk. We have them," she told him the exac instant his whole world went dark.

29

Phoebe Marleigh

Wilshire Boulevard
Beverly Hills, California

NEVER IN A million years did Riverstone ever believe he would meet the movie actress of his dreams, Phoebe Marleigh. Yet, there she was, real as life, sitting between Simon and him in their limo. Alice could have driven the limo through his gaping mouth. Like some magician's trick, she just popped out of nowhere. Simon had stopped to sign his comeback movie contract with his Hollywood agent, Saul, and after that . . . it was party time! They were curbside in front of Saul's office on Rodeo Drive in Beverly Hills, when Phoebe leaned into the open limo door, asking for a ride home. She said she was coming out of her doctor's office when she saw him getting into the limo. "My god, Simy, I can't believe it's you. Where have you been? It's been forever since I've seen or even heard of you."

"I know, Phoebs. Long story. Trust me, I can't believe how time flies."

"We'll have to have lunch and catch up. Are you back with Saul?

Another blockbuster?"

"I hope so, Phoebs."

"Would you be a dear, Simy, and give me a lift?" No one but Phoebe Marleigh could get away with calling Simon 'Simy,' and who in their right mind would turn down one of the hottest stars in Hollywood?

Simon waved her in. "Sure, Phoebs." He took her hand, scooted over and offered her a place next to Riverstone.

OMG! It's really her!

Shaking in his denims, red Lakewood football jersey, and blue Nikes, it was all Riverstone could do not to wet his pants from the excitement. She was even more glamorous in person. Her creamy smooth skin, long legs, and pink toes, contrasted beautifully across her white leather thongs, yellow designer sundress, blue-green eyes, and long flowing blond hair.

Phoebe slipped her hand under Simon's arm and snuggled close to him. Eleven years had passed, and she was still as hot as a teenage starlet. How could anyone deny her anything? "Is that cool, Simy? I can call an Uber if the Towers is out of your way."

"No problem at all, Phoebs. We would be happy to take you. As a matter of fact, Riverstone and I were planning a little night on the town to celebrate my new contract. Want to join us?"

She turned to Riverstone, stunned by his appearance. She had been so thunderstruck at seeing Simon, she hadn't noticed the handsome young man with them. "Whoa…you are a stud muffin." The freshness of her skin had already sent Riverstone's heart racing into hyper-light. "He looks like an officer even in a football jersey. Are you a spaceman like the famous Julian Starr here?"

Riverstone tried to find his tongue. "Yes ma'am."

Simon saw his difficulty and answered for him. "That's right, Phoebs, Jester…I mean Riverstone will be one of the co-stars in the next DG-III, To the Core & Back." 'DG' meaning, Distant Galaxy, the movie that Simon and the studios figured would make over a billion dollars in the first weekend alone.

Phoebe kept staring at Riverstone as if she were caught in a swift moving river of lust. "Have you picked a leading lady yet, Simy?"

"Well, yeah, Lara Allison. I thought you knew."

Phoebe didn't seem to mind that she wasn't in the running; after all she was still hot, just not the young starlet she once was. "How about a love interest with your co-star, here?" she giggled.

Riverstone's eyes pleaded for a yes from Simon. "Well, yeah, you'd be a natural for the part of Lara's mother. Is that cool?"

"I wouldn't care if I was a housemaid, Simy. As long as I have your co-star as my boy toy," she said, cooing over his tall good looks. Then, as if some uncontrollable force came over her, she took Riverstone's face carefully in her long delicate fingers and kissed him on the lips.

They continued their embrace, and would have stayed that way maybe forever, if Simon hadn't grown so uncomfortable he couldn't stand it anymore.

"Hey! Hey! Come on you two! Take a breath!" Simon cajoled. "I'm going to ride up front with Alice if you keep that up!"

Neither Phoebe nor Riverstone heard a word Simon was saying. They had entered a world of their own, and no one else was invited. When they finally came up for air, Phoebe said, "Wow, you've been around, huh, kid?"

"If you only knew," Simon replied for Riverstone, whose chest had yet to fill with enough air to talk.

"I'm so sorry," she repeated. "I'm acting like... Well, like a little schoolgirl."

Simon figured that was the first time in her life Phoebe had ever apologized for anything. What had come over her, he wasn't sure. But for whatever reason, she had Riverstone in her sights. Of that there was little doubt.

Riverstone didn't let her finish. He gathered her in his long muscular arms, and they kissed again, only this time, the kiss was more tender and giving. Simon didn't say a word. He patted Riverstone on the shoulder and gave them their space. He wanted to crawl through the window and sit with Alice, but he couldn't without stopping the car. Instead, he went forward to an empty place and acted like a potted plant that someone had forgotten to water.

30
Papa

Mertzig, Luxembourg

THE AFTERNOON SUN was bright and radiantly warm, when Father Espinosi, dressed in a traditional black cassock and zucchetto hat, entered the Café um Stamminée expecting to rendezvous with a special patron. Except for the dogs that barked at who knows what, Mertzig was a peaceful, medieval town in the middle of Europe where cows and sheep grazing in the meadows was common.

"*Puis-je vous aider, Papae?*" the girl asked in French.

"*Oui, Papa, s'il vous plaît, mademoiselle,*" Father Espinosi replied.

The girl pointed across the street at a small elderly man casually tossing breadcrumbs to the pigeons. He had white hair, a light blue polo top, dark khaki pants, cream colored walking shoes, and appeared all alone in the park.

"*Merci,*" Espinosi said, and walked across the street to the park.

* * *

When he wasn't feeding pigeons in the park, Papa oversaw the most powerful banking cartel on the planet. Only a privileged few in the world knew Papa's real name, Evelyn Du Bear. The Du Bear empire of banks and financial institutions was spread out across the globe, in every major city on every continent, including Antarctica. His influence controlled governments, elected presidents, prime ministers, powerful senators, and heads of state. His corporations on Wall Street, Brussels, Hong Kong, London, and Zurich, manipulated stock markets and elected political bodies that passed laws and changed the economics of regions for the sole purpose of protecting his global banking interests. The alien ship, code name "Caesar," or rather the boys who controlled the ship, had disrupted the Du Bear influence a decade before. The so-called boy captain had dissolved the Internal Revenue Service of the United States, the most devastating known arm of government to control a population anywhere, and he did it in a single day. When it was learned that Caesar was no longer a threat to their power, the Zmaji Cartel returned with a vengeance to control the planet again. Whether by accident or design, Caesar had vanished. Why, no one knew, not even Du Bear's vast intelligence resources could understand the disappearance. The Cartel, however, saw their opportunity and took it. An old Chicago politician once said, "Never let a crisis go to waste." The Cartel immediately launched a financial attack on the American economy, bringing down the Delmonte administration in less than a year. A month after that, the IRS was reestablished with the Internal Revenue Act of 2020 by an overwhelming 90 to 10 vote in the Senate. The House, with its spineless political lackeys followed suit the next evening by a similar margin. Caesar had taken the Cartel's power once before. It would not happen again. Evelyn Du Bear and the Cartel would do anything to keep their stranglehold on the world: assassinate kings, presidents, and dukes, and rape, pillage, and plunder entire continents, create economic depressions, fund world wars, all to preserve their power. And he would do it without remorse, guilt, or pity, just like his family had been doing for over six hundred years!

Father Espinosi bowed slightly, as he timidly approached Du Bear. "Good morning, Papa," he said respectfully in English, knowing Papa preferred to do business in a common language they both knew well.

Du Bear felt the sun's warmth on his face. "Indeed, Father, a lovely morning. Did you have a pleasant trip?"

"Yes, Papa."

"Good, good, and was your meeting with the Holy Father gratifying?"

"He is quite concerned. The beings are here, Papa. The ship has already landed in Nevada."

"Yes, Caesar has returned," Du Bear said quietly.

Father Espinosi was surprised. "You know this?"

Du Bear serenely removed more crumbs from his small paper bag and tossed them out to the hungry fowl. "Of course, that is my business, Father. To know things others do not."

Father Espinosi was taken aback. "But how?"

Papa smiled, but behind the smirk lay something far more evil than his frail body portrayed. "Let us leave it at that, Father. You may tell the Holy Father his empire shall remain intact, but there will be a cost, of course."

"Of course. We are all good patrons of the Cartel. The Holy Father will accept your terms, as usual."

"No omissions or exceptions."

"No exceptions."

"Or omissions," Du Bear emphasized.

"No omissions, *Monsieur Papa.*"

"You have the helix samples with you?" Du Bear asked.

Father Espinosi patted the envelope under his arm. "Yes."

"And what of this strain of human are you so fearful, Father? Why do we need to fear them? Are they not human? They bleed like us, oui?"

Father Espinosi turned grave "Yes, they bleed, but they are a Wild Strain of human, Papa. Our research has determined they are descendants of an extremely rare genome from the master species, creators, if you will. We believe with certainty, they are returning to Earth to reestablish themselves as the dominant specie of the planet. We cannot allow this to happen, Papa. We must eradicate them before they take control over all God's creatures."

Du Bear bent down, pushed a weak bird away from the pack, and continued only feeding the strong in the flock. "A Wild Strain?"

"Yes, they are a predatory race of beings we cannot allow to survive," Father Espinosi said, trembling.

Du Bear tossed the remainder of his crumbs onto the lawn. "If what you say is true, we must indeed act quickly. Goodbye, Father."

Father Espinosi bowed. "Thank you. Thank you, Papa. The Church will…" When Father Espinosi rose, Papa had already left the park. Du Bear's footman opened the rear door of a vintage black Rolls Royce that had silently rolled to a stop curbside. Papa stepped in, the door closed, and the Rolls pulled away as quietly as it had arrived.

Father Espinosi felt a tap on his shoulder. It was a man in dark sunglasses, casually dressed in a jacket that concealed a large caliber pistol beneath it. "The packet, Father," the man requested directly.

Father Espinosi wondered from where the man had emerged. He saw no one in the park before. Nor was there anyone standing on a street corner the entire time he was with Papa. "The packet," the man said again, more forcefully.

Father Espinosi stuttered, "Oh, yes the packet." He handed the large envelope over to the man who then stepped to the same curb and was picked up by a black, late model Mercedes 500.

Father Espinosi inhaled a deep breath, pondering on whether he had done the right thing. He would pray twice as long tonight. It was in the hands of the Holy Father now, he thought. He looked over at the Café um Stamminée across the street. The coffee smelled comforting.

31

Why On God's Earth

Location Unknown

TIMMER SAT WITH his legs off the edge of the comfy bed, wiggling the wrist and ankle that he swore up and down he had broken during the storm. Earlier, when he went to the bathroom, he checked his face and body in the mirror for scrapes and bruises. Nothing. There wasn't a mark on him. Even the hammertoe he had been suffering from the last six months was completely healed. More than that, all the nails on his toes and fingers looked like he had spent time with one of Darlin's manicurists. They were all perfectly trimmed, and polished.

Cool...

Relieved there was nothing wrong with his body inside or out, he stood up in dark blue shorts, not his, and stretched, feeling fully refreshed, like he had slept for a week. He looked around and wondered who undressed him and put him in the five-star hotel room. The accommodations were fabulous. If Dutch could see me now, he snickered. He was unable to conjure up a single synapse of memory that brought him from the campsite in the storm to here. Not one. The world was entirely a blank, except for the angel. He would never in a zillion years forget get that babe. Not only was she the hottest heroine he had ever laid eyes on, fiction or non-fiction, she rode circles around Lara Croft on that steed with the big horns. She snatched him from certain death and lifted him onto…? He tried to think again. A horse with horns? Go figure. Not even unicorns have claw feet, do they?

He walked through a sliding doorway into a beautiful, blue-carpeted corridor, marveling at the hotel's modern decor. Like his room, everything was first cabin. The carpet felt soft between his toes, and the ceiling lights were so natural, he could grow his stash all year round, he mused. Nice touch.

Suddenly, his thoughts turned to Searle and Enihoo and their condition. Had they survived the storm? Were they still out there in the desert? The last thing he remembered was Enihoo diving after Searle in the swirling waters. Wow… His heart skipped a beat, still thinking how lucky he was to be alive and all in one piece.

He swallowed hard and pushed the worst thoughts of last night behind him to find the others. He went across the corridor and knocked on the door.

"Enihoo! Searle! You in there? It's me, Timmer."

He continued knocking on doors until he thumped on the fifth door. At first, it was like all the rest of the doors, with no one home. He started for the sixth when Enihoo slid it open, yawning and scratching his crotch. He asked, half asleep, "Whassup, Lane?"

Timmer looked at him, somewhat annoyed. "Oh, I don't know, Maxi, the last time I saw you, you were flopping around like a beached whale, sucking on sage brush and mud. How did you—" He corrected himself. "How did we get here?"

Timmer followed Enihoo into his room with the same five-star, blue décor accommodations. "The only thing I remember…" The Sergeant's voice trailed off like he was talking to himself.

Timmer urged Enihoo to continue. "Go on, Maxi. Whatever wild-ass story you're thinking, I have one crazier."

Enihoo glanced at him twice. "Okay, the only thing I remember was this big black dude lifting me out of the water like I was a sack of perlite and throwing me on this giant horse with horns. He tied me down so I wouldn't fall off and went after Searle. I swear, I don't know how he found him. It was pitch black out there."

"He found Searle in that mess?" Timmer asked, relieved.

Enihoo continued: "Yeah, he did. Before the horse and I took off, I saw Searle being thrown on that hippo thing we saw earlier. The beast stood against the water like an Abrams, with the black dude holding on to Searle, and tying him down like me." Enihoo settled back on the bed with his hand behind his head. "Top that, Lane."

Timmer smiled, knowing he was holding all aces. "Same with me, but I was rescued by a twelve grade angel on a scale of ten," he bragged. "She put me on one of those horned things you saw and brought me here."

Enihoo wasn't buying it. "Sure, pal. When I believe in leprechauns."

Timmer raised his right hand. "God's honest truth, Maxi."

Enihoo laughed out loud. "Just like you to come up with a babe in the middle of a storm, Lane."

"Would you gentlemen care for some breakfast?" a soft-spoken woman's voice asked.

Standing in the doorway was the most gorgeous looking female the Airman and the Marine had ever laid eyes. Blond hair way past her shoulders, soft, slightly tanned skin, not a blemish, or imperfection anywhere, and a wide, welcoming smile, with green eyes that could launch ships at the snap of her fingers.

"That's her…" Timmer said in awe, not caring whether he ever took one more breath. He could die now, a happy man. "That's my guardian angel, dude."

Enihoo leaped up on the bed like he was goosed with an icicle, taking the sheet with him for cover. "I take it all back, Timmer."

"Are you gentlemen hungry?" she asked.

Timmer couldn't care less about clothes. Going to breakfast bare-chested in shorts with her was perfectly fine with him. He dressed like that most of the time anyway when he was home "entertaining." "Yes, ma'am, starving," he replied.

Enihoo wasn't so boorish. He was a U.S. Marine and would never embarrass the Corps in the presence of a lady. Their hostess must have understood his reluctance and said, "When you're finished dressing, Sergeant, I'll meet you in the corridor."

"But…" Timmer tried to say, as she pointed to an android stickman standing beside him with two folded changes of clothes in its hands. Neither Timmer nor Enihoo could figure out where the android came from. It just appeared out of nowhere and handed them their clothes.

"Excuse me," Timmer said, before she walked away. "We had a third man with us."

She waved and Searle came into view, grinning and already dressed. "Miss me?"

Timmer turned up his nose. "Like a boil."

Timmer couldn't wait. He hopped out the door, slid into his blue jumpsuit and stepped into his cool blue slippers. As long as he was the first one to the babe, he didn't care how he looked.

She giggled, watching him dress in front of her. "In a hurry?" she asked, standing beside a large golden disk.

"To see you, absolutely," Timmer replied. "Are you our tour guide? This is the coolest hotel I've ever seen."

She laughed again. It was cute, infectious, and charming all at the same time. "Feeling better, I see."

"Much! Thanks for saving our butts out there. How did you know we needed help? We didn't think there was anyone for a hundred miles."

"Our sensors picked you up," she replied.

"Really? Wow, is this some secret government installation?"

"No, it's private."

"I see." Timmer finished closing the front of his jumpsuit and was amazed at how easily the garment came together with no buttons, zippers, or Velcro. "Nice threads. What's it made of?"

"A special blend of dura-fiber," she replied.

"Everything seems kinda blue around here. Carpet, décor, even the lights have a blue tint to it." He looked at her eyes. "Except your eyes. Those are some wild contacts." He stared closer trying to analyze her eyes up close.

"Thank you."

"God, you're gorgeous." He offered her his hand. "My name's Timmer. You are…?"

"Leucadia."

"Leucadia, wow, cool name."

"My friends call me Lu."

"I guess after what we've been through, we qualify as friends," Timmer said.

Lu took his hand, just as Searle and Enihoo joined the party. "That would be nice, Timmer."

"Did we interrupt anything, I hope?" Searle inquired, cracking a sly smile.

"Yeah, you did," Timmer shot back.

Lu giggled. "You sound like Harlowe."

"Who's that? Your boyfriend?" Enihoo asked, hoping to dig a knife into Timmer's score.

"Yes. You could say that," Lu replied.

Searle and Enihoo's mouths flew open with laughter. "Oh, man," Enihoo howled, "you just shot a hole into Timmer's heart big enough to fly a C-134 through."

Timmer's pride shrank like a popped balloon. "Jerks."

"Please, gentlemen, if you would all step on the disk," she directed, stepping onto it first.

"What is it?" Searle asked.

"We call it a blinker."

Everyone followed Lu's instructions and gathered close together on the disk. Timmer tried to hold himself together, as he nudged close to her body and smelled her outrageously fresh scent. He thought of sweeping her in his arms and kissing her, regardless of her attachment to any "boyfriend." After all, he was a trained soldier and could take care of himself. Searle leaned over and whispered in his ear. "You try anything stupid, and she'll tear you a new one, Lane."

Timmer sighed. Searle was right. The way she picked him out of the water took a tremendous amount of strength. But one taste of those lips… he swallowed the heartache. He would pay a king's ransom for one small kiss.

* * *

In an instant, they were somewhere else. The room they were in was bright and full of yellow sunlight coming through a massive window that arched over the top of the room.

They were all awestruck. "What the…" Enihoo was stunned like Searle and Timmer.

Lu stepped off the disk, leaving the three soldiers to get used to their new surroundings. "The buffet against the wall has eggs over easy and scrambled, cheese blintzes, bacon, sausage, toast, potatoes, and several different kinds of fruit. Coffee, raw milk, and juices are at the end of the table. If you need anything else, or want something you don't see, just ask Betty, and she'll get it for you."

"Betty?" Searle wondered, looking around. There wasn't another girl in the room. "Who's Betty?"

Lu pointed behind them at the stick-like droid wearing a dark wig. "Betty is your servant."

Looking beyond the window, it felt like they were fifty stories up, overlooking a magnificent view of the desert and mountains, all spread out before them.

"This isn't a hotel, is it?" Searle asked, apparently already aware of where they were.

Lu's smile was reserved. She seemed more business-like now. "You are aboard *Millawanda*, our ship, three hundred feet above the valley floor, and looking northeast toward South Shoshone Peak. It's 0932, one day after your Chinook helicopter dropped you five point six two miles south of here."

"So this is the UFO that came to Earth four days ago," Timmer assumed.

"A Gamadin ship, to be precise," Lu corrected.

"You seem human," Searle said.

"We are."

"You're not human. Not with those eyes," Timmer pointed out.

"No, my father was human but my mother was from a planet over three hundred light-years from here."

"Interesting. I—"

Lu cut the questions short. "I know you have a lot of questions, but I have things to attend to at the moment. So if you will excuse me. I will talk with you at a later time."

Lu was about to step on the disk when Enihoo asked the elephant-in-the-room question. "Are we prisoners?"

Lu looked at them with caring eyes. "No. You're free to leave anytime you wish." She pointed out the window. "However, you might want to look closely at the valley floor."

The three stepped closer to the window and looked down. They saw movement but whatever it was, was too far away to see anything clearly. They looked like tiny ants.

"Who are they?" Timmer asked.

Although he was unable to see detail, Enihoo knew what they were. "They're soldiers."

"They're after this ship," Searle stated.

Timmer had another opinion. "Not enough bodies. If they were after this ship, there would be a battalion out there. No, they're after us."

"Who then? Not Air Force. The General sent us here, no one else," Searle said.

"Beats me. Somebody's looking for us," Timmer said.

"They're hot on our trail, too," Enihoo added.

"I wish I had my binos," Searle said.

No sooner had Searle asked for a visual aide, than Betty handed him a pair of binoculars. Searle took them cautiously. "Thanks…ah."

He forgot her name so Timmer helped him out. Remembering girls' names was a passion of his. "Betty, butthead."

Searle put his eyes to the optics and nearly fell backwards. "Whoa!"

"What happened?" Timmer asked concerned.

"I looked right at a guy's face," Searle replied, holding up the binos. "I could count his nose hairs with these."

Timmer took the binoculars and had a look-see for himself. "Nice… They came locked and loaded. Enihoo's right, they're out for blood."

Then Enihoo took his turn and was more concerned over what he saw than the optics. "They're not ours, either. Wrong camos. New stuff I've never seen before."

Searle took the binos back. He made an adjustment and pronounced, "Swiss."

"Why would the Swiss be after us?" Timmer asked, incredulous.

Enihoo didn't care. He only saw black and white and didn't care about motive. The Swiss were out to kill him, and that's all that concerned him.

Still looking through the optics, Searle went on describing what he saw. "They have long distance German HK's and Zeiss Victory HT 2.5-10x50 scopes with illuminated reticles."

Enihoo scoffed. "How do you know that, Captain?"

"I'm reading it off the scope, Sarge," Searle replied. After that he observed, "They can't see us either. The guy in the lead is scouring the valley and looked right at us." He lowered the binos and added, "He never stopped scanning."

Enihoo looked to Lu for an explanation. "We're invisible?"

She stood near the disk. "A magicians trick. Our force field hides us."

"But I saw you with my gravity wave device," Timmer pointed out.

Lu smiled graciously. "Yes, you did," and then she stepped on the disk and blinked away.

Timmer looked over at Enihoo and Searle. "She just dissed my wave device like it was nothing. What's up with that?"

Searle shrugged. "Maybe it's a toy to her." He went back to the optics and zeroed in on the Swiss soldiers. After a moment he looked up stunned. "Those dudes are Swiss Guards from the Vatican."

Timmer looked at Enihoo. "Well, I didn't see that one coming."

"Me neither," Searle added.

Enihoo went straight for the buffet and picked up a crisp piece of the bacon. "Man, this is to die for."

Timmer bowed slightly, allowing Searle to go first. "After you, Captain."

Searle ignored the buffet. He went back to the window with the binos, mulling over the idea of why on God's earth would The Church be out to kill them?

32

Delmonte's Mine

Abandoned Mine
Milepost 17, Hwy. 574
North of Aztec, N.M.

DODGE ADDED MORE nutrients to the hydroponic reservoir tub and adjusted the LED grow light a smidge lower over the lettuce plugs. Satisfied the lighting was correct, he measured the acidity of the water, added a few drops of pH Down, and measured the water again. "Perfect," he said to himself. Being a hundred twenty feet down inside an old silver mine, there was no one to talk to but himself. His mom, Tinker, was still up top, recuperating in his stepdad's father's old one-room shack. After seventy-five years of abandonment, the broken-down cabin was a weather beaten relic of a distant past. When they first arrived six years ago, fleeing from the government manhunts, it appeared the place was one stiff wind away from being blown to the next county. How it had survived this long was a conundrum. They found the front door lying splintered off the side of the porch. All the windows were broken. The holes in the floor could swallow whole bodies, and if they looked

164

up, they could view the entire Milky Way through the roof. But with the help of Clicker, the personal robob Captain Starr had given him as a kid, Dodge and his mom repaired the ancient cabin enough to make it livable and warm, until they completed a more hidden and secure living space deep down in the mine. They left the exterior of the cabin pretty much untouched for fear of people accidentally driving by and discovering the shack was occupied. Even though their mine quarters became quite livable, Tinker could only stand just so much underground living. She needed sun and fresh air even during the darkest and coldest months of the year. When she went below ground too long, she was prone to coughing fits that scared Dodge to the point he wondered if she could survive another winter. The drugs he brought back helped a little. She could sit up and drink fluids, like chicken broth, but nothing too solid. She was still terribly weak and pale. Seeing his mother this way when all his life she had been the titan of strength and courage for the family, sickened him to think she was a mere mortal like the rest of humanity, and could die.

Dodge picked the vegetables he needed for the soup he planned for his mom. He put them in a basket on the platform that went down into an inkwell of nothing for another two hundred feet. That done, he walked back through the brightly lit tunnel, past another garage size room of hydroponic plants and went into the first room of their underground living area. Off the living room were two smaller areas they used for bedrooms and a niche they dug out for their single bathroom. He found the spices he was looking for and walked back through the tunnel following a water trough that flowed from its source a hundred yards further back in the mine. There, a waterwheel, fed by an underground aquifer, turned a generator that gave them enough power for all their needs. Not far from the living room was Clicker's charging station. The robob stood against the rock wall, where two small power hooks held him up while he re-energized his system during what Dodge called the robob's off-the-clock time. Clicker lasted for two years before Dodge saw the degradation in the android's power. He acted like he was aging, unable to perform his normal activities without stopping to rest or sit in the sun to absorb its photons. That worked for another three years. But gradually, even the sun wasn't enough, so Tinker figured out a harness for him and wired it to the main generator. Incredibly, it worked. After three hours of charge time, he was his old self again. That was six months ago. Now the robob required twelve hours of charge time to make it through five-hours of up time. The down side was he required so much energy, the generator motor brushes were deteriorating from the overuse. As of five days ago, the generator's output dropped another 60% from what it was only a month earlier. Finding another generator, then, was critical, or all their work below ground was history.

Dodge lifted Clicker off his hooks and tapped him gently on the head. "All right, big guy," (The robob was actually sixteen inches shorter than Dodge.) "wake up. Time to go topside and take Mom some fresh veggies, pard."

Clicker's headband flickered briefly before becoming a steady blue glow.

"That's the spirit." For a short ways, Dodge supported the robob until he was fully capable of walking on his own. They passed by the living room and were strolling through the first garden, when Clicker's headband began to flicker in an alarming way. Dodge understood the meaning. It was not a low power warning and didn't happen often. Maybe a few times a year, but Dodge was trained to take any warning from Clicker as life or death. Robobs have built in sensors that can detect all threats to the beings they are assigned. Clicker's headband kept blinking like a strobe and wouldn't stop. If anything, it was blinking fast because the threat was already on them. If Dodge hadn't awakened Clicker when he did, they might have been caught by surprise.

Before hoisting himself up the mineshaft, Dodge sprinted back to the living room, found the emergency device in the center of their small dining table, and ran back to the platform. It was all part of the training they practiced weekly.

Clicker hit the up switch the moment Dodge hopped onto the platform. The servomotor engaged, and the platform rose. Dodge looked up, urging the hoist to reel faster, but it only had one speed... slow. A black military helicopter thundered overhead, and Dodge couldn't wait any longer. His mom was his only concern. He leaped up, grabbed the hoist rope holding the platform, and climbed like a sticky-fingered monkey the remaining hundred and fifty feet to the top of the shaft. He then swung himself out and over the metal guardrail, and hit the ground running. He made a beeline for the cabin, hurdling over sagebrush, boulders, and open pits in the earth. Soldiers had already reached the ridgeline, weaving their way toward the cabin as a second and third platoon of soldiers scattered along the dirt road double-timed up from the highway. The instant they saw Dodge they opened fire. Bullets whizzed by his head. Others kicked up dirt all around him. He kept running, speed his only ally. A bullet hit his shoulder, twisting him around. He went down but got right back up. A second bullet got him in the leg, and he stumbled on. Still another got him in the hand. That was nothing. He flung the blood away in defiance and hobbled forward, limping badly. He was almost there. He thought he wouldn't make it until the crack of two plas firing Gamadin pistols began mowing down soldiers like targets in an arcade. He looked up and saw Tinker shooting both weapons, and yelling, "Step on it, Dodge!"

Out the corner of his eye, he caught a glimpse of two solders kneeling, holding a long tube. A hand-held missile launcher, he figured. He reached into his pocket for the device, fiddled for the activator and launched himself at the open window. He felt a strong hand grab the back of his pants and haul him in, just as the missile rocked the cabin.

Between fits of coughing Tinker asked, "Where did they come from?"

"I don't know," Dodge replied. "Clicker saw them first."

Tinker zoned in on Dodge's bleeding wounds. "They got ya, Hon."

Dodge shook his hand. That one hurt the most. "Thank God they can't shoot like Marines," he jested with a grin.

She handed him a damp towel with which to wrap his hand. "Who are they?" she asked, helping him with his wounds. Another missile struck the wispy blue force field and exploded. She covered her eyes from the flash as the cabin shook, but nothing penetrated the rock solid energy field. They never had to use it before, but like their weekly prepper drills, they tested it often. "I don't recognize their camos," she remarked, squinting at the soldiers down the road.

"Why now?" Dodge asked. "I thought they forgot about us."

"Obviously not. Something's got them torqued, all right."

"The President's in jail. You can't mean that much to them now," Dodge said.

Tinker mused over the possibilities. "I know, but no telling what that no-good she-devil Shame, has going." She slammed her fist down on the table. "No one ever saw the treason sting she pulled on poor Peter, either. If only…"

"I know, Mom, if only Harlowe were here he would take care of all the bad guys."

Tinker lifted Dodge's leg to her lap. "I don't believe even Harlowe understands how deep the corruption runs in our government." She wrapped his wound and tied the bandage tight with a hard yank to stop the bleeding. Dodge cried out. "Ahh, did that hurt, Hon?"

With nothing but his pearly whites gritting away the pain, Dodge replied, "Nah, didn't feel a thing."

She smiled proudly. "Good boy."

Suddenly, after several more missiles died a pathetic death against the blue wall, the air went eerily quiet. Another few minutes went by, and a commanding voice boomed, "Come out now, and you'll live, Mrs. Delmonte!"

Tinker opened the front door and stepped out. She turned away briefly for a coughing spasm, spit, and then faced the voice defiantly. "Sorry, I've been a little under the weather. Here's the deal, go back to the slime hole you crawled out of before I embarrass you in front of your men."

"Last warning, ma'am!"

She shut the door and looked at Dodge, who had gotten off the floor to look out the window. "Was I rude?"

"Dad would have torn him a new one," Dodge said.

Tinker smiled as she checked over his wounds making sure the bleeding had stopped. "Yes, he would have." She pointed at his shoulder. "That round shattered a few bones, Dodge. You're going to need a doctor."

"Clicker will…" Dodge voice trailed off, suddenly remembering his robob was right behind him. Fearing the worst, he went back to the window and saw a dim blue light lying face down in the dirt. A soldier kicked Clicker's head and then hit him with the butt of his AR. Dodge seized one of Tinker's pistols and blasted the rifle from the soldier's hand, cutting the weapon in half. "Touch that droid again and the next one is yours, chump!" Dodge shouted. The soldier raised his hands and backed off, but sadly Clicker's light had already gone dark.

Tinker put a loving hand around Dodge's neck. "Those Gamadin make things tough. He'll be okay, Hon."

Dodge wiped away a tear, his eyes hoping for a glimpse of blue light, when all hell broke loose again. This time it wasn't the military shooting at the cabin, it was automatic gunfire, explosions, and hundreds of plas rounds coming from all directions at once. It was an all-out war outside, and strangely, nothing was hitting the force field.

When the discharges stopped, Tinker helped Dodge hobble out to the front porch. A smoky haze hung close to the ground as the acrid odor of spent ammo replaced the fresh smell of sage. A tall, broad-shouldered young man, who was easily a full head taller than the soldier, and dressed in blue jeans and sneakers, held a carbine in his right hand and a camo-clothed soldier by the collar in the other. The man proceeded to slap the soldier across the face twice, sending his beret off into the bush. The child-like futility of soldier's resistance was shocking. The soldier's boots left the ground with such force, and with such ease, he went limp the instant he was eye to eye with the man. The soldier's head seemed to vibrate up and down or shake sideways, depending on the riot act directives he was being given. After the one-sided conversation was over, the man tossed the soldier into the brush like discarded trash. The man then turned and strode coolly toward the cabin with a big-eared purple-haired creature by his side.

"I'll be a son-of-a…" Tinker gasped. Dodge's mouth dropped open as he switched off the barrier. They needed no introduction to this young man. They recognized the swagger and the mutt from halfway across the galaxy. With outstretched arms, Tinker ran coughing and crying tears of joy, yelling, "Harlowe! Harlowe!" She was nearly in his arms when a shot rang out.

"Mom!" Harlowe cried out in disbelief. Tinker fell into his arms. Miraculously, she didn't seem hurt. He looked up as Dodge lowered his weapon. On the ridge, the soldier who tried to ambush Tinker, fell to the ground.

Stunned, Harlowe quickly covered his mom with his arms, protecting her from any more ambushes as he looked at the crack shot who saved his mother's life. "Dodger?" he asked, wondering.

"Dodge," Tinker corrected. "He's all grown up now, Hon."

33

The Missing

White House
Washington, D.C.

SOMETIMES THE MORNING briefing began at 0800, sometimes at 0830. Rarely did it begin on time and never before 0730. But today it began at the unheard of time of 0600, when President for Life Shame marched into the Oval Office under a full head of steam. Without acknowledging any "Good morning, Madame President" salutations, she went directly to the Krispy Kreme table and plucked a hot glazed ring of heaven off the stack, as a servant handed her a voluminous mug of steaming hot Dunkin' Donuts coffee, black! While the morning attendees stood watching, she downed the entire donut, took a long drink of black ooze, and snatched two more donuts on her way to the Presidential chair between the two couches.

Shame looked over her cabinet, wondering why some of her people were absent. "Where is everyone? When I walk through that door, I expect everyone to be here, ready to go!"

General Drgastin spoke first. "Everybody was notified of the early start, Madame President."

"Well, obviously there's a lack of communication around here, Sledge," Shame retorted.

"Yes, Ma'am."

"Where are my Homeland Security Chief and my Secretary of State?" Shame roared as she reeled around to her Chief of Staff, Joe Boland. "I expect Director Logan to be the first one here, and he's a no-show, Mr. Boland."

Boland stuttered briefly. "White House limo picked him up thirty minutes ago, Madame President."

After a string of profanities, Shame directed her fire at the head of the National Security Agency, Director Judie Lougheed. "You're supposed to know everything that goes on in this country, Ms. Loughheed. so where is my CIA Director, and where is my Secretary of State?"

Director Judie Lougheed had the answer, but it was nothing Shame wanted to hear. "We don't know Madame. Secretary Minott was due in at Andrews (Air Force Base) early this morning. Her plane never arrived."

"Well, where is it?" Shame asked.

"It just vanished, Ma'am. Radar records show it suddenly blinking off the radar screen at approximately 0511," Loughheed reported. "The pilot reported nothing unusual during his descent from 30,000 feet, and then it was gone."

Shame wasn't buying it. "That's a bunch of crap. That plane had to go somewhere."

"I agree. We have search parties out combing the flight path as we speak, Madame President."

"And Logan?"

"The Director was picked up by White House limousine at 0624. As an added precaution, Secret Service has taken him to straight to Langley. He'll be available by video conference in twenty minutes."

Shame glared at the three faces left in the room as she downed her coffee and passed her empty mug to Loughheed for a refill. "What's going on here, people? This is no coincidence. My Secretary of State Minott is missing, and I want to know why."

After an array of "Yes, Madame President," the topic moved on to the former President. Loughheed handed Shame's mug to a servant and faced the President with the bad news. "Nothing, Madame President. We don't know how President Delmonte or General Branch escaped. It's like they walked right through walls and vanished into thin air."

Shame pointed a hot finger into Loughheed's face. "I never want to hear the title President used with that treasonous traitor again. Do you understand me, Director?"

"Yes, Madame President," Loughheed replied.

"How about his wife?" Shame asked. "Anyone?"

Loughheed glanced at Drgastin for his take. The General stepped in and replied, "She escaped."

"She what?" Shame gasped angrily at them both. "How? You had a hundred crack Rangers on her."

"I know. Someone took them out," Drgastin replied.

"Killed them?"

"No, Ma'am. Stunned them."

"You're pulling my bra straps, General. How do a hundred of our best soldiers lose the former first lady and that pissant kid of hers when they had them?"

"We have a soldier who knows, Madame President. It seems he was manhandled by one of the enemy who assisted the escape. He's in debriefing now. As soon as we have his story we'll have it to you."

You could fry an egg on Shame's forehead. She leaned back in her chair to gather herself. After a long pause, she reached down beside her chair and pulled up an amber bottle of whisky. She poured a large quantity into another coffee mug before she went on to the super-secret problem on everyone's mind. "So where's our ET, General? My guess is you haven't found it yet, either, or you would have told me," she snarled, clearly staring at the highly decorated soldier for his incompetence as she stuffed the fourth donut into her mouth whole.

Drgastin met her critical stare. "No Ma'am, but we're close. ET is in Nevada."

"How do you know that?"

"We tracked three of General Van Dyke's personnel to an uninhabited section of the state: a Marine, one of his top aides, and his number one astrophysicist. He wouldn't have sent them there to stargaze, Madame."

"No he wouldn't. That traitor sent them to make first contact."

"Yes, Madame. He's no green lieutenant. He's searched out Admiral Meads, too, for a reason."

Shame found that odd. "Meads? Why him? He's in the mid-Atlantic, steaming for Asia with a boatload of nukes for the Chicoms."

"They grew up together in Lakewood, California. They go way back, Madame President," Drgastin explained.

"Crap! Sounds like we need to take care of those two."

"Yes, Madame."

"All right, once Van Dyke's boys locate that ship, you know what to do. We nuke that alien salad plate!" Shame ordered.

"Yes, Ma'am unless the Vatican's Guards beat us to it."

Shame stood up and slowly walked across the Oval Office until The Church's role with the aliens finally struck home. "Well that Pope wants ET more than we do, doesn't he? Gotta love those religious types. It doesn't matter who they are. They don't want a thousand years of religious servitude down the toilet. Well, we'll show them what the next coming is all about, people. Wait and see."

Drgastin grinned slyly. "Yes, Madame President, let the fanatics do all the heavy lifting."

"You got that right, General, finally a bit of good news for the home team. Let them think they're ahead of us on this. I like your style, Sledge."

There was quick knock at Shame's personal secretary's door. The door opened slightly, and a grey-haired lady with glasses hanging between her large bosoms said, "You wanted to know when your guests arrived, Madame President."

Shame sipped her mug and put it on the coffee table. "Briefing's over, people. Meet back here after lunch. Loughheed, I want to know where my missing Secretary went, or heads will roll."

"Yes, Madame President," Loughheed replied, gathering her briefing papers.

As the others cleared the room, Drgastin asked, "Would you like me to stay, Madame?"

"No, Sledge, you have work to do. I want a full accounting on Van Dyke's boys, and especially those Catholics. I want them at arm's length and no farther."

"Yes, Madame."

Drgastin was headed out the side door when Shame called after him. She wanted their conversation only between the two of them. "What about that sub, Sledge?"

"The *Seawolf* found the *Ron Paul* an hour ago."

The news brought a smile to Shame. She lifted another donut off the tray and pointed at the floor. "Send those treasonous SOBs to the bottom, and shut the door behind you."

"Yes, Madame President."

34

Hudson Deep

USS Ron Paul
Grand Banks
231 Nautical Miles due East of Charleston, N.C.

ADMIRAL MEADS AND General Van Dyke were having breakfast at 0734 hours East Standard Time as a robob served another plate of scrambled eggs and hot, crispy bacon. "Thank you, Miles," Meads said to his personal droid.

Van Dyke snapped off a bite of crisp Applewood bacon. "You sub boys sure know how to eat, Huey," he said, savoring every mouthwatering chew.

As cabins go on submarines, even an admiral's quarters were Spartan. Just a tenth of the size of his cabin on the Gipper, Meads would have traded it all to have his old sub command back again.

"How do you rate having your own personal droid, Huey?" Van Dyke asked.

"It was a gift."

"Lucky you. From whom?"

Meads smiled. "A friend."

Van Dyke looked at Meads, questioning his motive. "I know that look. There's more to this droid than crispy bacon."

"A bodyguard and a taster," Meads admitted. "Shame couldn't force me out so she sent some of her pitbulls to take me out Plato style. Miles discovered the poison and the sailor behind it, twice."

"She's a real dirtbag all right. How did you know about ETs landing? I thought Space Command had the only intel on them," Van Dyke stated.

"I know them," Meads replied calmly.

"Them who? Space Command or ET?"

"The Unidentified, Dutch. I know the ETs. I've been in contact with their captain since they landed."

Van Dyke stared at Meads like he was conversing with someone wearing a tinfoil hat. "You're serious?"

"Very."

"Are they friend or foe?" Van Dyke asked.

Meads chuckled. "They're boys, actually. They're not even old enough to vote. A little green in the way they see the world, perhaps, but make no mistake, they are a force of good for all of us."

Van Dyke sat back and laughed. "You're talking like they're one of us."

"They are. They're human just like you and I. Harlowe, their captain, was born in the Naval Hospital at Pendleton. His father and mother were both U.S. Marines."

"You've been nipping that bottle of Glenlivet too much, Huey."

Meads eyes riveted their seriousness. "Why would I risk having your sweet puss come here? What I'm telling you is the God's honest truth, Dutch. The fate of our planet rests in the hands of these teenagers."

Van Dyke looked up at the ceiling and laughed. "I've just crossed over to the Twilight Zone."

Meads laughed along with Van Dyke. "I know. It's stupid to think someone is more powerful than we are, but it's true. Remember the world-wide takedown of our military over a decade ago?"

"I sure do. It led to that idiot Sandborne offing himself. I was on the tarmac when my B-1 suddenly shut down in 110 degree heat just before takeoff. I thought I was going to die in that cockpit."

"The boys were behind that. They got Pete Delmonte to run things, until Shame came along."

Van Dyke instantly went somber. "So where have they been? If they are so high and mighty with God and country, why did they let Shame come to power?"

"Bad luck, mainly," Meads replied. The Admiral went on to explain when the boys returned from repairing their ship, unbeknownst to them, eleven years had passed. "They're trying to make things right, but so far they haven't figured out how to make it happen. Harlowe has an idea he's working on, but needs our help to pull it off."

"Harlowe?"

"He's their captain."

Van Dyke kept shaking his head. "So the fate of the planet rests with a—"

A knock on the Admiral's door stopped the conversation as Meads acknowledge the caller. The cabin door slid back revealing USS *Ron Paul's* commander, Captain Alexander, who apologized for the interruption. "Excuse me, Admiral," as he also acknowledged Van Dyke, "General. I thought you would like to know we have a sonar contact five miles off our stern, Sir."

"One of ours, Gayle?" Meads asked.

"Yes, Sir. Sonar made positive ID. It's the *Seawolf,* Sir," Alexander replied.

Meads stood and wiped his mouth with a white cloth napkin. "Nootzy sent her best attack sub after us, Dutch. Care to join the party?"

Van Dyke nabbed two more pieces of bacon as he left the table. "Wouldn't miss it, Admiral."

On the way to the bridge Van Dyke asked, "How good is that *Seawolf* crew, Huey?"

Uneasiness spread across Meads' face. "I trained their captain myself. Mike Jackson served on this boat for two years. He knows everything there is to know about *Ron Paul's* capabilities."

"Can we lose them?"

Meads thought for a second. "If we can make the Hudson Deep, there's a chance."

"How deep can they go?"

Meads grabbed hold of the ladder that led to the bridge. "A lot deeper than we can."

On the bridge, the OOD, officer on deck, First Lieutenant James Sterbentz announced in a hushed voice, "Admiral and Captain on the Bridge."

Sonar said to the OOD, "The *Seawolf* is closing fast, Mr. Sterbentz."

"*Seawolf* closing. Roger that, Mr. Gingrich," Sterbentz acknowledged.

"How far to the Canyon, OOD?" Meads asked.

"Less than a mile, Admiral," Sterbentz replied.

Meads carefully studied the bank of computer screens that displayed the angle on the bow, present depth, speed in knots, and the red blip that represented the *Seawolf* related to the *Ron Paul's* in blue.

A sharp ping sounded outside the hull.

Van Dyke leaned over to Meads. "I know that sound."

Meads' mouth went sideways in a tight smirk. "Jackson found us on the first ping."

"You're a good teacher. Nice work, Admiral," Van Dyke quipped.

Meads cussed under his breath. "We're not going to make it." He stepped over to Alexander. "Level the boat, Gayle."

"But, Sir, if we do that, we'll lose speed and never make it," Alexander warned.

"I know, Gayle. Mike's warning us not to test him," Meads conjectured. "There's over a hundred and fifty good sailors on this boat. We can't risk it. Bring her topside."

Van Dyke stood with Meads. "If I were Captain Jackson, I would wait until were over the deep part of the canyon and let us have it there."

Meads gave Van Dyke a stern eye. "We have our hands up. He won't shoot."

Van Dyke glared at Meads, suspecting naiveté. "I hope you're right, Admiral. For the sake of your men, I sure hope you're right."

Sonar announced, "*Seawolf* opening number one tube, Mr. Sterbentz."

"Copy that, Sonar," Sterbentz acknowledged, as he looked back at Meads.

"Shouldn't they be closing that door instead of opening it?" Van

Dyke asked.

Lines of worry appeared on Meads' forehead. "Yeah, they should be." He turned to the OOD. "How far to the Canyon deep, Mr. Sterbentz?"

"We're over it now, Sir."

"Only one tube?" Van Dyke asked, alarmed. "They're going to use Grand Slam on us, Joe."

"You know about Grand Slam?" Meads asked, surprised. "That's even above my pay grade, Dutch."

Van Dyke bit his lower lip, shaking his head. "My boys at Skunk Works developed it in less than a week. The Navy wanted a one shot, one kill torpedo, and that's what we gave them; a low yield nuclear warhead. Anywhere close will do, Admiral."

"Any suggestions?" Meads asked.

Van Dyke had a one-word piece of advice. "Yeah, if he fires it... pray."

Meads glared at Van Dyke. "He doesn't have the authority to fire unless Drgastin..."

"That's right, and he gets his marching orders from Shame. What do you think our chances are now?"

Meads looked over the crew of the bridge with heartbreak in his eyes.

"Fish away, Mr. Sterbentz," Sonar declared.

"Fish away, Sonar, aye," Sterbentz acknowledged.

"*Seawolf* is turning, heading away at flank speed, Mr. Sterbentz."

"*Seawolf* turning, flank speed, aye, Sonar," Sterbentz countered.

"Time to detonation, Sonar?" Alexander asked.

"Ninety-seven seconds, Skipper," Sonar replied.

Van Dyke tapped Meads on the shoulder. Their eyes met. There were no more commands to give, no more reasons to be on the bridge. "How deep is this Canyon?" Van Dyke asked.

"About 8000 feet, give or take," Meads replied.

"Our crush depth?"

"About a thousand, give or take."

Van Dyke sighed, resigned to the grim prospects.

Miles appeared on the bridge with a plate of crisp bacon. "Dutch?" Meads offered.

Van Dyke smiled graciously, removing a piece from the offered plate. "Thank you, Admiral."

35

G-coin

"FOR YOU, MADAME PRESIDENT," Shame's secretary said, interrupting the meeting with her two guests, Richard Tucker from Dothan, Alabama and Leslie Cardé from New York City. The two were board directors of the Zmaji Cartel. Cardé oversaw the media arm of the Cartel, that included all the major newspapers, television, radio stations in the U.S., while Tucker handled the financial institutions that included Wall Street banks, the top 500 corporate enterprises, and insurance conglomerates. As board members of the Zmaji Cartel, they were each powerful in their own right and were the quintessential top of the food chain, the puppet masters of their domain. They called the shots. No one was above them, not even the President for Life.

Shame took the sealed envelope that read: "For POTUS Eyes Only," dismissed her secretary, and waved the envelope at Tucker and Cardé. "This better be good news." She opened the envelope and quickly read the single page document, racing to the bottom of the page for the conclusion. She broke out in a malicious smile and slapped the paper.

"Good news, Nootzy?" Cardé inquired.

"You got that right; two less headaches in my officer corps." Shame went to a nearby paper shredder and slid the document into the slot. Returning to her guests, she asked, "So what's this crypto whatever that has you two tied in knots?"

"People call it a G-coin. It's short for Gamacoin," Tucker replied, showing her the blue card in his hand.

"What people?" Shame asked.

"Everyone. You haven't heard?" Cardé asked accusingly. The Cartel had put Nootzy Shame into power. They could just as easily remove her from office like they did Delmonte.

"Excuse me, Ms. Cardé, I've been busy tracking down an ET that just landed in my backyard," Shame shot back. "Are you aware of that?" She quickly answered the question herself. "Of course you do. Papa knows everything. Even things my own CIA doesn't know."

"And what are you doing about it?" Cardé asked.

Shame reached down and picked up the paper, holding it in front of their faces. "I just sent a nuclear sub to the bottom of the ocean with an admiral, a general, and a crew of a 130 sailors who tried to conspire with the ETs to take down this government. That's what I've been doing, Ms. Cardé."

"Does that include General Van Dyke?" Tucker asked.

"And Admiral Meads, a particular thorn in my side."

"Their deaths were confirmed?" Cardé asked.

"Well, I didn't personally check their pulses at the bottom of the Hudson Deep, but I can assure Papa, they're talking with Davy Jones in his locker as we speak. Now, what does this have to do with this coin thing you're all in tizzy about?"

Tucker answered first. "Can you imagine a world without banks, Nootzy?"

"No I can't, and neither can you, Mr. Tucker, or who would pay for your Dreamliner to go hobnobbing around the globe on?"

It was Cardé's turn next. "Okay, how about something you can imagine. How about a world with no governments and no Nootzy Shame as President for Life?"

Shame hesitated. She started to laugh at the absurdity, but when she saw the seriousness in their faces, she knew they were serious. "You're saying this Gamacoin has that kind of potential?"

"Correct!" Cardé replied.

Shame spread her hands out. "Then I'll outlaw it. There, problem solved."

"It's not that easy," Cardé shot back.

"Why not?"

"Because it's gone worldwide. We tried containing it with our own systems and failed. The Gamacoin is affecting North America, Europe, and it's one jet aircraft away from Asia, if it isn't there already. People are taking their money out of banks and converting it to Gamacoin by simply swiping their cash cards across the Gamacoin card. Their funds transfer automatically. They can now use a Gamacoin on any network in the world with complete privacy. No third parties, no banks, and no government intervention."

"How is that possible? We have the best programmers on the planet to hack that kind of activity," Shame pointed out.

"Our computer specialists have studied the code. It's like nothing they've ever seen before. So far, even our fastest quantum computers are unable to crack it," Tucker explained.

"Where did it come from, and who's behind it?" Shame asked.

Cardé initiated a holograph screen from the small pad she removed from her purse. After a few hand swipes, she found the video she wanted. "We believe it was at this fast-food restaurant in Barstow, California where it all began."

The video fast-forwarded through the two young men stopping a child kidnapping. Shame stopped the video. "Where did you get this?"

"The Vatican secret service," Cardé replied.

Shame wanted to spit acid. "Them again. The Church has been ten steps ahead of my intel the whole way. I should hire them and fire those incompetent boobs we have running our intelligence agencies."

Tucker motioned for Cardé to continue with the video. "We're very aware of that, but this is what we're focused on now." She stopped where the muscular hunk handed the mother of the kidnapped little girl a blue, holographic card. "There! That card he handed to that girl. It's like the one in Richard's hand. We're certain that's where the G-coin infected the system."

"All right, so who are these guys?" Shame asked.

"They're your ETs, Nootzy," Cardé said.

Shame's cynical eyes darted between her two guests. While she was digesting that information, Tucker had Cardé rewind the video to show the hunk's face close up. "Recognize that hottie, Nootzy?"

"No, not to put a name to it, but he does look familiar," Shame admitted.

Cardé added a still photo of a decade-old sci-fi movie poster beside the hunk. "How 'bout now?"

"SIMON BOLT?" Shame exclaimed. "I was so in love with that guy. Julian Starr was my hero. But then he just . . . disappeared." She pointed at the video still. "You're telling me he's an ET?"

"That's right. And look closely at his face. He hasn't aged one day since the day he fell off the face of the Earth."

Shame leaned forward, studying the stills more closely. "You're right. Nothing's changed about him." She faced them again. "So what's the plan? What do you want me to do?"

Cardé removed a thick folder from her briefcase and placed on the coffee table. The top left corner read: Level 9 Top Secret. Below that, in large black block letters, was the single word: CAESAR. "Are you familiar with Caesar, Nootzy?"

Shame's eyes turned evil. "Caesar was responsible for my brother's death."

"Now you can get your revenge, Shame," Tucker stated with a twisted smirk.

"These are the same boys who destroyed my brother?" Shame asked.

Cardé put five more stills of four teenage boys and a beautiful young woman on the screen. "They were all in on it. The leader is the young man on the left. His name is Harlowe Pylott."

Shame's eyes exploded. "Why that's…"

"That's right," Cardé nodded. "He's Tinker Delmonte's son. Pylott was her late husband's name."

"Small world, ain't it," Shame seethed, pointing at the other photos.

"So who are these other snot-noses?"

"That one is Matthew Riverstone. He was the second young man in the restaurant video," Cardé said. "Ian Wizzixs, next. The black man is Monday Platter, Bolt's bodyguard."

Shame gasped and realized she recognized someone else. "I know her, too. Leucadia Mars. She was the head wench of the Mars Corporation."

Tucker laughed. "Bingo! You campaigned against her right-hand man, Jefferson Braxton."

Cardé sneered. "He would have beaten you, too, if it weren't for his untimely crash in the Pacific."

Shame gave them both a guiltless nod of appreciation, as Tucker added, "Fortunately, the typhoon scattered any trace of his plane to the bottom of the Marianas Trench."

"So why now? Where have these people been, why are they showing up when we're about to nuke the Chicoms?" Shame asked. "To see mom and dad and have a couple of yuk-yuks with the family?"

Cardé gave the okay for Tucker to add, "We believe they returned to take back the government of the United States."

Shame grunted. "Do tell."

Cardé added another wrinkle. "The Vatican has studied their DNA."

"So."

"So, they're not normal humans."

"These boys aren't human? Come on."

"Oh, they're human, all right, straight off the California beaches," Cardé said, "but according to Vatican geneticists, the boys are an offshoot of the human race. The Church has discovered they are a Wild Strain of humans with the same DNA found in a hair lock of Julius Caesar, Alexander the Great's crown, and Genghis Kahn's wolf coat. They fear if they are allowed to survive, and people discover alien life really does exist beyond our own planet, the Church will cease to exist, and so will the governments of the world."

Shame's eyes narrowed to razor sharp slits. "And don't forget the bankers, right, Mr. Tucker?"

Tucker grinned defensively. "If this Gamacoin succeeds in eliminating the banks, we will all be sucking face with Davy Jones, Madame."

Shame added the last drop of whiskey to her mug. "Then we better find that ship and take those pretty boys out. For the good of all mankind, of course," she sneered.

36
Al Di La

Hollywood Blvd. & Vine St.
Hollywood, California

RIVERSTONE PAUSED AND sighed deeply, looking up at the side
of the building. "She's always been the girl of my dreams," he remarked
to Simon, as they strolled down Hollywood Boulevard together. After
a full day's work shooting the trailer for Simon's new sci-fi blockbuster,
they were looking for a place to eat, but it was the huge billboard covering
nearly the whole side of a twelve-story building, that caught Riverstone's
attention. The movie ad featured his new heartthrob Phoebe Marleigh's
latest movie, *War of the Forgotten*, with her leading man, James Bastion,
just opening in theaters across the nation.

"You sure swept her off her feet, dude," Simon said, slapping him
on the back.

Riverstone smiled, dreamy-eyed. "She swept me off my feet the first
time I ever saw in *The Night of Abduction*."

"She was only fifteen then."

"Yeah, and I was twelve." He wanted to see her again so bad. "I can't believe she hopped into our limo like that."

Simon saw his pain, so he did what any friend would do…fix things. "I'll ask Saul to arrange a lunch for you two between shoots. Will that work?"

Riverstone grabbed Simon's arm. "Will it! You could do that?"

"Slam dunk, pard."

Riverstone could hardly control himself. "When?"

"Hold on." Simon pulled out his cell phone and dialed his agent. "Saul. Need a big favor. Riverstone… Yeah, Jester. Set us up a lunch with Phoebs. Have something Italian whipped up from Marceli's and brought to the set." Simon listened briefly to Saul's reply. "Perfect. He is?" Simon covered his phone mic and whispered to Riverstone. "Her agent's on the other line with Saul." Back to Saul, Simon continued, "All right, give me a call back when you're done. Later, dude."

Riverstone was stunned. "It was that easy?"

Simon chuckled. "Yep, Saul's putting the final touches on getting her a part in the movie."

Riverstone leaped in the air. "You're the best, brah!" He gawked at the billboard again, Phoebe dressed in a World War II nurse's uniform trying to protect the male star, James Bastion, from the German soldiers. Her face was a little dirty, and her uniform a little torn from running through the woods chased by soldiers, but Riverstone didn't care. The tiny flaws made her more beautiful than ever. She could wear a tarp, and all he would see was her gorgeous brown eyes and long blond hair.

"She's a lot older now, you know?" Simon pointed out.

Riverstone returned a wink of confidence back to Simon. "I don't care. I like older ladies, remember?"

Simon laughed. "Oh, yeah, I almost forgot about Sharlon. She was a lot older. A hundred years maybe."

Riverstone smiled approvingly, thinking back to the older lady he had a short affair with on the planet of Tomar, in the Omini Quadrant. She didn't look a day past thirty. "Not quite, but close," he admitted.

"So how was she?"

Riverstone turned thoughtful as he stared across Hollywood Boulevard. "What goes on in the Omini Quadrant stays in the Quadrant."

"Good answer."

Riverstone playfully pushed Simon along the street. "Come on, I'm starved."

They walked for another mile to one of Simon's old hangouts, Miceli's, a family-owned, Italian Restaurant on Las Palmas Avenue. Inside the eatery, the ceiling was full of hanging, basket-covered Chianti bottles. The rich wood décor was straight from the old country, complete with red and white checkered tablecloths. But what drove anyone crazy the instant they came through the front door was the smell of the wood-fired oven pizza, coming from the kitchen. In the old days (a decade ago), Simon would walk into Miceli's, and he would be greeted like an A-lister star, even though at the time he was considered a B-lister. Carmen Miceli, the owner, would kiss him on both cheeks and show him to "His" table by the window, where he could look out at the street, enjoying the many freak shows walking by. But today, a new generation had taken over the business, and no one knew Simon from next guy off the street. "Do you have a reservation, Sir?" the maître d' asked Simon.

Simon nodded politely and asked, "Are you Carmen's son?"

"No, I'm his grandson, Giuseppe," the young man replied. "Did you know my grandfather?" he asked.

"I did." Simon pointed at the empty two-topper by the window. "That was my table over there. Back then I never needed a reservation," Simon informed the young Miceli.

Giuseppe displayed a slight smirk, having heard the same line many times before. "I'm sorry, Sir, it might be a couple of hours before we can seat you."

Riverstone caught sight of a waiter singing something Italian at a table, and suggested, "You should know Mr. Bolt, here, used to sing for your grandfather."

Miceli smiled with small hint of disbelief, as he gave Simon a second look. "Really?"

"Yeah, that's why all his meals were free," Riverstone bragged.

Since it was early, and the dinner crowd had yet to come in, Giuseppe giggled. He was up to the challenge, and offered Simon a chance to prove himself. "The floor is yours, Mr. Bolt, sing away. Let's see how good you really are."

Riverstone walked over and asked a musician if he might borrow his violin. "I'll give it right back, I promise." He strummed it once. It wasn't quite the Stradivarius he normally played, but with a little tuning, it became an acceptable instrument again. He gave Simon a nod. "Good to go, *Signore* Bolt. What key would you like?"

Simon winked. "C major is cool." Riverstone showed off a little bit, playing an incredible intro. Without even clearing his throat, Simon began the first verse in full Italian.

Al di la; del bene piu prezioso, ci sei tu.
Al di la; del sogno piu ambizioso, ci sei tu.
Al di la; delle cose piu belle.
Al di la; delle stelle, ci sei tu.

He repeated the first verse in English.

Beyond; Of the most precious asset, there you are.
Beyond; Of the most ambitious dream, there you are.
Beyond; Of the most beautiful things.
Beyond; Of the stars, there you are.

By the time Simon completed the first line of the first verse, he had the entire restaurant in tears, including Giuseppe, whose whole attitude had changed. After the third verse, Simon had the young Miceli wrapped around his finger. Giuseppe graciously led them to the two-topper window table and said, "Order anything you want, *Signore* Bolt, our house is yours. I've never heard anyone sing so beautifully in all my life," he said, wiping his eyes with a white cloth napkin.

* * *

Toward the end of the meal, two gentlemen in dark suits entered the restaurant. The change in Giuseppe's demeanor was instant.

"I've seen these types before," Riverstone said to Simon across the table. "They're called Nootzy's Hoods." He explained they were government agents who dropped by various businesses to shake them down for added revenue.

A brutish hood grabbed Giuseppe by the shirt and began to threaten him.

"Excuse me," Simon said, walking up to the register. "I'd like to pay for my check now if you don't mind."

"Buzz off, grunt. Can't you see were busy here," the tall Hood said angrily.

"I wanna pay now," Simon insisted.

The smaller Hood poked Simon in the side. "Do you know who we are, chump?"

Riverstone stepped forward, as Giuseppe stood back and looked on, confused. "You didn't hear my friend. He said wants to pay now."

The small Hood went for his shoulder holster, when his weapon was snatched away in a blink. His pistol was now pointed at his gut. The tall Hood saw this and released Giuseppe, as he also went for his gun. But incredibly, the Glock was taken away and stuck in his side, just like his partner's. The two backed off and were about to raise their hands.

Riverstone touched the arm of the second hood. "Tut, tut, keep your hands down, gentlemen, and act all peaceful like. We wouldn't want to disturb our guests, would we?"

Simon handed Giuseppe a blue Gamacoin card. "Give yourself a good tip, *Signore* Miceli, say two hundred new dollars." Riverstone shook his head, indicating that amount wasn't enough. "Yes, you're quite right, Jester, make it 500 dollars on top of the bill."

"But that is way too much, Mr. Bolt," Giuseppe said.

Simon wouldn't hear of it and handed the card to Giuseppe again. "Take it and run it through. It's on the company tab, my friend."

Giuseppe followed directions, running the card through the reader and handing it back to Simon. "Thank you, *Signore*. Please come back anytime."

After a bear hug from Giuseppe and many more thank-yous for the wonderful dinner, Simon and Riverstone led the dejected losers out the door. Already parked behind their big, black SUV was the Gamadin limo, with Alice patiently waiting in the driver's seat.

Simon and Riverstone ejected the ammo clips from the Hoods' weapons, cleared their chambers, and returned them to their shoulder holsters. The tall Hood attempted to hit Simon across the face, but was stopped instantly by a grip so powerful, it brought the thug to tears. He collapsed to the pavement grimacing in pain. "Now," Simon began, "I know what you're thinking. As soon as we leave you're going to go back in there and make Giuseppe pay big time for what happened to you this afternoon. That would be a huuuuge mistake." Riverstone held up their wallets. The small goon grabbed his coat, stunned that his pocket had been easily picked. Simon continued: "We have your names, and we know where you live. If we hear that even the slightest hair on Giuseppe's head was harmed, or that his restaurant has even a dish broken, we will come looking for you." Simon released the beast's arm, bending down to him. "What will happen to you?" The Hoods remained silent as Simon went on, "Well, I'm glad you asked." He looked over at Riverstone and asked, "Melt it?"

Riverstone nodded. "To the pavement."

Simon pointed at the SUV. "Total it, Alice."

Alice touched an activator on the dash. Hardly a heartbeat later, a powerful blue beam above the windshield struck the vehicle, promptly melting the entire SUV into a heap of molten metal.

"Get the point?" Riverstone asked.

Speechless, their heads vibrated up and down.

"You will clean this up, right away...yes?" Simon asked politely.

More vibrating heads.

Simon turned back, smiled, and waved to Giuseppe, who had seen it all through the front window. The Gamadin then stepped into their limo, and Alice drove them away.

37

Rick's Place

Millawanda
Nevada desert

TINKER CAME OUT of the med room looking feeble. Her eyes were red and teary, her face solemn, full of worry. Her once physically tough body had become frail and weak. She took one step and faltered, but Harlowe was there and caught her before she fell.

"Sorry," she said, apologizing for his having to help her. She had always been the strongest one in the family. She cleaned scrapes and cuts, hugged them when they tried their best and failed, picked them up when they were down, and slapped them on their rears, reminding them never, ever to give up. She made the best guacamole known to mankind, grilled steaks, hamburgers, and hot dogs to perfection, made French toast and pancakes to die for, topped with homemade ice cream. Not only that, she was the only person alive Harlowe ever feared. But lately, watching her come out of the med room looking so fragile, she seemed ready to crawl between two sheets and let nature take her.

"How about a little sun, Mom?" Harlowe asked.

She sniffled back her tears, as Jewels appeared and handed her a white hanky. "Thank you," she said to the robob. She blew her nose, allowing Harlowe to keep her steady while she wiped her face. She took a long hard look up at him. She wanted an answer with no softball replies. Whatever the truth was, that's all she wanted. "Will he make it, Harlowe?"

Harlowe covered her with his arms. "Six hours ago, we almost lost him. But since you've been here, Lu says he's doing much better."

"He hasn't moved, Hon."

"He knew you were there the moment you took his hand."

"He's not your father, bless him, but he's a good man."

"I know Mom. A hundred million people know that, too. They never stopped believing in him."

"I don't want to lose another good man."

"You won't. He has the best care of anywhere in the galaxy. But no medicine I know can replace you, Mom. I know that for a fact."

She seemed to accept his answers and appreciated his candor. That's how all Pylotts drank reality–straight, with no ice. Out the corner of her eye, she looked him over. On the trip back to *Millawanda* from New Mexico, they had barely spoken. After the fight with the soldiers, when she saw it was Harlowe who saved them, she had collapsed on the cabin porch from the relief that her oldest son was alive and well. Once they were inside the ship, Harlowe laid her in the med unit next to Delmonte, and that's where she slept and received nutrient injections and nanobots that destroyed any remaining disease in her body. All she needed now was rest.

"You've grown a lot since I last saw you," she commented, and reached up and took his chin in her hands, gliding her fingers across his face. "How come you're not shaving yet? A man twenty-eight years old should be shaving. What has life as a Gamadin done to you, son?"

Harlowe motioned to Jewels, and almost instantaneously, a floating chair slid behind Tinker. Harlowe guided her to it, and replied, "I'll explain later."

She accepted the put off for now. She was too weak to make an issue of it. But she would have her answer. Marine moms' memories were long.

Still holding onto her hanky, she looked around the chair and saw something missing. "I don't see any wheels!"

"It floats, Mom." He pointed at the nearest armrest. "To make it go forward, press the front of the arm. Right, left on the side and back… well, you get the idea."

Tinker touched the front, and, in her normal Marine way, pressed too hard, sending the chair off like a rocket. Harlowe ran after her and shouted, "Take your hand off the arm!" She was a hundred yards down the corridor before she let up on the throttle. Harlowe finally caught up with her and chuckled, "Take it easy, Roadrunner."

"Okay, okay," she said, admiring the chair. She tried again and went slowly forward this time. "Nice. How does it do that?"

"It's a gravity thing. Mr. Prigg can explain it better."

Tinker began eyeing the arched ceiling and soft blue carpet between her toes. Nothing was familiar but everything was first cabin. "Where are we, Hon?" she asked.

He laid his hand over her shoulder as they approached a golden disk on the floor. Jewels handed Harlowe a pair of sunglasses. "You might need these," Harlowe said, placing the shades over her eyes.

"Are we going somewhere sunny?"

Harlowe led her forward onto the blinker. "Let me show you."

A wink later, and they were on top of *Millawanda*'s hull, overlooking a beautiful desert valley, bordered by a long line of jagged mountains. Far below, a herd of elk had gathered around the oasis, rubbing noses with Pigpo. The sky was blue and cloudless, and the white-yellow sun overhead felt warm and radiant on their shoulders.

"Wow…" Tinker gulped, bringing her arms to her chest in awe. Her posture changed, and she was more alert. She leaned forward, as if wondering if this was all a dream. She wanted to see it all.

Harlowe stopped her from going too far. "Allow me." He touched the arm of her chair and they rose together, floating, turning round and round ever so slowly, taking in a drone's-eye view of *Millawanda* from a thousand feet above her dome.

Tinker's eyes grew big and round. "So this is Millie?"

"Yeah, isn't she the coolest thing you've ever seen?" Harlowe bragged, and pointed at the dome. "Those three big windows are the bridge. The smaller windows along the right side are my cabin. When you're ready,

I'll give you a five-star tour."

"That would take a lifetime on a ship this huge."

He hugged her. "The nickel tour then."

Tinker continued to stare, awestruck. "She is so much more than I ever imagined." As they drifted down to the upper hull, she began to see her son in a totally different perspective. Even when he visited her at the White House, he was still her son, who never graduated from high school, who wore flip-flops, old No Fear swim trunks, and could be found on any good surf day at 42nd Street. Commanding an alien starship was cool, saving the Earth from the Daks was heroic, and so was hyper-lighting around the galaxy putting out fires, but he still didn't have a high school diploma. A decade ago she would have grounded him until he did.

Until now…

Now, as her feet touched down on the warm, golden surface of the ship again, she finally understood what she was asking made no sense at all. *Millawanda* had transformed her son into something greater than any diploma could ever make him: a force for the good for all life in the galaxy. "Thank you, Millie," she said to Her.

* * *

They sat for another hour in the sun, sipping Blue Stuff, holding hands, laughing a little, and reminiscing over lost time. Jewels delivered a floating table of small sandwiches, drinks, chips, and guac. Tinker especially like the Blue Stuff. The herd of elk had moved on and a small group of prairie antelope had come in for their turn at the watering hole. It all looked so peaceful. No one fought over a place at the trough. There was enough for everyone. It was then that Harlowe explained how the time difference had affected them and why he had not aged or shaved yet in eleven years. He spoke of their journey to the galactic core to fix Millie and returning to discover that Saturn had moved. Of course, he wouldn't tell her everything. Sometimes parents are better off not knowing "everything" in their children's lives. A son's or daughter's near death experiences can cause undue heartache and are best left for discussion many years afterward. She said to him, "You're planning something, aren't you? I see it in your eyes, even if you don't say it. It's there in the way you talk to me. Your dad was the same way. He didn't want me to worry."

There was no reason to involve her. Her well-being and the care and recovery of her husband were enough for her than any scheme of his. "It's more like a dream than a plan, Mom," he said.

"You're going after Shame, aren't you?"

"She's on my list," Harlowe admitted.

"The corruption runs deep, Hon. It's so vast, not even God knows all the players. Shame is a puppet. All presidents are puppets to the real masters of power. Peter slew many dragons, but he could not slay them all, and he still lost. Their evil is deep and hidden in the dark. They don't play by nature's laws. Their rules are not from heaven but from the darkness below. They have ways to stop you, that can't even be imagined. I saw it firsthand. The families that rule our planet have been entrenched for centuries. They are unstoppable. I'm afraid your ship, as powerful as She is, cannot stop them. Your father tried, Harlowe, and he died for it. I don't want to lose you, too."

Tinker saw that her words seemed to go unheard. "Did you hear anything I said, son?"

Harlowe took her hand and squeezed it confidently. "I heard." He stood. It was time to go. He had things that needed his attention, and Tinker needed to return to the med room for Peter. "One of Dad's favorite movies was an old black and white film about a hard-ass restaurant owner named Rick."

Tinker smiled. She knew the movie well. *Casablanca* was Buster's favorite. If she saw it once, she saw it a thousand times and could recite every line of dialogue Rick preached.

"Well, the odds were always against him. The German might was overwhelming. They, too, were unstoppable. But that didn't stop Rick. When he was asked why he fought against such odds, he said, "…*If we stop breathing, we'll die. If we stop fighting our enemies, the world will die.*" He put his arms around her. "Mom, I wasn't raised by one Marine, I was raised by two Marines. Our world will not die." They touched knuckles together. "Ooorah!"

At that same moment, Monday appeared and saluted Tinker. "Ma'am."

Tinker knew the two had important matter to discuss and didn't want to be a bother. "Good to see you, Mr. Platter. This isn't a social call, is it?"

"No Ma'am." Monday turned to Harlowe. "We have incoming spacecraft entering the neighborhood, Captain."

Jewels appeared at Harlowe's side as he asked, "What's their position?"

"Two A.U's out. Shall I recall Riverstone and Mr. Bolt, Captain?" Monday asked.

"No. Let them go. We'll have to make do with the crew we have. Where is Dodger? I mean Dodge?"

Monday pointed across the valley at the two white tigers and two long horned ceffyls with riders. They were racing across the desert in fifty-foot strides, leaping and pounding back and forth, jumping over each other, having a blast, and enjoying a morning ride.

Tinker couldn't believe her eyes. "That's my Dodger? Holy crap!"

"Call them in, Mr. Platter, we'll need their help on this," Harlowe ordered.

"Aye, Captain."

Monday winked away as Harlowe came back to Tinker. "Gotta go, Mom. Jewels, here, will take you back to Peter."

"How serious is it?" Tinker asked.

"Uninvited guests are always serious."

He gave her a hug and kiss before he stepped on the nearest blinker and was gone.

38

When Pigs Fly

LeBeau Park, NV

DODGE LAY PRONE along Molly's back, holding onto a special harness he and Prigg had fashioned from strips of dura-cloth fabric. Timmer had the same rig for Rhud. The only addition was the belly cushion Timmer designed so they could absorb the bounce during the cat's great leaps over the narrow gorges, boulders, and dry riverbeds. But on the open stretches of terrain, riding the cats was like riding the ceffyls, smooth as glass.

The morning had started out slow, until Leucadia introduced them to Dodger's Place. Timmer had asked her if there was a place they could work out to pass the time while they waited for the Swiss soldiers to clear out. Leucadia apologized for being a neglectful hostess, and showed them the swimming pool. Timmer's eyes lit up. "Wow, you have a pool here?"

"We do. I'm sure you'll find it to your liking. If you would follow me," Leucadia replied.

All Timmer could focus on as they walked with her and smelled her flowery scent, was seeing her in a bathing suit that fit in a Band Aid box. It was the same neverending dream he had since the moment he saw her;

198

just the two of them on some sunny desserted island, eating coconuts and grilled fish, and never returning to civilization ever again. He kinda wished they could have gone to the pool alone. Leucadia thought he was adorable for suggesting some time alone together. "Your boyfriend wouldn't mind, would he?"

She laughed. "Oh, my God no, he never gets jealous."

Timmer found that incredible. "Never? Doesn't he care about you?"

"He cares. It's just that he's so busy, he has little time to think about being possessive."

"I would always have the time for you, Lu."

"You're so sweet. I bet you have several lady friends back home, Mr. Lane."

"Come on, Lu, call me Timmer."

"Okay, Timmer."

"When do we get to meet your dude?" he asked, strutting tall and cocky as they walked. "Is he hot like me?"

She smiled graciously, "He'll do."

"Big and tall?"

"Six-foot-nine, I think, and around two-hundred and ninety pounds."

Timmer's heart skipped a beat. "Holy-cow, girl, he's Tarzan on steroids."

Her eyes went somewhere distant for a dream-like moment. "He is amazing." They stopped beside a door. "Here we are. I believe this is Mr. Searle's room."

Searle and Enihoo exploded out of their rooms in five seconds flat when they heard the ship had a pool. They were thinking lap pool, or something one might find in a 24 Hour Fitness gym. But when they walked through the large doors, it was like no lap pool they had ever seen before. It was an enormous natatorium, surrounded by lush plant life of unknown species, colorful flowers, and bright flying things that chirped and sang as melodically as any Earthly fowl.

Suddenly, someone shouted out "Do it, Betty!" and a wave rose up carrying a tall man on a surfboard. The surfer gracefully cut back and forth until the wave played out and he floated ashore. That's when they first met Dodge.

"Is that your boyfriend?" Timmer asked, figuring the hunk paddling fit her description perfectly.

"No, that's his little brother," Leucadia replied with a giggle.

Timmer stood frozen in shock. *Little?*

She greeted Dodge on the beach with a warm hug and introduced him to her guests.

The four became instant friends, explaining how they came to be on the ship, and how they almost died in the sudden storm. Timmer, who was nearly the same age as Dodge, even spoke the same hip language. "Hey, brah," they said, touching fists. Although Timmer had never surfed, he always wanted to learn, and when he mentioned he rode horses on his uncle's ranch, the two struck a bargain; Timmer would teach Dodge how to ride, and Dodge would teach Timmer how to surf.

"You'll love riding my brother's ceffyls, Timmer," Dodge said proudly.

"Ceffyls? What are ceffyls?" Timmer asked.

"Probably the most magnificent mounts you'll ever see," Dodge replied.

"Here? You have horses here on this ship?"

"Well, they're sort of like horses but different."

Timmer was intrigued. "Alien, huh?"

"Very." Timmer started to get up. "No, stay right there. I'll call them." Dodge blew a loud whistle that caused a few creatures to take flight. "Delamo! Josie! Come here!" he called to them. Hardly any time went by when the tree branches parted and two magnificent horned beasts came bounding toward them, leaping high over the tallest ferns. Enihoo and Searle bolted for the water. They hadn't shared the conversation about riding horses and were a little freaked out by the ceffyls sudden appearance.

Timmer was instantly awestruck. "They are amazing." He noticed their feet right away. "They have claws."

"They came from a planet with a lot of rocky terrain," Dodge explained, and then he asked everyone if they would like to go riding.

Timmer was the only one to raise his hand. "I'm in!"

When it was obvious they wouldn't be skewered by the massive horns, Searle and Enihoo slowly came out of the water. The two were in ankle-deep water when two, car-sized white tigers sauntered out of the bushes to join the party. This time Timmer joined Searle and Enihoo bolting for the water.

It took some sweet-talking and a trip to the restroom, but gradually the three gathered enough courage with the animals, including a big-eared creature that jumped into Enihoo's arms like a little lap dog. Enihoo petted his newfound friend. "For a strange looking critter, it sure is friendly. What's its name?"

"Mowgi," Dodge replied.

Enihoo pointed at Mowgi. "Now if they were all this size, I wouldn't have a problem."

Dodge laughed. "Just keep him on your good side."

"No worries. We're buds, right, Mowgi?" Enihoo stated.

The undog yipped twice.

So this is when the conversation began to go south. There were only two ceffyls to ride, and four of them.

Searle pointed at Timmer and Enihoo. "You two will have to stay here while Dodge and I take the first ride."

Timmer wasn't going for it. "It was my idea, Butthead, I get to go first. Besides, what do you know about riding anything but a Walmart rocking pony?"

"I've ridden plenty, Lane," Searle countered. "In high school, I worked in Colorado for Granite Mountain Outfitters in the summer."

"You rode horses for Sue Applegate?" Timmer asked.

"Yeah. You know her?"

Timmer thought that was cool. "Yeah, I know her. Okay, you can ride. If you didn't know how to ride before you rode with Sue, you did afterwards. No question."

Enihoo didn't have a problem with letting everyone else go first until Dodge posed the question, "Can you ride, Sergeant?"

Timmer reached up and laid an arm over Enihoo's thick shoulder. "Don't tell me you rode for Granite Mountain, too?"

"No, but I've ridden a horse, Lane," Enihoo defended. No respectable Marine wants to feel like he's a rookie at anything.

Timmer was shocked. "You have? Where?" Enihoo refused to

answer. "Come on, Maxi, where have you ridden a horse?"

Dodge began to laugh.

Enihoo didn't see the humor at all. "What are you laughing at, civilian?"

"It was Disneyland, wasn't it?" Dodge asked.

Timmer laughed out loud. "You talking about those nags at Frontierland?"

Enihoo glared harshly at them all. "So?"

That was when Enihoo tried to show how tough he really was by walking up to Dodge and giving him a chest butt. Dodge, standing bare chested, stood his ground as Enihoo slammed into the young man like a steam pile driver. But what happened next was difficult to explain. Enihoo bounced off Dodge and fell down on the sand, grabbing his chest in pain. The last thing Dodge wanted to do was hurt his new friend. He knelt beside him and asked Enihoo if he was all right.

Enihoo tried to hide his embarrassment as he kept rubbing his chest. "Yeah, I'm okay," he coughed.

Dodge gave Enihoo an alibi while helping him to his feet. "I think you slipped on the wet sand, Sergeant."

"I think it was more like a brick wall there, dude," Timmer uttered more credibly.

Searle checked the dazed Marine's eyes. "I think you should stay here, Maxi," Searle suggested.

A tubular android appeared out of nowhere holding a glowing blue sphere in its metal hand. "Let Clicker touch your chest, Sergeant," Dodge suggested.

Enihoo backed away. "No way. I'll be okay. Just give me a moment," he said, bent over and wincing.

Dodge nodded at Clicker, and before Enihoo could stop the robob from touching him, the droid put the blue ball to the Sergeant's chest. It was like draining a balloon full of air. Instantly, the pain magically subsided. Enihoo looked at Clicker, stunned. "How did it do that?"

Timmer touched the ball. He didn't feel anything, not even a little tingle. "The pain's gone?" he asked Enihoo.

"Like it never happened."

"It's a med ball," Dodge explained. "I'm not sure how it works, either.

It just does. The blue light has something to do with it. It just works."

Enihoo stood up, ready to take on the world. "Gentlemen, lets ride!"

* * *

After the first mile, no one cared whether they were on a tiger or a ceffyl. The speed, agility, and grace of all four alien beasts went far beyond fun. They were an experience of a lifetime. To feel something that powerful beneath them, capable of running all day, as fast as a car, was exhilarating beyond belief. The four rode to the top of South Shoshone Peak, a twenty-mile ride one way, before turning back for home. They were halfway across the valley when Monday called out "CYBOF!" over Dodge's ear-com. It was a made up Gamadin word that meant "Cover Your Butt Or You're Fried." In other words, immediately drop what you were doing and return to the cover of *Millawanda*'s force field, or you'll be dead by an enemy attack. But as time went by, on several occasions a threat of a different nature arose that forced the CYBOF alert to evolve into a general emergency signal. That incident occurred when a meteor shower struck one of Jupiter's moons the Gamadin crew was exploring. If Ian hadn't called out the CYBOF alert when he did, *Millawanda* would have lost a captain, and Julian Starr, actor of *Distant Galaxy,* would never have received his Oscar. So today, regardless of the reason, when a Gamadin hears the warning, it means gather all forces and return to the ship…NOW! No questions asked.

Dodge pointed back to the ship. "RETURN NOW!" he cried out several times to make sure everyone understood.

Timmer saw where they were headed and shouted, "AMBUSH!" They were about to run straight through the oasis where they knew the Swiss soldiers had staked out the pool after finding their belongings.

Dodge pointed at himself first and then at the ship, so that everyone knew to follow him. The tigers and ceffyls were so fast and quiet, their feet hardly made a sound when they broke through the cottonwood grove and leaped across the fifty foot pond like it was a wading pool. The Swiss forces were caught completely by surprise as the four flew past their stakeouts, and disappeared behind the force field like flashing ghosts.

* * *

A soldier, covering the oasis pool from his bivouac, ran out into the open with his AK-47, trying to get a bead on the creatures that blew past him like the wind.

The squad leader cried out, "What are you doing, Warfel?" He was angry that the soldier had blown their cover.

Warfel kept his cheek to the stock of his rifle, searching for his target. "Did you see them, Sir? They went right over us!"

Several others came out of their hidden blinds. "See what?" they asked.

"I saw them leap across the water, Sir," another said, backing up Warfel.

"I heard something, too," still another said.

"Describe what you saw," the squad leader ordered Warfel.

After it was obvious the targets were gone, Warfel lowered his rifle and said in all seriousness that he saw, "Two white tigers and two horses with big horns. They all had riders, Sir."

A few soldiers, ones who never caught a glimpse, began to laugh. The squad leader wanted to laugh, too, but the mission was too critical for banter. Three American soldiers were still out here, and if they somehow got away, the Church would condemn them. "Get back to your places," he ordered.

"I saw what I saw, Sir," Warfel insisted.

"When pigs fly, Warfel," the squad leader snapped.

Suddenly, a giant creature resembling a pig rose out of the pool like a breaching whale and took flight above the trees. At that same moment, a stiff gust blew two soldiers into the water. Warfel pulled the squad leader out of the pool and asked him to explain what he saw. No one laughed.

39

No Show

Blue Bayou Restaurant
Disneyland, California

THE BLUE BAYOU Restaurant was the perfect setting. Riverstone had two fabulous dates with the girl of his dreams so far, but both times they were never alone. Simon and his agent, Saul, had tagged along both times. That got old fast. This time, however, Simon was in meetings all day with producers, so he and Phoebe had the table all to themselves, that is, when she showed up. He and Harlowe had floated by the Blue Bayou many times with their dates. It was their favorite ride to snuggle up and play kissy-face, as they drifted in the frolicking darkness of barmaids, singing pirates, and treasure chests filled with gold doubloons and silver pieces of eight, along the watery canals of old Montego Bay. To this day, they had never once eaten at the restaurant because they could never afford it, and had envied the love-struck couples that could. Dining in the perpetual twilight under strings of magical lanterns, while crickets chirped, frogs croaked, and fireflies winked overhead was, for Riverstone, a romantic setting he never thought would ever come true. Yet, here he was, his perfect place for his dream date with Phoebe Marleigh.

Riverstone glanced at his watch for the umpteenth time. She was late…by more than an hour. He had offered to pick her up in the limo, but she insisted on meeting him here after her appointment…whatever that was.

"Would you like another Phoebe Marleigh?" the waitress asked, taking his empty glass. In his parent's day, a 7-Up with a splash of cherry juice was called an Angelina Jolie. In his grandfather's day, they called the same non-alcoholic drink for the underaged a Shirley Temple.

After three generations of tall ones, Riverstone waved his hand. "No thanks, I think I'll—"

"Is that a Phoebe Marleigh?" Simon asked, pointing at his empty glass.

"Yeah, it was," Riverstone grunted. "What pirates' chest did you crawl out of?"

Simon ordered two more Phoebes and took a chair. "It's not healthy to dine alone, you know."

Riverstone didn't have to ask how Simon found him. Alice would have driven him here, and the rest was a slam-dunk. "So far Phoebe's a no-show."

"Bummer. Did she call?"

"No, but then how would she call me? We don't have phones with numbers, remember."

Simon pulled out his com. "But we can call her."

"I know, but I didn't want to…"

"Disturb her?"

"Yeah, something like that."

Simon spoke to his com. "Call Phoebs."

Riverstone half-heartedly tried to grab the com from Simon's hand, but missed. He felt embarrassed calling her if she wasn't coming.

Simon slapped his hand away. "I'll take care of it, Jester. No worries." He listened and waited for Phoebe's cell to ring seven times before he said, "She's not picking up. That's not like her. She always answers my calls."

"She's an important lady. Maybe something came up. Dark matter happens, right?" Riverstone said, defending her.

Simon reached for a menu lying on the white tablecloth. "I'm starving. Let's not spoil the moment, honey."

When the waitress delivered their drinks, Riverstone grumbled, "I'm not hungry."

Simon took his eyes from the menu and looked at the waitress befuddled. "What happened to the fillet mignon?"

"We don't serve meat anymore," she replied.

"WTF? No meat? What are you talking about? That was my favorite entrée," Simon protested. "What's up with that?"

"I'm sorry, Sir, I was told government regulations caused the price of meat to skyrocket. No one can afford it so they removed it from the menu. People don't want to pay two hundred dollars a plate for three ounces of steak," she explained.

Simon had never heard of such a thing. "That's outrageous. I don't blame them."

"I know, Sir. Sorry."

Simon glared at Riverstone. "Can you believe that?"

Riverstone patted Simon's hand. "Now, now, Mr. Bolt. It is what it is."

The waitress bent down and looked at Simon close up. "That is you. You're that old-time movie actor. I loved your films," she swooned.

"That still won't get me a fillet, will it?" Simon asked.

"I'm afraid not, Mr. Bolt. It would take a whole day of filling out papers to get your order. I could ask the manager, though."

"No," he said, glancing at the menu again, "that won't be necessary. Give us two Royal Street jambalayas…to go, please."

"Yes, Sir, Mr. Bolt."

After the waitress left, Riverstone leaned over the table, "I told you, I'm not hungry."

A boatload of rowdy teenagers, drifting by the Blue Bayou, began whooping and hollering obscenities and causing a general disruption for the entire restaurant. Flying across the lagoon two small butter plates careened off the foreheads of the two most disruptive teenagers, causing them to slump down inside their boat.

Simon and Riverstone clinked their Phoebe Marleighs as Simon whipped out his blue Gamacoin card. "Relax, Jester, we're paying with this. Remember what Wiz said, spend, spend, spend."

40

Welcome Aboard

Millawanda

WHEN HARLOWE STEPPED from his cabin onto the bridge, Monday began with his usual announcement, "Captain on the... bridge...," but trailed off when he realized he was the only one on the bridge who heard it.

"Where is everyone?" Harlowe asked, going to his center command chair.

"Present, Captain," Leucadia replied, stepping off the blinker. "I was checking on the President."

"How is he?" Harlowe asked.

She continued to her seat to Harlowe's left. "Better. I think he'll make it."

"And General Branch?"

"Ready for action, Captain," Branch announced, following Leucadia off the blinker.

"You're looking fit, General," Harlowe said approvingly.

"Where would you like me, Captain?" Branch asked. "I hear you're a little short-handed."

"Mr. Platter. Would you show the General the weapons station, if you please?"

Monday smiled. "Gladly, Captain. Right this way, General."

As Monday was cluing the General in on the finer points of the ship's weapons array, Harlowe turned back to Leucadia. "Are Dodge and our guests back yet?"

She touched his arm. "They're changing now. I invited them to the bridge. I hope that's okay?"

Harlowe accepted her forethought. "Can't hurt. Think they can handle it?"

"They seem capable enough," she added, just as Dodge and the three guests materialized onto the bridge.

Harlowe rose from his command chair to greet them. "Welcome to the bridge, gentlemen."

"This is Captain Harlowe Pylott, commander of the Gamadin starship, *Millawanda*," Dodge said proudly, as he introduced his brother. The two airmen were dressed in Gamadin regular blue uniforms with no signatures of rank on their collars or sleeves. Enihoo, on the other hand, wore dress Marine Corps blues, complete with sergeant stripes, three hash marks, mirror polished shoes, white gloves, and a gleaming, brass-handled parade sword at his side.

Harlowe addressed the Sergeant first. "Sergeant Max Enihoo, is it?"

"Yes, Sir. Dodge said I should dress formally for my first bridge appearance, Captain. I hope this is appropriate attire."

Dodge chuckled. "I said normal, not formal, Maxi."

"Miscommunication, Sir, it's the only formal attire I know," Enihoo said.

Harlowe pinched a tiny piece of lint off the Sergeant's sleeve. "Perfect Sergeant. True Marine Corps spirit. If my mother sees you dressed like this, be prepared for a marriage proposal."

"Yes, Sir."

"But please decline her graciously. She's already married to the President of the United States," Harlowe pointed out.

The group laughed.

"Thank you, Sir, I'll keep that in mind."

"She is a former Marine D.I. Need I say more?"

"No, Sir," Enihoo glanced at Timmer and Searle, "she eats airmen for breakfast, Sir."

Harlowe laughed uproariously and shook the Sergeant's hand. "Good answer, Marine. Welcome aboard."

Harlowe stepped in front of Timmer next, looking down at him. Timmer wasn't often intimidated by anyone. Even four-star generals caused him little concern. Harlowe may have looked too young for his position as an alien ship's captain, but his physical presence and cock-sure demeanor more than made up for his youth. His steel blue eyes and undeniable knightly good looks, humbled Timmer. The boy-captain was not at all what he had envisioned.

"Airman Lane?" Harlowe inquired.

Timmer offered a slight correction. "Yes, Sir. I go by Timmer mostly, Sir."

"You do?"

"Yes, Sir."

Harlowe's eyes appeared to look straight into his soul. "This is the bridge, Mr. Lane. It is a sacred place of duty for my crew and me. So anyone who graces this hallowed ground will be respectful at all times while they are here."

"Aye, Sir. Understood, Sir."

"I understand you have eyes for one of my crew?"

The question caught Timmer off guard. "Well, ah, ah... I didn't know..."

Harlowe smiled, eyeing Leucadia with a tender wink. "Relax, Mr. Lane. Half the world and two of my own crew have those same dreams. Good luck."

"Ah, aye, aye, Sir."

"I also hear you are a man of science, and that your device found our ship, even when she was cloaked."

"Yes, Sir. It detected your gravity wave distortions."

"You detected Her gravity distortions," Harlowe corrected, emphasizing the proper pronoun "Her." "Our ship is the hottest, most powerful, gorgeous, magnificent woman in the galaxy. Always remember that, Airman."

"I will, Sir."

It was then that Prigg stepped onto the bridge, spooking the three soldiers with his three wayward eyes. They had never seen a Naruckian being before. Harlowe put his hand on Prigg's shoulder. "Mr. Prigg is one of the finest minds anywhere in the Galaxy. Respect him as you would me."

"Yes, Sir," the three said in unison.

Harlowe asked Leucadia. "Do they have their language implants, Ms. Mars?"

"They do, Captain," Leucadia replied.

"Cool." Harlowe returned to Timmer. "Mr. Lane, when time permits, please explain your gravity device to Mr. Prigg. I'm sure you'll both learn a few things together, and he will make several improvements."

"Thank you, Captain," Timmer said.

Searle was beside himself. He had never seen or heard Airman Lane act so intimidated by anyone since he had known him.

Prigg tugged on Harlowe's pant leg. "Your Majesty, Pigpo is still outside."

"In the oasis pool?" Harlowe asked.

"Yes, Your Majesty, I believe so."

Harlowe's lips pursed. "Where else would he be?"

"Only there, Your Majesty"

"Don't worry, Mr. Prigg, we'll lift him out before we leave."

Prigg went on to his navigation post. "Yes, Your Majesty."

Harlowe stepped left and faced Searle. "Captain Searle."

"Yes, Sir."

"No disrespect intended, Sir, but why are you here? You don't seem to be a specialist. What is your claim to fame?"

Searle gestured at Timmer. "I'm his babysitter, Captain."

Harlowe glanced at Timmer. "I see. A worthy cause, I'm sure."

"Not really, Sir, but he's the monkey on my back."

"The General over there would say the military can never have enough good men like you, Captain." Harlowe glanced Branch's way, and received a right-you-are salute back. Harlowe shook Searle's hand and said, "Welcome aboard, Captain," then stepped back and added, "Mr. Platter and Dodge will show you gentlemen to your stations. I'm afraid we don't have a lot of time for a systems education, so what you learn will have to be on the fly, literally. Regardless, I want to thank you all for being here on such short notice."

"Yes, Sir," was the collective reply.

Harlowe returned to his command chair and ordered, "Mr. Platter, is our warbird ready for flight?"

Monday accepted the command. "Aye, Captain, all systems positive. Warbird ready for flight."

As the others dispersed, a second woman's voice announced, "I heard we were short-handed."

"Tinker?" Leucadia gasped, surprised by her appearance. She came dressed in her Marine Corps camos.

Leucadia turned to Harlowe for help on what to do. For what seemed like an eternity, he was silent, like he was trying to figure it out himself. Tinker shrugged with disappointment when no one seemed to acknowledge her. "All right, I can see I'm a little late to the party," and started to leave.

"Stay right were you are, Ma'am," Harlowe commanded. "Sgt. Enihoo."

"Yes, Sir."

"Please escort, Mrs. Delmonte, to her chair next to me," Harlowe said, pointing to the right side command chair.

"Yes, Sir, I would be honored." Enihoo placed his white hat under his left arm and stepped smartly to Tinker's side, extending his right elbow for her to take. "If you would allow me, Ma'am."

Tinker's eyes widened with admiration, as she gladly took his arm. "My, my, you're a handsome Marine. Are you married, soldier?" she asked.

"Not yet—" A hard eye from Harlowe cut him off quick. "I mean, yes Ma'am, I'm happily married."

"A very fortunate girl, I'm sure."

"Yes, Ma'am."

Tinker nodded to the crew as she went to her chair and took her place on Harlowe's right. "My, this is comfortable. Thank you, Sergeant."

Harlowe sat down and patted his mother's hand. "Thanks for being here, Mrs. Delmonte."

"Thank you, Captain."

"Mr. Pylott," Harlowe said in addressing Dodge, "are you squared away with departure procedures?"

"I am, Captain," Dodge replied.

"Sensors ready, Mr. Prigg?"

"Sensors ready, Your Majesty."

"Take her up then, Mr. Pylott."

"Aye, Captain, taking her up."

Leucadia slipped out of her command chair and sat in Wiz's seat next to Timmer. Timmer leaned over and said to her quietly, "He's nails," he said of Harlowe.

As her fingers swiftly went over the console in front her, her eyes alone displayed her feelings. "Yes, he is."

"Do we have our wayward pet located, Ms. Mars?" Harlowe asked.

"Yes we do, Captain. Pigpo is back home and in the pool," Leucadia replied.

"Follow the course on the overhead, Mr. Pylott. Quarter light until we pass the moon, please."

"Aye, Captain, course engaged. Quarter light until we pass the moon," Dodge acknowledged.

Through the massive front windows, *Millawanda* silently slid over the valley floor for only a second before She tilted upward, passing 10,000 feet over the North Shoshone Peak, headed for deep space. Timmer felt no perceptible sensation of movement as the sky turned dark, going from deep blue to night before the second hand of his watch ticked once. As they passed through the upper ionosphere into space, the stars lost their glitter, turning to tiny pinpoints of scattered dots across the galaxy. The moon now grew exponentially, until it winked past them off the starboard observation window. It then grew tiny again on the rear view holo screen above. Timmer made the calculation in his head; a million miles in two seconds and they had just left the starting gate, he marveled. He had seen it all with his own eyes, and still he couldn't believe what he had just witnessed. The speed of their climb was off-the-charts cool. He didn't feel a thing, not one perceptible sensation of motion at all. They might as well have been watching an Imax movie. He looked over at Searle for his reaction. His mouth was still wide open in awe from the second they left the desert floor.

"Proceed to five light, Mr. Pylott," Harlowe ordered.

"Aye, five light, Captain," Dodge answered.

As *Millawanda* scooted to light-speed and beyond, suddenly the little star dots glowed bright white like someone slid the dimmer switch to full intensity. The holographic screen changed to a graphic of the solar system that displayed a small blue dot moving fast past Mars' orbit in less than a minute. A little longer, and a giant striped beach ball blew by, followed by Saturn, and the orbits of Uranus, Neptune, and Pluto until they were well inside the Oort cloud.

"How are you holding up, Mr. Lane?" Harlowe asked, noting the far off stare of the airman.

After a blink to collect his thoughts, Timmer twisted around in his chair. "Well, Sir, I was just thinking from a military standpoint, any force on Earth that tried to stop you would be like a B-2 Stealth Bomber against a paper glider. What they believe they can do to this ship is laughable."

"All stop, Mr. Pylott," Harlowe ordered.

"Aye, Sir."

Harlowe pointed out the forward window. "Compared to that ship out there, Mr. Lane, are we the paper glider or the Stealth Bomber?"

Timmer about leaped out of his chair. "Holy bejezus, Captain!"

The size of the alien ship far surpassed *Millawanda*, who appeared tiny as an ant standing next to an elephant.

41

The Trespassers

The Oort Cloud

FROM BOW TO stern the alien ship measured 9.32 miles long by .5 miles wide, not including its extended star-drive pods. It was one of the largest ships they had faced. Heavily armed batteries of plas-cannons were spread strategically across the entire superstructure.

"Are they parked, Mr. Platter?" Harlowe asked.

Enihoo stood next to Monday as he read his displays. "She's all stop, Captain. It appears they've been sitting there for some time."

"Waiting for an engraved invitation, I presume," Harlowe speculated. He then inquired, "Power surges, Mr. Lane?"

Timmer looked over his console for the readout he needed for his reply. Seeing his confusion, Leucadia pointed at the appropriate screen. "Power is constant, Captain," he replied, glancing at Leucadia for her approval.

"She looks bigger than a Mysterian ship, Mr. Platter," Harlowe noted.

"She is. Three times bigger, Captain, with ten times the mass."

Harlowe whistled low. "She's a big one, all right."

Tinker leaned over and spoke softly in Harlowe's ear. "You've seen ships this big before?"

"Somewhat. This is the biggest one so far."

Tinker's mouth dropped open. "My God, son."

Harlowe gave her a gentle, steady-mom, pat on the arm and looked at her straight in the eye. "Captain, not son, Mrs. Delmonte," he corrected her.

His sternness took a second to sink in. She leaned back and took a timeout at having been disciplined by her own son. After a calming breath, she gave him the go-head to continue. "Yes, Captain." It was a minor slip and one she would try her best not to repeat, that is, if she could help it. But man, the alien ship scared her plenty, as it did everyone else, except the Gamadin crew. To see them cool as ice, facing the gargantuan ship like it was an everyday problem, made her wonder what other threats they had faced during their voyages. Even General Branch, for whom she had great respect, was taken aback by the overwhelming size of the alien ship. Tinker had faced death before, suffered through Buster's murder, but this? What chance did they have against something this powerful?

"He's waiting for us to make the first move," he said softly to Tinker. Back to the bridge he said louder, "Open a line if you please, Mr. Searle."

Leucadia watched the airman follow his lessons to a tee.

"Aye, line open, Captain," Searle replied confidently, but one eye was never removed from the alien ship.

A short crackling, and the screen went haywire. Harlowe patted Tinkers hand again.

"They're charging their forward weapons, Captain," Monday announced.

"Anything we need to worry about, Mr. Platter?" Harlowe asked.

"If that's all they have, no worries, Captain."

"General, give them a short burst at three percent, between their third and fourth drive pods, as a thump on the noggin."

"Aye, Captain, three percent between the third and fourth uprights," Branch replied.

A brilliant bolt of blue light shot from the saucer rim and crossed the hundred thousand miles of open space in a blink, passing between the two drive pods, exactly where Harlowe had instructed.

Timmer came around to Harlowe in disbelief. Searle had the same look, but Timmer was first to express himself. "That was three percent, Captain?"

Harlowe winked. "We don't want to show them our best hand yet, Mr. Lane." To Branch he praised, "Nice shooting, General."

Branch acknowledged with a two-finger wave of appreciation.

"They're powering down, Captain," Leucadia announced.

"And we have contact, too, Captain," Monday added.

"Put 'em on, Mr. Platter," Harlowe directed.

Another crackling hum preceded a fuzzy shape that cleared to reveal a strikingly handsome human-like being with light brown hair, bright yellow eyes, and cream-colored complexion. Tinker sat up. "Well now, a hot alien." Harlowe snapped a sharp scowl her way. "Sorry," she said, and slipped back in her seat.

"*Greetings. I am Commander Sextonis from the Crodo Quadrant by authority of the Dawash group of planets. And you are?*"

"He speaks perfect English, too," Searle blurted out.

Harlowe glared at the airman. Leucadia leaned over and whispered, pointing at the back of her left ear. "Millie translates in real time." She followed her quick clarification with a keep-quiet finger to the mouth.

"It doesn't matter who I am, Commander. What matters is you're far from home and playing in my backyard, and I want to know why," Harlowe charged. He had no intention of being sociable.

"*We were on a normal patrol route when our number five power drive began to leak fuel. We detected a category three planet where we planned to do our repairs. If you have no objections, that is,*" Commander Sextonis explained.

"Anything wrong with the Commander's number five power drive, Ms. Mars?" Harlowe asked Leucadia.

"Not a thing, Captain. All alien power drives are functioning properly."

Harlowe returned to Sextonis. "That's a no go, Commander. I ask you to leave this quadrant immediately, or you will have drive problems."

Monday had his eyes glued to the alien ship's power levels, when they suddenly spiked. *Millawanda's* shields snapped on the instant before a phalanx of photon missiles exploded from their launch bays across the entire bow the ship, nearly a hundred in all. Without a single word, a short nod from Harlowe gave Branch permission to retaliate. The General vaporized every missile before they reached the halfway point between the two ships.

Harlowe wasn't finished. There were lessons to be made. He pointed two fingers at the ship's outer drives. "Take them out, General," Harlowe ordered. The General fired two more intense bolts that ripped through the massive struts like cheap toy parts. The huge appendages broke away from the main fuselage and drifted into space. Their broken ends sparked with brilliant flashes, sending huge arcs of charged energy into space, away from the mother ship.

The screen went suddenly blank as Harlowe asked Monday, "Power levels, Mr. Platter?"

"Dropping fast, Captain. Diverting what they have left to their remaining drive pods," Monday replied.

"Very well, Mr. Platter. Remain here until they're a parsec out," Harlowe ordered.

"Aye, Captain, remaining here until alien ship is a parsec out."

"Nice work everyone. General, you da man," Harlowe added with a thumbs up.

"Thank you, Captain. It was a pleasure to be of service."

"So much for diplomacy," Tinker grumbled upon Harlowe's return to his command chair. "You didn't give them much of a chance. The Commander's drive could have been damaged. You don't know."

Harlowe noted her concern. "Walk with me, Mrs. Delmonte." He took her by the hand and led her to the blinker. They winked away, and in the next instant, they were strolling under a serene moon along a sandy shore. There were no ripples on the water. No gurgling of waves from "Do it Bettys" rolling across the lagoon. Not a single bird cawed or flew. The ceffyls grazed silently on the knoll, while Mowgi and the cats slept peacefully at the top of the cliff, overlooking the pool. Except for an occasional snort from Pigpo, and the crickets chirping in the background, all was quiet inside Dodger's Place.

"Mom..." Harlowe began. "do you trust me?"

"Of course I do. I'm so proud of you. But..."

"You cannot second-guess me . . . ever! When we're on that bridge," he said pointing up, "you don't question my decisions, not even you."

Tinker sighed. "Because you're the king."

"That's right. I rule with absolute authority here."

"With no dissent."

"When it is appropriate. You, of all people, should know that."

Tinker crossed her arms in front her, and she glared up at the heavens. "Your moons look so real. Are they taken from somewhere?" she asked.

"From a planet called Gazz. A big blue one will be up shortly. It will amaze you."

"Everything amazes me, son. You've accomplished so much." Harlowe let her talk and waited for her to face him as she humbled herself and said, "I overstepped, didn't I?"

"You were being my mom." He took her in his arms. "I'm afraid moms aren't allowed on the bridge."

Tinker thought for a moment, her gaze returning to the still waters of the pool. "You're right. I should know better. I'm a Marine. I follow orders. I'm so sorry, Hon. Your crews' lives depend on you. The survival of this ship." She wanted to cry, but she sucked it up. This was no time to be weak; humble yes, but not weak. "I'll stay away from now on. Millie is your ship. Your responsibility. Seeing you against such odds... I just... I was scared for you."

Harlowe put his hand around her shoulders. "I know. It scares me, too, but that alien ship out there was here for a reason. They were testing us. They would have killed us in a heartbeat with no remorse, no guilt, no shame, if we didn't stand up to them. We've crossed this galaxy and have seen what powerful starships can do to a planet. It's not pretty. They will inflict terrible pain for one reason...power."

It wasn't necessary for Tinker to reply. She knew Harlowe was right. Power was the only reason empires existed.

"You want to know what we discovered 35,000 light-years from here?" Tinker kept to herself, and let Harlowe continue. "An entire planet that was peaceful, prosperous, and free." Harlowe looked at her all crazy-like. "It was a place called Orixy. The entire planet had zero rulers. There was no one who controlled anyone. No one told me I couldn't surf here or there. No one told Wiz he couldn't drive his gerbid on the beach, or told Lu she couldn't ride Josie anywhere she wanted. And no one hovered over you and said 'Tinker, you can't put your feet in the pool'."

"You're joking? No government at all?"

"None. The people lived happy, productive lives because they didn't have some authority telling them how to live. It was complete freedom."

"Wow…I never thought of it like that. But it makes perfect sense. What is it that governments touch that they don't screw up?"

"N-O-T-H-I-N-G!" Harlowe stressed.

She turned to her son, with a stern motherly look, like he had forgotten to take out the trash. "Don't you ever abuse your power, son, or there will be hell to pay," she warned him.

They stepped into the pool together with their shoes on. "Everyday I'm up there on the bridge making decisions, I see you and Dad watching me, making sure I don't cross that line. So trust me when I say that if I ever abused my command once, I know you'll be there to throw me out that window like you did when I was nine."

She waved an accusing finger in his face. "You deserved it, too, you little devil!"

They laughed, and talked a little more, sloshing their feet in the water until it was time for Harlowe to return to the bridge. "Are you coming with me, Mrs. Delmonte?"

Tinker declined. "I need to check on my man, Hon."

He gave her a thumbs up. "Breakfast tomorrow with Lu and me?"

"Maybe."

He kissed on the forehead. Tinker looked up, uneasy, and said, "That ship wasn't random. It was sent."

Harlowe winked at her. "I know. Someone from Earth called them."

"How do you know that?"

"Prigg intercepted the transmission."

"Do you know who?"

"Not yet. We'll let them play the game a little while longer before we pull their chain."

"Are we going back to Earth now?" Tinker asked.

"Soon," he said, with a cheesy grin. "First we have to drop some things off at Tinkerville."

"Tinkerville?" She smiled. "I like the name. What is it? A surprise?" she asked.

"For some." He walked over to Delamo and Josie, patted them good night, and winked away.

On the bridge, Leucadia waited impatiently for Harlowe to step off the blinker. "Can we talk?" she asked him.

"My cabin?"

"Please."

As the two of them walked toward his cabin, Harlowe asked Monday for a status report on the alien ship.

"They left the Ort cloud, Captain at a very reduced speed," Monday replied.

Harlowe stopped and thanked everyone again for a job well done, before he opened his cabin door and allowed Leucadia to go in first. When the door closed behind them, she leaped into his arms, pressing him against the door. When their lips finally separated, she moaned, "What took you so long?"

Harlowe gave her another, longer kiss before replying, "We had boundaries to discuss."

"Are the Pylotts all good now?"

He grinned. "It's never all good."

"With me on your left and your mom on your right, what could go wrong, Pylott?"

Harlowe rolled his eyes. "Don't get me started." He yawned, leading her to the observation couch where they could relax and watch the vastness of space through his cabin window. It had always been a good place for him to step back and think things through, visualizing the direction he was taking his crew. It was also a time for them. Curling up together, holding on, touching and talking things through, confiding, complaining, and sharing thoughts on what was coming. They needed to think things through. There would be consequences. There always were. From here on out, things would get dicier, so any time they could steal for themselves, they took it. Jewels brought them comfort food. For her, a glass of warm chamomile tea and white chocolate cookies, and for Harlowe, a double chocolate shake, which he only looked at.

"They'll be back." Leucadia began.

"I got that impression."

"You don't seem too concerned. They know where we live, Pylott."

He yawned again, only not as long. "We'll take out four drive pods next time."

"They won't try to reconcile will they?"

"Nope."

"Maybe we should go there and pay them a visit," she suggested.

"If they have a beach with waves, I'm all in."

"What else do you know?"

"Not much."

She elbowed him in the ribs. "I'm serious. We should go to this Crodo quadrant. Maybe they will have beaches." She giggled. "You could give them a surfboard, as a token of our friendship." He didn't answer. She felt his slow rhythmic breathing next to her. "Harlowe?" Her nose wrinkled. He was out, sleeping like he hadn't slept in days, which he probably hadn't. She didn't disturb him. Jewels covered them both with a blanket. She thanked the robob, kissed Harlowe on his fluttering lips, and then laid her head down on his chest and closed her eyes.

42

The G Team

East China Sea

LEUCADIA HELD UP a photo of a dashing, middle-aged man with dark manicured hair, and intelligent eyes, posing against a wood-paneled wall with his arms folded in front of him like a GQ model. "His name is Jefferson Braxton," she said to Dodge, Timmer, Searle, and Enihoo. The four were already suited up in their SIBAs for a personal mission for her. "Years ago he was my loyal attorney and confidant. His private jet crashed somewhere over the Kerama Island Archipelago in the East China Sea, right before President Delmonte was accused of treason. There's just too much coincidence, gentlemen, for this to be an accident."

Team leader Dodge offered, "I read the story, Lu. The papers said his plane went down without a trace. No wreckage or bodies were ever found."

Leucadia had read the same reports, but there were gaps in the conclusions. "Mr. Prigg and I went over the radar logs in the area. We believe either by design, a payoff, or sheer incompetence, the Okinawan authorities searched the wrong group of islands. Our research shows Braxton's plane went down a hundred and fifty miles northeast of the search area, near the island of Zamami. That's where your search will begin. Braxton is a resourceful man and was an army Ranger in his youth. If he's still alive, you'll find him there. I'm sure of it. Regardless, find the truth for me. I have to know."

Dodge looked over the search equipment they were taking with them. Coms, Gamadin pistols, assault rifles, extra mags, full Gamabelts that included thaders explosives, communication devices for extract, and DNA samples of Braxton's hair for I.D. purposes. "We'll find him, Lu."

Enihoo checked his sidearm. Unlike the Gamadin crew, when they were 'low-life' recruits on Mars, the Marine sergeant was thorough in his gear inspection. "Dodge is right, ma'am. If your man's out there, we'll find him."

For the last three days, sixteen hours a day, the military guests had been honing their skills with the Gamadin gear. Being the trained soldiers they were, they caught on quickly. A month more preparation would have been nice, but Harlowe informed them three days was it. Riverstone and Simon had gone dark for too many days. More training would have to come on the fly like their recent bridge assignments.

"Five minutes to the drop point," Harlowe's voice said over the air.

The four slipped on their packs, secured their belts, and, together with Leucadia, they headed out the utility room door to the center foyer of the ship. Molly, Rhud, Mowgi, and Prigg were already waiting at the edge of the open hatchway. The cats had their parachutes strapped to their backs, Mowgi required no added equipment, and Prigg was there just to give Dodge a sendoff.

"Stay safe, Master Dodger," Prigg said. Leucadia had mentioned several times to the little Naruckian about Dodge's name change, but like Harlowe and "Your Majesty," it went in one ear and out the other. Tough to teach old Naruckians, as they say.

Timmer pointed at the undog. "Where's his chute?"

Dodge tapped the side of his neck deploying his SIBA headgear and the others followed his lead as he explained, "Mowgi doesn't need one."

Timmer found that kind of strange. Was Dodge going to carry the tall-eared little critter in his arms?

Below, through the open gap in the floor, it was total night. The muted reflection of a quarter moon somewhere out of view reflected little diamonds off the East China Sea. From two miles up, the islands of the Kerama Island Archipelago appeared like small, black blotches of mud splattered across a sparkling surface.

Mowgi answered Timmer's question when he dove straight off the foyer deck. He wasn't waiting for anyone. Just below the hull he mutated into his dragon alter ego, his gossamer thirty-foot wings stretching outward, gliding free as he spiraled down toward the planet. The three military guys had never seen the undog go full-on dragon before.

"Holy-moly!" Enihoo gasped. "That dog's full of surprises."

"And to think you were playing kissy face with him thirty seconds ago," Timmer joked.

Searle asked, "He's with us, right?"

"All the way, Captain," Dodge replied. He gave Leucadia and Prigg quick hugs and dove.

Leucadia gave Molly and Rhud large squeezes. "Off you go now." They leaped out like they were stepping off the side of the pool. Their chutes deployed automatically five hundred feet below the ship. Piece of cake.

Searle, Enihoo, and Timmer stood in awe watching, spellbound by the ease of Dodge and the animals flying. They made it look so easy.

"You better hurry. You'll lose them," Leucadia urged.

Timmer jolted to life. "Right, right. Gotta go." He tapped the side of his neck and tally-ho, diving headfirst like a missile with his hands at his side. Searle and Enihoo went together, as Leucadia and Prigg's waved goodbye from the ledge with worried eyes, watching their A-team of humans, tigers, and a dragon disappear into the darkness.

* * *

When the team landed in the open rice field, Timmer made contact with the ship, letting Leucadia know everyone was down, safe and sound. The only problem they had was minor. The tropical trades blew Molly and Rhud off course. Dodge and Timmer were able to guide Molly back to the island while she was still in the air. But Mowgi had to grab Rhud's chute and carry him over to the rice field. Enihoo marveled over the undog's size and strength, as he put the big cat down with seemly little effort. "Love that dog. Any more like him?" he asked Dodge.

"No, he's one of kind," Dodge replied as they watched Mowgi shrink to a less frightening size.

Searle kept looking at him in disbelief. "Where did he come from?"

Dodge shrugged. He and the undog had been playing together since he was nine. Mowgi was Mowgi. He had never thought about his origin. "Some unknown planet is all I know. He was Lu's mother's pet, and from what she says, her mom didn't know either. She was some kind of elite soldier, and during one of her missions, she found him lying near death in a gully surrounded by a bunch of dead creatures. She wouldn't let him die and brought him back through a swamp to safety, and he never left her side after that."

"Crazy," Searle said.

Timmer agreed. "Yeah, crazy by ten."

"Ready?" Dodge asked the team. Everyone signaled go. "Com check."

Searle held up his device. "How secure are they?"

"Nothing on this planet can tap them," Dodge assured them.

"Range?" Timmer asked.

"Inside our solar system, we're cool," Dodge replied.

"You're kidding?" Enihoo questioned. "Out to Pluto?"

"So I'm told. We'll be connected to Millie the whole time we're down here," Dodge explained.

Harlowe's voice broke in. "Yeah, so stop talking. Lu has new intel on Braxton. I'll let her explain."

"*After further study,*" Leucadia began, "*Mr. Prigg discovered the earlier radar reports were several years old. We now have him on a small island south of you. If that's the case, he's still alive, Team.*"

"Are you picking us up?" Dodge asked.

"*No, we have deliveries to make. We'll be out of com range soon. So, you're on your own.*"

Harlowe broke with a quick order. "*Find a boat—*" and then there was dead air.

"I guess the local cell tower dropped the call," Timmer quipped.

Dodge stared across the rice paddies, wondering where they would find a boat. "No, it means *Millawanda's* gone to hyper-light."

"And we're stuck here until they get back?" Searle considered.

Dodge checked his bugeye nav screens to get their bearings. "We don't need a boat. There's a jungle road over that hill leading south. We'll take that to the other side of the island."

"Molly and Rhud will be hard to explain," Searle noted.

"We'll deal with that later. Follow me," Dodge waved. He took the first twenty-foot leap with his SIBA enhanced gravs and struck his head on a low hanging tree branch he didn't see. Twisting like a top in midair, he ended up in a fern patch full of jungle creatures. Fortunately for him, the slithering serpents that snapped at him were unable to bite through his tough, dura-fiber suit. Timmer and Enihoo helped him out of the bushes, pulling off two anacondas that wanted a piece of him for disturbing their sleep. "Got a little carried away there, huh, team leader?" Enihoo inquired, behind a snicker.

"Embarrassing," Searle added.

Dodge stood up unhurt. "Don't tell Harlowe. Promise?"

"What goes on in Zamami, stays in Zamami," Timmer replied, flicking a hand-sized spider off his shoulder.

Dodge launched a land crab stuck to his boot and set off again. "That way, team," he directed, mindful this time of the obstacles overhead.

43

French Connection

Southeastern France

THE UNMARKED B-5 stealth bomber carrying President for Life, Nootzy Shame, had already landed and remained in a low idle, off to the side of a secret airfield near the little wine-country commune of Saint Jeannet, France. Coming in for a landing, the small, also unmarked, private jet touched down and taxied to a stop, where Shame awaited its passenger. A dozen heavily armed elite mercenaries stood by, providing her security. Except for the mercenaries and her B-5 bomber crew, she was alone.

"Papa's jet, TL?" she asked the Team Leader, standing nearby.

"Yes, Ma'am," TL replied crisply.

It was early morning. The sun was just peeking above the forest-covered hills to the east. The cool air felt invigorating after being cooped up in the tiny pilot's rest area behind the cockpit of the supersonic three-hour flight from Andrews.

The cabin door of the private jet opened, and two large, bodyguards, armed with short barrel assault rifles, stepped out onto the small platform and canvassed the runway for threats. After checking with Team Leader that the area was secure, a guard signaled inside the cabin, giving the all-clear. The two guards then proceeded down the short stairway, and a small, elderly gentleman in a dark suit came down the steps and was greeted by President Shame, who kissed his hand.

"It's an honor to meet you, Papa," Shame said, almost reverently.

"We have important matters to discuss, Madame," Papa said directly as if he had little time for her.

"Yes, Sir," she said, and led him to a waiting limousine. Mercenaries opened the heavy, foot-thick, bomb resistant doors for the two elites. When they were both seated, they shut the doors but the limousine remained parked and did not move.

Inside, Shame poured herself a stiff drink, no ice, as Papa began, "Have you found Caesar?"

"No, not exactly. We've narrowed the search to Nevada, but its precise location is, as of yet, unknown," Shame replied.

"We have no time for incompetence. We must find that ship," Papa said with urgency in his tone.

"Believe me, Papa, we have all our resources on it. Its stealth technology has our boys scratching their heads. We'll find it by the weekend, I'm told, or heads will roll. How are Chancellor Milberg of Germany and Circosta of Spain? Do you have them on board?"

Papa's hazel eyes hardened with intensity. "They've been warned. They will join our one-world government or be annihilated. Are your armed forces prepared for war?"

"Once my top generals are eliminated, the others will fall in line," Shame assured Papa.

"Admiral Meads and General Van Dyke? They will never accept our order."

"They're both accepting God's order now, Papa," Shame stated coldly.

"Then the reports of the *Ron Paul's* sinking are true."

"And confirmed. Seven thousand feet down."

Shame hoped for some expression of gratitude from Papa, but he remained impassive. To him, even good news was simply business. If there was one thing a half-century of lessons had taught the old banker, it was that there were no mistakes, only lessons, and those lessons were always repeated until the obstacles were removed. Cheering over one success was unproductive when the goal was a one-world ascendancy that had yet to be achieved.

"And the alien crew? You received the reports from the Vatican emissary, Father Espinosi?" Papa asked.

A lost look of confusion came over Shame. "No. We received no reports from The Church. We were told a representative was en route, but the Vatican jet never arrived at Andrews, Papa."

Papa turned his head, blinking with surprise. "That is impossible. It was seen leaving daVinci late yesterday afternoon. The plane should have arrived many hours ago."

Shame had no explanation other than, "The jet never arrived, Sir. Truly. And there have been no reports of a missing plane, either. Maybe his plane had mechanical problems."

"The plane has all the latest avionics. If it would have flown anywhere else, The Church and the world would have been alerted."

Shame thought a moment. "Unless the plane was diverted by force. Who else would have known about the jet? The Chicoms? The Ruskies?"

"No one but you, the Zmaji...and The Church..."

"Surely they have no reason to take down their own plane," Shame said.

Papa glared at her accusingly. Shame held up her hands. "I swear, Papa, the U.S. had nothing to do with the missing jet."

"Your secret agencies, perhaps?"

Shame poured another three fingers of whiskey into her glass and drank before she answered, "No, I would have heard about it. We have eyes everywhere." She held her glass up as she spoke. "But I will find out what happened, Sir. Our satellites track every flight on the planet. If the Church plane was diverted, went down, or landed at some other airport, we'll know." She drank again. "But I've been having problems myself. Three of my cabinet people have been missing for over a week, and no one knows what happened to them. My Secretary of State, Linda Minott, disappeared last night on her way to a Broadway play."

"No trace?" Papa asked.

"Nothing. Like she dropped off the planet. Limo and all."

"Peculiar."

"We did locate the Pylott kid and his girlfriend," Shame said, changing the subject slightly.

Papa's eyes brightened. "Where?"

"At one of your banks in Manhattan. They made a large deposit."

"In Gamacoin…" he asked.

"How did you know?"

"The coin has infected our banks across the globe."

"The Fed, too. It's wreaking havoc with our balance sheets. People are using that cryto-coin instead of dollars, bypassing the banks altogether. They're buying cars, real estate, even making loans to other people, all without banks or financial institutions overseeing their transactions. Your man Tucker is going crazy. The people love it, and his banks are losing money. The IRS is unable to track the users of the coin. NSA, CIA, and the FBI are all on it, but their brightest geeks have no way to stop it. Without the control of the money supply, we're in deep trouble, Papa. Can you help us?"

"Not at this time. The coin has gone viral here."

"We know the source. Two males were seen using the Gamacoin card in California," Shame said, and then added, "We also obtained this photo yesterday of the couple from your New York bank." She held up her iPhone 17, activated her holo-screen, and displayed the picture of a young couple talking to the new accounts manager. Papa's face instantly turned bright red. "Do you know them?" Shame asked, seeing his ire. "They're the one's who used the coin to deposit millions into your bank."

"I know the girl," Papa said in a slow, deliberate voice. "It all makes sense now."

Shame wanted to know what Papa knew. "How so, Sir?"

Papa pointed at the photo. "The girl. How old does she appear to you?"

Shame stared but saw nothing usual about her except she was exceptionally beautiful and poised for someone her age. "She's a looker all right, like the young man. Twenty?"

Papa looked at Shame in all seriousness. "This is Leucadia Mars and she is over seventy-five years old."

Shame nearly fell out of her limo seat. "No way is that woman that old."

"I knew her parents, Harry and Sook Mars. Leucadia and I played together on swings and built sandcastles on the beach when my father traveled to their estate in Newport Beach. They never joined the Cartel, no matter how much pressure we put on them. They had no time for us. They were always involved in a worldwide search for an ancient artifact. My father first thought it was Alexander's Tomb, or some such thing. But when he managed to infiltrate their inner circle, he discovered it was an artifact that could destroy worlds: an ancient alien ship they called *Millawanda*. But up until the day he died, he believed the Mars family never found it."

"Are you talking about the same Mars family that ran Mars Corporation?" Shame asked in disbelief.

"Yes."

"She was Braxton's financial backer. She left him in charge of the Corporation when she went missing," Shame remembered.

Papa knew him, too. "Jefferson Braxton."

"He was one of Delmonte's White House advisors and my biggest headache when I was running for President." She patted Papa on his forearm. "Thank you for handling that for me, Sir. His accident was timely."

Papa did not acknowledge her comment, only replying, "We must find Leucadia Mars, understand? And we absolutely must find *Millawanda*'s location before it's too late. That ship is the key to our survival."

"We'll find it, Papa, and when we find her, we'll put an end to her family once and for all," Shame assured him.

"The Zmaji have a better plan. The movie star Simon Bolt and another young man, Matthew Riverstone."

Shame knew the names. "We have had them under close surveillance since California, Papa. All we need is your order to take them."

"No, the Zmaji will handle this."

"You're certain? Special Forces teams can have them locked up within the hour."

"That will not be necessary," Papa said sternly.

"Okay. I will clear the way for your men."

"That is all that is required."

Papa tapped his window, and a black uniformed mercenary opened the door. Papa climbed aboard his jet and took off without a word.

44

Repairs

Hudson Deep Canyon

GENERAL VAN DYKE reached out and touched the shimmering blue field before him. "It feels mushy, not solid at all," he commented to Admiral Meads, who stood next to him. Awestruck, the General followed the massive field that totally covered the submarine. "No drips, no errors, no leaks. How does it do that?" he wondered aloud.

"Give it a hard rap, Dutch, and see how it feels," Admiral Meads directed.

Beyond the field it was dark as night. No light could penetrate this far below the ocean surface of the Hudson Deep Canyon. Stretched out behind them, the long grey, and damaged side of the USS *Ron Paul* lay on the ocean bottom surrounded by a protective energy dome that served two purposes: first, it kept the crushing depths of the Atlantic Ocean at bay, and second, it produced enough soft light to allow walking around without the need of external lights from the boat.

As Meads suggested, Van Dyke struck the field with a sharp rap of his knuckles. "Ouch!" he said, shaking his hand. "Like concrete." The General glanced back at the damaged *Ron Paul*. "It's hard to believe that little box of yours is protecting us. How deep are we now?" Van Dyke asked.

Meads reared back in wonder at the dome, equally as amazed as Van Dyke. This was the first time he ever used the alien device Harlowe had given him. "We don't have gauges that go this deep, but the charts say this section is 7,236 feet deep, maybe more."

"Unbelievable. How long do we have?"

Meads glanced back at the conning tower with uncertainty. "I don't know. I was never given an instruction book."

"No guarantee either, I bet," Van Dyke said with a forced grin.

"I didn't ask."

Van Dyke looked down at the olive green, calf-high muck boots they were both using to slosh around on the wet ocean floor. At this depth, the sandy bottom was rather featureless. Small, colorless mounds had the appearance of crushed sandcastles. Incredibly, there was life, but nothing like they were portrayed in the movies. These organisms were tiny shrimp-like creatures, and wiggled around harmlessly on the other side of the field. "So where is all the air coming from? The *Ron Paul* can't produce that much," Van Dyke pointed out. Besides their boots, they each wore matching grey sweatshirts over black, rubberized pants, and USS *Ron Paul* baseball caps. The air inside the dome was cool, staying a constant 60 degrees Fahrenheit, even though beyond the barrier the water was a nippy 35 degrees.

Meads touched the barrier with an open hand. "The field produces enough air for everyone."

"Sucking it out of the water?"

"That's my guess."

"Food?"

"Ship's stores have four months supply left."

Van Dyke kept looking around, insecure, as if believing that any second he would be crushed to the size of a pea. "If that battery lasts..." He sidestepped a tiny wiggly thing with stick-like legs as he added, "But as long as we have bacon, I'm a happy camper, Huey."

Meads laughed and slapped the General on the back. "We'll run out of air before we run out of bacon, Dutch."

Van Dyke kept shaking his head, wishing he had a strip of bacon right now to calm his nerves. "Who's going to save us, Huey? Your boat's stuck on the bottom. Look at her side. Who's going to fix her at this depth?"

"Maybe they will, Dutch," Meads said, pointing upward toward a circular band of slow pulsing blue light. It seemed to grow larger and brighter as it drifted toward them.

Van Dyke stared, fixated at the circle of light. "What the...? What is it?"

Meads stood with his hands on his hips. "I can assure you, it's not one of ours."

The circle of light was massive, hovering over the dome, revealing the undersides of a golden, saucer-like ship that dwarfed the *Ron Paul* many times over in its size. Although Meads had never seen the Gamadin ship, he had felt its power many years ago, when it overpowered his nuclear submarine, causing it to float to the surface deep inside a super secret Chinese harbor. According to General Van Dyke's reports from Arecibo and a Marine sergeant's sighting of a UFO over Colorado, what else could it be? No power on Earth had the ability to cruise so effortlessly at this depth.

The crew on the gangplank began to panic, racking their assault rifles and loading their 20 mm cannons when a curtain of blue light shot down from the perimeter edge of the saucer and covered the dome. A cubic mile of ocean water suddenly began to be expunged through the new barrier, and when it was totally empty, the protective field over the *Ron Paul* expectantly shut off, further terrifying the crew, including Meads.

Captain Alexander on the catwalk was understandably anxious for the safety of his men and his boat.

Alexander hollered down, "What is it, Admiral?"

Meads stepped lively over to Alexander to help calm his fears. "A friend," he replied, and waved to the boatmen to lower their weapons. "Stand down, Captain!" he ordered.

Guardedly, Alexander followed orders, while at the same time everyone watched as a wide, circular hatchway opened under the saucer, and an enormous ramp, that was as wide as an eight-lane highway, deployed out from the center of the ship and touched down not two steps from where Meads and Van Dyke stood. Light from the saucer's hull grew brighter and brighter until it was like daylight everywhere. Four human beings, two males and two females, dressed in dark blue uniforms walked out through the open hatchway and began walking down the ramp.

"Who's the one in charge there?" Van Dyke asked, studying the group coming toward them.

Meads pointed. "The tall, dark-haired young man in the lead."

"Rather young, isn't he?"

"Don't let his looks fool you, Dutch. He's got his act together." Meads then added, "And if I'm not mistaken, that is General Ivan Branch..." The Admiral questioned his eyesight for a second, "and I believe that's the former First Lady, Mrs. Delmonte. Now how did he pull that off?"

Van Dyke was dumbfounded as well. "Intelligence has tried to find her for years."

"I've never seen the blond, either," Meads said.

"She's a dish and a half."

"Roger that."

While the two senior officers waited for the small group, Van Dyke took the opportunity to size up the tall young man he would be facing. The young man's swagger was hardly soldier-like, yet it was bold, confidant, and in-your-face imposing, like he knew he was the two-ton gorilla in the room. His own teenaged son would call him bad-ass cool, his daughter would think he was hot and begin purring like a kitten over his striking good looks, his intense blue eyes, and a stunning blue uniform with skintight pants and light touches of gold trim. The girl walking beside him was just as striking as the young man, only cut from a different cloth. A rare silk cloth, he figured. She was beautiful, far beyond even Timmer's pay grade. Her straw-colored hair, flowed straight past her shoulders, framing her flawless, lightly tanned face, and large green eyes, that seemed to grow brighter as she floated softly beside her leader like an equal.

The young man extended his hand to Meads first. "Admiral," he began, "nice to see you again, Sir. Are your boatmen okay?" He was extraordinarily polite and seemed genuine in his concern, as well.

"Likewise, Captain Pylott. Yes, all but the boat are in good shape," Meads replied.

Pylott scanned the *Ron Paul's* damaged hull. "I understand, Admiral. We'll have your boat up and running in no time." He then extended his hand Van Dyke. "General Van Dyke, a pleasure to meet you, Sir. General Branch says you're the best of the best."

Van Dyke thanked the young man and asked directly, "I understand you are in charge of all this, son?"

"Yes, Sir. I am. This is my ship, *Millawanda*." He turned to the young woman beside him. "And this is my science officer, Ms. Leucadia Mars. She keeps me in line." The two officers exchanged handshakes as Pylott continued with the introductions. "This is…"

"Mrs. Delmonte," Van Dyke interrupted. "We know who you are, Ma'am."

"Please, call me Tinker, General," Tinker insisted as she turned to Branch, "And you know, General Branch, of course?"

The officers shook hands. "Ivan, good to see you again," Van Dyke said.

Meads said, "We never met formally, General."

Branch smiled graciously. "But your reputation precedes you, Admiral. I personally recommended you for command of the Pacific Fleet."

"So I can blame you for my hair falling out then?" Meads joked.

Branch continued with the banter. "It was either that or keep you at Pentagon with Drgastin."

After a short laugh, Pylott got down to business. "Sorry to break this up, Gentlemen, but we have work to do. We need to get your boat fixed, Admiral, and on its way."

Van Dyke stared at Pylott as if he was loony as a politician. "And how are you going to do that, son? This boat's in a helluva mess."

General Branch stepped forward and into Van Dyke's space. "Captain Pylott, Dutch."

Pylott understood there were more important matters than protocol. He put a guiding hand on Branch's shoulder. "That's okay, General," as he faced Van Dyke and Meads. "It will take some doing, but my repair crew," he pointed back up the ramp at a squad of stick-like droids clanking down the ramp with large pieces of sheet metal in their mechanical hands, "will have the *Ron Paul* good as new in a few hours.

In the meantime, won't you join us for lunch in my cabin, gentlemen?" Dropping from open doors in the hull, more pieces of metal floated down to waiting robobs, that handled the replacement sections of the hull like they were in zero gravity. "Please, if you follow me to the disk over here," he said pointing a few steps away, "we'll transport up, and maybe we can even find General Van Dyke some crispy bacon."

Van Dyke blinked. The young man indeed had his act together.

* * *

Toying with his slice of crispy bacon, General Van Dyke asked the elephant-in-the-room question everyone wanted to know, "So what is your plan, Captain?" he asked Pylott. They had just finished a sumptuous lunch, sitting around a large conference table. The young Captain met the question head-on. Van Dyke's question required courage to answer for it had worldwide implications concerning the human race. "Do you understand the consequences that this will cause, if the population of the planet finds out about you and your ship?"

Pylott finished his sip of chocolate shake and set it beside his plate. From his right was Leucadia, followed by Tinker, Admiral Meads, General Van Dyke, and General Branch sitting to his left. "I do, General."

"There will be mass hysteria on a scale the world has never seen before," Van Dyke stated forcefully.

"Yes, Sir."

Van Dyke continued his rant. "Our brightest minds have studied the big what-if question since the day man looked up at the stars, and asked, are we alone out there?"

"We're not, General; it's a very crowded galaxy."

"You know this?"

"My ship and my crew have been seen worlds you can only dream about. Life in the galaxy is common, not rare, Sir. We must prepare Earth for this fact."

"By causing the deaths of millions, perhaps billions of people?"

"No, by saving the human race. My crew and I have been 35,000 light-years and back across this galaxy. We've met more aliens than you can imagine, played with them, fought with them, and learned from them a lot more than they have of us." His eyes met the beautiful blond next to him, "And yes, fell in love with them, too. Trust me when I tell you,

General, there are those out there who would destroy us and our planet as easily as you would step on an ant."

"So you're going to make that decision as to whether the people of Earth are ready to meet these ETs?"

"I am."

"People will comment suicide, jump off cliffs, businesses will shut down, markets will collapse, and there will be total worldwide chaos."

"Yes, for a time there will be pain, confusion, and fear," Pylott admitted. He leaned forward and asked, "So would you rather deal with it now or continue with the Earth being run by nut jobs like Shame and the Zmaji Cartel, who control this planet? As we sit here they are planning an all-out nuclear war! How many billions will you sacrifice then, General?"

Van Dyke remained unfazed, already knowing the decks were stacked. "It is out of our hands. The Russians and the Chinese forces are in position. There is no turning back."

"I will not allow the total destruction of the planet, Sir," Harlowe stated sharply.

"Shame is a total nut job, I'll grant you that," Van Dyke admitted, "but she would never turn our military forces on the planet."

"You don't really believe that, Dutch," Meads aid.

"Shame would do it in a heartbeat, General," Harlowe spread his arms out, "all she needs is *Millawanda*."

General Branch chimed in, "As Presidents who came before her did at Fort Sumter, the Lusitania, the Maine, Pearl Harbor, 9/11, or President Delmonte's trumped up charges of treason, she will, like them, use the discovery of an alien ship as a threat against all of humanity. So what do you think will happen when Shame releases the Arecibo report to the world?"

Admiral Meads replied, "The populations of the world will be begging for someone like her with her mighty forces to rush in and save us all from the alien invasion."

Branch concurred. "That's right, Joe, all governments across the planet will band together as a single power to fight the alien invasion. This ship and its crew will be their excuse to complete their total takeover of the planet. The people will plead for the governments of the world to save them from what The Church is calling your crew...the Wild Strain. The Church believes they have evidence we are descendants from a Wild Strain of human beings that have returned to Earth as conquerors. Tell me, General, who will the people of Earth believe? Us or the Church?"

Tinker faced Leucadia. "Tell them, Lu."

Leucadia stood and stared at Van Dyke. "That's right, General, we're the Wild Strain. Shame and her military might, and with the power of the Cartel behind her, will search us out to kill us. They want this ship for one reason only; to control the planet in perpetuity."

It was Van Dyke's turn to sit back in his chair, completely stunned by the revelation. "Do you have proof of this, Ms. Mars?"

Leucadia touched an activator at the edge of the table and a holographic image appeared above the table. An elderly gentleman appeared from the cabin door of a private jet and began stepping down the stairway where Shame stood as she greeted him like he was her king. In the background was a large military jet that sat at the end of the runway with its engines at idle. Van Dyke recognized it instantly. "That's a B-5 stealth. No one has permission to use that jet. Not even me."

"But Shame does," Branch stated.

"Who's the old guy?" Van Dyke asked.

Leucadia knew him well. "His name is Evelyn du Bear, an old friend of my family, General, and arguably the world's most powerful man."

Van Dyke found that hard to believe. "That old man? That pencil-neck?"

Leucadia continued: "Within the inner circles of the power elite, he is known as Papa. Through his family's financial company in Luxembourg, Du Bear, Ltd., he controls every central bank, in every country throughout the world. All wars and local conflicts, since the Hundred Year' War begun in 1337 by the House of Plantagenet, rulers of the Kingdom of England against the House of Valois, and rulers of the Kingdom of France, the House of Du Bear has financed every conflict. You've heard of the House of Medici?" Leucadia asked the table.

Admiral Meads was a student of history. "Of course. They were powerful Italian bankers from Florence in the fourteenth and fifteenth centuries. Led by Giovanni Medici, the family began a political dynasty that ultimately became the largest bank consortium in Europe by the fifteeth century."

"Correct," Leucadia stated, "but who do you think was behind the House of Medici's rise to power?"

"Du Bear?" Meads replied, as a guess.

"Correct again, Admiral, the father of world influence, Marcus Aurelius Du Bear. He was not only the brains and the money behind House of Medici, he supplied the capital behind the rise of The Church."

"That goes against all the history books I've read on the Medicis and The Church, Ms. Mars," Meads pointed out.

"Yes, Admiral, 'He who wins the war writes the history.'"

"So what you're saying is that this Du Bear's family has been running things since the fourteenth century?" Van Dyke asked. "That's over 600 years. Hell, most nations don't survive that long."

"Are you saying all wars, Ms. Mars? The American Revolutionary War, War of 1812, World War I, World War II, Korea, Vietnam, and the Middle East?"

"Don't forget the Civil War and the Spanish American War, Napoleonic campaigns, Columbus' expeditions, all of it. Wherever there was money to be made, the House of Du Bear was behind it."

"What kind of mind could organize such a powerful business that takes over the known world for over six centuries?" Meads marveled in awe.

The Admiral's question piqued Tinker's interest, too. "Good question, Admiral." To Leucadia she asked, "How did they do it?"

Leucadia made sure she had everyone's attention before she dropped the bomb. "With a mind that's not from this planet."

"They're ETs!" Van Dyke exclaimed.

"That's right, General. They're ETs, and they came here hundreds of years ago with one thought in mind…to control the planet."

"So this Papa is from somewhere out there?" Branch said, waving at the sky. "Do we know where?"

"No," Leucadia replied, "and we don't care. Marcus could have been from my mother's home planet—"

Van Dyke suddenly went slack jawed. "You're an ET?"

Leucadia smiled politely. "Yes, General, I'm an ET."

Harlowe qualified her statement. "Half an ET. Her dad was an

Earthling."

Leucadia confronted Van Dyke on another matter. "But why act surprised, General? You've known for years about ETs. You wouldn't have been placed in charge of Space Command unless you were fully aware ETs have existed on this planet for centuries."

Van Dyke's eyes drifted around the table, looking like his hand was caught in the cookie jar. "How do you know that?"

From the holo-screen in the center of the table, Leucadia produced Top Secret document after document, signed by every President since Truman, along with the top military brass at the time of their origination. The last few documents, as recent as three months ago, had General Van Dyke's signature, indicating that when he took over Space Command, he was brought up to speed on all things extraterrestrial within the government, including the alien bodies recovered at the Roswell and Aztec crash sites in 1947.

"We have all the documents ever produced, General. There is nothing secret on your computers that we can't extract," Leucadia said.

Harlowe saw the anxiety in Van Dyke's face at being exposed. "Relax, General, we know you're one of the good guys. Whatever you've done in the past has always been for the good of the country. If you had ordered our destruction from the onset, you wouldn't be sitting with us now. The fact is, you didn't. Since the day your man Timmer showed you the Top Secret documents from Arecibo, you've been after the truth, not trying to suppress it. And for that, we welcome you aboard." Harlowe then announced to Meads, "I believe your ship is ready, Admiral."

Meads was stunned. "So soon?"

"Aye, Sir, you're good to go," Harlowe replied.

"Where will we go?" Van Dyke inquired. "There's not a port on the planet where the *Ron Paul* can escape Shame's satellites."

Meads agreed. "That's true. Satellites will have us the moment we surface."

Harlowe put a hand on Branch's shoulder. "The General, here, will show you a safe harbor, Admiral."

Van Dyke and Meads stepped over to Tinker to say farewell. "It was an honor to see you're safe and sound, Mrs. Delmonte," Van Dyke said, taking her hand. "We both wish the President...the true President," he emphasized, "a quick recovery."

The door to Harlowe's cabin slid back and a deep, familiar voice asked, "Did I miss the party?" President Peter Delmonte stepped through the doorway, aided by two girlbobs in platinum blond wigs.

Tinker scurried over to his side and relieved the girlbobs of their assistance. "Not at all, Mr. President."

* * *

The reintroductions were brief. After taking everyone's well-wishes, and nice-to-see-you-up-and-abouts, the former President excused himself. The sight of real food was almost too much for him to bear. After nothing but a prison diet for five years, who could blame him. The fate of the planet could wait. Tinker guided him to the table of delights. The first thing he grabbed was a fry. Shaking uncontrollably, he tried putting it in his mouth, but dropped it before his tongue could touch it. Tinker quickly snagged a second one with a small dab of catsup and placed it in his mouth. He sat down to savor every slender morsel, too exhausted to stand any longer.

Knowing the lunch was over, everyone left the room, leaving the two of them alone to enjoy their meal. On the way back to the *Ron Paul,* Van Dyke asked Harlowe again, "Why, Captain? Why are you doing this? There's no good ending for this. You could leave Earth with your ship and your crew and never have to worry about Shame and the Cartel ever again."

Harlowe stopped at the top of the ramp and replied, "It's not about me and my crew, General. Earth is our home. To survive it must mature. To do that, people must have control of themselves, not governments."

The Generals had never heard of such a thing. "Do away with government?" Van Dyke asked for all of them.

"Yes, the sooner the better. Stop the control, and the people with prosper. Stop the control, and they will govern themselves. The Invisible Hand, Sir…works! I've seen it myself. Have you ever been to a dog park?"

The question caught Van Dyke off guard. What did a dog park have to do with anything? "No. My wife's allergic to pet hair."

Harlowe grinned before going on: "If you had, you would have seen dogs playing peacefully with no leashes inside the park. Why is that?"

Van Dyke had no clue, but Meads did. "Because they have no

leashes."

Harlowe tapped Meads on the shoulder. "Excellent, Admiral. You get a gold star. 'Because they have no leashes.' Put a chain around their necks, and they become hostile and territorial. They fight. If no one stops them, the big dogs will kill the little dogs. But once you give them back their freedom and take away their leash, they become serene and peaceful again." Harlowe folded his arms. "All the answers to the world's problems are right there in that dog park, Gentlemen."

Van Dyke nodded thoughtfully. "No leashes, huh? That's your answer to world peace?"

"That's right, General, remove leash that stops our planet from maturing so she'll be ready to greet our neighbors when they come calling."

"So you believe less government is humanity's only hope?" Van Dyke asked.

Harlowe stared back convincingly. "Not less, General. I'm shooting for none."

"That's never happened in the history of the world," Meads pointed out.

"And look at the oppression and all the millions of lives lost in wars throughout the centuries. We've tried it with a leash, Generals. We're going to try it without it this time."

Van Dyke wasn't convinced. "If it's not power you're after, then why do you need us?"

Harlowe's eyes drifted between the two generals and the admiral. "To help slay the dragons, Sirs." He didn't elaborate, or wait for another question. He gave them a confident wink, and added, "If the Earth is to mature, we must slay the dragons first." He left it at that, turned away, and went back to his ship.

45
The Rules

Millawnda Deck

HARLOWE DIPPED THE mop into the bucket and splashed the sudsy water across an already spotless surface. *Millawanda* was back at their original putdown in Nevada. It was early morning, and the sun had yet to peek over the eastern mountains. Since leaving the *Ron Paul* in the middle of the Atlantic Ocean, Harlowe had yet to find time to sleep. He kissed Leucadia good night, but instead of going to bed himself, he grabbed his bucket of soapy water and a mop, and did what he always did when it came to thinking things through: he swabbed the deck. A three-quarters full moon subdued the normal riot of stars to a dull luster. There was plenty of light, though, for cleaning, and pondering, and mopping, and calculating, and cleansing the world. Once or twice he glanced up at the ship's bridge. Prigg had the night shift. He was seated in his science chair, his three eyes looking this way and that, always appearing to be in perpetual motion. One eye, usually the upper middle one, oversaw the big screen. The second, and sometimes they switched, scanned the numerous small screens. But the third eye was always, always glued on His Majesty out on the deck.

Harlowe tipped his mop toward Prigg. It didn't appear the little Naruckian saw him. He was twisting around in his seat very busy like. Harlowe counted to three, and by the time he reached three, without skipping a beat, Prigg saluted back. Harlowe snorted a small chuckle. God, he loved that little guy, and that was pretty much all the recognition he required.

The entire crew knew, unless it was life or death, when Harlowe was swabbing the deck, he was never to be disturbed. It was his quiet time. Riverstone, on the other hand, apparently never got the message. He appeared on the deck at the exact moment Harlowe tossed out a mop full of water.

"You didn't bring a mop," Harlowe said accusingly upon seeing his First Officer.

"That's your deal, not mine. Alice does my cleaning," Riverstone replied.

"Good thing, too, or you wouldn't ever find your socks."Riverstone pointed at his shoes, and smiled. "We don't need no stinkin' socks with these 54th century shoes, brain."

Harlowe glared at him. "That's Captain Brain, Mister." He then asked, "So what brings you back to the desert. Actors Guild give you some time off?" Harlowe caught a twitch in Riverstone's nose, a sure sign that all-was-not-well on the girl front. "Oh, wait! I get it now. Phoebe dumped your mug." He jabbed him in the shoulder with his mop. "You know, I knew there was something I liked about her."

"She has three months to live…maybe less," Riverstone said straight out.

The revelation caught Harlowe off-guard. Up to this point, it had all been normal ragging, but Riverstone's announcement shook him. "Wow…" was all he could say without sounding pathetically stupid.

"I want to bring her here," Riverstone said.

Harlowe laid his mop to one side, "Of course," he said without hesitation. "You don't need my permission for that."

"I know."

"You're wondering how you're going to do it."

"Yeah, it's not like I can go up to her and say, I've got this ancient spaceship that's pretty good at fixing things. Want to give it a shot?"

"Whatever it takes, we'll make it work."

Jewels brought out two low beach chairs and they sat down like they were sitting on a sandy beach somewhere.

"Stage four?" Harlowe asked.

Riverstone nodded. He appeared strong, but on the inside Harlowe knew his gut was tearing him apart. "Inoperable. They told her to go home and get her affairs in order."

"Does Rerun know?"

"Yeah, he told me. He had Prigg check up on her when she didn't show up for our date."

Riverstone regarded Harlowe's bucket and mop. "So what has you kinked. I thought you had everything worked out. Your mom's ok. Dodger is now Dodge. Delmonte's on the mend. What's not to like? Wiz's wave maker on the blink?"

Harlowe folded his arms in front of him. "I've been thinking."

Riverstone rolled his eyes skyward. "Oh no, you've been thinking?"

"We've only been gone eleven years, Earth time, right?"

"Something like that. What's the point? What's done is done."

"The point is, it only took a few years for the good people we left in charge to get totally screwed over by the toads that run things. Did you see all the businesses that are closed? The homeless begging on the streets? You can't do this. You can't do that. You need a permit to do this. A permit to do that."

"My parents can't even go to Me-N-Ed's without getting the shakedown."

"Nootzy's Hoods?"

"You know them?"

"We had words."

Riverstone pointed at himself. "Me, too. Twice. You know the Blue Bayou doesn't serve steak anymore."

"What?"

"They took it off the menu because it costs too much. You have to get special permission to order it a week in advance. What's up with that?" Riverstone pulled out his Gamacoin card. "Good thing Wiz came up with this, or we'd be starving. If you don't have a money card, you ain't nothing, pard."

"Yeah, good thing."

Riverstone leaned forward, grabbing both handles of the chair. "So what are we going to do about it? You've got a plan, right?"

"I'm toying with ideas," Harlowe admitted.

"Well, it better be quick, and better than your the last idea. That one only lasted a couple of years before Delmonte was canned."

"I was thinking of making some rules."

"Rules? Rules for what? We've hated rules all our lives. Why start now?" Riverstone asked.

Harlowe stared off in a quandary. He really had no idea where he was going with the thought, only that he felt compelled to set some boundaries. "Not for us dummy. For the planet."

"Oh, like the Ten Commandments. I don't want to bust your bubble, pard, but there was a guy called Moses who got his rules copyrighted before you."

"I'm not talking about people rules. Ten is enough. I'm thinking of rules for toads that want to play God. Rules for those who want to control everything. Those kind of rules."

"You're not making any sense. My dad is always talking about the Constitution. He says if government would just follow those rules as they were written, we wouldn't have the problems we have today. But as you can see, everyone is corrupt these days from the top down. They're like us. They don't follow the rules, either. It's just a bunch of words on old paper."

Harlowe understood that. "Yeah, but we're honest rule breakers. Our rules will have teeth. If they're broken, then the bad guys will be dealt with the old fashioned way."

Riverstone slid a finger across his throat. "I like the sound of that. Keelhaul them, Captain! Now you're talking my language."

Harlowe thought that went too far. "Not quite, but there will be consequences."

"Like when you didn't take out the trash, and Tinker tossed you out the window."

"Yeah, like that. Tinker rules. If you break them, you'll be tossed out with the garbage."

"With no time off for good behavior."

Harlowe stuck a finger in the air. "Exactly!"

Riverstone was all in. "Okay, when do we get started? What are the rules?"

"I have a few in mind, and Lu has some ideas she wants to add."

"Start with the Declaration of Independence. It was good enough for Quay when she read it. It changed her life. I always wondered what happened to her."

Harlowe wondered, too. There would always be a place in his heart for the girl he rescued from a burning ship on a distant moon, far, far away from here. He often wondered if she had never left on her search for freedom, would Fate have taken him away from Leucadia? Would he have returned to Earth? So many possibilities. So many what-ifs. He had no regrets, though, none at all. He and Leucadia were soulmates, and that's the way he wanted them to be for the rest of time. Still, there were moments he thought of Quay and the sacrifice she made. To search for the self-determination for all God's creatures to be free from tyranny everywhere was the highest goal obtainable.

Riverstone was on to something, though. Thinking of Quay and her quest made sense. She had figured the real meaning of freedom before they did. But how did she know so quickly. After all, she was like Lu; she had lived longer than all of them put together. She saw the world through the eyes of a centenarian, not as a teenager. Maturity may be the key to it all, he reckoned. So how could he bring adulthood to an entire planet? Was it nuts to even think about such an undertaking?

He sighed, heavy with the weight of an entire planet inside him. That's what Quay sought, and that's what he wanted. Freedom! Not just for a city, a state, or a country, but freedom on a planet-wide scale for everyone. That was the place in his heart where she would always be and never leave.

Like a revelation suddenly hit him across the face, Harlowe bolted upright in his chair. "All right, we'll start with the Declaration. But we have to make it fit the times. It's got to last, pard."

"Check out Millie's database," Riverstone suggested. "Our new friends on Orixy seemed to have it pretty good. They've been around awhile, too. We also need to keep it simple enough for Rerun to understand."

"Good point. No longer than a page."

"Simple sentences. Subject, verb, object."

"My dad called it KISS. Keep It Simple Stupid."

"And it needs a good title like The Rules of Earth," Riverstone suggested.

Harlowe spread his arms out. "Bigger! Much bigger. We have to make it for everyone, all life across the galaxy."

"You're going for the whole enchilada, huh?"

"Dream big, be big!" Harlowe stated.

"Rules for the universe then!" Riverstone declared, knowing nothing else that infinite.

Harlowe slapped Riverstone with a big high-five, giving his approval. "The Universe!" he echoed, and coined the title of their new rules, "How does, Absolute Laws Pertaining to the Ruling Bodies of the Universe, sound?"

Riverstone turned his nose up. "Way too complicated, pard. KISS remember?"

"Yeah, yeah, you're right. So Rerun can understand it."

"Now you're talking. A code of some sort."

"A Gamadin code."

Riverstone grabbed Harlowe by the shoulders and barked, "Gamacode, brah!"

Harlowe jumped out of his chair. "That's it! The Gamacode!"

"KISS to the max!" Riverstone stated.

Harlowe and Riverstone were in sync. "Exactly. For Rerun!"

All was well and good, except Riverstone's happy face sobered when one particular problem came up. "Not even God can stop bad behavior, pard. Remember the apple. There are a lot of bad apples out there, and that's never going to change. That's just the way it is. We can't take them all out."

As much as Harlowe felt with all the power he had beneath him he could remove the corruption like a bad habit, Riverstone was right. No Gamacode ever written, now or in the future, would stop corruption. Even if he could do it, it would be a brief fix. The bad in humanity would always come back. The apple had already been eaten. There was no turning back. To think otherwise was naïve. History was against him.

"Okay, we can't play God. That's a given. Moses took care of the first part, we'll have to take care of the freedom part. Everywhere we've ever gone in this galaxy, what's the one thing we've always, always fought against?"

"The chief buttheads," Riverstone answered straight out.

"YES! Every time. They're always the ones who force their stupid rules on everyone. Now they're going to have to live under our rules, or they're outta here."

"And how are you going to get them to play by our rules? You can't even get Tinker and Lu to obey yours. Think of it as a world full of them. Now what? Not even God would touch that one."

Harlowe stood up. "I'm a toad for even thinking it, huh?"

"This is why you're out here, isn't it? You haven't found an answer yet, and you're scared."

"I'm scared big time, as much as I've ever been scared of anything. What if we make these rules and the world suffers more? There are going to be costs, Matt. Things we never even thought of will happen. Things that could destroy what we wanted to fix."

"Harlowe, the bad guys are already destroying the planet. It's up to us to make it right again. You know why?" Harlowe waited for Riverstone to drop the other shoe. "Because we can."

Harlowe put his chair down three times and picked it up again three times before he agreed with Riverstone. "You're right. If we sit here and do nothing, then bad guys win every time. We'll do whatever it takes, because we can."

They walked with their chairs to the perimeter edge of the ship, and looked east. The sun's pink light was just peeking over the mountains. Jewels brought the breakfast burritos and Blue Stuff shakes. It looked like a good day to stay positive.

46

Tiramisu

Hollywood, California

IT WAS NIGHT. Only a couple of dim lights were left on inside Phoebe Marleigh's palatial, 6,500-square-foot ranch house. She wanted it that way. Dark. Morbid. Uninviting. She slipped off her shoes and walked barefoot out into the backyard that was one of a kind. The ten and a half-acre estate in the Hollywood hills was devoted to spreading trees, palms, a riot of colorful flowers, herbs, vegetables, and fruit, all surrounding a long lap pool of clear water. In the daylight, it was lush and green. At night it was her hideaway from the fame, the agents, the directors, and recently her doctors. On one side of the property was a greenhouse full of tomatoes, peppers, basil, orchids, arugula, kale, and spinach. To the other side, a stone walkway led to a fruit orchard of avocados, juicy peaches, oranges, lemons, and limes all along the back fence. It was Satoshi, the best gardener money could buy, who always kept her sanctuary of small waterfalls, gurgling brooks, and hundred-year-old Koi, beautiful and lush and far from the maddening fear of doom.

She dipped her foot in the cool water of her pool. Maybe she would take a swim, she thought. It was a perfect night, the air heavy with futility. All she had to do was slip out of her silk shift and float to the middle of the pool where she could sink to the bottom and no one would ever care.

She wiped her tears. The doctors all agreed. This was it. In a few short weeks, or less, her walks through her garden would end. She couldn't believe it. She was really mortal. She felt betrayed. She had done everything right. She hardly drank. She loved salads and fruit, and ate like a bird to keep her weight in check. She exercised daily, took her vitamins, and got a little bit of sun for color. So why was she dying? In a fit of rage, she grabbed a clay pot of yellow daffodils from its stand and hurled it in a high arch, breaking it into a zillion pieces against the far side of the pool, muddying the water.

She heard clapping behind her on the stone walkway. "You almost made it," a familiar voice said. "Will the pool filter have it cleaned up by the time we go swimming?"

She came around to the voice and couldn't believe it was the young man, Matthew, whom she met with Simy. He sat calmly at a table with two chairs, covered with a white tablecloth, wine glasses filled with blue liquid, red and white wrapped burgers, a tray of fries, guacamole and chips, all on a cut crystal platter. A single candle in the middle of the table was the only light.

"How did you get in here? I have security everywhere," she asked as she sauntered over to the table.

"I tried the door but no one answered," Matthew replied.

"There's a reason for that. It means I don't want to be disturbed," she said bluntly.

"Really? I thought it meant 'I'm feeling sorry for myself, and I want to wallow in my soup bowl of self pity alone.'"

She looked at him oddly and pointed at the table. "What's this?"

"Comfort food," Matthew replied. He wore jeans with holes and frayed ends, flip-flops, and a red and white football jersey that read Lancers and the number 17 on the front.

"Nice touch with the candle. Walmart?" she asked.

Matthew's eyes giggled. "Close. Dollar Store."

"Do you always dress so formally for a romantic dinner?" she asked.

"Well, you should have seen me at the Blue Bayou. I was dressed to the nines then." He pointed up at the night. "There were balloon lanterns overhead, a river gurgling in the background, fireflies, and crickets. All that was missing was you."

"I'm sorry about that."

"You should be. And you know what the worst part about it was, besides your no show?" She kept quiet and let him rant because he was right to be upset. "There was no filet mignon on the menu."

She allowed him a trivial smile, gazing over the table and chairs. They were not hers. The entire set appeared to be held up by slender pieces of metal so thin she could barely see the support between the round base in the dark. As she felt the chair, it was surprisingly sturdy and made of a soft, golden metal. His weight was probably twice that of hers, and yet the chair seemed to support him easily. She decided to risk it and sat down. "No filet, huh? That's always a problem these days," she commented, stunned by the chair's comfort.

Riverstone continued venting. "That's right, a big problem. The first world kind. It never used to be that way. What happened?"

"Where have you been? On a desert island somewhere? Ever since the overthrow in D.C., everything has gone downhill. For the good of the country, they said. Right. We gotta cut back, tighten our belts for Shame and her Hoods."

"I've met them twice."

"And you survived? They'd toss you down a manhole just for looking at them wrong."

"I got that impression."

Phoebe took a chip and scooped a small taste of guac. Her eyes lit up with surprise. "That's really good. Where did you get the avocados? I thought they were restricted, too."

"I have a source. Try the fries," Matthew offered. "They'll blow your socks off."

She took one and stared at it. "I wish we had some catsup."

"Hold on." He glanced behind him, and spoke to someone out of sight. "Alice, a little catsup for the lady, if you please."

Hardly two seconds went by, when a stick-thin droid with a dark brown wig, sashayed from behind a tall fern holding a small dipping cup of the red sauce. She placed it on the table in front of her and left like she entered. "This is illegal, too."

"Catsup?"

"Yeah, can you believe it? I grew up on this stuff." She waved her finger at him in jest. "But I won't tell. Does the droid cook, too?" Phoebe asked cynically, as she dipped her fry and tasted the perfectly cooked fried potato.

Matthew pulled a chip from the pile and scooped a healthy portion of guac into his mouth. "She made everything you see here."

"That's insane. You think I'm going to believe that? What do you think I am? Some blond-haired twit?"

"What? You don't believe me, huh?"

"No, I don't."

Riverstone met her doubt head on. "Okay, what do you want for dessert? Name it, and she'll make it for you," Matthew boasted.

"Even if it's forbidden?"

"Even better."

"Tiramisu," she ordered. "Forbidden enough for you?"

"From the Florence region or Southern Italy around Naples?" Matthew asked.

Phoebe laughed out loud at the absurdity. "The chefs at Wolfgang's couldn't do that!"

"Northern or Southern, Phoebs?" Matthew insisted again.

She took the challenge. "Southern, only instead of Naples, I want it from Sorrento."

Matthew smiled like someone holding four aces. "With a small glass of Limoncello as a chaser?"

"Of course."

A whole minute went by, that turned into fifteen. It seemed every second that went by without the droid only added to the tension. Phoebe broke the tension with a small joke. "Shame's thugs must have caught Alice raiding the cocoa powder."

To that Matthew said with self-assurance, "That would never happen." Another half minute went by, and Alice finally emerged from another direction with a dessert plate in one hand and a small glass of yellow substance in the other. "Ah, there she is. I think she had to nab a few of your lemons first. I hope that's okay?"

Phoebe tapped the table with her dessert fork. "Anything for the cause."

Alice placed the dessert and drink in front of Phoebe. She toyed with it with her fork but didn't indulge. She looked around her yard like she was searching for some hidden camera videoing her doing something illegal.

"Go on, no one is watching us," Matthew assured her.

Phoebe offered her fork to Matthew. "You first."

Matthew happily took the fork and sliced through the layers of mascarpone cheese, cocoa, and coffee flavored layers of Italian cake. Sliding his tongue across his lips, he announced, "Not bad. The Northern has a little more cocoa, but I like this. Not bad," he said, returning her fork.

"You're so full of it, Matthew." She dove into the layers and took a bite of the Italian sweetness. She gasped. "That's it! That's from Sorrento. I'll never forget that taste. It was so perfect then, and now this…" She picked up the Limoncello and sipped. "Oh my God! Are you kidding me? Chilled to perfection, too. How did you do that?"

Matthew played innocent. "It wasn't me, Phoebs. It was Alice."

Phoebe kept shaking her head. "This is stupid. Stupid! Stupid! I can't believe this is happening. And you!" she said, pointing her fork between his eyes. "You're crazy, you know that? Why are you doing this to me?"

Riverstone came out of his chair, stood her up, and kissed her while she still held onto her fork. "Because you're hot, you're beautiful, funny, marvelously intelligent, quirky, crazy, and not a bad actress, from what I understand."

She kinked her head up. She was a tall, five-foot ten-inches, but he was a foot taller, like looking up at a point guard for the Lakers. He was three times her size, too, and not an ounce of fat on him. "I'm supposed to die in a few weeks. So how do I look now?" Phoebe asked.

He brushed back the hair that had fallen across her face. "Like you need a swim to calm down."

Still in his arms, she said, "But I thought you don't like dirty water."

"I don't."

She turned to the pool. The water was crystal clear and not one speck of dirt or broken pot anywhere. So many odd things were happening around her, she became numbed by their effects. "Alice again?"

"She's a little obsessive-compulsive that way."

"Did you bring a bathing suit?" Phoebe asked.

Matthew moved his eyebrows up and down. "I forgot, but Alice—"

Phoebe cut him off, as she pointed at the fern. "Alice!" she ordered sternly, "Don't move!"

47

Butts

Fururamami Beach
Zamami Island, East China Sea

DODGE AND HIS team of beasts and men made it to the south tip of the island before noon. The jungle was insufferably hot and infested with blood sucking insects so big they could have been made at Lockheed. If it weren't for their SIBAs, sloshing through the island jungle would have been excruciatingly difficult. Upon reaching the shore, the cats kept to the shade of the coconut palms, while the humans dove in the ocean to cool off with their clothes on. Mowgi parked himself near Molly and Rhud in the shade. Earthly weather never seemed to affect him. Whether the climate was desert hot or arctic cold, it was always 72 degrees as far as he was concerned.

A machete wielding island gang greeted them as they came out of the water, looking for whatever they had of value, their weapons for starters. Dodge walked up to the gang of six and said quite calmly, "We're looking for an American who might have crash landed here six years ago—"

The gang leader barked, "Hand over your weapons, kid, or be shot," nodding behind at the three other gang members hidden in the jungle undergrowth with their AK-47s pointed right at them.

With blinding speed Dodge drew and fired three shots, melting the barrel ends of their AKs. The gang, seeing they were totally defenseless against the stranger's pistol, tried to run, but Molly and Rhud cut them off. The leader, in a futile attempt to protect himself, pointed his machete at Rhud's nose.

Dodge came to the leader's side. "If you threaten him, he will swallow you whole, and use your blade for a toothpick."

The others dropped their machetes immediately, but the leader continued to hold his, more out of fear than rational thought. "He will kill me anyway. I will die an honorable death by a beast so magnificent."

"What's your name?" Timmer asked.

"Butts."

The three glanced at each other, trying not to laugh.

"Butts?" Timmer repeated.

"Yes, I am called Butts. You have a problem with that?"

Before things got out of hand over Butt's name, Dodge intervened and said, "Listen, no one has to die. The cats are with us. Sheath your blade, and they will not harm you or your men. All we want is to locate our friend. Help us, and you can go."

"Except Butts," Searle said, as he relieved the leader of his machete. "He stays with us. If he wants to lead us down a rat hole, we'll let him die . . . honorably."

Dodge agreed. He opened a pouch and showed Butts a picture of Braxton. "Have you seen this guy?"

"No," Butts replied, a little too fast. The look in his eyes told them he knew something about the picture that he wasn't telling them.

Searle took over at this point. He had experience squeezing bad guys. "See that mutt over there, Butts. He's our lie detector. Tell us the truth and he barks once…"

Dodge cut in. "It's more like a yip, Robby."

After being corrected, Searle went on with Butts. "Okay, he yips once for—"

"Twice for yes," Dodge corrected again.

Searle faced Dodge. "That doesn't make sense. Everyone knows that once is yes."

Dodge shrugged. "What can I tell ya? Where he comes from two yips is a yes."

Searle sighed at Mowgi, then went back to Butts. "Just tell us what you know and," he waved at Dodge, "he'll translate." He held up the picture again for Butts. "You've never seen this guy, huh?"

"No," Butts replied again.

Mowgi yipped once.

"That's a lie," Dodge translated.

"Try again, Butts, or we'll hand you over to the mutt. Did I tell you he hates liars? I mean, eats liars?"

Butts let go a short laugh. "Too bad."

Searle went back to Dodge and asked, "How do you get him to, you know, get big?"

"Just ask him," Dodge replied.

"No magic words like abrocodabra?" Searle wondered.

"Nope."

Searle faced the undog and said, "Show Butts your alter ego, Mowg."

Dodge pulled Searle and Timmer back a ways to give Mowgi room to expand. As the undog grew, saliva dripped from his swelling green tongue, sizzling the sand. The other gang members took off screaming. They didn't even seem to care about the tigers anymore.

Timmer commented to Dodge, "He is frightening."

Dodge looked on with controlled amazement. "You don't know the half of it." He took Butt's machete from Searle and placed it where drops of Mowgi's slobber could hit it. The spit ate right through the steel. "How's your honorable death look now, Butts?" Dodge asked him.

Butts couldn't shut up. He described everything he knew about the plane that crashed years ago, when he was just a kid. As he went on with his story, Mowgi returned to his small size, yipping mostly twice whenever Searle would ask for confirmation on Butts' story. If Butts did stray from the truth, a single one yip gave him a shot of religion, and he quickly returned to honesty.

Searle pointed south, across a long sandbar that served as a shallow land bridge to another island. "You're telling us he's over there?"

"Yes, he is there. You will see," Butts stated.

Searle looked at Mowgi. "Do we let him go, Mowgi?"

When the undog yipped twice, Butts' collapsed in the sand, relieved that his fate was not in a pile of sticky goo.

* * *

They left Butts where he fell and sloshed their way the few hundred yards across the shallow sandbar to the other island. It was part of the same chain of islands, so the terrain was much like what they had already crossed, except there were no roads cutting through the dense jungle to shorten their journey. They had to make their own way, breaking trail the old fashioned way, using the machetes the gang had obligingly left behind in the sand. Molly and Rhud made their own paths. Traipsing through the thick jungles was natural for them. They would disappear for a short time then return from nowhere just when Dodge began to worry about them. Mowgi, however, stayed with the team, preferring to walk behind and let them do the clearing for him. After three straight hours of cutting, they were still only a quarter of the way through the island. It was already dark, so Dodge called it a day. They made camp, hanging their jungle sleeping hammocks from trees, rather than on the ground, where hungry land crabs ate their way across the jungle floor at night. By morning, the continuous jungle sounds of crickets, birds cawing, and flying insects suddenly went silent. Timmer awoke in a start from the abrupt soundlessness.

"Pssst," Timmer whispered over to Dodge. "Hear that?"

Dodge peered through the mesh of his hammock at a hundred plus pairs of eyes looking at them. "Yeah, we have company," he whispered back.

48

Code is Law

WKBZY TV Building
290 N. Foster Rd.
Dothan, Alabama

*N*O ONE WOULD ever suspect the small, southern city of Dothan, Alabama was the home of North America's most powerful banker and financier. The tallest office building in the city stood unassumingly at seven stories high in the middle of town. Granted, it was small by any city standards, but perfect for Richard Tucker who owned it. His chief concern was keeping his vast holdings of timber, cattle, real estate, railroads, shipping fleets, South African diamond mines, and most importantly, his domestic and global banks discreet. Tucker Corporation made no Fortune 500 list of the world's wealthiest companies, or America's either. He was on no one's list. Although he was, by far, the richest individual in the country, surpassing Buffet, Gates, and Bezos by over a hundred and fifty billion dollars, being isolated from the public eye allowed him to lead a normal life of anonymity, far from the noise of the mainstream media and the ruckus of big city scrutiny. He owned five-star hotels by the bucket full in New York, Chicago, Los Angeles, Atlanta, and Dallas, and wanted nothing to do with their daily operations. Power was his goal. Pulling the strings of his puppets was his thrill. Judges, U.S. Senators, Governors, Congressmen, and CEOs of top corporations in the world were all his marionettes, and he was their undisputed master. Even the President for Life was at his beck and call.

The day began on a downward trajectory the moment Papa had awakened him at three a.m. with the bad news; the Gamacoin had now infected their Asian banks, and people were withdrawing their funds and placing them into the new untraceable, unhackable G-coin, which was more secure than any bank. The Gamacoin exchanges that had sprung up overnight around the globe were a feeding frenzy of monetary conversion, 24 hours a day. Du Bear banks were losing a billion dollars every day, and increasing. Losses at Tucker Corporation banks were no less painful. In the last five days, to help stop the bleeding, his Dothan home office closed a record 190 branches in Mexico, Puerto Rico, and Panama alone. The following week it would be closing another 460 more from California to Florida. Unless the Gamacoin obsession was stopped, by month's end Tucker Corporation's Du Bear holdings would need to be liquidated in order to stay solvent. Today's meet up on the seventh floor war room was a make or break moment for the North American arm of the Zmaji Cartel. What happened here today would also affect Du Bear's worldwide stranglehold on the planet.

Zmaji representatives from Du Bear, Switzerland, China, Brazil, India, Canada, and a special Zmaji tech from California's Silicon Valley, sat around the conference table with bottled water and yellow note pads in front of them. The three empty seats were from Russia, France, and the Vatican. They were late.

"Roxanne, honey, have you heard from the other members yet?" Tucker asked his secretary over the intercom.

"*No, Sir. As far as we know, they were en route and should have landed an hour ago. Even the Russians left early, but their jet dropped its locator signal over Greenland two hours ago. Strange, is it not, Mr. Tucker?*" Roxanne questioned.

"Very…" Tucker answered, and released the talk button, mumbling to himself, "Strange indeed." So much so, he knew it was not a coincidence.

Security was tight around The Tucker Building. No one entered the building, except those cleared by the cartel with both DNA and retina scans. Personal assistants and private security guards were prohibited. They had to remain inside their planes and were not allowed to disembark, or Tucker's elite mercenaries would shoot them.

When they could wait no longer, the lights dimmed, and Tucker called the meeting to order, minus the absent Cartel members. Time was critical. The Cartel had already suffered too many losses. Some doubted if they could even recover.

As the room darkened, their faces remained visible in the low light. It was the way Zmaji meet-ups began. It stood for the power they brandished behind the scenes, never exposed to the light of day. Leslie Cardé spoke first. She represented three of the largest business structures of the planet: drug, oil, and the media. "Why haven't we stopped this Gamacoin?" she asked the table. "This crypto-currency will be the end of the Cartel if we don't stop it. Must we shut down the Internet to eradicate it?"

A young California tech, Mozy Huddelston, known by everyone as Mo, spoke next. "It doesn't matter," he said calmly.

"What do you mean, it doesn't matter? It certainly does matter," Cardé shot back. "Without the control of the world's currency, we will lack the funds to place our people and control the governments. You know this, Mo. Without the banks, we're finished. Already, the island districts in the Caribbean have stopped taking our government-backed currencies. They now only accept gold, silver, and this Gamacoin. We must shut down the Internet and stop the transfer of our wealth from the central banks, or we will be little people, like the rest of society."

Mo looked smugly at the table of cheerless faces. "You could do that. You could shut down the Internet all day long, but it won't make any difference. Code is law. You can't change it. This coin is like gold and silver. The Gamacoin does not depend on the Internet to exist."

"The coin spread by the Internet, it can die by the Internet," said a voice from Asia.

Mo replied, "True. However, we are an Internet dependent world. To shut it down for even a few minutes would put businesses in a tailspin, including us. What you believe will solve our problem, would only make matters worse. Unlike our banks, the Gamacoin has no known source. It does not depend on any authority to make it work. Like I've been trying to explain to the members around this table, and to Papa, The Code rules because it has no governing body. It is everywhere and nowhere at the same time. And like precious metals, it is finite. Our research has discovered its limit of 21 million units. Once it reaches that limit—"

"It will die a happy death," Tucker quipped.

"Hardly. Each infinitesimally bit-sized coin will increase in value, and the more money your banks create out of thin air, Mr. Tucker, the more expensive the Gamacoin will become. It is a store of value that will not go away over time. If the Earth would suddenly go dark, the Gamacoin would survive. Let me repeat, the Gamacoin code is law. It will endure forever unless we can find its source."

"Destroy it then!" Tucker boomed. "Destroy every card out there. Pass laws to make it a crime against humanity."

"It doesn't matter," Mo countered. "We tried cutting the cards in tiny pieces like Mickey Mouse cut up the broomsticks in the movie Fantasia. And we all know what happened there."

"The splinters turned into more broomsticks," the man from India said correctly.

Mo giggled at the Indian. "Yes, a lot more. Go to the head of the class, Gandhi."

The Indian shot back hard. "Don't patronize me, Mo."

Tucker immediately sliced through the tension. "Get over it. We have more important things to worry about than bruised egos." Once the calm was restored, he asked the young man, "So you're telling us we're up the creek? There's no way to stop it?"

Mo replied, "Unless we can find the source of the G-coin, yeah, we're screwed. Our best minds have been unable to crack its code. It's beautiful beyond anything we've ever seen before."

Tucker grunted angrily. "Beautiful is not what I would call it, you little twit!"

Mo matched Tucker's scowl with his own. "Look, I can't help it if you don't like the messenger. That's your problem, Mr. Tucker. You buttheads are the ones who screwed things up when you became too greedy. What do you expect the world to do when people discover your banks have stolen their wealth? For them, this Gamacoin is survival."

Mo reached in his pocket and pulled out a blue card, waving it at their faces. "I have coins myself. Right here." He tossed it Tucker's way. "Go ahead. Tear it up. Burn it with a blowtorch. It won't make any difference. I'll get another card, put in my code that I keep right here," he pointed at his head, "and it will be like I never lost it. That card is society's survival, and they know it." He glared at the table. "You are all behind the power curve. This genie is out of the bottle worldwide. Like it or not, this crypto is the future, and we have to find a way to deal with it, or the Zmaji is finished as a cartel. They won't need us anymore. Banks will go the way of the horseless carriage, because the money supply will be theirs, not ours."

Changing the subject slightly, the Canadian asked, "Did the Wild Strain create this?"

Mo turned to the Canadian hearing something that made perfect sense for the first time. "The Wild Strain? What's that?"

The Brazilian replied, "We thought you knew. The Vatican Observatory discovered an alien ship that came to Earth two weeks—"

"Alien ship?" Mo was astounded that he had been kept in the dark about such an earthshaking event. "Why wasn't I informed of this?"

Cardé explained it was not the members' intention to keep him uninformed. They were waiting for confirmation that the ship was indeed of an extra-terrestrial origin before divulging their info to the group.

Mo glared up at the ceiling in disgust. "You idiots! Do you realize what you've done by not sharing this information with the science arm of the Zmaji? Idiots! Your arrogant secrecy has just signed our death warrants."

"It can't be that bad," Tucker retaliated.

"Oh yes, it can. What is this Wild Strain the Canuck mentioned? Some form of DNA?" Mo wondered.

"Why, yes," the Canadian replied surprised. "How did you know?"

Visibly upset, Mo angrily replied, "Again, it doesn't matter. You've already screwed this up royally, so tell me the rest, and don't leave out a single detail. I need to know everything!"

The Canadian glanced at Tucker and Cardé, who gave him the okay to proceed.

Mo shot back, "Don't look at them. Look at me. They don't know squat. Tell me what you know."

The Canadian went on describing how the Vatican members tracked the alien ship when it entered the solar system and landed in Nevada. Through sheer luck, two of the aliens foiled a kidnapping and left some of their body fluids behind. Swiss intelligence, at the direction of the Vatican, obtained and brought it back to Rome, where The Church scientists analyzed it.

The Canadian was about to continue, when Mo stopped him. "Don't tell me. Let me guess. They weren't purple people eaters with three eyes and bald heads. They looked and behaved just like us."

Cardé removed a couple of photos from a file and handed them to the techie. "Better than that. They were really hot young men."

Mo scrutinized the photos of the two young men at a fast-food restaurant and a second one of another tall young man with a big-eared, purple-haired mutt. "They're human, all right, but did anyone bother to check out the origin of that creature?"

The faces around the table said no.

Mo slapped the photo with the back of his hand. "Holy crap, people, are you that stupid not to recognize an alien species when it's staring you right in the face? There's not an animal on this planet that even comes close to looking like this thing. Where is this guy? Do we have him in custody?"

"No," Tucker mumbled.

"Why not?" Mo asked sharply.

Cardé added: "Nootzy's people tried to arrest him, but he shot fourteen Hoods before they could draw their weapons."

Mo was impressed. "FOURTEEN? Wow, that fast, huh?"

The Canadian added, "They may be human, but their DNA is different than ours. Church scientists likened their DNA to a wild dog found in South America."

Mo chuckled. "I get it now. What the Church is really saying is, they're scared they'll be put out of business like the rest of us, right?" The Canadian's silence answered his question. Mo tossed the photos back to Cardé , as he said to Tucker. "Cool, Tuck, now we're getting somewhere. We found the source of the Gamacoin, and it's these dudes."

Tucker accepted Mo's premise. "Bingo, Huddelston!"

Cardé put aside the bad news. She wanted a solution. "All right, we screwed up. It's done. As Mr. Tucker would say, the horses are out of the barn. What do we do now, Mr. Huddelston?"

Mo had two solutions, neither of which were acceptable. "We either make peace with these guys, or we kill them and destroy their ship, because obviously, the coin's power is the alien ship."

Tucker grunted his disdain for both alternatives, but he did have a third option for the table. "What if we kill them and take their ship? We'll have the best of both worlds: control of the Gamacoin and the power of the ship."

Mo pointed a finger at Tucker. "That would work, if you could capture it."

"Papa is working on it," Tucker added.

Mo had his doubts. "Good luck."

Cardé sighed, looking at the photos Mo had returned to her. She kinda liked the idea of having a couple of young aliens for pets. Knowing the futility of her dream, she said, "And so they're going to just hand over the keys, right Richard?"

Before Tucker replied, Mo had one big caution. "Don't treat these pretty faces lightly, people. They possess tech far beyond ours. No one wants our stinking dollars anymore. This Gamacoin has proved that. So whatever plan we have, it better be a good one, and one that won't fail. We won't get a second chance."

A heavy silence fell around the table. What else was there to say? The problem was identified. Its source was known. The only solution the Zmaji had left was to kill the human Wild Strain or die.

Tucker called on the Swiss member of the Cartel when he raised his hand. "You're on, Kaufman."

"*Ja! Ice tue*, Frau Cardé " Kaufman replied.

"In English, Herr Kaufman," Tucker snapped, weary of roadblocks to any solutions to his banks going into default.

"*Ja*, I do have an answer," Kaufman said with a heavy Swiss accent, "As you are aware, our FIS (Federal Intelligence Service) returned from the States two days ago."

Tucker interrupted. "Yeah, empty handed. They said a dragon chased them out of the desert. Now, that I can believe," he snarled.

Kaufman returned a self-assured grin. "Yes, but they also found a device that our researchers believe can help locate the alien ship."

Tucker traded doubtful glances with Cardé. "Well, where is it? Did you bring it with you or leave it in Zermatt?" Tucker asked.

"*Ja*, it is on my plane, Herr Tucker," Kaufman replied.

Tucker pressed an activator under his the table, and tall rock of a soldier in black fatigues, black boots, and a Glock sidearm, emerged from a hidden door somewhere in the dark. "Leader, here, will take you to the airport to retrieve the device. If it is what you say it is, Herr Kaufman, you can go home and continue sucking on your favorite schnapps." Tucker grabbed the soldier's sleeve. "Did you get that, Leader?"

In a low authoritarian voice, Leader replied, "Every word, Sir."

* * *

It took less than an hour for Leader to make the round trip to the airport and bring the device back to Tucker. No one left the meeting. They wanted to see the device that would save them from themselves. Leader put the Samsonite case on the table.

"This is it?" Tucker asked, touching the case and unlatching it.

"YesSir," Leader replied, standing at a soldierly attention.

"Did you open it?" Tucker asked, wondering if Leader had checked it for any explosive device. He had enemies, lots of them, even within the Zmaji, who wanted him off the power grid.

"Good to go, Sir. Checked it myself."

"What do you make of it, Leader?" Tucker asked, opening the lid. "It looks like something my grandson made with a science kit."

"DuckFart examined it, Sir."

"That's your whiz kid, right?"

"Tops in his field, Sir. He checked it over. It's the real deal."

The techie removed the device from the box and began securitizing the instrument. After a few minutes, he agreed. "Wow, I'm impressed. It's some kind of gravity wave device. Cool. If it works, and that's a big if, and if that alien ship is as big as Ms. Cardé 's files suggest, this device will locate it. All we have to do is get within twenty miles of the thing, and we'll have her."

Tucker shut the case and snapped the latch shut. "Take this back to DuckFart, and let him play with it a while. I don't want him learning on the job."

"I'll tag along for backup," techie volunteered.

"Good idea," Tucker agreed.

"Everyone set?"

"YesSir, good to go. We have a C-130 ready at the airport."

"Nevada?"

"No, Sir, Burbank. We need to pick up some insurance first, before Nevada."

Tucker smiled greedily. "I like your style, Leader, get 'er done. There will be a huge bonus for everyone, and triple for you, when we capture that salad plate."

Leader picked up the case and headed for the secret door along with techie. "YesSir."

49

Throwing Bananas

Du Bear Bank, U.S.A.
New York Main Branch
New York City, N.Y.

IT WAS HIGH noon in mid-town Manhattan. The skies were clear and reasonably clean after an early drizzle. Harlowe couldn't ask for a better day to be holding hands with Leucadia along Fifth Avenue, one of America's most expensive streets. Fresh from the clothiers, he wore a sharp, dark blue suit with subtle grey pinstripes, that had been custom tailored for him at Martin Greenfield Clothiers in New York City. It wasn't the first time he had ever worn a suit. Several times, in the days before *Millawanda*, when they were first dating, he had to wear a suit just to get in the door with Leucadia at the elite restaurants she frequented. Still, an $18,000 suit was no substitute for his surf-worn No Fear swim trunks or an In-N-Out double-double, fries, and a shake. They walked from the Wollman Ice Skating Rink in Central Park where they landed their Orixy transport. The platform was fast and easy. Its stealth properties allowed them to fly a thousand miles per hour across the country with ease, without being detected. Right now they were on their way to Du Bear Bank to open an account. If they had time, and he would make sure they did, he wanted a few slices of New York Pizza before returning to Nevada. It was the last item on his bucket list. After that, whatever Leucadia wanted to do, he was just along for the ride.

So far, their return to New York City was a huge disappointment. The Wollman skating rink, where they spent their one and only Christmas together, had closed for good. The ticket office windows were broken, graffiti-sprayed walls defiled the rink, and tall weeds were sprouting between the cracks in the concrete walks. And oh my God, the odor of human waste everywhere.

"Remember when we came here last Christmas?" Leucadia asked, when they first stepped off the platform an hour ago.

"You mean twelve years ago," Harlowe reminded her.

Leucadia laid her head against his shoulder. "Hmmm…the snow was coming down in big, fluffy flakes that winter, and you tried to do a full, flying twist and fell flat on your back."

Harlowe stretched one way and then the other like he was working out a kink. "Embarrassing."

Leucadia caressed his head. "You poor thing. Does it still hurt?"

"Scarred for life."

She pulled him down and kissed his head. "Does that help?"

"A little."

* * *

They kept walking. It seemed the "out-of-business" storefronts outnumbered the ones still open, but now with reduced hours. Nine to one in the afternoon was common. "How long will this take?" Harlowe asked, loosening the tight collar and tie away from his neck.

Leucadia, dressed to the hilt as usual, had no trouble trading in her Gamadin uniform for a black Dara Lamb suit, with an all cotton, white and black polka dot blouse and matching Manolo stilettos. "Not long," she replied. "Depends on how many ID checks they're going to make us hop through." They came to the front of one of the tallest buildings on the Avenue. "Here we are," she said, looking seventy-two stories straight up.

Harlowe grunted. "Nice place," he remarked, unimpressed by the gold leaf, brass, smoked glass, and Vermont granite siding. If there were a beach nearby, he might have given it more thought.

She fixed his tie and straightened his collar, making sure there was nothing out of place. "You are so handsome in a suit," she purred.

"How about when I'm not in a suit?"

Her green eyes sparkled. "I'll never tell."

"I bet you say that to all your Captains."

"Only one."

"Good answer," Harlowe said, playfully high-fiving her.

She stared at the giant, solid gold Du Bear Bank marquee and commented disapprovingly. "Mars Corp used to own this entire block."

"You think they'll recognize you?" Harlowe asked.

Leucadia opened her purse and put on a pair of designer sunglasses. "Recognize me now?"

Harlowe grinned. "I would recognize that body all the way from Pluto."

"Lets hope they're not as observant as you."

Harlowe opened the door for her, and they walked into the lobby. A customer service woman met them inside the foyer and asked if she could be of assistance. "New accounts, please," Leucadia replied.

She led them to a middle-aged man with stylish grey hair. "This is Mr. Ellingsen. He will help you with your new account."

After the normal introduction Harlowe asked Mr. Ellingsen if he was the same Bruce Ellingsen who pitched for the Dodgers. "That's me. Not a lot of people remember me, nowadays," Ellingsen admitted. But he was genuinely delighted that Harlowe recognized him.

"My pals and I do. You had the biggest banana curve I've ever seen," Harlowe said.

"You saw me throw? That was years ago, son. You probably weren't even born yet."

A sharp elbow from Leucadia told him to watch his conversation. "Old films. My dad had a collection, and you were in it."

"A Dodger fan, huh?"

"Big time. He nicknamed my brother Dodger after the team."

Ellingsen beamed with pride and offered them both chairs. "Please, sit down Mr. Py…"

"Pylott. Harlowe Pylott," Harlowe said, helping Leucadia first, then taking a chair himself.

"What can I help you with today?" Ellingsen asked.

"We want to open an account at your bank," Leucadia said.

"Have you banked with us before?"

"No," Leucadia replied, "this our first account here."

"Are you married?"

Harlowe covered his mouth to hide his laugh as Leucadia answered for them, "No, I'm Mr. Pylott's personnel assistant."

The way Ellingsen's eyes ogled Leucadia, then back to Harlowe, there was little doubt that he knew they were an item. "I see. And how much will you be depositing with us today?"

"One hundred million should do for a start," Leucadia said in all seriousness.

Harlowe thought he might have to catch Ellingsen before he fell over backwards in his chair.

After he collected his thoughts, Ellingsen asked, "You have those kinds of funds to transfer?"

Leucadia removed a blue card and handed it over to Ellingsen. "It's all there in the card."

Ellingsen studied the card in wonder. "I've never seen a card like this. Where did you get it?"

"It's made special for my Gamadin Corporation," Harlowe replied.

"And what is your occupation, Mr. Pylott?" Ellingsen asked.

"Space travel," Harlowe replied.

Leucadia handed over a file from her purse. "Here are all the documents you need to verify Mr. Pylott identification."

Ellingsen leafed through them, making sure each document was authentic and notarized. "Everything seems in order."

"It is, Mr. Ellingsen, I assure you," Leucadia said.

Ellingsen closed the file and laid it on his desk. "I guess all we need to do now is transfer the funds."

Leucadia tapped the top of the blue card on his desk. "Go ahead, Mr. Ellingsen, we have a 4:31 flight to catch."

"Of course." Ellingsen brought his reader closer and punched in the new account number along with his own security code. When the flashing green light went steady, he asked, "Would you like to do the honor, Ms…"

"Ms. Mars. Ms. Leucadia Mars. No, you go right ahead, Mr. Ellingsen."

Harlowe pointed a finger at Ellingsen. "As long as you don't transfer the Gamacoins to your Cayman Island account, that is, Mr. Ellingsen."

Ellingsen's face suddenly lost its color.

Harlowe tapped the reader. "That's okay, Mr. Ellingsen, we all have our little secrets, don't we?" Ellingsen nodded, his mouth open and dry. Harlowe winked. "And yours is safe with us, Sir. Go ahead. Transfer a few thou for baseball. My dad would love that. We'll never tell."

Ellingsen nervously slid the card through the reader and waited for the green light to go steady again. After checking the balance in the new account, Ellingsen confirmed, "It's all there, Mr. Pylott."

Harlowe rose, taking the card back. He handed it off to Leucadia and said, "Well, enjoy my money, Mr. Ellingsen, it was a pleasure to meet you." Harlowe tossed him a fake pitch and added, "It's good for the circulation."

* * *

Ellingsen watched the couple leave, all the way out the door. He looked around to see if anyone was watching before he asked himself, "How did he know about the Caymans?"

50

Braxton

Amuro Island
East China Sea

THE BIG MAN with an AK-47 motioned for Searle, Dodge, and Timmer to drop down from their sleeping hammocks. Although their spears, blowguns, and AKs would never penetrate their SIBAs, and their numbers were no real threat, either, since the weapons they had, and the animals in the bushes could easily take out the whole lot of them, they followed orders with no resistance. The Team was after information, not confrontation.

For the most part, the natives were young, darkly tanned, and oriental in appearance. They were shirtless and barefoot, but they wore normal shorts and a variety of cutoff pants, which seemed odd for the jungles of a secluded island like Amuro. They were also quite fit, like swimmers. A few wore gold and silver earrings, some even had gold necklaces, but most had charms and ornaments made of seashells. The fact that none of them had bones through their noses was a relief to Timmer, who whispered, "They don't appear to be cannibals."

Timmer had obviously seen too many jungle horror films. A scowl from Searle told him to zip it.

"Braxton," Dodge said aloud to the group. He didn't know who the leader was, but when a shaved head guy in his mid-twenties stepped forward, parting a sea of natives, he felt he was talking to the right guy. "Braxton," Dodge repeated. "We are looking for Braxton."

"I don't think he understands English," Timmer whispered.

"I understand English just fine," the front man said in an obvious New York accent.

Searle made a guess, "Brooklyn?"

"Queens, 113th Street. Now tell me why I shouldn't kill you three right now?" Frontman threatened.

Dodge replied coolly. "Because even if you could kill us, our animals would eat you. Not a good way to start a friendship. Right, guys?" he said to Timmer and Searle.

"Horrible. Definitely not a good way to go," Searle confirmed.

Frontman looked around and smiled. "What animals?"

Dodge nodded behind Frontman. "That one there," he said, pointing out the massive white tiger with bright blue eyes, staring at Frontman like he was the next meal. "Or that one over there. She loves dark meat."

Frontman and his band froze. Out of fear, an islander fired off a long lance at Rhud. Dodge blew it away before it had hardly left his hand, impressing even Searle and Timmer. "Tell your boys to stand down or it won't be pretty." Suddenly, from out of the jungle, a huge, saliva dripping purple monster came through the canopy, breaking branches as it stepped into the clearing, overshadowing them all. "Oh, I'm sorry. I forgot Mowgi. He doesn't care about white or dark meat. He just likes to eat."

In his native tongue Frontman ordered everyone to drop their weapons. NOW!

Searle stepped forward to relieve Frontman of his AK, but Dodge motioned to let him keep his weapon as he asked for the third time, "Braxton?"

Frontman pointed his AK at a jungle path where Molly stood in the way. "Don't worry about her, pal," Timmer warned, "worry about your head if you lead us to anywhere else but to Braxton."

Dodge pushed Frontman forward. "After you, big guy."

* * *

A few yards away, mushing through the jungle became easy. Frontman led them to a path that seemed well used. The Team followed next, followed by Mowgi and the rest of the natives with their eyes wide, alternating between the tigers walking beside them and the canopy, searching for the dragon they knew was still out there, lurking. Everyone was allowed to keep their weapons, with the understanding that one misstep would cost them their lives. With the fear of a gruesome death hanging over their heads, no one made any attempt at martyrdom. After another hour of walking, they came to an island village the Team found astonishing. They were expecting movie set grass huts, lean-tos, or at the very least, something fabricated out of driftwood and tied together with braided palm leaves. Not so. The structural layout of the village and how the huts were built put all their preconceived ideas of island living to shame.

"This place rocks!" Timmer exclaimed, clearly impressed by the huts that were raised several feet off the sand. They were more like small cabins, nestled under tall, spreading, tropical trees to protect the occupants from the hot sun. The walls and roofs of the cabins were made of bundled palm leaves over a superstructure of tough, three-inch thick bamboo, tied together with palm rope. Inside, the flooring was tightly woven strips of grass. There were no glass windows. Instead there were square, shuttered openings, that allowed a cool cross breeze to enter and exit the cabin. An island stream running through the village provided plenty of water. Downstream, a water wheel provided the energy needed to power a small generator for the pump that fed water to a hidden field a short distance away, where they grew a variety of fruit bearing trees, pineapple, and all kinds of edible plants. At ground level, walking through the village, there was plenty to see, but because the cabins, fields, and activity took place under the canopy, prying satellites shooting pictures of the island from above would be hard pressed to see anyone was living there.

"Holy moly—" Timmer about lost it, when his find-the-prettiest-babe-on-the-island radar suddenly zeroed in on a gorgeous black-haired number walking by. She had come from the orchard of mango trees, carrying what appeared to be a heavy basket of fruit. As she gracefully sauntered by, everything about her, her olive skin, her long silky hair, long dark legs, seashell necklace, and skimpy, colorfully flowered sundress, froze Timmer in place. And when she gave him a jaw-dropping smile, he couldn't help himself. He rushed to her side and asked with a beam in his eyes, "Can I help you with this, Miss?"

She giggled and trotted off into the village, leaving Timmer wanting more...a lot more.

Timmer went back to Dodge and Searle. "Did you see that?"

Dodge replied, "Awesome."

Searle pointed at Timmer's chin. "Wipe that drool off. You're embarrassing us."

Timmer stepped in front of them. "Babes like that are only found in dreams, guys. Maybe she has sisters." Suddenly the search for Braxton had taken a back seat.

Always the business mind of the three, Searle said, "Stay focused, Lane, this isn't the time for trolling."

Timmer kept his eye on the target. "There's always time for trolling, Captain."

Frontman interrupted the conversation to inform Dodge that Braxton was ready to see him, but Searle and Timmer had to stay behind. "Only you are allowed," Frontman said.

Dodge told them not to worry. He was taking Mowgi with him. Maybe so, but just to be safe, Searle wondered where the cats were. He figured they were close by, but where? He was still uneasy with knives and spears still in the hands of the natives. Timmer, on the other hand, wasn't at all worried about the cats. His only concern was the location of the mango girl.

"They're always close, Captain," Dodge replied, and then he and the undog went off with Frontman.

* * *

Frontman led Dodge to a field where several people in white linen shirts were kneeling on the ground, attending to the lines of healthy green crops. The corn was especially tall and heavy, with thick ears pointing skyward. Dodge was envious of the yield, since he was only able to grow corn half that size in the mine.

"Sir," Frontman said respectfully to a man on his knees, pulling weeds.

A man in his fifties turned to him. It was difficult to tell with the thick, dark beard covering his face whether he was Braxton or not. The man was slender and fit. It was hardly a body that had suffered over years on an isolated island in the East China Sea. However, he nodded, accepting the interruption, as he scrutinized Dodge.

Frontman stood back a distance, giving them privacy. Extending his hand, Dodge asked, "Are you Braxton?" The man sat crossed-legged on the ground and offered Dodge a place next to him. The undog wagged his whippy little tail, and completely out of character for him, leaped into the man's lap. Dodge smiled. "Yeah, you're Braxton. Mowgi would never do that to a stranger."

"Yes, I'm Braxton," the man admitted, continuing to stroke the undog. "I recognize you now. You're the hellion that gave the Secret Service fits playing hide and seek in the White House. My, how you've grown."

"I've calmed down a might since then, Sir."

"Leucadia? She...what happened to her?"

Dodge told Braxton all that he knew. For the most part, Braxton was caught up on the world news that was brought over from Zamami City. It was over a year after the crash that he learned of Delmonte and the fall of his administration. As for Leucadia, he never heard a word about her and Harlowe. The short version, for now, was they had returned from a long journey to fix *Millawanda*, but at a cost, losing a eleven years of Earth history, and found a planet full of corruption and imminent war.

"So why find me?" Braxton asked.

"To bring you home, Sir. Leucadia needs you."

Braxton smiled pleasantly. "She believes I'm alive?"

"She doesn't know for sure, but she knew you. She felt if anyone could survive a hit job, it was you."

"We were fortunate. We ditched our plane in the bay out there," he said, waving at the ocean, "with only two lives lost." He wiped his nose before saying, "They were good people, too. The ten of us who survived are still here, rescued by the fellow who brought you here and his village." Braxton made a sly grin. "You must have really scared him to give us up so easily."

Dodge smiled back. "It wasn't his fault. Mowgi and the cats have a way about them."

"So I've heard."

"So you'll come with us, Mr. Braxton?" Dodge asked.

Braxton looked across the field at a beautiful oriental woman in a straw hat surround by kids, who were helping her tend the tall shoots of sugar cane. "I have a wife and three children. They're the only things important to me now. The thought of returning to Washington has no place in my life, son."

Even if he could, Dodge would not try to talk him out of it. This was Braxton's home. Over the years, his priorities had obviously changed. Here was a small, peaceful community. He worked with his hands, grew his own food, fished, swam in a clean sea, and lived happily with a wife who loved him and his children. Why would anyone want to go back to politics, power, and dishonesty only to be a hunted man again, and possibly spend the rest of his life in jail?

"You're doing the right thing, Mr. Braxton. I don't blame you at all," Dodge told him.

He looked around at his little paradise. "Thank you for understanding." Braxton stood up and helped Dodge to rise with a strong hand. "In the meantime, please enjoy our hospitality for as long as you want. I'm sure you and the two young men with you could use some rest."

"Yes, we would like that."

"The cats? Are they nearby?" Braxton asked, as they strolled along a bushy path to the village.

"Yes, Sir."

"Can you call them? I've heard so much about them from Leucadia. I would like to see them."

"They can be quite frightening, Mr. Braxton, especially to the villagers. They are not like any cat on this planet, Sir."

Braxton eyed his children splashing across the nearby stream. They seemed so innocent and free of fear, and re-thought his request. "Perhaps you're right."

"We could meet with them privately, though," Dodge suggested.

Braxton was ecstatic. "Wonderful. A little later, perhaps. After breakfast?"

Dodge stepped toward a thick overgrowth and pulled back some of its fronds. "How about now, Sir?"

"Oh, my God!" Braxton cried out, grabbing his chest. "I see what you mean."

"Mr. Braxton, meet Molly." As he pulled more branches, there were three small children riding on her back, surprising even Dodge. "I guess they haven't frightened the children much." Rhud was right behind them, with four more youngsters on his back.

Braxton went over to Molly and began stroking her mane of soft white fur, as he looked up at her glowing blue eyes and listened to her purr. "I've never seen such beautiful animals. They're huge, and even more magnificent than I ever imagined."

"Yes, they are."

51

The Interview

HARLOWE'S STOMACH WAS growling. All he could think about since leaving the bank was the dripping, gooey, cheesy slices of New York pizza: tomato sauce, oregano, mozzarella, on a thin, crisp, stone baked crust that was like no other in the world. When they walked in to Marty's Pizza Diner, incredibly, it was lunchtime, and yet, the diner was void of patrons.

Harlowe was about to ask where everyone was, since the last time he and Lu were there the place was packed. But behind the counter, the girl's sad face spoke volumes. He had seen the same face at Bunker Burgers and a number of businesses where he recently traveled across the nation. Marty's Pizza was only one of the thousands of businesses affected by the depression.

Looking down at the selection of pizzas, Harlowe saw how small the pies had become. Back in the day they were twenty inches across and thick with toppings. But now, the selection was slim and the size was cut down to a small eight-inch pie. Nevertheless, Harlowe salivated over the entire line up of three pies under the heat lamps.

"Can I help you?" the girl asked.

Harlowe couldn't make up his mind, so the answer was simple. "I'll take them all," he replied, waving his hand over the pies.

"A slice of each?" she asked.

Leucadia answered for him. "No, whole ones. He'll have them all."

The girl's eyes went wide. "Will you be sharing?"

"No, they're all his, but you can give me that salad bowl, please," Leucadia replied, pointing at the glass refrigerator door.

The girl tallied the purchase on her display and said, "That will be $230.25, please."

Harlowe was astounded. He felt like he had a dot on his forehead the read "sucker." "You're joking?"

"Plus a 25% city tax," she added.

Leucadia was more practical. "How much does the diner take in?"

"I'm not sure, ma'am. My dad handles those kinds of things. But he says that after we pay for all the city, state, and federal taxes, there's not much left."

Harlowe handed her his Gamacoin card. She looked it over and said, "I've never seen a card like this. I'm not sure we take this."

Leucadia explained, "It's new. Your card scanner should handle it just fine."

The girl inserted the card into the scanner, and it was recognized immediately. "Oh my," she said surprised. "that was fast. It usually takes a full minute or two to post the funds."

"Like I said, it's new," Lu said, taking the card back from the girl.

Harlowe carried the stack of pizza boxes to a round table by the window, where they had a good view of Central Park. He gave Leucadia her salad first, then dove into his pepperoni and cheese. He bit down and closed in eyes in ecstasy. "This is sooooo good," he cooed. By the time Leucadia took her second bite of salad, Harlowe had plowed through his pepperoni and was halfway through the Hawaiian pineapple and ham, when a reporter and his camera crew entered the diner. It was easy to see the reporter was an ex-football player type: thick neck, broad shoulders, size 19 shoes, who towered over his camera crew by over a foot. He paid for everyone's meal and took the table next to Harlowe and Leucadia. It wasn't long before the entire crew, including the reporter, began staring at Leucadia like she was eye-candy.

"You folks enjoying the city?" the reporter asked.

"Just arrived," Leucadia replied.

"Whereabouts?"

Harlowe and Leucadia traded glances. "West," Leucadia answered.

"West? Flew in this morning then?"

Harlowe opened his third box. "Yes, a lot has changed since we were here last," he replied, and asked the reporter what happened to the ice rink in the park.

"No funds to keep it up," the reporter replied, indifferently.

"How can a city that charges a 25% sales tax run low on money?" Harlowe inquired.

"The wealthy are leaving. Taxes right? They don't want to pay the freight. So they leave because they have connections, or they pay the freight."

Harlowe responded with an sensible fix. "So lower the taxes."

"Then who would pay for the police and fire and all the other services the communities need?" the reporter retorted.

"If you don't lower the costs of living here, you won't have a community to service, dude," Harlowe explained.

The reporter looked outside with pride. "They'll always be a New York."

"That's what they thought about Rome, too," Leucadia said, "but when they raised taxes beyond what people could pay, Rome fell from a city of beauty and a million inhabitants, to a rat-infested city of 15,000 in a few short decades."

Harlowe looked across the street. "That ice rink over there? Think of it as Rome."

"So what would you do to fix it, young man?" the reporter said.

"Well, for starters—" Harlowe began.

The reporter held him up. "Do you mind if we get this recorded?"

Harlowe liked the idea. "Sure. Go for it."

The reporter reached out to introduce himself. "My name is Michael

Stenkman. I'm a reporter for the New York Daily."

After Harlowe responded in kind, introducing himself, Leucadia asked, "Does Clarence Miller still own the newspaper?"

Stenkman seemed emotional about the question. "No, he was caught evading taxes. His newspaper and all his holding were forfeited to the government."

"I never knew Clarence to have a dishonest bone in his body. He was always very meticulous about such matters," Leucadia said.

"You knew him?"

"Yes, he was a very generous and kind man."

"Well, the authorities didn't think so, and now he's somewhere in a Federal prison in Colorado, I think someone said." He then asked Harlowe, "Ready?"

"Ready."

Stenkman motioned for his cameraman to begin recording. When the camera's red light switched on, Stenkman began the interview. "Hello and good evening New York, this is your man-on-the-street reporter, Michael Stenkman here. Today I'm at Marty's Pizza Diner on Fifth Avenue with a young couple from out West visiting our fair city for the first time."

"No, we've been here several times," Harlowe corrected.

Stenkman continued without missing a beat. "Welcome back, then ah…can you tell our audience your names?"

"Harlowe Pylott and Leucadia Mars," Harlowe replied, smiling innocently at the camera.

"Okay, Harlowe, when we were talking earlier, you felt the city had changed a great deal. Is that right?"

"Yes, it has, for the worse. We used to go to the skating rink in Central Park, and now it's closed. People are living in the Park in tent cities. That never happened before. Businesses are shutting down everywhere. We used to find pizza diners on every block. Now most are closed because they can't afford the taxes and regulations to stay open. So I'll ask you why have you allowed this to happen to your City, Mr. Stenkman?"

"Our City is still the best place in the country in which to live."

"By whose standards? Your corrupt city officials? They squeeze the taxpayers out of every dime they earn. They have large expense accounts and live in gated mansions with servants and chauffer-driven cars, all paid for by the revenue they steal from the people."

"How do you know this? New Yorkers elected their government and they believe they're doing a wonderful job."

"The elections were rigged, Mr. Stenkman. They've been rigged ever since Shame became President."

"Stop recording," Stenkman said to his cameraman. He said to Harlowe. ""Do you know what you're saying, son? The authorities can arrest you for inciting misinformation."

"What happened to freedom of speech, Mr. Stenkman?" Leucadia asked.

Harlowe added, "It's not misinformation if it's true, is it?"

"You can't prove the elections were rigged," Stenkman insisted.

"Turn the cameras on. I'll show you," Harlowe said.

A hushed fear came over Stenkman's face. "Can we talk about something else?"

"You asked. Are you scared of the truth?"

Leucadia saw something deeper. "No, it's not fear, Harlowe, Mr. Stenkman knows what you're saying is true. He can't report it, or his job is in jeopardy. Isn't that right, Mr. Stenkman?"

Stenkman looked at them both. "Who are you? You're not really tourists, are you?"

"Roll the camera, Mr. Stenkman, and we'll give you the story of the century," Harlowe said.

Stenkman looked on, feeling he was being taken for a sucker. "I'm supposed to believe my crew and I walk into a pizza diner, and out of the blue we meet a couple that can change the world?"

Harlowe smiled. "Roll the camera and find out. If what we say is nothing, then you don't have to run it on your newscast. But if you're as good a reporter as we think you are, you'll want to know what we know. Are you game, Sir?"

Stenkman went from friendly to serious in an instant. "Give me a hint at what you have first."

"Do you have a phone tied to the Internet?" Harlowe asked.

"Of course. Silly question."

"Look up Leucadia Mars. Tell us what it says."

Stenkman removed his cell from the breast pocket and spoke into the device, asking for any information on the individual Leucadia Mars. The search cautioned Stenkman there was so much data on the subject he needed to be more precise in his search. "Just give me a brief paragraph on the subject," Stenkman ordered.

The cell stated out loud, "Leucadia Mars, female, age unknown, daughter of Harry and Sook Mars of the Mars Corporation. After the untimely death of her parents, she became the world's richest individual. Her holdings included five casinos in Las Vegas, including Harry's Hotel and Casino, Mars Airlines, Mars Corporation and all it sub corporations, Mars Banking Corporation, Mars Land Holdings in all fifty states of the Union, two islands in the Hawaiian chain, four islands off the coast of China, three islands and one million acres in Antarctica, Mars Energy Conglomerate with oil field in—"

"Stop!" Stenkman called out, "I get it. This Mars lady was uber-rich. But it says here," pointing at his cell, "she disappeared eleven years ago, and all of her great wealth was forfeited to the state because she was part of the conspiracy to overthrow the government of the United States. So what does she have to do with us here today?"

"The conspiracy accusation was a complete fabrication," Leucadia said, forcefully.

"I'm sure. Everyone says that when they're guilty."

"But I was not guilty of anything."

The cameraman cracked, laughing, "Oh, so you're Leucadia Mars?"

Stenkman added, "Right. And I'm Santa Claus."

Harlowe pointed at Stenkman's phone. "Pull up her picture. See for yourself."

Stenkman tapped his screen, and a holographic image of Leucadia Mars hovered over the table for everyone to see.

"Wow!" the cameraman exclaimed. "She's hot!"

"Who's the dude with her?" a second assistant asked.

Stenkman and his crew had yet to connect the dots between Leucadia and the picture as he read the caption aloud. "It says he's a movie actor, Simon…" he hesitated, recalling the name vividly. "Bolt…"

Harlowe's nose crinkled up. Of all the photos of Leucadia on the Internet, the first one that popped up was the one where she and Simon were on a yacht together off the coast of Southern Italy. It was the cause of their breakup and the reason he never went to the prom that night because she went to Italy. Jewels, her human servant, stopped by his house and picked him up in the Mars' limo to console him, bringing a stack of In-N-Outs with him. But even burgers at the beach wasn't enough to soothe the pain in his gut that night.

"Bolt was super cool," a cameraman said. "He had some pretty good flicks. Got an Oscar, I think."

Stenkman grunted is disdain. "He was overrated."

"He kicked your ass, didn't he?" Harlowe said with a knowing grin.

The cameraman added, "Yeah, the story was all over the Hollywood Reporter. He made you a star, Stenkman."

"He sucker punched me when I wasn't looking," Stenkman defended.

Leucadia giggled as she removed her sunglasses. "That was a horrible picture."

The cameraman pointed. "Oh my God! That's her!"

"That's who?" Stenkman asked, still holding his cell with the holograph above it.

"It's Leucadia Mars, Stenkman!" the cameraman exclaimed. "Look at her eyes. It's her!"

Stenkman was stunned, but remained cool on the outside, as he said to her, "Well, it really is you, isn't it?" But as calm as he tried to be, it was obvious he knew he had stumbled onto something big.

Leucadia crossed her legs in a relaxed pose. "Yes, I am."

Stenkman gave a nod to his crewman, who suddenly had an urge to go to the bathroom. He excused himself and the girl behind the counter directed him to the back of the restaurant. While his assistant was gone, Stenkman began recording again, starting with her name.

"So why are you here in New York, Ms. Mars?"

"To reclaim my property which was stolen from me by the government and the banks," she replied.

"I thought the government seized your property when it was discovered the Mars Corporation was involved with President Delmonte's treason," Stenkman stated.

"There was never any trial," Leucadia countered.

"There must have been some type of hearing. The government can't just take property without due process."

"Look it up if you don't believe me. It's called Civil Asset Forfeiture. There was no trial, no hearing, no due process."

"So how do the banks enter into this? They don't have the power to seize property," Stenkman pointed out.

"The banks own the world, Mr. Stenkman. They are the masters. The government, the people who make the laws, create money, and tax you from the day you are born to the day you die, are all their puppets. Surely you must know that."

"They don't own me," Stenkman said frankly.

"Oh, do you own a car, a money card, make house payments, and do you have a student loan you're making payments on?" Leucadia asked.

"Yes, to all those questions, Ms. Mars. Most people do."

"Then you're a slave to them."

"I'm beholden to no one. I told you that."

"What would happen if you stopped making those payments?" Harlowe asked.

"Well, of course…"

Harlowe cut Stenkman off. "They would take it all away, wouldn't they?"

Stenkman straightened his back, "So what do we do about it?"

Harlowe replied calmly, as he bit into his third pie. "I'd get rid of the dragons."

"By dragons you mean the banks?"

Harlowe gestured a thumbs up, and replied, "We're on the same page."

"That's absurd. How would society function without the banks?"

Harlowe held up a blue Gamacoin card. "They would function just fine with a card like this. This will make banks everywhere obsolete."

"No way that would happen."

Harlowe continued: "Right now the central banks own the world. They are the masters of the planet. They make wars. Topple governments. Elect presidents. Buy politicians. Control markets. They make all the rules. This has been going on for centuries. Whoever controls the money, controls you. They're dragons, and they believe the Earth is theirs, Mr. Stenkman."

Stenkman sat back looking clever. "All right, say you had all the power in the world, Mr. Pylott. How would you go about ridding us of these dragons?"

"If I had all the power in the world, huh?" Harlowe asked.

"Yes, if you had all the power in the world, how would you deal with the dragons, Sir?" Stenkman questioned.

Harlowe smiled back. "I would gather them all up and take them someplace far away so they can't come back."

"And the politicians? You would take them, too?"

"I would start with them. They're the toe-jam of the dragons."

Stenkman laughed. "That is bold, Mr. Pylott, even if it is wacky. That's about as likely to happen as a flying saucer landing in Central Park."

"You don't believe in extraterrestrials, Mr. Stenkman?" Leucadia asked.

"No, I don't, Ms. Mars," Stenkman said firmly.

"Looks like we have a non-believer here, Lu," Harlowe said, as he handed her a glass of water.

"Stenkman has been selected for a trip to the International Space Station," the cameraman boasted.

Leucadia clapped. "Congratulations, Mr. Stenkman. You must be excited and honored?"

"This interview is not about me, it's about you two. I want to know more about you, Ms. Mars," Stenkman said. "Where have you been this last decade?"

"Traveling across the galaxy," Leucadia confessed, honestly.

"With Mr. Pylott, I presume?"

"Indeed. With Captain Pylott to be more precise."

Stenkman chuckled. "Oh, I suppose you're the captain of a spaceship, like that fraud Julian Starr?"

Harlowe looked at Leucadia first, before turning back to Stenkman. "How did you know?"

"And you're friends with Simon Bolt, right, Captain?"

"He's a member of my crew."

"And what crew is that?"

"The Gamadin crew. Our ship is called *Millawanda*."

"*Millawanda?* What kind of name is that?" he scoffed.

"A very old and proud name, Mr. Stenkman. A hundred-and-seventy-century-year-old name, to be exact."

"Your ship is 17,000 years old?"

"She just had a major tune up, so she's like brand new now."

"So you're an alien?"

"No, she is," Harlowe said, nodding at Leucadia. "Well, half an alien, anyway. Her dad was an Earthling."

"Where were you born, Captain?"

"Lakewood."

"Colorado?"

"California."

"Do you surf?"

"That's my passion."

"Now let me get this straight. You're a California surfer who commands a 17,000-year-old flying saucer with an Oscar-winning movie star, and one of the world's richest women as part of your crew?"

"You're batting a 1,000, Mr. Stenkman."

"That's such a crock of..." Stenkman started to say when a horde of dark grey utility vehicles came to a screeching halt in front of the pizza diner. Dozens of black-clothed men in helmets, boots, and masks, wielding assault weapons, exploded out of their SUVs and pointed their weapons directly at the diner.

The assistant returned from the restroom, and upon seeing the mass of armed police said with a happy grin, "That was fast."

Stenkman snickered. "Welcome to New York City, Captain." To Leucadia he added, "There will be a nice reward for you, Ms. Mars."

Harlowe faced the cameraman and said, without looking at all like he was upset about the deception, "I'd copy that video before the dragons take your camera, Stinky."

The cameraman scoffed. "This is America, Spaceman. We're not some third-world country. We have rights."

Stenkman reached over and patted the camera like it was a dear pet. "This will be on tonight's news world-wide, pal. You can take that to the bank, Ms. Mars."

Two thick black uniforms entered the front door, pointing their assault rifles at everyone, including the news crew. "Face down on the floor! All of you, NOW!" they shouted.

Everyone followed orders and dropped to the floor facedown, except the assistant. He stepped up to the black uniforms and said with a smug, dutiful face, "I'm the one who called you."

Whap!

The rifle barrel slammed across the back of the assistant's neck and down he went, out cold.

"What did you do that for? He's the one who got you here," Stenkman said.

A rifle barrel jammed into the side of Stenkman's head. "Shut up, diphead!"

Striding through the front door, another huge black uniform growled, "Where are they?"

A boot slammed into Stenkman's side. "Is it these two, butthead?" the policeman growled, aiming his barrel at Harlowe and Leucadia.

Stenkman gutted out, "Yeah, that's them."

Five more police came through the door. The uniform-in-charge motioned, "Zip-tie their hands and put them in the wagon."

"Yes, Sir!"

Within seconds, Harlowe and Leucadia's hands were zip-tied behind their backs, and they were hauled out the door.

"Can we get up now?" Stenkman asked.

Another boot slammed into Stenkman's side. "You talk when I tell you to talk, dunce."

The uniform in charge went directly to the cameraman and grabbed his camera. "What's on this?"

The cameraman replied, "The interview."

Uniform-in-charge pointed at the street. "With the two we hauled off?"

"Yeah…"

"Any copies?"

"That's our property," Stenkman defended.

Uniform-in-charge grabbed the cameraman by the neck and lifted him off his feet. "Any copies?"

Barely able to breathe, the cameraman gasped, "No…"

Uniform-in-charge slammed the cameraman against the wall, where he collapsed to the floor, unmoving, next to the assistant. He waved his men out the door, taking the camera with him. "We're done here."

* * *

Wheels of the black police vehicles screeched away, as Stenkman crawled to his crew, lying motionless on the floor. He checked them over and was relieved to find them still breathing. Seething with anger, betrayal, and disbelief that he and his crew had done all the right things, yet they had been treated like common criminals. It just wasn't right. Now his only thought was Pylott's words, "They're dragons, and they believe the Earth is theirs, Mr. Stenkman.

52

Got 'Em

White House War Room
Washington, D.C.

PRESIDENT SHAME NEEDED a drink and needed it fast. She was seething. The Gamacoin was driving her crazy, and the young aliens who were behind it all had eluded her most powerful elite agencies, ever since their discovery. They had to be found and eradicated before the Big G, the people's crypto-coin they were calling it, killed the banking systems throughout the world and turned them into useless enterprises. It seemed whenever she thought they were about to apprehend them, the alien boys had somehow escaped. The Gamacoin was now the de facto world currency. For the first time in history, people of all walks of life, rich or poor, were their own banks and in complete control over their own financial privacy, all because of the Big G. They trusted it. They could make loans and send money across continents without passing through an "approved" entity. The governments of the world tried to shut it down, outlaw its use, and program it out of existence. But whenever they tried to stop it, Big G mutated into whatever currency the demand required, and did it instantly. Revenues to tax authorities suddenly tanked. How could they tax something that was untraceable? Finding the source was the only way to control it. A global effort to locate the ship became the greatest hunt the world had ever seen. For them, it was survival. If their rule was to continue, if they were to remain in control of their countries and populations, destroying the alien ship was the answer. Death to them, or the masters themselves would become the slaves.

Shame was on her way to the elevator inside the underground bunker beneath the White House when the call came through. "What do they want, General?" Shame fumed.

General Drgastin held the phone up for her. "New York City Chief of Police. They found the Pylott kid and Leucadia Mars."

"They what?" she barked back with skepticism. She had already had so much bad news over the last week that even hearing good news was difficult to swallow.

"They got 'em, Madame President. They apprehended Harlowe Pylott and Leucadia Mars. The alien ringleaders."

Shame stepped out of the elevator and slowly made her way to Drgastin in a state of shock. "You're sure?"

"Yes, Ma'am," Drgastin replied with a hearty grin. He led her to a large wall display that showed a young couple, in real time, sitting handcuffed and manacled to chairs and a table in a featureless room, with only one window looking out on the afternoon Manhattan skyline.

"Yesssss, that's the boy, all right." Shame recognized him instantly, from the video taken in Colorado. Leucadia Mars was easy. There were millions of photographs of her all over the Internet from the days she was a powerful socialite and corporate head of the Mars Corporation. "She's a looker. Are those green eyes real?"

"Yes, Ma'am."

"She can't be human then. How old is she? That should tell us something."

Drgastin picked up a file and read the front page on Leucadia Mars. He found it hard to believe she had no recorded birth certificate on file. "This picture of her does have a confirmed date of April 4, 1951."

"That puts her well past 70 years old. That's impossible," Shame calculated. "She's older than I am."

"It's a confirmed photo, Madame President."

Shame stared at the General with cold, brown eyes. "Well, we don't need to debate whether she's alien or not, do we?"

"No, Ma'am."

"What about the boy? Is he human?" Shame asked.

The General switched out the files and leafed through Pylott's history. "We have a birth certificate. According to this he's 29 years old."

"That baby face is not 29 years old," Shame protested.

"We have everything on him until eleven years ago, including a complete medical history with x-rays of broken bones and removal of his tonsils. He's definitely human."

"Have they done a DNA test on him?"

"Yes, Ma'am. We have. His Wild Strain is off the charts," Drgastin stated.

"Take care of them right now, and do it wet. Both of them!" Shame ordered, practically jumping through the screen to get at the pair. (Wet meaning a government term to off someone.)

Drgastin didn't think that was wise. "Tucker is en route to New York, Ma'am. We have to keep them alive long enough until he gets there. Papa's orders, Ma'am. We need the location of their ship. Without it we don't have a chance to stop the Gamacoin."

"All right, what else?" Shame was hoping she had enough time for a drink, but Drgastin had more.

"This just in. Our sources in Okinawa say Mrs. Delmonte's youngest son was seen on Zamami Island in the East China Sea."

Shame stood gawking at Drgastin. "What is he doing down there?"

Drgastin didn't know either. "He was spotted with three other males."

"That seems too unusual. Who were the other three?"

"We have a sketch. The informant got a name, too. Timmer." Suddenly, Drgastin's eyes popped out of their sockets. He slapped the paper with the back of his hand. "I know that young man. He's no civilian. He's General Van Dyke's go-to astrophysicist. He's Air Force, Madame President. And I'll bet the farm the other two males are military."

Shame kept mulling over all the possibilities in her mind, but could think of nothing that made sense. Drgastin, however, recalled an incident in the air years ago. "Wasn't that the area where President Delmonte's personal lawyer went down?"

A light blazed hot in Shame's mind. "Braxton..." She slammed her hand down on the table. "My God, Braxton. If he somehow survived that crash, that's where he would be all right."

"They never found his plane, Madame."

"That doesn't mean squat." She waved her hands like she was swatting a hive of hornets. "It doesn't matter! They found Braxton, you idiot!" She went to the satellite wall screens. "I want eyes on that island and everything around it. Get a team down there, and take care of business, General."

"Yes, Ma'am."

Shame's hands were shaking. Her world was back on track again. She could have that drink now. She deserved it. She headed for the elevator, like an Abrams tank cutting across the desert. Two Marines at their posts saw her coming. They reacted with typical military precision, opening the elevator doors for her as she stepped into the lift and continued barking orders.

"Non-military, General. We don't want any blowback on this."

"Understood, Ma'am."

"Call me the instant Tucker arrives in New York."

Drgastin saluted as the door closed. "Yes, Ma'am."

53

Mahi-mahi

Amuro Island
East China Sea

KEKE, THE ISLAND beauty he had met upon their arrival, took Timmer by the hand, and led him toward a remote getaway in the jungle that she wanted him to see. He was giddy with anticipation, having waited all day for darkness to come. After sunset was the only time she could get away from her chores, which suited his plans just fine. That same morning, while Dodge and Braxton were catching up, and Searle was taking a swim, he helped her pick fruit and haul water to the cistern. After lunch, he even pitched in with the laundry. Whatever it took to be close to her, he was at her beck and call.

"How much farther?" Timmer asked Keke, as he pushed aside jungle fronds along the path.

"Not far," she replied. But she always said that. He had already asked her three times, but each time the answer was the same. "Not far, Tim-tim," she called him.

He paused in the middle of the path, unable to go any farther without a little incentive. He said to her, acting like he was exhausted, "Time for a pit stop, Ke."

She knew what he wanted but played the game anyway. For someone who had lived her whole life on a remote island, he thought Keke seemed well educated in the ways of courtship. She let him take her in his arms as she asked, "What is a pit stop, Tim-tim?"

They touched lips briefly at first. Nothing heavy. Just a simple, tender peck. "This is a pit stop." She put her hands around his neck. He couldn't remember ever kissing someone so stunningly sweet and innocent. His girlfriends had all been experienced, and at times, quite aggressive. But Keke was different. She was unhurried and delicate. Her soft breath was fragrant like the island flowers they had gathered during the day. Yet, as gentle as she was she was, not frail. He felt the steadiness in her arms and hands. She was strong. There was nothing about her that needed to be protected. He took a breath and his legs suddenly became wobbly.

"Are you okay?" she asked, looking at him with concern.

"Yeah, I've been wanting to do that all day," Timmer confessed.

"Come on," she said, pulling him farther up the path. "Not far, Tim-tim."

"If we didn't go another step, I would be happy for the rest of my life."

Keke giggled. "No, no, we must go to our place. You will like it, I promise."

He didn't resist. He let her lead, following the path that eventually led to an incredible waterfall that splashed and gurgled over rocks into a starlit pool. Behind them, nearly a mile away, was a magnificent view of the beach and the moon, glittering off the ocean.

"Wow…" Timmer marveled. She was right. The trek had been worth every step.

"It's about time you got here," Searle's voice said over the splashing waterfall. "What did you do, make a pit stop?"

Keke giggled, surrounding Timmer with her arms to belay his disappointment that they were not alone anymore. Another familiar voice in the darkness said, "Come on you two, the mahi-mahi is almost done." Dodge waved them over, where he and another island beauty were cooking fish on sticks over an open fire. Mowgi and the cats sat nearby. The undog's thin, whippy tail wagged, hoping for a piece of fish. The cats, on the other hand, were pretty much content. They had feasted earlier on some of the island's plentiful game.

Searle and his date, holding hands, passed in front of them. "You snooze, you lose, Lane."

Timmer's plan, deflated. His visions of being alone with Keke, swimming together in their own private pool, suddenly went poof! The place was teeming with human beings. "What is this, Grand Central Station?" he fumed.

Keke took Timmer's hand, and kissed him on the cheek, to help cool his jets, as she pulled him toward the fire. "Come on, Tim-tim, we eat now." He was hungry, too, but not for food. He went along grudgingly, his lower lip sticking out like a spoiled infant who was denied candy.

* * *

Timmer had to admit Dodge's grilled fish was as good as any high-end restaurant he had ever patronized. "Don't thank me, thank Clicker. He's the chef," he said of his robob servant.

Still, he would have traded it all to be alone with Keke. Time was running out. They were due to leave the island soon. Dodge had contacted Leucadia, and he gave her the whole story on Braxton. The news that he was staying was disappointing, but she understood and was gloriously happy he was alive and well and living a contented life with his wife and family. "Tell him I love him, and he will be missed dearly," she said. She had often dreamed of such a life with Harlowe, but under the circumstances, a contented future of peaceful living was a fantasy. But while she and Harlowe were taking care of business in New York, Monday would pick up the Team on the backside of the island before sunrise.

According to Keke, the rendezvous point was another hour away on foot. With two hours to go before *Millawanda* arrived, Timmer had to act fast, or he would lose his chance with the hottest babe in the East China Sea, possibly the planet. With everyone else busy around the campfire in their own little worlds, touching noses and making silly small talk, he doubted anyone would care if they slipped away. A quick nod to Keke, and she understood. She was as eager as he was to get away. They made it to the other side of the pool, when Mowgi and the cats suddenly took off. The wind from the undog's giant wings, flapping into the starry night, blew Timmer and Keke off their feet. Looking up, Mowgi was in full dragon, flying straight for the village. Molly and Rhud were just gone. He didn't know why the animals had reacted the way they did, but he knew being alone with Keke was history. Dodge was already up, strapping on his weapons, telling his date to stay put. He looked up at Timmer, "CYBOF Team!"

Clicker tossed Timmer and Searle their Gamabelt belts, as Dodge gave him a verbal lashing for leaving his weapon behind. "Where were you going without that?"

Timmer could think of no excuse worthy of his stupidity. Letting loose a string of profanities, he strapped on his belt and managed a quick peck for Keke before the first *RAAAAP! RAAAAP!* burps of automatic weapons exploded from the village.

54

Abduction

Rodeo Drive
Beverly Hills, California

THE DAY WAS too amazing to be riding in a car. So after a fantastic sushi lunch at Sugarfish, Riverstone and Phoebe left the limo behind and went strolling, hand and hand, along Rodeo Drive, seeing nothing behind the glass. They would link up with Alice later at William Morris/ Endeavor Agency, where Simon and Saul were inking the final nine-figure deal with Somnus Studios for the next Julian Starr movie.

"Do you think I'll get the part in Simy's movie, Matthew?" Phoebe asked, looking beyond a Gucci handbag behind the window. In the past, if she saw something she wanted, all she had to do was point, and the store manager would have it sent to her house within the hour. But today, shopping was far from her mind. When a person has only months to live, the small things in life like a savory meal, a bright, cloudless day, playful thoughts, and meandering the streets of Beverly Hills with a handsome young gentleman were all that mattered.

"Bolt has your back, Phoebs, count on it," Riverstone replied.

"Simy didn't seem to care that I was…" She didn't quite know how to say "might not finish the production."

"That's because he knows you're going to beat this."

"I could shoot my scenes first so when I'm…well, you know, laid up, my part will be done. It won't stop the production."

Riverstone brought her close, touching her mouth gently with his finger. "Stop it, Phoebs. No more talk about this. I told you everything is going to work out."

She smiled, genuinely happy to be in his arms. "You're something, Mister. I wish I would have met you ten years ago."

"When I was eight?"

She slammed a playful fist into his chest. "No, silly man. When I was twenty, not you. You're not allowed to get younger, only me."

He tapped the top of her head with an imaginary magic wand. "There. Your wish has been officially granted."

She sighed regretfully. "If only that were true, my knight in shining armor." After a small kiss, she asked, "Who are you really, Matthew? You're not a movie person. I could see that from the moment we met."

He touched her nose, playfully. "Oh, yeah. How's that?"

She scrutinized him up close and personal, like she was studying a script of his soul. "There's an honesty about you. You're still a kid in many ways, yet there's a suffering in your eyes. Where does that come from, young man? It's like you've lived a thousand lifetimes and experienced things no one has ever seen before. Yet, it hasn't made you haughty or arrogant. No, quite the contrary, whatever you've been through has made you mysteriously poised and cool, like I've never felt in someone I've been this close to. I saw it in Simon, too, since the last time we saw each other. So who are you really? What do you do when you're not dating movie stars? Hmmm… How did you become so…so together for someone so young?"

Riverstone suddenly lost his boyish grin. He knew she deserved an answer, but how would he begin. How would he tell her without sounding flip or coming across as a nut job? "It's complicated."

She saw the stress in his eyes. "I'm sorry. I didn't mean to pry." She tugged on his arm to keep him walking, not wanting to spoil the afternoon.

"No, it's okay."

"You don't want to tell me. I understand."

"It's not that. I do travel a lot."

"You're military?"

Riverstone smiled defensively. "Yes and no."

"Secret Service?"

"No, and I'm not a spy or secret agent, either."

"You work for the government?"

"Oh, God, no. Not even close."

Phoebe kissed him on the cheek. "Thank God for that." Her legs buckled, stepping over a small crack in the sidewalk. He caught her in his arms. The treatments she was receiving were making her weak. Making it to the next block was iffy. Alice pulled up to the curb, and he guided her to the door, that opened automatically when they approached. Once inside, Riverstone poured her a glass of blue water and nodded for Alice to drive on.

Phoebe took a long sip and said, "What happened?"

"You fainted."

She stared at the glass, already feeling its medicinal affects. "Is this the same stuff as the other night?"

"Yes."

Phoebe sat up, squinting her eyes, as she took in a fresh breath, realizing where they were. "Your limo."

"It was nearby," Riverstone said, holding her. "You're okay now. We'll pick up Simon, and then we'll take you home."

She looked at him tearfully. "I want to stay with you. I don't want to go home."

"You need to rest."

"I'm all right. Do you have more...stuff?" She couldn't recall its name.

Riverstone reached for the decanter and refilled her glass. "Blue Stuff," he replied.

"How quaint. What's in it?" she asked, taking the glass. "It kinda perks you right up, doesn't it?"

"It has amazing qualities," Riverstone admitted.

"Can I buy it online?"

"No."

She turned, frustrated. "Why not?"

It was another one of those Hobson's choices. If he told her a lie to make himself look good, he would be disrespecting her. If he told her the truth, she wouldn't believe him. It was lose-lose for him either way.

"You can't tell me, can you?"

"It's not that."

Again, the pain in his eyes was evident, and she understood. "It's an illegal substance?"

"I'm sorry."

She slid her arms around him, pulling him closer than ever. "No, I'm the one who's sorry. You've risked so much for me already. Our dinner the other night, a part in Simy's movie, and now this," She held up her empty glass. "I'm so lucky you're here, Matthew."

They kissed, and by the time the limo had pulled curbside in front of William Morris/Endeavor Agency, Phoebe had her third refill of Blue Stuff. The security guards at the front door didn't bother to tell Alice she couldn't park there. After a weeklong negotiation, everyone at the Agency knew the car was the VIP limo that belonged to their A-List star, Simon Bolt.

"Look!" Phoebe said excited, "there's Simy now. Is that Saul with him?"

Riverstone glanced outside the window at the short man with a big nose and thick-rimmed glasses, wearing a curly, bright red toupee that appeared to combed with a jolt from a light socket. "That's Saul, all right. You could see that head from the moon."

Phoebe laughed. "It certainly is bright. They look like a very happy couple, don't they?"

"They do. I bet he got that hundred mil he wanted," Riverstone added.

"Plus residuals and a cut of all the Captain Starr action figures," Phoebe figured.

When Simon and Saul finished talking, Saul's bright head went on its way, while Simon headed for the limo.

"Did she get the part?" was the first thing Riverstone asked Simon, as he sat down beside them in the back seat.

Simon threw his arms around Phoebe before answering any questions. "Phoebs, so good to see you. You look incredible."

She kissed him lightly on the cheek. "Thank you, Simy."

Riverstone wanted an answer, now. "Rerun, did she get the part?"

Simon took Phoebe's hands and looked in hard in the eyes. "Of course she did, pard."

Phoebe clapped with excitement. "Oh, my God. I did?"

"You did."

"And who's your leading lady?"

"Lara Allison."

"You're kidding. She is soooo good. How did you get her to sign on to a sci-fi movie? I thought she was strictly mainstream."

"I saw her in the hallway. It turns out she's a Julian Starr fan from way back. She wanted the part and wouldn't take no for an answer."

Riverstone congratulated Simon with a high-five slap. "You da man, Rerun. How many mil?"

Simon grinned, showing off his bright pearly whites. "All of it plus a signing bonus of twenty more."

"WHOA!" Riverstone shouted out. "Well, you're buying dinner tonight, my man!"

Phoebe turned Riverstone around and kissed him full on the lips. They continued their embrace, until Simon grew so uncomfortable he couldn't stand it anymore.

"Hey! Hey! Come on you two! That's disgusting," Simon cajoled. "I'm going to ride up front with Alice if you keep that up!"

Neither Phoebe nor Riverstone heard a word Simon was saying. They had entered a world of their own, and no one else was invited. When they finally did come up for air, Phoebe said, "I'm so sorry," she repeated. "I'm acting like...well, like a school..."

Riverstone didn't let her finish. He gathered in his long muscular arms, and kissed her again, only this time, the kiss was more tender and giving. Simon said nothing. He patted Riverstone on the shoulder and gave them their space without interruption. He wanted to crawl through the window and sit with Alice, but he couldn't without stopping the car. Instead, he casually slipped to an empty seat toward the front. As he was about to reposition himself, the limo came to a screeching halt. Everything that wasn't tied down went flying, including bodies. The Gamadin trained reflexes, however, saved anyone from getting slammed. Simon released his hold on a nearby grab bar that saved his face from the divider window, while Riverstone's quickness held Phoebe in check.

"Are you okay?" Riverstone asked Phoebe, as he steadied her on the seat.

Phoebe looked at him blinking her light brown eyelashes. "What happened?"

"I'm not sure." Then to Simon he asked, "Rerun?"

Simon turned to Riverstone with a thumbs up. "I'm cool," he replied. "You?"

Riverstone gave Phoebe a quick once over. He didn't find any cuts or bruises anywhere. She was still flawlessly beautiful. "Good to go." He then looked up at Alice, wondering why she had stopped the limo so fast, when black uniforms began surrounding their vehicle. Loud masculine voices shouted orders at them, as Simon opened the door to confront the problem and was met by the barrel of a 9mm HK MP5 pointed at his forehead.

"Get out of the car! Now!" the gruff voice ordered. "Face down on the sidewalk!"

He must have taken a moment longer than he should have, because a black-jacketed arm swung the butt of his MP5 between Simon's shoulder blades, knocking him to the pavement. "Face down, I said!"

He went down hard and stayed there.

While the first black booted military thug kept his MP5 stuck in Simon's back, two more barrels with green laser dots found Riverstone and Phoebe in the back seat.

"Out, you two! Now!" shouted the rapid-fire command. "Face down on the deck!"

"What's the meaning of this?" Phoebe protested, as her long tan legs extended out first. "Do you know who I am?"

A black-gloved hand grabbed her and yanked her forcefully out of the limo. A rifle butt was about to cold-cock her across the back of the head, when a strong hand caught the weapon and held it. The burly black suit tried to break away, but the grip was far too powerful. The hand wouldn't release its hold on the weapon.

"Don't touch her," Riverstone warned.

A third barrel pointed at Riverstone's temple. "Release the weapon, prick!"

"Don't hurt her," Riverstone said.

A fourth, fifth, and sixth barrel pointed at Phoebe.

"Release the weapon, I said," the deep voice ordered. There was cold death in his tone.

Riverstone calmly pushed Phoebe toward the pavement, as he released the barrel and went to the ground with the others. In the next half second his, Phoebe's, and Simon's hands, arms, and legs were zip-tied together. Phoebe kept protesting her treatment, threatening the thugs with every lawsuit imaginable, when another huge glove covered her mouth with duct tape, reducing her loud cries to muffled grunts and protests.

"What do you want?" Simon asked.

"Shut up!" came the instant reply, followed by another strip of grey duct tape over his mouth. Riverstone remained silent while his mouth was being taped.

Heavy boots came from the front of the limo. "No driver, One."

"No driver? What do you mean no driver?"

"No driver, Sir. No one was under the seat, either. No hidden compartments. No one."

"He got away then," Leader concluded.

"No one left the cab, Sir."

"That's BS, Awol! There has to be a driver."

"Nothing, Sir. Must be an auto-drive limo." The black-gloved hand held up a muted gold colored cylinder. "We did find this."

One uttered a string of profanities, as he peered out the round holes of the black, hooded mask that coved his head. "Put it in the sack with the rest of their things." To another black ops thug, he ordered, "All right, get them secured, DuckFart, and move out."

A thug covered Riverstone's, Simon's, and Phoebe's heads with black hoods, then the soft prick of a hypo touched Riverstone's arm. Five seconds later Phoebe's muffled outbursts went mute.

55

Do the Right Thing

New York City

LESLIE CARDÉ, RICHARD TUCKER, and his tech-savvy Zmaji cohort from California, Mozy Huddelston, boarded a private jet from Dothan, Alabama and flew immediately to New York City, after they received word of the Wild Strain capture. A Du Bear limo picked them up at JFK International Airport at 1:05 a.m. From there, a police escort took them immediately to One Police Plaza.

Tucker was in a fighting mood, as they rode along and the city slept. "We're stopping these ETs and their dirt coin if I have to cut off every one of their fingers and slice them up like French fries to do it," he howled at whoever was listening.

Mo snorted.

"Wipe that smirk off your face, Mr. Huddelston. Why do you keep laughing?" Cardé wondered, clearly up to her eyebrows with his arrogance.

"Because he thinks we're in way above our heads, don't you Mo?" Tucker presumed.

Mo stared at them both. "That's right."

"You're wrong," Tucker said with confidence.

"Have you read the Caesar dossier on this alien ship? Either one of you?" Mo inquired.

"Parts of it," Cardé admitted.

"It's sitting on my desk," Tucker confessed.

Mo looked away, musing over a drunk stumbling along the sidewalk. "What part? Did you get past the introductory page?" he asked Cardé, because he knew from the look on her face she clearly hadn't read any of it either. "So think about this: Imagine a ship 17,000 years old. In laymen's terms that's five times older than the Pyradmids at Giza. She even survived the comet that melted a two-mile thick ice sheet over Northern Hemisphere in days, not centuries, killed off the mammoths and the human race, the subsequent flood, and the four-hundred foot rise in the oceans twelve thousand years ago. And well, what do you know, she still flies. Imagine, too, this same ship can travel to any planet in our solar system in mere minutes, and to other star systems many times faster than light-speed. Imagine, also, this ship can cook our entire planet from a million miles out with its ray cannons, like we were chickens on a spit. All of that was in the Caesar file neither of you bothered to read." He pulled a blue Gamacoin card from his shirt pocket. "And then imagine this unstoppable cyber-coin was created by that same 17,000 year-old technology, and now, Mr. Tucker here, is telling us he's going to fix things like 'Ray Donovan.' " Mo laughed out loud. "Yes, Ms. Cardé, that's laughable."

"You think we're going to lose this battle?" Tucker asked.

"I know we are," Mo snapped. "Listen, nothing scares us more than something we can't control. I get it. But you're all behaving like this is some sci-fi flick, where the Earthlings always get the upper hand by the end of the movie, even though the aliens are way smarter and far more advanced than we are." He waved the blue card in their faces. "This is reality, folks. This is kindergarten stuff to them. For all we know, it could even be something one of their crew dreamed up as a lark."

Cardé fumed. "That's no joke, Mr. Huddelston!"

"Not to us, but to them it might be."

"But not now?" Tucker asked.

"No, not now. Now we've abducted them. Now we've shown our

hand before the game had a chance to play out. Now we're the prey, Mr. Tucker," Mo replied.

Tucker scoffed as Cardé continued, "What do you suggest we do then, Mr. Huddelston?"

"We stop being arrogant fools. I've told you a thousand times, Leslie. We apologize. Say we're sorry. We ask them to forgive our sins or whatever they want us to do to make amends."

Now it was Tucker's turn to laugh. "You want to give them a piece of the action?"

"I want to survive."

"That's not living. That's surrender."

"Well, it's either that or they kill us. Take your pick. Isn't that what the Vatican told us? Isn't that what Papa's report from the Church told us? That these humans are a special breed...a Wild Strain of beings? So far, they haven't come here with their guns blazing. All they've done is land, have a few hamburgers, save a child, and beat up a few government thugs, over pizza."

"No, fourteen were gunned down in Colorado," Tucker reminded him.

"Yeah, after Nootzy's bad boys cornered him. I read that report, too, Mr. Tucker."

"What about the G-coin? That was provocative. You can't deny that," Cardé said.

Mo grinned. "There's that. But I would bet all your banks that it was an accident."

"Where did you get that idea?" Tucker asked.

"Because if you would have done your homework instead of looking at Cardé's breasts, you might have watched the video of two of them ordering hamburgers. They tried to give them actual cash money, but they were turned down. They didn't know we've been cashless since Shame signed that stupid decree. If they could have paid for it with currency, there would never have been a problem. Instead, they had to use what was available to them." Mo held up the card again. "This! The Big G."

Cardé sat back in a huff. "This is stupid, Ricky. There is no negotiation with these aliens. I, for one, will not sit back and let a bunch of adolescents take our world from us."

Mo relaxed back in his seat, placed his sound buds in his ears, and submitted that, "A little bit of something is a whole lot better than an awful lot of nothing, ma'am." He then switched on the music, turning up the volume to an old rock tune, Blue Sky, by the Allman Brothers Band.

* * *

The Mayor, the Chief of Police, and a police escort were waiting when the Du Bear limousine rolled to a stop in the underground parking garage. The escort had their back to the Du Bear occupants for security reasons. Only the Mayor and the Chief of Police were allowed to face or talk to the Zmaji members, since they were also on the cabal payroll. There was no small talk, no chitchat. Everything said was strictly business. There were no long explanations, no excuses, no run-on accounts or descriptions unless they were asked.

"Have they caused any trouble?" Tucker asked, stepping away from the limo.

"No, Sir," the Mayor replied. "They've been surprisingly well behaved, even friendly. The boy even asked how the Yankees were doing this year."

"Yep, like they hadn't a care in the world," Mo added.

"Yes, Sir. Exactly like that," the Mayor replied, surprised by Mo's unexpected answer. "How did you know?"

"Didn't. Just a guess."

"The girl has been positively identified?" Cardé asked, as the entourage walked briskly toward the waiting elevator.

"Yes, ma'am. Leucadia Mars," the Police Chief replied.

"And the young man is Harlowe Pylott?"

"That's correct. Positive I.D. He is the former First Lady's son," the Chief answered.

Mo walked behind the four, not really caring where he was in the pecking order. He had nothing really to contribute, other than a short one-liner here and there. He was mostly along for the ride, and some comic relief.

The small entourage stepped into the elevator, and the Mayor himself, pressed the up button. "The two detainees are on the fourteenth floor, under 24-hour surveillance behind two-inch thick, ESG blast proof glass."

"Sounds tough," Mo quipped.

The Chief grunted. "Tough enough to support steel beams and concrete from collapsing."

"Cool."

"Secure enough for you, Mozy?" Tucker asked.

"Secure enough for me, but I'm not the one in the cage, Ricky," Mo replied with a smirk.

"Have they said anything worthwhile?" Cardé asked.

The Chief took the question. "The boy has done most of the talking. Like the Mayor said, its mainly sports questions. He wanted to know who won the World Series for the last ten years, and did the Dodgers ever move out of Chavez Ravine? Now why would anyone want to know that?"

"Maybe he's been away for ten years?" Mo suggested.

The Chief shrugged. "So where's he been, on Pluto? Everyone with an Internet connection knows the Dodgers went back to Brooklyn three years ago."

"Bingo," Mo responded.

The elevator glided to a slow stop, and the doors opened. The Chief led the party down a long hallway. He passed a security card over a scanner and placed his hand on a lighted pad. Once his I.D. was verified, the door lock released, and he opened the three-inch thick, solid steel door. They went through two more vault doors before coming to a large room with a wide, one-way glass window. On the other side of the window, the two detainees, Leucadia Mars and Harlowe Pylott, were inside a glass cubical, talking casually, just passing time. The moment the entourage entered the room, the two detainees turned to the window like they could see right through the mirrored glass.

Tucker pointed at the glass. "Isn't this one way?"

"Yes, Sir. They can't see us," the Chief assured them.

The Pylott young man stood up and said aloud, "Hello Mr. Tucker. How are you this very early morning? Hope we didn't wake you."

Tucker's face turned hot. "Well, it appears he didn't get the message, Chief."

Mo chuckled, and shook his head, looking at the floor.

The Chief was beside himself. "I don't know how he could know, Sir."

Pylott waved at the room. "It will be much easier to talk with you, Ms. Cardé, and it's Mozy Godfrey Huddelston, isn't it? You know, you two should listen to him."

Mo nearly lost it. "I'll be a son-of-a—" He looked at Tucker and Cardé. It was the first time either of them had ever seen him so stunned. "Papa doesn't even know my middle name."

Tucker pointed at the door to the high security room. "Make it easier on everyone, Chief, and open it up."

The Chief quickly followed Tucker's orders. When the group walked in, Pylott and Ms. Mars greeted them all with welcoming smiles. "I was wondering how long it would take you to get here."

"Are you in a hurry, son?" Tucker asked.

"As a matter of fact, we are, Mr. Tucker," Pylott admitted.

"Need to feed the cats?" Mo joked.

Pylott smiled at Mo. "No, they're on assignment. My horses."

"You have horses?" Mo asked.

"Well, they're not exactly horses. But close."

"They're not from Earth, obviously."

"No, they're ceffyls. They have horns and padded claw feet from a planet 1000 light-years that way," Pylott pointed. Leucadia corrected him by pointing over his right shoulder instead of his left. "Sorry, about that."

Mo was intrigued. "You were on a planet 1000 light-years from here?"

"Yeah, about two months ago, before our journey to the galactic core."

"The core. That's 30,000 light-years from here," Mo figured.

"The far side of the core, actually, add another 5,000 to that," Pylott said.

Mo kept pressing questions that even Tucker found relevant. "But you didn't know who won the World Series for ten years?"

"It's complicated, but coming home lost us eleven years," Pylott explained.

"Space-time differential. You didn't compensate for the relativity constant."

Pylott shrugged. "Yeah, we missed some stuff."

"And you were there two months ago?"

"That's right. Our ship needed repairs, so that's where we had to go to get her fixed. But I would advise taking the long way around Cartooga-Thaat and missing the Zabits. They'll eat you alive, if you're not careful."

"Sounds like a bunch of horse hockey stacked twenty feet deep, son," Tucker said.

"You say you're ship is fixed, Pylott?" Mo inquired with genuine interest.

"She's good as new. Like she just drove off the showroom floor," Pylott replied proudly.

"So where is she now?"

"Somewhere in the South China Sea, I believe."

Ms. Mars corrected him again. "East China Sea, Pylott."

Pylott tilted his head toward Ms. Mars. "Talk to her, she knows."

Tucker had enough back and forth ship talk. He wanted answers to his own questions. "The Gamacoin. I want you to stop it."

Pylott lost some of his coolness, as he faced Tucker. "I'm not sure how to do that. It wasn't part of our plan."

Mo nodded acceptance. "I figured as much."

"What was your plan, boy?" Cardé asked, her face showing her contempt for the detainee.

Pylott eyed her curiously. "You're the media part of this league of misfits, aren't you?"

"We're not misfits. We're leaders for a better world," Cardé countered.

Pylott snickered. "That's funny. The world I left was in far better shape than the one I see today."

"Answer the question, son," Tucker directed.

"Our plan? Our plan was to come home and have a little rest, go surfing, and catch a movie or two. Say hello to folks, maybe even graduate from high school. But you changed all that when you took down President Delmonte. Now we're going to clean house and put you and your Zmaji swampdaks out of business. Unless…"

"Unless what?" Tucker interrupted. "Unless we submit to your demands?"

"I haven't made any demands . . . yet, Mr. Tucker. Unless the Zmaji does the right thing and divests all their holdings, banks, and corrupt polices, it will not end well for you and your swampdak friends."

"You dare to threaten us?" Cardé charged.

Pylott didn't hesitate with his reply. "It's not a threat, Ms. Cardé. It will be the biggest takedown of corruption the world has ever seen."

Ms. Mars stepped forward. "Within weeks, the final nails will be driven into the coffins of your businesses, government collection agencies, banks, and financial institutions for good."

"You're talking about shut down of all governments, including the United States?" Mo asked.

Harlowe nodded. "We are."

"Wishful thinking, son," Tucker interjected.

Harlowe countered. "It's not a wish, or a dream, Sir. It will be a reality."

"And who will lead this country then? You as king, emperor, or god?" Tucker snickered at Pylott.

"No. I am not a king or god, nor do I have any deSire to be one. I'm just a guy who loves his country and the ideals it was built on: freedom, liberty, and justice for all. All those quirky principles that people today find so yesterday. Well, I want them back for me, my family, and my planet."

"You don't have that kind of power, boy," Cardé stated, like she would kill him if there were no glass wall between them.

Pylott's eyes focused on her so hard, the hairs on the back of her neck rose. "Ma'am," he began, "I have more power than you can imagine, and I'm not afraid to use it. In a few weeks, even the King of England will be standing in the same soup line with you and the President of the United States. The Gamacoin is only a simple example of what we can do." Pylott glanced at Mo. "Tell them what they're up against, Mr. Huddelston, because you know, don't you?"

Mo stood with his back against the wall. His arms were crossed in front of him; his shoulders were round with futility. "I tried, but they won't listen."

Pylott came back to Tucker and Cardé. "He's the only one who gets it. Do the right thing, Mr. Tucker," he said, glaring at them all like a scolding parent, "Close your businesses. Give up your power. Stop the corruption. Turn yourselves in. Take your medicine, while you still can."

Tucker laughed to disguise his fear. "You're the ones behind the glass wall, son. Not us. Your life is in our hands." The Chief walked to the opposite wall, where he opened a panel of switches and waited for Tucker to give the go ahead. "All the Chief has to do is flip a switch, and the air inside your cubicle will be sucked out and you'll die a horrible death."

"Not today, Mr. Tucker. Well, you've been warned," Harlowe said.

An insidious frown came over Tucker. "No, you were warned. After we kill you, we'll start on your crew. Would you like to see a picture of two of them?" Tucker nodded at the Chief, and a nearby closed-circuit screen brought up a scene of some dark room where Riverstone and Simon were tied to chairs. Their faces were swollen and bloody. Lying on the concrete floor was a female body. Whether she was alive or dead was impossible to tell, but she was lifelessly still. A rock hard fist slammed across Riverstone's face, sending him and his chair to floor. A second fist hit Simon, and he slumped over, out cold, with a possible broken jaw.

Pylott's face turned volcanic. "You'll pay for this!"

Tears flowed from Ms. Mars as she cried out. "Stop it! Stop it!"

56

Brutus

White House, Situation Room
Washington, D.C.

POTUS FOR LIFE Shame, General Drgastin, NSA director Lougheed, Director Logan, and Chief of Staff Joe Boland sat comfortably in theatre chairs, staring up at a big screen. Besides the usual finger foods and snacks, Shame had her usual whiskey highball in the cup holder, while the others drank sodas and water. In reality it was not a movie at all, but a direct satellite feed from the Top Secret East China Sea operation called "Brutus." Brutus had only one goal: kill or capture Jeffery Braxton and the four soldiers connected with the overthrow of the world's governments. The seven-foot screen was divided up into ten smaller screens surrounding the large center one, depending on the particular view that one wanted. Drgastin held the remote control, and with a click of the button, he could switch instantly to any one of the ten screens or expand a single view to take up the entire screen.

"How many men have landed, General?" Shame asked.

"Three squads, for a total of one hundred and three, Ma'am,"

Drgastin replied. "Squad One is leading the ocean assault directly to the village. Squad Two landed north of the village. Squad Three put down on the eastern side of the island and is positioned to take out anyone escaping the backside of the village."

Lougheed pointed at the lower screen that displayed a green night vision helmet and the tips of automatic rifle barrels pushing back the thick underbrush. They seemed to be making good time. "Cameras 3-A, 3-B, and 3-C are squad Three?" she asked.

Drgastin replied: "That's right, Director. Squad Two to the left and Squad One, the main unit, have the remaining screens."

"Which one is the operation leader?" Logan asked.

"The center screen, Sir, designatied 1-A," Drgastin replied.

"He seems to be offshore in a boat. Why isn't he with his men?" Logan asked.

"See that lower screen? His SOC (Mark V Special Operations Craft) has that same view as we do. He can coordinate and watch the attack unfold, so if anyone tries to escape, like Braxton or the soldiers, he'll direct his men to where the support is needed."

"No escape then?" Boland inquired.

"No, Sir, the village is covered," Drgastin answered confidently.

Shame downed a big gulp before she asked the General, "So where are the villagers, General? I thought the village was full of people."

"They're there, Ma'am."

A half naked male body flashed across the center screen, followed by sudden burst from a full auto assault rifle. A second and third human form bolted from the behind the bushes and quickly disappeared again into a grove of palms.

"They're sneaky little buggers, aren't they?" Logan remarked.

Drgastin changed the screen to one of the soldiers on the beach and brought it up on the main screen. "Yes, Sir, the soldier is after them now."

The sound of boots in the sand, heavy breathing, and soldiers communicating between one another, wearing their gen-7 night vision optics, made the jungle seem bright as day. This brought the White House viewers directly to the action like they were actually there instead of twelve thousand miles away.

An ungodly loud screech thundered through the White House speaker system.

Lougheed tried pulling back from the screen. "What in God's name was that?"

Shame grabbed her whiskey, downing all of it in a single gulp. "Did anyone see what it was?"

"I saw something white flash by the screen, Madame," Drgastin answered.

"Which screen was that, General?" Logan asked.

"3-B, Director."

"There!" Lougheed called out. "Upper left. 1-C. I saw something definitely white and glistening."

"Did you see what it was?" Shame asked.

"No, but it was a big animal; I know that."

The General pointed out an irrefutable fact. "Whatever you saw it wasn't the same animal. Screen 1-C and 3-B are over a mile a part. It has to be two animals."

The screech blasted through the speakers again, and followed by an incredibly load roar.

"Oh my God!" Lougheed cried out again. "Did you hear that?"

"What is that, 1-A?" Drgastin inquired of his mission leader.

"Unknown, General. Intel reports no large animals inhabit these islands," 1-A replied.

Suddenly, a human-like figure leaped out of the ocean and onto the bow of the SOC. He resembled something close to the *Creature From the Black Lagoon*, an old horror movie. The fearful creature was big and muscular, with big bulbous eyes and covered by a dark skin. The General was shocked. "Kill it, 1-A!" he ordered. One-A and two other crewmen ripped off a dozen rounds through the small portholes of the bridge cabin before the bug-eyed being drew his weapon and blew away everyone's HKs. The projectiles fired were not bullets, but searing bolts of blue light that easily penetrated the bulletproof glass of the SOC Bridge. The being told 1-A and his crew in perfect English to shut down the engines and step outside onto the rear deck. A crewman told the being to stick his weapon where the sun doesn't shine.

"You can step outside now or you can deal with my friend," the being said.

The SOC was suddenly slammed by something extremely heavy, making the boat plunge for a brief moment beneath the water. If it weren't for the shallow coral bottom, the SOC would have easily swamped. Huge claws tore into the top of the cabin and ripped the roof off, revealing a giant dragon with devilish yellow eyes, drooling hot spit from its green, whip-like tongue and long incisors. From the size of the beast, it could easily swallow 1-A and his crew in a single bite. With no further discussion, 1-A and the SOC crew moved quickly to the back of the boat.

The sea being petted the creature as he faced the SOC crew. "Call your men back from the village."

"Or what? Death is the risk we take. Give us Braxton, and the village will be spared," 1-A sneered.

"You don't get it, toad. I'm not worried about the village. They're safe. I'm giving you the opportunity to save your own men. None of them will make it off the island alive unless you cooperate. Call them or lose them. Your choice," the being explained.

"You're bluffing. We know what you have. There's only four of you," 1-A said.

"General Drgastin, look at screen 2-C. Tell 1-A what you see," the Being said.

Five weaponless soldiers were kneeling in the sand in front of a large black man with an assault rifle pointed at their heads. Behind them was a massive white tiger, eyeing the soldiers hungrily.

"Show them what you got, Rhud," the being said.

A blood-curdling roar thundered across the island, stopping hearts all the way back to the White House.

"Do it, 1-A. Call your men back," the Drgastin ordered.

Shame jerked up from her chair, knocking over her glass and countermanding the General's order. "NO!" she shouted in a burst of anger. "Complete your mission! Take out Braxton! Do whatever you have to, sacrifice to the last man if you have to, but take out Braxton! That's an order from the President of the United States! Do you hear me, 1-A? GET BRAXTON!"

57

Get It Done

Abandoned Warehouse
Location unknown

SOMEWHERE IN A dark underground bunker, the black leather fist collided with Riverstone's jaw, spinning his face sideways. He spat blood along with pieces of teeth his parents had spent thousands to straighten when he was in junior high. The hours of no sleep, water boarding, electric shocks, crushed toes, and broken fingers had all taken their toll, but he was still alive. He gutted out "That hurt," wincing and licking his swollen, cut lips to find moisture for his dry throat.

"I'm just getting started, kid," Leader said, breathing heavily into Riverstone's ear. "Tell us how to enter the ship or that hurt will be more painful than you can imagine."

"What ship?" Riverstone wheezed.

SMACK!

The jaw broke back in the opposite direction, splattering more blood, bits of tongue, and upper lip tissue.

Leader motioned to DuckFart to play the video again. The

subordinate placed the iPad within two inches of Riverstone's nose and touched the small triangle at the bottom of the screen. For the umpteenth time Riverstone and Simon were shown the video. They saw themselves walking through an invisible barrier, dressed for a night on the town, slapping high-fives, laughing it up as they climbed into a stretch, dark blue limo driven by a mechanical being. A high-flying military drone clocked the speeding limo at 300 M.P.H., heading west at across the Nevada desert without touching the ground.

DuckFart pulled the iPad away. "How did you do it, kid? How did you walk through the barrier unimpeded?"

"Tell 'em, Jester. You can't take any more. It's not worth it, brah," Simon pleaded.

"Listen to your friend, son, and stop this madness before someone dies," Leader urged.

Riverstone stretched his one good eye and found Simon, sitting shackled in chains and plastic wristbands like he was. His face was unrecognizable. Blood smeared down his new white shirt that was now torn in ragged threads around his body. His nose was broken in at least three places and was bent to one side. His front teeth were missing so he talked with a lisp through his bloody gums. The whole right side of his face was puffed outward the size of a grapefruit. It hurt Riverstone terribly to see him suffering through so much pain.

"Do you know a good plastic surgeon, Rerun?" Riverstone uttered slowly.

SMACK!

A mercenary thug unbolted the heavy door, interrupting the beating. He saluted crisply and waited to be recognized.

"What is it, Awol? Papa again?" Leader asked, keeping his temper in check. He tore off his bloodied glove and slammed it against the wall where it stuck briefly before it dropped to the floor.

"Sir! Papa wants an answer immediately or our bonuses will be recalled from the bank," Awol stated.

"These two kids have taken everything we've dished out. What does he want me to do? Kill them?"

"Papa is waiting at the site, Leader. He doesn't care how you do it. He wants in that ship by daylight. Get 'er done or else, were his last words,

Sir."

Leader picked up the golden cylinder lying on a nearby table and began hitting his open hand with it. He smashed the end into the reinforced concrete wall, making a fist-sized dent in the once smooth surface. He was about to hit Riverstone with the next blow when DuckFart stopped him, blocking his hand from crashing down on Riverstone's head. "Sir," the mercenary said, looking into Leader's death-filled eyes, "there's a better way." Leader waited, his lungs pumped, wanting to finish the blow to the head. "...the girl, Sir."

"She's not one of them," Awol pointed out. "She doesn't even know about the ship or who these two are."

DuckFart smiled. "Yeah, but it doesn't matter. When he stopped you from hitting her, I saw the look in his eyes. He cares about her. That's his weakness, Sir."

Awol nodded, remembering the altercation. "DuckFart's right, Sir. He cares about the babe."

"Another bleeding heart, huh?" Leader grunted, musing over Riverstone's pathetic face. He stepped around the side of the chair and slapped the side of Riverstone's legs with the cylinder to get his attention. "Is that what you want, pretty boy? You want me to bring your hot little movie star in here and watch her scream when I cut her face in slices?"

Suddenly Riverstone came alive, lifting up, breathing and hissing, fighting to break loose of the bonds that held him. "Touch one hair on her, butthead, and I swear, I'll kill you!" he seethed. "UNDERSTAND ME? I WILL KILL YOUUUUU!!!"

Leader smiled, approving the request. He had found the way in. He smacked the cylinder twice before he ordered, "Get the babe."

58

Timmer Down

Braxton Village
Amuro Island, East China Sea

DODGE CAME OUT of the water and onto the beach, leaving the SOC launch anchored beyond the reef. Mowgi fluttered down, his great wings coming to a smooth landing, dropping a limp 1-A onto the sand next to Dodge. With his hands tied with his own zip ties, 1-A fell forward on his knees. Dodge lifted him up and threw him forward toward the waiting area, where the rest of his weaponless mercenaries were gathered in a circle guarded by the Team.

"What are we going to do with them?" Enihoo asked Dodge, as he tossed 1-A into the pile.

"Let them go," Braxton said, walking toward them. "They want me. The village will never be safe if I'm here."

"Smart man," 1-A grumbled.

Enihoo swatted the mercenary across the back of his head. "Shut up, chump, nobody asked you."

Searle walked over to Dodge and pointed at the head cameras on the various mercenaries. "He's right. Whoever sent them has a real-time video feed on what's happened here. They won't stop until Braxton's taken out."

"That's right, scumbags," a cruel voice said coming out of the jungle. "Braxton for the ladies." Five other mercenaries followed behind the first black-clad soldier. They had their dates zip tied together with knives across each girl's neck. The girls had been roughed up. Keke's right eye was puffy, her hair disheveled, and her sundress torn. The other two girls were in similar condition, but Keke had suffered the most.

Seeing Keke, Timmer lost it. He rushed the mercenaries. A muffled shot rang out and he went down hard. The mercenary had a second round for the back of Timmer's head but a fury of intense blue bolts stopped him. One bolt sizzled between the mercenary's eyes, while five more rounds dispatched the others before their brains could react, leaving the girls standing alone. Dodge re-holstered his weapon as Searle and Braxton went for Timmer. Enihoo bounded for the girls and cut their ties. In the next breath, Keke was at Timmer's side, her swollen face full of tears crying out, "Tim-tim!"

During the distraction of the melee, a few of the mercenaries tried to escape but Molly and Rhud were on them. When Molly bit off the head of one of them, the others hastily returned to the group with no more thoughts of escape.

Searle rolled Timmer over. He had entry and exit wound through the fleshy part of his side. It was bleeding badly, but the wound wasn't life threatening. "Ke…" Timmer said, gritting in pain.

"I'm here, Tim-tim," Keke said, putting her hand over his injury to stop the bleeding.

Searle was about to announce it was just a minor flesh wound when Braxton pulled him aside and said, "Let them be."

Keke kept fawning over Timmer, like a mother fussing over a hurt child. The Airman was in heaven, soaking up every moment of attention, and at times, gutting out the pain, playing his part to the hilt. "No…" Searle replied, with a thoughtful grin. As often as he and Lane had butted heads in the past, especially these last few weeks, and the experiences they had survived together, he had not only grown close to Dodge and Enihoo, but as hard as it was for him to believe, he'd grown even closer to Lane. Riding in an alien ship, a trip to the end of the solar system, and the subsequent destruction of a hostile alien ship so massively huge it boggled his mind to think about, to their mission to find Braxton, and saving the village and the girls they met. They were all brothers who had fought side-by-side together and survived. Although he would never admit it to his face, when he saw Lane go down, a piece of him nearly died with him. He was so grateful that the mercenary's shot had missed anything vital. He also he found himself shaking, realizing what might have been if the bullet had been an inch to the right.

"Excuse me," Searle said to Braxton, and ran into the jungle to throw up.

Dodge came to Braxton's side. "What's with the Captain?"

"A personal matter. Nice shooting," Braxton congratulated. "Who taught you how to shoot like that? Harlowe?"

"My mother," Dodge replied coolly.

Braxton understood. He knew all about Tinker and didn't doubt him for a second.

Dodge handed Braxton a folded paper. Dawn was breaking over the island, with enough light to see the words on the page. "Lu wanted me to give you this and asked for your feedback. It might give you part of an answer about what they're planning."

Braxton read aloud the word, "Gamacode," at the top of the page. After reading the entire page, he smiled like someone does when they see the merit of the words, but putting it to work was a fantasy. "They're not serious? Congress will never pass these laws. It's too radical. You're asking every politician and banker in the world to jump off a cliff."

Dodge understood the doubt Braxton had about passing rules that would ultimately tear down every government on Earth. "I can't tell you this for sure, but knowing my brother the way I do, I don't think he's expecting any vote at all."

"By decree?" Braxton asked.

"By a Gamadin decree."

Braxton guffawed. "And they want me to oversee this code?"

"I know you want to stay here, but Lu says there is no one better for the job."

Braxton stared out at the ocean, his thoughts looking far beyond the horizon and the mercenaries that were released, swimming out to their SOC never to return again. "Oh my God…"

59
Nikto

"NIKTO!" HARLOWE CALLED out. This was a code word the Gamadin crew borrowed from an old sci-fi movie, The Day the Earth Stood Still when Klaatu, the alien, summoned his robot, Gort. Pylott held out his hand to Ms. Mars. "Time to go, Pylott." She took his hand and faced the ultra-security door like it was about to open for them.

"You're not going anywhere, son," Tucker sneered. He turned to the Chief and ordered, "Suck the life out of them if they try anything at all."

The Chief placed his hand on the air reduction switch. But before anything else happened, a wide crack formed around the door frame, and unexpectedly, the door itself was yanked out of the wall. Two stick-like droids entered the room. One droid carried weapons, the other had two round medallions with chains.

"We never go anywhere without them," Pylott remarked with a smile.

The Chief drew his sidearm and fired at the triangle-shaped heads. The bullets ricocheted off the alien metal, walls, and eventually striking the Mayor in the chest and Cardé in the leg. The Mayor fell to the floor, bleeding. Cardé grabbed her leg, screaming that she was hit. Tucker saw the damage, and before anyone else was hurt, he slapped the weapon out of the Chief's hand. "You idiot!"

Unfazed and unharmed by the bullets, the droids stepped to the front of the glass cell and burned through the hinges and locking mechanisms with intense beams of blue light. When they were finished, Pylott kicked the door, slamming it down on top of the Mayor. Tucker confronted Pylott, as he and Ms. Mars came out of the cell and was tossed the gold medallions by the droids. Behind the cell wall, Pylott appeared too young and unintimidating to worry about, but once he stepped out in the open, his size was shocking. "Are you going to hit me, Mr. Tucker?" Pylott asked, as he draped the medallion around his neck.

With Cardé and Mo looking on, Tucker's ego overwhelmed his common sense. "You punk son of a…" He threw a fist at Pylott's jaw. The punch struck home but had no effect. Tucker's hand cracked like he struck concrete. He threw a punch with his other fist, but it was caught and held fast in front of his own face. No matter how hard Tucker tried to free himself from Pylott's grasp, his hand was frozen. In the ensuing moment, bones inside Tucker's hand began to break like brittle bones under the intense pressure. Sweat flowed down the side of his face, as his legs collapsed under him, and he cowered on the floor like a baby.

Pylott called out another code word, "Klaatu," and the droids went to work on the outside window, burning a large hole in the glass with their blue beams. With their task complete, the droids reduced themselves into cylinders. Ms. Mars touched the medallion around her neck. Instantly, an unknown material covered her entire body, including her head. She picked the cylinders off the floor and placed them in a sleeve on her back. Her large faceted eyes glanced at Mo and Cardé before she casually dove out the open window. Pylott released Tucker and shoved him back into the cubicle. He then touched his medallion and was covered by the same dark material. He said goodbye and followed Ms. Mars out the window.

Mo ran to the window to see where the two had disappeared. As Cardé limped over to check on Tucker, Mo turned, his face aghast. "Holy crap! They just grew wings and flew north toward Central Park!"

60

Welcome to InZeeOut

USS Ron Paul
Amundsen Sea, Antarctica

IT APPEARED THE *Ron Paul* was headed straight for the massive Pine Island Glacier, that stuck out far from the land and into the Amundsen Sea. If the sub didn't come to a full stop or change course soon, the long escape voyage was over. The boat had been running on stealth mode, all the way from the Mid-Atlantic, hugging the ocean floor. Captain Alexander and Admiral Meads had used every trick they knew of underwater warfare to evade all contact with naval sensors and listening devices spread across the world's oceans. More than a dozen times, ships and subs from Russia, China, Japan, and Great Britain were detected, but each time they switched on the alien device, covering their boat with its protective shield, the *Ron Paul* became invisible to any sonar ever made. Cruising all the way from Hudson Bay Deep without detection, had worked. The first time they surfaced was in the Amundsen Sea, fifty miles from coast and only a thousand yards from the Pine Island Ice Shelf. It was a moonless night. Off in the distance, the two thousand foot cliffs of the Ice Shelf glowed mystically white against the dark, starlit heavens. Up on the conning tower, the air was a chilly minus ten degrees Fahrenheit. It made one's nose hairs stiff as pins stabbing the nasal passages. The *Ron Paul* had surfaced briefly for a bit of fresh air and a cigar break for the officers. With the alien device still on, they figured it was safe to go topside and enjoy a brisk view of the Down Under continent.

"Have the OOD come right five degrees, Captain," General Branch ordered Alexander.

Admiral Meads passed his cigar tin to General Van Dyke, who graciously helped himself. Captain Alexander relayed the course correction, as Meads bit the end off his Bolívar Super Corona and lit up. He took a well-deserved draw and exhaled the aromatic Cuban nice and slow. "So why are we here, Ivan?" Meads asked Branch. "Not a lot of places to moor here."

Branch wasn't sure himself. "Part of Captain's plan, Huey. He called it a holding area for some of our friends."

"Friends?" Van Dyke question, dubiously.

Branch chuckled. "I don't think it's the kind of friend you're thinking of, Dutch."

Van Dyke understood the meaning. "Oh, those kind of friends."

Meads smiled. "These boys don't play by our rules. Who knows what they're up to."

Branch removed a pair of high-powered binoculars from the case. "That's a big block of ice there, gentlemen." He handed the binos over to Meads for him to look.

"And no signs that read '"To Port this Way,'" Meads cracked.

"We're not docking outside the ice pack, gentlemen, we're going under it," Branch clarified.

"How far under?" Van Dyke asked.

"Nearly two hundred nautical miles," Branch replied.

"That would put us inside the continent?" Van Dyke asked.

Branch agreed. "I know. It's a leap of faith."

Captain Alexander interrupted their discussion. "Time to go below, gentlemen."

Meads and Van Dyke took one more draw before dousing their

stogies on a piece of ice that had stuck to the conning tower.

* * *

The officers reconvened on the bridge, and to Meads' and Van Dyke's surprise, the human steerage crew had been replaced by Gamadin droids. Captain Alexander had his doubts about the replacements, and kept the OOD, First Lieutenant Baker, looking over their tubular shoulders to make sure there were no screw-ups.

"How did they get aboard?" Meads asked. "I thought I was the only one with a droid."

"I brought them," Branch replied. "They're going to guide us the rest of the way in. The Captain calls them robobs."

"Robobs? You have three?" Van Dyke asked surprised.

Branch smiled. "Jealous, huh Dutch?"

Van Dyke glared at Branch. "You bet I am! I have as many stars on my shoulder as you two, so where's mine? Mrs. Dutch would love one in her kitchen."

"Still burning the meatloaf, Dutch?" Meads jibed.

Van Dyke rolled his eyes and nodded. He had one of the prettiest wives in the Air Force, but cooking was never her strong point. Over the years he'd learned to eat steak well done. "If she ever found out you knew about that, Huey, she'd slit my throat and call it justifiable homicide."

Branch noted, "What goes on in the *Ron Paul*, stays with the *Ron Paul*."

Meads gave Van Dyke a comforting squeeze on the shoulder. "We're committed to top level secrecy here, Dutch."

"The robobs have leveled off at one-niner-seven feet, Captain," Baker announced.

"Speed nav-com?" Alexander asked Seaman Gingrich.

"Speed seventeen knots, Captain, and holding."

"Thank you, Mr. Gingrich."

Baker asked the station next to steerage. "Sonar reading, Mr. Walters?"

"Under the ice pack, Sir. Looks like were headed for a deep water canyon dead ahead," Walters replied.

Lieutenant Rich approached Alexander with concern. "We've lost global positioning, Captain, without it we're going into unchartered waters."

Alexander glanced at Branch, wondering if he should be worried. Branch returned a nod of approval. Alexander turned back to his officer. "Concern noted, Lieutenant."

"Aye, Sir."

* * *

Twenty-nine minutes later, Walters at sonar reported the *Ron Paul* was entering an underwater tunnel off the canyon. "Looks too small for us, OOD," he warned.

"What's our clearance, Mr. Walters?" Alexander asked.

Walters had his doubts. "We might need a shoehorn, Mr. Baker."

"Speed, Mr. Gingrich?" Baker asked.

"Speed unchanged, OOD. Seventeen knots," Gingrich replied.

Alexander leaned over to Meads, blowing out a long, slow breath to calm himself as he spoke in a low voice, "Maybe these robobs aren't sweating, but I'm dripping enough for all three of them."

Meads understood the anxiety. He felt it himself, but they had little choice but to go with the hand they were dealt. "They've got us this far, Gayle."

"Entering the tunnel now, Captain," Walters announced.

Five minutes into the tunnel, the sound of scraping was heard throughout the bridge.

"That can't be good," Van Dyke whispered.

Seaman Walters informed the officers, "It's the long-wave communications antenna on the con, Sirs."

Alexander inquired, "Hull to tunnel bottom distance, Mr. Walters?"

"Bottom distance to tunnel six feet, Captain," Walters replied.

"Speed, Mr. Gingrich?"

"Speed steady, Captain, seventeen knots," Gingrich replied.

Van Dyke kept rubbing his hands together, wishing he had something to chew on. "How much farther?"

"Need a little bacon, Dutch?" Meads kidded. "You sound like my grandkids."

"Fifty-one miles to objective, General," Rich replied.

"There ain't enough bacon on this boat to satisfy my need, Huey. I'll die of a cardiac arrest before this is over," Van Dyke insisted.

Alexander wasn't feeling any better. "I'll join you in a drink myself, General, when we get through this."

"You're on, Captain, and I'll buy."

* * *

Another thirty minutes passed. The *Ron Paul's* speed, depth, and course headings were announced every five minutes, with no change. Finally, Seaman Walters announced, "We're heading into warm water, Captain."

"Confirm that, Mr. Rich," Alexander directed.

Rich went to an alternate sensor station and confirmed the measurement. "Aye, Captain, water temperature has changed. In the low fifties and rising."

"What could account for that?" Meads wondered, glancing at Branch.

Branch shrugged, but Van Dyke had a possibility. "There are several hotspots around the globe. We could be entering a place where underground magma vents have percolated up from the mantle, similar to the Yellowstone region in Wyoming."

Walters announced, "*Ron Paul* has cleared the tunnel, OOD. It's like we've entered some kind wide-open bay. The ceiling is now a thousand feet above us."

The officers all traded looks of astonishment, as did every human on the bridge. There was even a round of applause for the robobs. But they didn't react. The trio of droids just went along with their business of bringing the *Ron Paul* safely to wherever, wherever was.

"Can we surface?" Meads asked.

OOD Baker reported, "The robobs are already taking us up, Admiral."

"Confirm that, OOD," Walters replied with assurance. "Topside is clear."

Alexander turned to Rich. "Outside water temperature, Lieutenant."

"Outside temperature seventy-one degrees, Fahrenheit, Sir."

"*Ron Paul* has surfaced, gentlemen," Baker announced.

Gingrich further added, "Boat has slowed to five-knots, OOD."

"That was smooth," Meads remarked.

"Let's see what's out there, gentlemen," Alexander said to the officers as Rich readied a large flat screen.

"What? No periscope?" Van Dyke asked.

"No Sir," Rich replied. "We haven't used periscopes for twenty years. The *Ron Paul* has the latest high-def photonics mast, although the thermal and night vision won't be necessary. There seems to be plenty of light outside for normal viewing."

"Where's the light coming from? There should be five thousand feet of ice pack over us."

"Unknown, Sir."

Mouths dropped open in awe the instant the outside environment came into view. "What's the ceiling overhead, Mr. Walters?" Meads asked.

"Con to ceiling twenty-one hundred ten feet, Admiral," Walters replied.

It was soon apparent the *Ron Paul* was cruising slowly inside a vast under-the-icepack cavern that grew wider and more vast by the mile, like the Grand Canyon in reverse.

"Outside temperature, Mr. Walters," Meads inquired.

"Outside temperature a balmy seventy-four degrees Fahrenheit, Admiral," Walters replied.

Meads tapped Van Dyke and Branch on their respective shoulders. "Join me topside, Gentlemen?"

"I think I'll have one of those Cubans of yours, Huey," Branch requested.

Meads reached into his shirt pocket and handed Branch a cigar tube. "My pleasure, Ivan."

As they climbed their way to the outside observation deck, Van Dyke asked anyone who had an answer, "What are we celebrating, Gents? We had the President of the United States trying to kill us. Survived that. Another sub tried to sink us. Survived that. An alien saucer fixed us, and things called robobs brought us ten thousand nautical miles to an unknown place under the Antarctic ice pack reminiscent of something out of Jules Verne. And for what? Aliens, UFO's, and national security? Where is this all leading? Anyone got a clue?" His eyes traveled between Branch and Meads. Both faces were twisted with blank gazes. "Ivan, you and Huey know more about these boys than I do! What's going on? Am I the only one who didn't get invited to the party?"

A boatman opened the hatchway to the observation deck, and they climbed up the remaining ladder steps to the outside. Branch was about to give some kind of nonsensical answer since he was as clueless as Van Dyke or Meads. He had been given a directive by the young Captain Pylott to bring the *Ron Paul* to Antarctica, but there were no details on why. Beyond that, he had no more understanding of what the young Captain's ultimate goal was than the Man in the Moon, and he told them so.

"That really eases my mind, Ivan," Van Dyke said cynically.

It was Mead's jaw dropping stare that caught Van Dyke's attention next. "Stop it, Huey, you're giving me…" he turned to see what all the hoopla was, and when he did, he finished his sentence almost choking on his words, " . . . the creeps." Two pyramids, each three times the size of the great pyramid of Khufu that Van Dyke and his wife saw in Egypt, flanked both sides of the channel. "My God…" Van Dyke gasped. Not only were these pyramids massive, they glistened a golden hue in the dull light, like they were built yesterday. It was difficult to tell from the observation deck, but even the blue capstone had sharp defined edges. How old the two sentinels were was anyone's guess.

As the *Ron Paul* passed between the two structures, a city built on a series of rolling hills came into view. The buildings were round like glass yurts, but their sizes were quite large. Some were so big, the *Ron Paul* could easy fit through the front entry way of the largest buildings. Others were smaller and had several levels, but no buildings were taller than the pyramids. Coming up on the port side of the ship were mooring docks built for ships larger than the *Ron Paul*. There were others, too, on the opposite side of the river, but the robobs kept to port side and were guiding the boat to the nearest berth.

"I guess were holding up here for the time being," Meads figured.

"To what end?" Van Dyke asked, always wondering what the ultimate purpose of their voyage was.

"We'll soon see," Branch said as he pointed at the crowds of people inside the round structures pounding on the glass. It appeared they were locked up, and wanting out. There were no children, only adults. Not a single person, man or woman, bore a smile. Most, if not all, were downright angry, shouting profanities at the *Ron Paul*, calling them names, and warning them there would be hell to pay when they returned home.

The three officers recognized many in the crowd, either personally or by photographs. Most were clearly politicians, but others were bankers and members of President Shame's cabinet, all of whom were reported missing over the last few weeks. Still others were unknown, obviously from other parts of the globe, and even some were clergy.

Van Dyke turned to Meads and Branch after looking at the faces with the boat's binoculars. "You know, there's not a single face I see in there that I would release."

Meads laughed. "Maybe that's your answer, Dutch, a staging area for the scumbags of the world."

Van Dyke chuckled the irony. "Works for me."

Branch snickered, lighting up his Cuban. "Did any of you bother reading the sign?"

"What sign?" Meads asked.

Branch snapped his lighter closed and pointed at the large marquee above the glass structure containing the crowd of detainees. It read: WELCOME TO INZEEOUT.

61

Special Delivery

Skeet Shooting Range
Camp David, Maryland

"PULL!" PRESIDENT SHAME called out. Three discs shot out from behind a covered blind and three quick shotgun blasts later all three clay targets disintegrated in midair. A round of clapping by her entourage congratulated her. "Nice shooting, Madame President. Bravo! Nicely done!"

Shame's rosy red face bore only contempt. A Secret Service agent traded Shame's empty shotgun for another fully loaded one. "I wish they were the heads of those Caesar boys." She spat. "I'd be a whole lot better, Randy." She liked shooting skeet with Director Logan because he was a world-class skeet champion and kept her on top of her game.

"How 'bout five this time, Madame?" Logan challenged, holding the barrel his shotgun safely down.

"What's your personal high, Director?" she asked Logan.

"Nine, Ma'am."

"Boland? How 'bout you? What's your best?" she asked her Chief of Staff.

"Two, Ma'am. I'm not much of a shooter," he admitted.

A sly grin slid across her face. "All right, Boland. You sit this one out. Director Logan and I will play. We put twenty-five targets in the air at once. Whoever hits the most targets gets to ride to D.C. in Air Force One. Whoever loses, walks back."

Logan found the deck stacked against him. "You can't lose, Madame. Air Force One is by law your only form of transportation."

Shame's evil cackle echoed across the field. "Then shoot well, Director." She lifted her shotgun as Logan readied his. More shotguns were brought forward. When a shooter emptied their gun, an agent would hand them another. The bet was on. "PULL!" she shouted.

But before anyone could discharge a single round, twenty-five targets exploded in mid air, shattering into tiny bits of skeet across the field.

The shooters were stunned. "Who shot those?" Shame roared.

Logan was less alarmed by who and more troubled by how. "That's impossible," he said, as he looked across the field at a towering male, walking their way. The young man was still a hundred yards and reloading his pistols as he came forward. He wasn't hiding. He was out in the open and striding toward her like he was on a mission to do them harm. A dozen secret service agents surrounded Shame, cocking their MP-5's, waiting for the order to open fire.

"Don't wait for me!" Shame screamed. "Kill that SOB.!"

A fusillade of blue light exploded from the young man's weapon and twelve agents collapsed where they stood. The attacker wasn't finished. A dozen more blue bolts eliminated the other agents hidden in the nearby woods, and seven more were neutralized along the banks of the nearby river. When the gunman came within shotgun range, Shame, Logan, and Boland turned their guns on him to no avail. His sizzling bolts sliced their shotguns in half before they could fire a round. The residual heat was so intense, the three dropped their guns to the ground and watched in terror as they melted at their feet.

The young man, dressed in a dark exoskeleton armor that covered his body, became more intimidating the closer he came. With one quick motion he ejected his weapon's magazine, replaced it with another, and re-holstered his pistol, all in a blink of an eye.

"Pylott…" Shame fumed, recognizing the thorn in her side immediately. Nothing had ever scared her before, and she wasn't about to let some young punk frighten her now. She hadn't made it to President for Life by backing down, especially from teenage boys who hadn't begun to shave yet. Pylott stood confident like a soldier, although his eyes worried her. They were cool as ice and lacked any fear of her or her power.

"I'm making a special delivery for you, Madame," Pylott said to her.

"You got my attention, boy. Now what do you want before the Army, Air Force, and Marines take over?"

Pylott held up a single sheet of paper. "You're dissolving the government of the United States, immediately."

Shame scoffed as Logan and Boland laughed. "Oh, is that all. I thought you came here to shoot skeet."

"The government closure will begin Monday or—"

Shame interrupted. "Or what?"

"Or I will do it for you."

"Do you know what would happen if we closed the government?" Logan asked.

"I don't care. It's not just the United States, it's every ruling body across the planet. You're all being shut down for good."

"I'll say this much, when you go, you go all in, and you don't pussyfoot around," Shame glared.

"No Ma'am." Pylott shook the paper at her and said, "This here is the universal code of law for all ruling bodies. If you wish to continue, they will be followed, or there will be consequences."

Shame kicked the molten scrap metal out of her way. "You don't have that kind of power. So don't threaten me with your stupid ideals."

Pylott looked at Logan. "You know, don't you Mr. Logan? You were the Captain of the *USS Forrestal* when all power aboard your ship went dark."

Logan nodded, terrified. "I remember." He faced Shame. "I'm afraid he does, Madame. He had shutdown our armed forces world-wide before."

Shame pointed at Boland to take the paper from Pylott. "Let's see this code, boy!"

"We call it the *Gamacode*, Madame."

Shame grabbed the one page list from Boland and began reading. She barely made it past the preamble before she wadded the paper up and tossed it at Pylott. "Why don't you just ask me to shoot myself like you did my brother and become dictator?" she snarled, her forehead sizzling hot with hate. "You could be another Julius Caesar crossing the Rubicon."

"I'm not a dictator like you, Madame." Pylott pointed to the agents on the ground, who were beginning to move around after being stunned. "We have other means more effective than plotting your demise."

"You killed my brother because he didn't conform to your rules. I'll kill you for that!" Shame fired back.

"He killed himself, Madam, because he was unwilling to face the consequences of his actions."

"But you drove him to his death."

Pylott stared them all down. "You are a bunch of worthless swampdaks, no different than any crime syndicate throughout history. How you choose your downfall is entirely up to you. A bullet to the head, throw yourself off a cliff, or drown yourself in a pool of whiskey, I don't care. But down you will go."

"You'll never get that satisfaction. I don't die easily, punk," Shame hissed.

Pylott remained unemotional. He felt nothing. He was here to make his point, and that was it.

"So how will the people survive without government?" Boland asked.

Pylott faced Boland. "There will be hardships, even riots. The poorest will suffer the most, because they have suffered the most from your tyranny. But when the good people of the planet realize they are free, they will come together and rebuild. The world is compassionate and generous. They will take care of the needy. Given the responsibility and the freedom to live one's life as they choose, Earth will grow and prosper without the force of someone digging into their pockets and taking what they worked so hard to create. But that's not what really scares you is it, Mr. Boland? It's the fear of losing control over the beings you rule. For once, government will be shown for what it is: corrupt, irrelevant, and self-serving. Given the chance to grow without fear of tyrants like yourselves, the planet will realize no government can give them happiness or security as much as their own self-reliance. Governments everywhere will wither away and go the way of the dinosaur."

"People will always want someone to take care of them," Shame insisted.

Pylott saw the merit in the statement. "True. Some will always have that need. But it is a false security brought on by lies and inducement. There is nothing I can do or say to change human nature, for there is always a price to pay for security. Some of us, of course, have never found that course to our liking."

Shame turned her back on Pylott. "Ain't going to happen, boy. Get over it!" She faced Logan and Boland for their support. "Imagine anyone telling us we can't tax our own people, have a military, or own as much land as we want. Why that punk kid…" When she turned back around to confront Pylott again, he was gone.

"What do we do now, Madame President?" Logan asked.

Shame tossed what was left of her shotgun toward river. "We fight that SOB! He's human. He bleeds. He has faults and weaknesses, like everyone else. We find out his, and we use it against him. That's what we've always done. We fight back."

"For the good of the country!" Boland sang out in a fit of patriotism.

Logan and Shame traded humorless glances as they stormed off toward her waiting Air Force One helicopter. "Get Mr. Tucker on the line, Randy! I want to know why Pylott showed up here and wasn't in that cell in New York."

"Phone call is already in, Madame President," Logan stated.

* * *

Boland stayed behind to clean up the mess. Air Force One lifted off. The rotor wind blew the clumped up paper across the ground. He ran and snagged it. Curious, he read it with disbelief as his hands began to shake and his mouth cried silently, "OH . . . MY . . . GOD!"

62

Barrier Breach

LeBeau Park, NV

The twin, tilt-rotor Bell V-280 Valor helicopter touched down in a whirl of dust and sand. It was two hours until dawn in the LeBeau Park valley. A single, black-uniformed messenger jumped out of the open cargo bay, carrying a small satchel securely under his arm. He had no insignia of rank, or any patch that gave away his service affiliation. A black silk mask covered his face to guard his identity. The messenger ran to a waiting souped-up, all-wheel drive electric DPV (Desert Patrol Vehicle), that tore across the desert following a dusty wash. Upon his arrival at the pre-designated location two miles south of the massive, alien saucer, code name Caesar, the messenger delivered the package to Leader, the head soldier in charge of three dozen elite mercenaries.

"The device?" asked Leader, relieving the messenger of his satchel.

"Yes, Sir!" the messenger acknowledged crisply.

Leader, without opening the satchel, handed it to an elderly gentleman dressed in an expensive down overcoat, sable cap, knee-high Dubarry leather boots, and cashmere lined, lambskin gloves.

"Your key to Caesar, Papa," Leader said, handing the Zmaji patriarch

344

the satchel.

Papa casually took the bag, unfastened the security latch, and removed what appeared to be some kind of garage door opener. The device was dark gray, two by three inches long, with a large, light gray button in the upper center. Along bottom read the manufacturer's logo: Genie.

"Is this a joke?" Papa asked in a clear French accent.

"No, Papa. To save the life of Ms. Marleigh, both marks caved. They said for security reasons it was designed to look like a common door opener." Papa had is doubts. "If this fails, Sir, my men are standing by to end their lives," Leader assured the Frenchman.

"Do it, Monsieur," Papa ordered, returning the device to the Leader. "No one must know. This operation must be wet."

"Aye, Papa." Leader leaned over to his subordinate and made the call. Moments later the soldier returned with a positive nod. Leader went to Papa and reported, "It's done, Sir."

"Any movement from Caesar?" Papa asked.

"Nothing, Sir," DuckFart replied, keeping his eyes fixed on the wave device they had obtained from the Swiss. "No movement since the girl and the boy passed through the barrier in the flying platform at 15:32."

Leader faced Papa again. "We'll let you know when you can enter, as soon as we're in, Sir, and Caesar is secure."

Papa nodded in silence. He had nothing more to say until Leader's mission was complete. If the truth were known, he was as anxious as a young boy expecting his first bicycle from Santa. He would allow his elite forces to do their job. He and the other members of the Cartel, who were waiting in their Humvees a mile away, would remain a safe distance away until the soldiers had secured the ship. Being in the middle of an operation was unheard of for the head of the Zmaji organization. But Caesar was special. Papa wanted to oversee the operation himself and be the first Du Bear to capture the most powerful alien spaceship the world had ever seen. There had been other alien ships, of course, 1946, and 1947, 1951, two in 1969, 1981, and 2012, but none like Caesar. None that were so capable of destroying entire worlds, and none that could make a one-world government of Earth a reality for as far into the future as one could imagine.

Leader spoke into his throat mic. "All units. Converge at designated rendezvous point three Zulu. Watch for my signal. When Caesar is breached, all units will follow my lead into the ship. You have your assignments from there."

Clicks from the half dozen five-man squad leaders came back over the earpieces, signaling they were ready.

Leader checked his Glock 19 and the MP5 strapped to his chest, then motioned for his masked mercenaries to climb into their respective DPVs. The drivers switched from their gas engines to the all-electric stealth mode, as they rolled silently toward their objective. They raced toward Caesar's shimmering blue wall that protected the ship from any intrusion, and no atomic blast could penetrate. The other DPVs converged on their flanks, forming a tight wedge as they continued toward the three Zulu entry point. When the eight vehicles came within fifty yards of the force field, they slowed to a crawl until Leader's DPV came within a foot of the blue translucent wall. He stepped outside the cab and pointed the device at the barrier. He clicked the center button once, as instructed, and silently a hole opened up in the field large enough for their DPVs to drive through single file.

After driving two hundred yards beneath the saucer's hull, the squad of vehicles came to a slow stop in front of an immense ramp that angled upward toward the center underbelly of the saucer. Leader and five of his mercenaries exited their vehicles and inspected the incline for booby traps. No one found anything unusual. After marveling over the size of the ship, the ramp on which two A-1 Abrams tanks could drive side by side up the gangway appeared too frail to hold a single DPV. He had never seen anything like it. Remaining cautious, he ordered DuckFart to drive his DPV onto the lower section of the ramp to test its integrity. The ramp took the weight like it was made of thick, steel I-beams.

Amazing!

The inspection completed Leader signaled the others to follow his lead. The DPVs drove to the top, where they inspected the soft, golden hull of the ship. He wondered if they had brought enough C4 to blow open the ship's center hatch. "Where should we place the charges?" Awol asked, since there was no apparent seam of an entryway. Leader stood perplexed. He touched the surface. It was completely solid.

BigBoard stuck his head out the window and yelled, "Press the clicker again!" anxious to get the show on the road.

Leader figured there was nothing to lose and pressed the button again. Sure enough, a huge hatchway quietly open into the ship. "Son of a. . ." Before proceeding, Leader sent BigBoard, Awol, and Mongol into the ship for recon. After a long minute, BigBoard's voice came over the mic to informed Leader, "Clear, Sir!" and Awol waved them in.

Leader didn't like surprises. He wondered if it was his activation or if they were being set up. The knot in his stomach told him it was the latter. But Papa would never tolerate gut feelings. They had to go on. He gave the hand signal to move forward cautiously, and all the DPVs but one entered the hatch. As to the layout inside, Leader and his squads were flying blind. Their orders were to locate the ship's crew, neutralize them, to kill only if they resisted, and to secure the bridge.

Every mission had unexpected anomalies. Lights becoming brighter as they entered the ship were just the start. They soon discovered what lay beyond the opening was an immense, blue-carpeted room that was so plush and clean, it seemed almost unholy to drive on it with their dusty DPVs.

But time was of the essence. Papa wanted his prize secure. The ship was too vast to inspect on foot. Radiating out from the room were five huge corridors that led away from the center like spokes on a wheel. He sent one team down each corridor to look for the crew. A mercenary, called Psycho, and his squad were to locate the ship's bridge from a primitive map that was extracted from the captured marks. Leader and his squad would take the largest corridor, with the remaining teams searching the passageways for aliens. Whatever they found, even if it was nothing, they were all to meet back at the center room in thirty minutes.

* * *

With his teams dispersed and one DPV left behind to guard the hatchway, Leader and a second DPV drove into what appeared to be the main corridor. Both vehicles traveled a good distance, finding no one. It was like the entire ship was deserted. Reports from the other squads had no better luck. But when Leader's group slid open two giant doors at the end of the corridor, what they discovered was off-the-charts unimaginable. An immense natatorium, the likes of which no one had ever seen before, stunned them. There was nothing normal about it.

Unusual bright-colored birds fluttered from the foreground trees and flew across a body of water that was as big as six Olympic-sized pools. Surrounding the clear, blue pool was a lush indoor jungle, complete with hundred foot tall palms, ferns, trees, and beautiful blue flowers that matched the color of the carpet throughout the ship. Above it all, was an artificial blue-green sky with a bright yellow sun that illuminated the entire room. The air was wasn't too cool or too hot. It was fresh and heavy with a sweet flowery fragrance. One could almost imagine they had come upon a huge flower shop. A hippo-like beast grazed on grass at the water's edge. However, this was no Earthly species of hippo. Its sizable, round body may have been hippo in appearance, but its head was that of a pig with a wide flat snout and droopy ears. The creature paid them no mind, as it lumbered past them on its way to graze on more grass.

Suddenly, a loud roar broke the peacefulness of the room, raising the hackles on everyone's necks, including Leader's. The mission statement made no mention of any large predators. A second roar, equally as loud and fearsome, came from the other end of the pool, like the two were communicating with each other.

"*That didn't sound good,*" BigBoard whispered nervously in his mic.

Leader faced one of his mercenaries. "Awol."

"Sir."

"Who surfs?"

"Mongol and BigBoard, Sir."

Leader pointed the muzzle of his MP5 at the two surfboards along the shoreline. "Paddle across the pool. We need an O.P. (observation point) on top of that cliff."

"Aye," Awol confirmed, and directed the two men to take the boards and paddle their way to the opposite shore.

The two were halfway across the pool, when a devilish creature launched itself from the high cliff. It's body and wings seemed to grow exponentially as it dove down, scaring the bejesus out of the two boarders. They flipped their boards an instant before the creature's giant claws would have torn their heads off. The winged creature then swooped up to the heavens, nearly touching the sun, before it dropped back down and disappeared behind the cliff.

"*What in the name of God was that?*" the chatter began over the communicators.

"*My mother-in-law,*" Psycho replied dryly.

"Mongol and BigBoard, you okay?" Leader radioed as he watched his two soldiers scramble to their boards.

"*Aye, Leader, good to go.*"

"If that thing returns, you drill it. Ya got that?"

"*Roger that!*" Mongol yelled back.

Leader wasn't interested in any more anomalies. The mission was at stake. The off-world show was over. He had to button up the ship before sunrise. He came back to Awol and ordered, "Take two men that way. We'll meet back here in twenty. This place isn't as empty as it looks," he ordered.

"What if they're alien?" a mercenary named Clown asked.

"Then drag them back here by their antennas," Leader replied.

Awol led the two mercenaries into the undergrowth, brushing back ferns with their MP5s as they disappeared from the group.

VAROOM!

Leader looked up in time to see a wall of water appear out of nowhere. The wave swelled three feet high, coming straight at them. Looking in every direction, there was no escape.

DuckFart's voice shouted out, "HIT THE DECK!"

63

Two Captives

Aboard Caesar

IT ALL HAPPENED so fast, no one had time to avoid the wave before it slammed them. Bodies tumbled, weapons were ripped away from their hands, and helmets were torn from their heads. No one escaped the deluge.

Incredibly, no one was hurt, but the wave caused a ton of embarrassment for Leader and his men. Leader found his helmet under a fern, as the others picked themselves up, located their scattered gear, and began checking for damage.

"Sound off. Anyone missing?" Leader cried out.

"Klinker, here."

"Psycho, yo."

"AK, operational, Sir,…barely," he grunted.

"DuckFart?" Leader called out. "Where's DuckFart?"

There was a moaning between the ferns. Dripping wet, Leader, with a little help from Klinker, climbed to his feet. He walked over and lifted the soldier out of the bushes. "You with us, DuckFart?"

Groggily, DuckFart found his balance and replied, "Yeah, what hit us?"

"A frickin' wave, that's what," Leader snarled, glaring at the pool that was now calm as a windless morning. "I don't see BigBoard or Mongol out there." He called to them twice on the com, and got no response both times. He was about to give the next order, when Awol and his squad with two captives in tow broke through the bushes.

"What happened here, Sir?" Awol asked, staring at the disheveled mess of dripping mercenaries.

Leader glared down at the squad leader. "Don't ask. Did you see BigBoard and Mongol?"

"No, Sir."

He then looked over at the two captives with their hands securely tied behind their backs. From the photographs he was given at the briefing, he didn't need introductions. The tall kid was Harlowe Pylott, the presumptive leader of the crew. The babe was Leucadia Mars, the heiress to one of the world's greatest fortunes and Pylott's girlfriend.

"Good work, Awol. Where'd you find them?" Leader asked.

Awol pointed back over his shoulder. "They were eating breakfast over there in the jungle."

"It was good, too," Pylott said to the mercenaries. "There's still plenty of eggs Benedict, smoked salmon, toast, and fresh squeezed OJ, if you gentlemen would care to join us."

"Shut up, kid! Nothing comes out of that trap of yours unless you're asked," Leader scolded.

Pylott nodded that he understood. "Yes, Sir."

"Klinker!"

"Yes, Sir."

"You and Pyscho skirt the beach for BigBoard and Mongol."

Suddenly, two bodies dropped in the water. Leader and Awol waded out into the pool and brought the two soldiers back to shore. BigBoard and Mongol weren't dead. They were just shaken up. Klinker pointed at the huge winged creature they had seen earlier.

Leader was fuming. "What's going on here?" he scolded Pylott.

"Would you believe me?"

Leader grunted his distain and turned to the Mars girl. She was stunningly beautiful. Her olive skin and emerald eyes made his mouth go dry. Leader forced himself to take a breath. His men were equally awed. They gawked, still as statues, their faces slack, like they were staring at a real live mythological Greek goddess.

"What do you have to say?" Leader asked her.

She turned to the soldiers with her bright eyes and said, quite business like, "Good morning, gentlemen."

Leader had enough. They had to get moving if he was going to meet Papa's deadline. He pointed the muzzle of his HK at the open doorway and the two DPVs.

Pylott and Ms. Mars followed Leader's instructions without protest. Neither captive was dressed. The shirtless Pylott had on a pair of old swim trunks. The briefing notes on him were full of errors. His stat sheet said he was eighteen years old, six-foot-one, one hundred seventy pounds. He may have been eighteen, his face certainly fit the description, but his physique was hardly normal. He towered over Leader, who was six feet four, by a good five inches. His stated weight was obviously wrong, as well. Judging from the kid's muscular build, Leader figured two hundred-eighty pounds was no exaggeration.

Ms. Mars, as mentioned before, was a striking specimen of womanhood. Standing next to the kid, she appeared small, but then, the kid's size made everyone around him appear small. In reality she was quite tall, her long shapely legs could easily be seen strutting down a high fashion runway in Milan, he thought. She wore a revealing, dark blue bikini that left little for speculation. The silken fabric covered barely one percent of her body. Leader and his men were so transfixed by her, they never saw the approach of the droid wearing a brightly colored bow tie around his tubular neck. How the stickman showed up without being seen was unnerving. In its four-digit hand, it held a sheer, white silk robe and offered it to the girl.

"May I?" Ms. Mars asked politely, before taking the garment.

Leader nodded. "Please do." Anything to cover her from the distracted eyes of his men was welcome.

Ms. Mars accepted the delicate garment and graciously said to the droid as if it were human, "Thank you, Jewels."

The stickman nodded and then obediently left the area.

"Follow it," Leader ordered Klinker.

But when Klinker went to track the stickman, it had already disappeared.

Leader glared at the two captives. "Where did it go?"

Pylott answered, "That's always befuddled me, too."

"Befuddled?"

"Yeah, my mom always said that when she was confused—"

Leader cut Pylott off, fed up with the chicanery and still embarrassingly wet with damaged pride. "Are you Pylott?" he asked, as they walked.

"I am," Pylott replied assuredly. The kid was cool as ice. Leader gave him that much. He acted as if the assault weapons pointed at them were useless toys.

"Who else is here?" Leader asked his captives.

Pylott's face was expressionless. "Just us."

Under the circumstances Leader never assumed anyone spoke the truth. He stared at Awol with cold eyes. Awol's answer was direct. "We found no one else, Sir. Just birds and a small purple mutt with big ears."

"That would be Mowgi," Ms. Mars offered.

Leader found that odd. "We heard big animals."

"We saw nothing large, Sir."

"What about the hippo thing we saw coming in?"

Psycho pointed behind him. "He was in the pool, Sir."

Leader turned to Pylott. "Where did the mutt go?"

Pylott scanned the artificial sky. "He's flying around somewhere."

Leader felt like smashing Pylott's face in with the butt end of his rifle for his wiseass answers, but Papa wanted them unharmed. He needed their knowledge of the ship to get Caesar off the ground.

But Leader couldn't help himself and slammed a fist into Pylott's side. To his surprise, the kid hardly flinched. He hit him hard, too.

Leader recharged his fist and was about to take another swing at Pylott that would have ended a normal man's life when Papa called, interrupting the kid's comeuppance.

"*Leader? Are you fini?*" Papa's thick French accent asked over the com.

Leader kept a tense, fighter's stare on the kid. He didn't care how important he was. Pylott needed that schoolboy smirk left on the ground. "Not yet, Papa. All units have yet to check in."

"*My team is waiting, Leader. Please hurry, s'il vous plait.*"

"Understood, Papa."

Leader then went through the roll call. "Unit Two. Report."

"*Unit Two secure, Sir. The Bridge is ours.*"

"Very well, two. Any trouble?"

"*None, Sir. No one is here. The place is deserted.*"

Leader glared at Pylott. "I'll ask you again, where's your crew?"

"I thought they were with you," Pylott replied.

Leader didn't like that answer either. The kid didn't seem that concerned that two of his crew were chewed up pieces of meat. But he was under the gun, and went back to his roll call. Everyone checked in with no problems, a condition that he found uneasy for such an important mission.

Leader continued with Pylott. "Either you have the most undisciplined crew on the planet or you're hiding something big time."

Pylott turned slightly, displaying his plastic ties around his wrists. "My hands are tied, Sir. You have all the cards," he said, eyeing his MP5.

"If this is a ruse, you'll be the first one I shoot," Leader warned.

Pylott said nothing, looking at Ms. Mars often as if he was making sure she was all right.

Leader clicked on his mic. "Clear, Papa. Will meet you at rendezvous alpha."

"*Merci beaucoup,*" Papa replied, his tone giddy with anticipation.

As Leader and his soldiers came to their vehicles, Awol whispered in Leader's ear. "I saw paw prints, Sir. They were three hands wide, if they were an inch."

Leader groaned. Nothing was right. This was feeling like a major SNAFU for any logical reply. He ordered their captives into separate vehicles and closed the natatorium doors. If there were creatures inside that made the prints, he wanted them locked in so as not to cause any problems down the road.

Leader glanced at DuckFart, who looked like death warmed over. "Feel better?"

"Not even a little bit, Sir," DuckFart grunted, putting the DPV into forward gear. As they began to roll down the long corridor he added the observation, "That kid is way too cool about all this."

"Yeah."

"His dad was a Jarhead. Twice earned the Medal of Honor, all that. One badass SOB."

"I know."

"So was his mom."

"Your point?" Leader asked.

"He was raised cool."

"I get it."

"Not good, Leader. He should be in chains not plastic ties."

Leader knew DuckFart was right, but there was nothing he could do about it now. "Aye."

64
Papa's Prize

Aboard Caesar

As PLANNED, THE DPVs silently regrouped at the center room of
the ship. With the all-clear given, Papa's vehicle and two other Humvees
arrived, along with their escort of the last DPV from Leader's team.

Papa opened his door and bounced out a conquering hero.
"Magnifique!" he gasped, catching his breath over his glorious prize. He
continued onto the blue carpet, turning round and round with his arms
out, looking up at the soft glow of the ceiling. Others in his entourage
left their vehicles and joined his enthusiasm over the capture of the alien
saucer built to travel the stars. Papa knelt down, running his hands along
the soft carpet, caressing the fibers like it was a mink coat. Leader pulled
Pylott out of his DPV, and brought him to Papa.

"So beautiful and rich. How old is it?" Papa asked Pylott, marveling
at the towering young man's physical presence.

"Our guess is 17,000 years, give or take a few thou," Pylott answered.
Tucker and Cardé were just leaving the second Humvee. The instant
they saw him, vengeance filled their faces. Tucker's hands were heavily
wrapped, as was the limping Cardé's leg. Pylott greeted them with a

pleasant smile. "Mr. Tucker and Ms. Cardé, how nice to see you again. How are your hands, Mr. Tucker?"

"Not nearly as bad as your face will be, punk," Tucker shot back, full of hate.

Pylott looked past the couple. "What, no Mozy? I figured he'd love the cool stuff here."

Cardé beamed. "He thought our chances of getting this far were nil."

Pylott returned her smile. "He was obviously wrong,"

"Obviously."

Papa found the banter distracting. He couldn't care less about what went on in New York. He had his prize, and that was all that mattered. Pylott turned away from the couple, dismissing them as unimportant.

"How fast can she go?" a German gentleman from Papa's entourage asked.

Pylott grinned. "Fast, Herr Kaufman."

"Speed of light?"

"In first gear."

Everyone's eyes expanded tenfold.

There was dead silence before a feminine voice said to Papa, "Comment êtes-vous cette belle soirée, Evie?" in perfect French.

Papa's face sobered instantly. No one was supposed to know his name, much less speak it. There was only one person aboard the alien craft who knew him that way, an old childhood friend. Papa waited for the soldier to bring Ms. Mars to him.

Papa bowed slightly at the head. "Leucadia," he said, knowing they had to eventually meet. He snapped his fingers at BigBoard. "Untie her," he ordered angrily.

Leader gave the okay, and BigBoard reached around and cut her ties with his K-bar.

"Thank you, Evie. What brings you to Nevada? The water?" Leucadia asked politely.

Papa forced a smile. "I have come for your beautiful ship, Lu."

She gestured at Pylott with an open hand. "It is not my ship, Evie. She belongs to Captain Pylott, here."

There were a number of chuckles from the Zmaji group.

"A lot of responsibility for someone so young, hey, son?" a Russian gentleman remarked in a heavily accented voice. "You don't mind if the grown-ups take over, now, do you?"

Pylott smiled. "Are you taking my keys, dad?"

The Russian laughed. It was surprising how muffled the sound was in the vast room. There were no echoes at all. He winked back at the young man still dressed in a bathing suit. "I guess we are," he replied with a broad, self-assured smile.

Suddenly, the center hatchway began to close for no apparent reason at all, worrying everyone but the captives.

Several frightened voices cried out. "What's going on?"

Leucadia stepped forward. "It's an automatic closure, Evie." She tried to walk toward a nearby wall but Leader's goons stopped her. "Would you like me to reopen the portal, Evie?"

Papa nodded. "Let her go."

Leucadia continued over to the wall and touched an activator. The access hatch opened just like before. "It does this to conserve energy. You might think of it like keeping the door closed while the air conditioning is on."

The explanation made sense, and since the ship was secure, and since his team would be moving the ship to a remote underground African location anyway, Papa saw no harm in keeping the hatchway closed. He waved, giving her permission to close the portal again.

Addressing Pylott, an Asian woman asked, "You said the ship was capable of light-speed."

Pylott turned to her. "Yes, I did."

"To make travel to other star systems practical, one must go faster than light," she presumed.

"Considerably faster."

The crowd was awed. A black man with a South African accent asked the next question. "I thought faster-than-light was against the laws of physics."

"No, Sir, we do it all the time," Pylott replied.

Papa asked, "So that must take incredible power. What is her source?"

Pylott handed the question off to Ms. Mars. "She understands that better than I do."

Leucadia came forward.

Papa said, *"Mademoiselle. S'il vous plaît.* But in simple terms, if you would, for those of us who skipped our physics classes."

After the small chuckles, Leucadia answered, "Well, in simple terms, Millie—"

"Millie?" the Asian man asked, interrupting. "Is that what she is called?"

"No, Millie is what the crew calls her. Her real name is *Millawanda,*" Leucadia replied.

"*Millawanda?* Very nice. Beautiful even. Does it have a special meaning?"

"None that we have discovered yet."

Papa returned the conversation to back to physics. "Lu, please continue with Millie's source of energy."

"Oh, yes, her power." She spread out her arms. "Her power is infinite. It comes from the universe itself. It is everywhere."

"She gathers dark energy?" Herr Kaufman asked.

"Yes, because it is everywhere in the galaxy."

Pylott looked impatient, like he had somewhere else to be. "Come on, Lu. You know how Tinker gets when we're late."

"Whoa!" Leader protested, grabbing Pylott by the shoulder. "You're not going anywhere, punk."

"Sorry, Mr. Chance, but we're done with your little takeover game. I have to be in Lakewood by 9 a.m. for a meeting with my principal, Mr. Cross, or I'll never hear the end of it from my mom."

The Asian lady giggled. "Your mom? Mrs. Delmonte? The former first lady? How adorable. You still obey her?"

"I do. She's also a former U.S. Marine D.I. I learned at a very early age not to piss her off."

"You're not serious?" a voice from the Zmaji crowd cried out.

Pylott turned to the voice. "No. I'm quite serious, Sir. My mom insists I graduate from high school before my next offworld mission, or she'll ground me."

Papa waved to take care of the kid. Leader had a huge smile on his face. He had waited all morning to pulverize the snot out of Pylott himself. But before he could raise the butt of his MK5 and crack the kid's skull open, a giant, blue-eyed, white tiger leaped onto the roof of his DPV to protect him. Its maw of incisors was long as a man's arm, gleamed, ready to strike. A second tiger, white and blued-eyed like the first, landed atop Papa's Humvee ready to bite off the first head that would harm Pylott. Finally, as if that weren't enough, the winged dragon from the pool, appeared from main corridor and hovered above them. The creature let go the most godawful screech anyone had ever heard, terrifying them to the bone.

Leader tried to blast the creature out of the air, but his MK5 misfired every time he pulled the trigger. Even when he tried ejecting the cartridge, the rifle still wouldn't fire. He tossed it away like it was a useless piece of scrap, and drew his Glock Gen 7. *Click, click, click.* Not one round fired.

"They won't work. None of your weapons will work," Leucadia emphasized. "They were all neutralized when you went through the force field."

Awol slid next to Pylott, ready to slam the barrel of his HK against the kid's skull. But before he could touch him, Pylott grabbed the rifle and held it steady as a rock. Awol fought with all his strength to move his weapon, but Pylott overpowered him with strength far greater than his. He simply twisted it away from Awol's hands and shoved the 300-pound mercenary against a parked Humvee like he was a small child. Awol slumped to the floor and didn't move. "Take care of your soldier, Mr. Chance," Pylott said to Leader, and tossed the HK away.

Leader grew even angrier. "You're dead, kid." Spitting mad, Leader added, "When this is done, it's just you and me. *Mano a mano.*"

The kid's steel blue eyes did not flinch. He nodded at Awol. "Just do it."

Dead silence fell over the room, as Leader eyed the open mouth of the tiger. It came within six inches of his head before he motioned for DuckFart and BigBoard to pick Awol off the floor and put him into the DPV.

Pylott spoke to an unseen entity. "What's our 10-20, Mr. Riverstone?"

"*Parked and ready to accept our new guests, Captain,*" came the reply of another young voice.

"My men have your bridge," Leader pointed out.

Pylott turned and pointed at a squad of mercenaries walking from one of the passageways along with a tall droid and two smaller droids with fake long hair. The stick-bots had all the weapons. Right behind them was their DPV, driven by the droid with the bright bowtie. "I'm afraid what they thought was the bridge was only a simulator." He crossed his arms in front of him. "Did you really believe that you arrogant toads could possibly steal the most powerful warbird in the galaxy? This machine traveled the stars before our ancestors walked upright on this planet. You may be big dudes on Earth, but when you crossed that force field," he said, pointing his thumb toward the hatchway, "you entered my world. This is my ship. Now get your sorry butts off my ship."

Cardé found the directive bewildering. "You're letting us go?"

"Yes, Ms. Cardé, I'm letting you go. We are not killers. We are Gamadin. We protect freedom and liberty for all the beings in this galaxy, not just a few swampdaks that want to control the world."

"We can give you so much more," Papa offered.

"*Vous pouvez nous offrir rien, monsieur.* We are not interested in power, Sir. We have all that we need, and its everywhere, and infinite. Your time is up, dude! *Fini!* The people of Earth are taking their planet back."

"And I suppose you, a mere boy, will crown himself king?" Tucker asked, like he wanted to spit.

"No, Mr. Tucker, my mom would rip me a new one if I tried that. Besides, you're the small fish. We have a galaxy out there that's full of bigger swampdaks needing our attention."

Tucker scoffed at the idea. "If not us, then someone else will take our place. The lust to rule will always be the goal of man."

Pylott nodded in agreement. "True, Mr. Tucker. You are absolutely right. Even I, who have the power to be king, can't alter what has always been. I can only create an invisible hand to protect Earth and its people."

Tucker laughed at the thought of an invisible hand guiding the planet. "A la Adam Smith, I presume. That's a joke."

"Freedom has worked every time it's tried, Sir," Pylott responded. "Adam Smith was onto something: Allow the invisible hand of human nature to rule."

It was Cardé's turn to scoff. "There would be chaos everywhere."

"Only when governments end their rule. Eliminate them. Enforce the Gamacode. Problem solved."

"Gamacode. What is that?" Papa asked.

"The invisible hand, Sir."

"So who will be judge, jury, and executioner of this code? You?" Papa asked, irate.

"No, Sir, The Code. The Code is the law now. When you are gone, it will be the law that rules us all, including me."

"When we are gone? You keep saying that as if we will no longer exist," the Asian lady pointed out.

"That's right, Ms. Wong. When you and the Zmaji are gone," Pylott replied, and motioned the groups toward their vehicles as the portal to the outside reopened to the outside world again. "Like I said, time to go."

65

The Choice

Millawanda

EVELYN DU BEAR, Tucker, Ms. Cardé, Ms. Wong, Herr Kaufman, and the Russian packed themselves into the back seats of the lead vehicle. DuckFart held the front door open for Leader, who confronted Pylott one more time before getting in. "We're not done here, punk."

It happened so fast; no one saw the blow that sent Leader to the floor. "Oh yeah, we are."

DuckFart stared at the still body, aghast at the swiftness with which Leader was taken down. "Did you kill him?" DuckFart asked.

Harlowe motioned for the mercenaries to remove the body, and replied, "No, probably not."

Without delay, BigBoard and Psycho lifted Leader off the carpet and placed him next to Awol. That done, BigBoard approached Pylott, concerned over the other mercenaries that were being detained by a line of droids and the white tigers. "What about them?"

"They will have a choice to make. You don't."

"But—"

"Get in the car, dude." Harlowe's tone was definitely not a request.

The dragon ambled toward them, looking really hungry. BigBoard didn't hesitate. He squished in beside DuckFart and shut the door. "Step on it!" he barked. DuckFart slammed the shifter into drive, and off he drove through the open portal. The other Humvees and the five DPVs followed. The remaining six mercenaries stood anxiously around the last DPV, wondering why they were being singled out. As Pylott made his way over to the group, the droid with the bright colored bowtie met him with a change of fresh clothes. Pylott took the offered jeans, white and red Lakewood High School #7 football jersey, and blue tennis shoes from the droid, and continued on toward the group. He slipped behind the front vehicle and said, "Excuse me," as he began changing into his clothes. Peering over the top of the hood, he continued addressing the skittish soldiers. "You all can relax. You're not in trouble."

A tall, black soldier came forward looking rather annoyed. "Yeah… well, why are we detained then?" he said in a highly educated English-South African accent.

"Because each of you have a choice to make." Harlowe pointed across the black hood at the open hatchway. "They didn't."

The mercenary's face expressed his confusion.

Harlowe pulled his jersey over his head. "The answer is simple. You're not cold-blooded killers like the others." He smiled easily. "Don't get me wrong. You're not pure as the driven snow, either. You are all quite capable of taking care of business. But you don't kill for the pleasure. You do it, as you were led to believe, for God, country, and all the right reasons, Mr. Patosi."

The black man turned hostile. "No one knows my name, not even Leader."

"I know all your names," Harlowe said.

"We were told this ship would take over the planet if we didn't capture it. That our homes and families would be ruled by an alien force so powerful, it would be the end of mankind as we know it," Patosi clarified.

Harlowe zipped up his fly and stepped out from the front of the vehicle to join Ms. Mars. "I'm here to tell you that was all a lie. We are the good guys. Those swampdaks out there have been keeping you in the dark for centuries."

Ms. Mars waved at their heads, "So please, remove your masks, gentlemen and lady," she directed, acknowledging the only female in the group. "We know who you are," and proceeded to name them off individually, "Titan Taldoor, Luvo Patosi, Warus Knap, Thadeus Frank, Monsieur Hookan Yaakan and, of course, Izabel Barbara. And where you come from: the South Sotho tribe, Patty," the South African's call moniker, "Brazil's Rocinha, Tootie," she nodded respectfully. She went to Knap, "Nebraska farm boy, right Beast?"

Beast came stick-straight, showing his pride. "That's right, ma'am. Cornhusker born and bred."

And to the tall hunk, she smiled and said, "Thadeus Frank from Marfa, Texas. Welcome, Doodle."

Doodle gave her a disarming smile. "Thank you, ma'am."

Next was Titan Taldoor. "Kreetan from down under Australia, I presume."

Kreetan stepped out and turned to the small crowd. "What no applause?"

Patty gave him three unceremonious claps.

"You all have something against Aussie's?" Kreetan asked.

"Sorry, that's all you get, chum," Doodle replied.

Ms. Mars slid smoothly to her left. "And finally, our Swiss mountaineer, Yaa-man."

Yaa-man bowed elegantly. "*Merci, Mademoiselle* Mars. A pleasure."

All six soldiers were in their twenties and as physically fit as any elite soldier in the world. From what Leucadia could see, Papa had chosen the best of the best to be part of his assault team. But like Harlowe had mentioned earlier, they were all good soldiers, and good soldiers followed orders. Some were God-fearing, some were not, some had girlfriends and a boyfriend, but none were married or had families. They all loved their countries and their planet, and would fight to the death for all mankind.

Harlowe tied his shoes on the front bumper, addressing the group. "You are here because you have a choice to make before we leave this planet."

Kreetan stepped forward. He was equally as tall as Pylott and easily thirty pounds heavier, but like the others, there wasn't an ounce of fat on him. "Oh yeah, and what would that be Governor?" he asked.

Harlowe turned to Ms. Mars with a boyish grin. "Governor? I like the sound of that."

Ms. Mars rolled her eyes. "Stick with the program, Hon."

"Right," snapping out from his stupor. He returned to the mercenary and answered his question. "You can go with the swampdaks that brought you here, or you can come with us. The choice will be yours to make, Mr. Taldoor."

"Why are you giving us a choice? Why not just let us drive away? We know the way home, Governor," Kreetan said.

Harlowe grinned, knowing he had the best hand at the table. "Not necessarily, Mr. Taldoor. If you would follow Ms. Mars, she will escort you to that large disk over there. It is there you will find your answer, Sir."

They hesitated like they were being led to a gas chamber until one of the white cats lumbered up behind them a let out a low growl of encouragement.

"Now, Molly, be nice," Leucadia said, and gave the cat a big hug. "She's just a lovable fur ball, aren't you, girl?"

The mercenaries were taking no chances. They hurried along to the disk without further protest. When they were all on the disk, Leucadia nodded, and they all winked away.

66
Plains of Tall Grass

Unknown

THE FORCE FIELD was gone, so the vehicles rolled past the perimeter of the giant saucer without stopping. The Cartel vehicles drove on for a short distance before coming to a slow stop on the dirt road. The passengers began to exit, gawking up at a yellow sun that was somehow different. The unnatural green sky was the first oddity, the first of many things out of place. The morning sun wasn't right either. It should have been rising over the nearby desert mountains. But instead, the sun was overhead like it was high noon, and there were no nearby mountains. The mountains were now a massive range of snow-pack peaks, jutting upward like the Swiss Alps. Tucker tapped his diamond Rolex day-date watch. Even his watch said it was morning, not midday. Somehow even his watch was unaware of the passage of time. The ground around them had also changed. It wasn't the dry, brush-covered desert valley anymore. It was replaced by a lush green plain of tall grass that spread out all around them. The nearby oasis pool was gone, but off in the distance, there was a serene lake with a ribbon of white sandy beach surrounding it. The waterfowl swimming and dipping their bills for lunch were unlike

367

any birds he had ever seen. But the most amazing oddity of all was the three moons hanging above the horizon. That shocked everyone.

"Where are we, Sir?" BigBoard asked, coming to Papa.

With his hand touching his mouth, Papa stepped out in front of his Humvee, trying to make sense of it all. "I don't understand," he kept mumbling to himself. "We had it all worked out…"

"This doesn't look like Nevada, BigBoard," DuckFart stammered slowly.

Tucker overheard the mercenary and nodded in agreement. "It's not, son. We're on another world."

"But how is that possible?"

Tucker just pointed up at the saucer. There was no other way to explain it. Somehow in the short span of time they were on the ship, they had transported to an unknown world without any sensation that they had ever moved at all. They had not felt any force of acceleration, no movement up or down, no vibration, no motion, no engine sounds that would make them believe they had flown one inch away from LeBeau Park, Nevada.

* * *

"Oh mon Dieu. Ceci est impossible," Yaa-man gasped. The Swiss mercenary was the first to understand the change.

Doodle concurred, in his elegant Texas drawl. "This isn't Texas either, folks," he declared, tipping his hat toward Tootie.

"Where is here?" Beast asked.

"Not Earth, that's for sure," Kreetan answered, gawking at the moons, his eyes absorbing as much of the alien landscape as they could hold.

A terrifying beastly scream broke the silence. Whatever it was, lay hidden in the tall grasses of the plains.

"I'm not sure I like this place," Tootie confessed, inching her way back to the disk with one hand on her Glock and the other withdrawing her foot long knife from her belt.

Beast saw Patty stepping back on the disk. "Where are you going, stud? You're not scared of a little critter, are you?"

Patty replied as he made his way to the center of the disk. "I've made my decision. You can stay here if you want, but I'm going with the beautiful green-eyed lady." He looked around at his feet. "Where is the back button for this thing?"

A Jurassic carnivore over twelve feet tall with huge razor-sharp incisors leaped up from its lair and snagged a large fowl twenty feet off the ground before disappearing again into the tall grass.

Doodle pushed Beast aside. "I've seen enough. I'm with Patty and Tootie," he said, as the others hopped aboard, helping Patty look for any sign of a return button.

* * *

Two magnificent high-stepping horned steeds trotted down the ramp and made their way toward Papa and his entourage.

"Whoa, Delamo," Pylott said to his mount, as he rode up to their vehicles. "Welcome to Tinkerville, ladies and gentlemen."

Tucker found the name rather boorish. "Tinkerville? Really. This place is called Tinkerville?"

"Get used to it, Ricky, it's your new home," Pylott replied, pointing off in the distance at the high fence, surrounding a huge compound.

"And where would that be, son?" Papa asked, finally finding his voice.

Pylott smiled pleasantly, as he looked back over his shoulder at the lake. "On a planet, far, far, away, Monsieur du Bear," he replied, borrowing a line from an old *Star Wars* movie series.

Ms. Cardé stepped forward, holding her Cartier purse firmly at her side. "You don't mean to keep us here, do you?"

"I do," Pylott answered directly.

"For how long?" she asked. "I have meetings to attend this morning. My little Daisy must have her paws manicured, her coat trimmed and brushed for her showing this afternoon at the Westminster Kennel Club Show in Madison Square Garden."

"She'll be late," Pylott replied unconcerned.

"This is outrageous, young man. I protest!"

"*Ferme ta bouche, Leslie*," Papa snapped, and gestured BigBoard with a tweak of his head to silence her petulant voice.

"I will not shut my mouth, du Bear. I demand – " Ms. Cardé dropped unconscious into the soldier's arms after a slap to the jaw.

Papa came back to Pylott: "I would like to know that answer myself. For how long are you detaining us?" he asked.

Pylott squinted at the sun. "For the rest of your lives should do it," he answered, and then looked out at the lake again like it was calling to him.

The crowd of Zmaji protested as Papa shouted back in French, "*Vous ne voulez pas dire cela!*"

Pylott understood him perfectly. "Oh, but I mean every word, Mr. du Bear."

"Where is Earth?" DuckFart asked, still in shock over the moons on the horizon.

Pylott pointed at the middle moon. "Just to the right of that one, and about four and half light-years away."

"Impossible!" Ms. Wong shot back. "This is a movie set . . . a Hollywood stage, like the moon landing. You're tricking us. None of this is real!"

Pylott patted his steed and stated, "Like I told Herr Kaufman, Millie travels fast, and with her new upgrades, well, I hardly felt a thing, did you?"

Ms. Wong glared at the group, looking for support. "This is staged, I tell you!"

"Think what you want. But Tinkerville is your new digs." Pylott lifted his eyes toward a Grannywagon drifting down from the saucer's underbelly. A blond girlbob was driving the Generals Van Dyke and Frank in the back seat while Admiral Meads rode shotgun. All three were holding umbrella drinks, wearing bright colored Hawaiian shirts, and puffing on Cubans, listening to Vivaldi. "Sheila and the Gentlemen will show you the way to Tinkerville."

* * *

The Grannywagon came along side the Cartel vehicles. "Did you have a nice breakfast, Gentlemen?" Pylott asked the officers.

"The best I've ever had," Meads replied.

"How was the bacon, General?" Pylott asked Van Dyke.

Van Dyke blew him a kiss. "First cabin, Captain. Sylvia is the best!"

"She's yours when you get home, Sir," Pylott said.

"My wife will love you forever."

Herr Kaufman made a sour face. The officer's expressions seemed way too happy. "Why are they here?"

Pylott spotted Ms. Mars coming toward the group from across the grassy field, as he answered Tucker, "To inspect the complex and see that you have all the necessities."

"Why are they exempt? They were part of the leadership of the country," Tucker asked.

"Did they ever accept money from you?"

"No, they were all good 'Boy Scouts.'"

"That's why. There is good leadership, and there is bad leadership, Sir. These officers are patriots. They represent the best of the best. They were never swampdaks. They fought for our country and have stood in harm's way many times to defend us. They believe in a Constitution, freedom, and apple pie. You, on the other hand, do not."

"You think you've gotten rid of us? You haven't. Tinkerville is a bunch of hogwash!" Tucker shouted at Pylott.

Pylott met Tucker's angry eyes with his own. "Careful, Mr. Tucker, that's my mother you're insulting. If she gets wind that you called her hogwash . . . she'll break both your legs, for starters."

"What about the President?" Tucker asked.

"What about her?" Pylott countered.

"You think you can dispose of her? She'll take you down just like she did Delmonte."

Pylott leaned forward, holding onto the black sable mane with his right hand. "Mr. Tucker. You just don't get it. The reign of government is over, including hers."

Visibly shaken, Tucker lost it and came after Pylott with both cast hands flailing. "Time to meet your Maker, punk!" But before he could strike, Pylott's shoe snapped outward, slamming into Tucker's forehead. The banker stumbled back dazed, and collapsed to the ground.

"Not today, Mr. Tucker," Pylott observed, like he had just swatted a fly.

Leucadia walked up and saw Ms. Cardé passed out in the back seat of Papa's Humvee. "What happened to her?"

"She had a first world problem," Pylott replied.

"And Mr. Tucker?"

"The same."

Understanding that Pylott had everything under control, she asked,

"Ready?"

"Good to go." Pylott reached down and lifted her onto the second beast. "Anyone staying?" he asked her.

Leucadia looked over at the group of mercenaries who had been given the choice of staying or leaving. All six were frantically waving their arms up and down at her, trying to get her attention. "I'm pretty sure from the look of them that they're leaving with us."

"Good. Make sure they get something to eat," Pylott said, pointing his steed's head for the lake.

"Simon will be taking them to the forward piano room."

"Perfect." Harlowe leaned over and kissed her. "Nice work, Ms. Mars."

"You're most welcome, Pylott."

"Come on, I'll race ya to the lake."

"We don't have time, Harlowe," Leucadia said, and tried to warn him. "You know your mom. If we're late—"

Harlowe didn't care. "I know, I know, but look at the day, Lu. It's too nice. Besides, Delamo and Josie need to stretch their legs." The horned beasts pranced and bayed, as they waited eagerly to be let loose and run wild along white sandy beaches. "Are you going to tell them no?" he asked.

"How long do we have, Matthew?" Leucadia asked Riverstone, who was on the bridge.

"*Twenty minutes, Lu...tops, before we have to head back to Lakewood,*" Riverstone's voice replied aloud.

Pylott charged ahead. "Plenty of time, Lu!"

"You're cheating!"

67

Tinkerville

Unknown World

RIVERSTONE EASED BACK in the center command chair, observing the line of black ops vehicles and Humvees on the overhead. The Grannywagon led the way toward the gated settlement off in the distance. "And there goes the final batch of toads to Tinkerland."

"Tinkerville, Sir," Prigg advised.

Riverstone winced. The little Naruckian always corrected him for the slightest tweak. *All right, already!* "Whatever, Mr. Prigg," Riverstone mumbled, then replied normally, "It's all good riddance."

Simon twisted around in his console chair, rubbing his chin. "Next time we get used as punching bags, we call Nicto sooner. My jaw is still cockeyed."

Riverstone felt his nose. "Alice was awesome. Think your makeup babe can fix my nose for next week's shoot?"

Simon squinted with doubt. "Not that schnoz." He saw that Riverstone had suddenly lost his mirth. "What's wrong? Worried about Phoebs?"

"Yeah, she wasn't part of the plan, and I almost lost her."

"She surprised me how tough she turned out."

"They scared me, Simon. They were going to kill her."

"I know."

"Never again. People around us die if they're not . . ." Riverstone couldn't say it.

Simon understood where he was going. They had lost more than one relationship to bad luck. "If they're not Gamadin?"

"Yeah, if they're not Gamadin. Can we talk about something else?"

"Sure. How 'bout Dog. He did it. He pulled it off. Did we get them all?" Simon wondered.

"We got enough…" Riverstone replied. "That's all he cared about. The top of the food chain."

Simon still wasn't happy. "I want them all. Every last scumbag."

Riverstone looked at Simon, deep in thought. "I used to think that way, Mr. Bolt, until I was pulled over speeding in Harlowe's bug. Stop me if you've heard the story before."

"Go on. You're going to tell me anyway."

Riverstone continued with his tale. "So this officer pulls me over for speeding and I say: Everyone else was going faster than the limit, officer. Why me? He says: Son, when you go fishing, do you expect to catch all the fish in the lake? I said no, just the biggest one. He smiled at me as he kept writing out the ticket. Exactly, you're my big fish for today. He hands me the ticket and says: Have a nice day, and slow down."

Simon looked at Riverstone with a smirk. "Did you slow down?"

"Are you kidding? I had five more tickets before we made it back to Lakewood."

Simon's mouth dropped. "FIVE! How come you didn't go to jail?"

"Because Harlowe took over."

"I thought his license was revoked," Simon said.

"It was. But he was tired of getting stopped and wanted to get to the beach because it was pumping big time. And you know Harlowe when it comes to waves."

"Yeah, but I can't imagine him going slower than you," Simon said.

Riverstone laughed. "He didn't. And not just a little bit. He broke the sound barrier going through Seal Beach."

Simon looked at Riverstone with a whole lot of doubt. "And he didn't get caught?"

Riverstone just shook his head. "Nope." He snickered. "Well, two cops tried, but Harlowe, being who he is, ducked down the back alleys and into Harry's garage before they caught him."

Simon thought his whole yarn was a stretch.

Riverstone pointed out one glaring fact: "Trust me, there's not a cop in Newport that would enter the Mars garage without permission."

"You weren't afraid of crashing?" Prigg asked.

Riverstone's eyes displayed the memories of many such occasions. He took a deep breath and sighed, "When Harlowe's driving, you have a tendency to keep your eyes closed or you'll lose your lunch, Mr. Prigg."

Simon raised his hand. "I'll second that," recalling the race to save Leucadia's life, before they were Gamadin. With Daks chasing them and Harlowe driving the lead car, his brand new, quarter-million dollar Austin Martin was a total wreck by the time they made it to Utah. He still had nightmares over it.

Prigg's center eye began to go haywire. Riverstone laughed, returning his thoughts to Tinkerville. The circular compound, where the Zmaji would spend the rest of their lives, covered nearly five hundred acres. Plenty of extra room for growth, he figured whimsically. The large domed warehouse in the center stored the supplies and solar energy production they needed to survive in their new homes. Besides the Quonset-style living quarters around the dome, there were acres of fields for food production and grazing pastures for the goats, sheep, and cattle. They would be living like the "preppers" they often criticized in the media. Many of the occupants had never grown anything in their lives. But they would access a whole host of YouTube videos from which to learn new skills, or they would die. There was plenty of water and sunlight. Most of the year, which was twenty-seven days longer than Earth's, the weather was mild like the Mediterranean. It was only during the planet's winter months that temperatures drop below freezing.

If good weather and a well stocked supply house were Tinkerville pluses, there were also a few negatives. The population's main concern would always be the number of natural predators that inhabited the region. The twenty-foot high, electrified fence surrounding the compound wasn't built to keep the occupants in. It was built to keep the predators out. Dinosaurs still roamed here. They didn't die out from a giant meteor hitting the planet. Velociraptors, T-rex giants, and the most bloodthirsty meat-eater of them all, the *Spinosaurus*, all existed here, or some variation. They were as common as they were on Earth during the Jurassic Epoch. The ravenous carnivores now included humans who might wander out beyond the fence without protection as new entrées.

Riverstone checked the time on the upper screen. "Okay, gents, I'm off-the-clock in three, two, one, bzzzz," he sounded. "My time is up."

Simon looked around at the desolate bridge. "Where is everyone?"

Riverstone stopped halfway to the blinker to answer. "Dodge asked to borrow the limo to drop off Sergeant Enihoo and Captain Searle in Colorado. It seems they're going help Mrs. Dutch pack up and make the move to D.C., where the General will take over the Pentagon and help Braxton and President Delmonte in implementing the new Gamacode."

"He needs the limo for that?"

"He said he did."

"There are going to be a lot of unemployed bureaucrats come Monday morning. What about Admiral Meads and General Branch?" Simon asked.

"They're going fishing somewhere in Montana with someone called Hatchet."

"Timmer still recuperating on that island?"

"Dutch gave him a month off to recuperate before joining him in D.C."

"I saw a picture of his nurse. I'm giving five to one odds his bachelor days are over."

Riverstone fired a finger pistol back. "Can you blame him?" He turned to Prigg, as he marched to the disk. "How much time before we blow this Jurassic Park, Mr. Prigg?"

"If you mean this planet, Mr. Riverstone, not for another sixty-seven minutes."

"Perfect, my man. Thank you."

"Where are you going in such a rush?" Simon asked. Riverstone's happy grin increased ear to ear. "Never mind," Simon replied the instant Riverstone winked away. He knew exactly where he was headed.

68

Have a Nice Day

Tinkerville Gates
Unknown World

GENERAL VAN DYKE couldn't believe his eyes. "Well, looky there."
The blue and white symbol of American power throughout the world,
Air Force One, was parked behind the Tinkerville compound. All the
doors of the 797 Dreamliner were open, and only one escape chute was
activated. No flight crews or attendants were anywhere to be seen. The
plane was completely abandoned.

The three senior officers traded several bemused glances before
General Branch said, aghast, "If I hadn't seen it with my own eyes…"

Admiral Meads twisted around in his front seat. "You don't suppose
our dear Madame President was on it when the Captain nabbed it, do
you, Ivan?"

Branch snorted confidently, "Our young Captain would say, 'Count
on it!'"

Van Dyke tapped Sheila's seat. "Hurry, hon, let's get the rest of
these swamp-things booked so we can see who else the Captain snared."
Since leaving InZeeOut, the three officers had been giddy anticipating

377

what else the young "Captain," as they referred to him, had in his latest roundup of Cartel captives from around the globe. From the moment the *Ron Paul* docked at InZeeOut, and they saw the hundreds gathered behind the glass walls, they understood the unimaginable scope the young Captain's plans were for the future of mankind.

Stepping off the *Ron Paul*, they were greeted by the largest robob they had ever seen. The big droid didn't speak a lick but guided them over to another glass building where they ate like they were at a California beach party. It wasn't just finger food, donuts, coffee, sodas, vegetable plates, chips and dip, either. It was hamburgers, hot dogs, curly fries, shakes, sodas, and guacamole by the bucket. It was all wonderfully prepared and plenty of it. The girlbobs in their various wigs served it all up, and they never ran out of food. The new age delicacies kept coming and coming from a source no one understood. The Captain and Ms. Mars joined the party soon after everyone began chowing down. They flew in on a cool-looking platform that sat them right on the dock. The Captain asked the three officers, including Captain Alexander, to walk with him and Ms. Mars as they explained why they were brought to InZeeOut.

Meads had to know something first. "Where did you get the name, InZeeOut, from the hamburger chain?"

The Captain winked. "We borrowed the idea." He pointed at the Secretary of State Minott, who was pounding on the glass wanting out. From the way her mouth was pumping out unspeakables, she was clearly upset over the whole idea of being interned. "She comes 'in' and soon 'zee' will go 'out' on the next cruise to Tinkerville."

"Got it."

"Tinkerville?" Van Dyke wondered.

"Yes, that's her final destination," Ms. Mars replied.

Van Dyke realized his first prediction about InZeeOut was correct. "So this is a staging area?"

Ms. Mars answered again. "Yes. Swampdaks, that's what we call the Zmaji, are captured from all over the world and brought here first, before they are flown off-world."

"To another planet?" Van Dyke asked.

"Bye, bye," the Captain confirmed.

"For how long?" Meads asked.

"Forever, long enough?" the Captain replied.

Branch added his own finality. "With no time off for good behavior, I hope."

"None."

Van Dyke kinked his head up, scanning InZeeOut and the wonder of it all, the vast ice cavern, the glass structures, the pyramids, and the hoard of boats, planes, and limousines piled up in the distance, all in which the Cartel had been captured. "So how did you find this place?"

"Wiz found it," the Captain replied.

Ms. Mars saw the blank look on their faces and added, "He's our science officer. He had the idea that our ship, *Millawanda*, was coming back to a Gamadin station here on Earth. But by the time Millie arrived, the Earth had shifted its axis, making the continent of Antarctica a hidden frozen world covered by miles of ice.

"Antarctica was a sunny place at one time?" Branch asked.

"A tropical paradise. When Wiz heard that researchers discovered evidence of tropical vegetation here, he flew down, in a smaller version of *Millawanda*, and found it. InZeeOut was not only a Gamadin outpost at the edge of our galaxy, but a vacation destination for Gamadin crews during their off-the-clock time," she explained.

"Wow..." Van Dyke cooed as he touched the glass, ignoring Minott's constantly moving jaws and fists pounding on the wall. She could smack, kick, or slam herself against the glass all she wanted, but no one could hear a thing through the ancient material. She was a silent movie playing in the background. "It feels so new. It's hard to believe it's that old."

"So how can we help you, Captain?" Branch asked, returning to the business of InZeeOut.

"I want you gentlemen to oversee our operation. Design any changes to InZeeOut you think will be more efficient. We're going to be taking in a lot more Swampdaks in the coming days, so we'll need your help in making it work smoothly."

"No one dies, huh?" Branch asked with disappointment in his tenor.

"No one dies," the Captain affirmed. "As much as we would all like to see them sprouting wings, there is no need with our way. They had their chance here in heaven, now they can serve in hell, or they can take the coward's way out. You'll see what I mean at a later time. As for now, feel free to wander about in our five hundred century-old city," he said, tapping the glass that sent Minott raging all over again. The big robob that greeted them at the dock clickity-clacked up to the Captain who introduced him properly. "This is Bigbob. My right hand, dude."

"Yes, we met earlier. Serves a hellava meal," Meads complimented.

"He is amazing. You want a wall built, a table made, or a banquet served, he's your go-to guy."

Van Dyke tapped the big robob on its ball shoulder. "Can I get a small one for my wife?"

"Sure, anything for Mrs. Dutch," the Captain promised.

* * *

Sheila pulled up beside two people walking with their heads down away from the Tinkerville gates. "Good afternoon, Madame," General Branch said, recognizing the disheveled lady.

Shame's puffy red face looked up. Her eyes were swollen and bloodshot. She needed a drink desperately. But to her dismay, there was not an ounce of adult beverage anywhere in the compound. She couldn't even drink herself to death. She looked like she had been in a wrestling match and lost. Her clothes were unkempt, soiled, and torn along the sleeves. The gentlemen next to her fared no better. "I thought we killed you three," she grunted hoarsely.

"Almost," Branch replied.

"Sorry, we can't stay for dinner," Van Dyke chimed in.

General Drgastin flipped them off. "Next time."

Meads drew on his cigar as he pointed his thumb over his shoulder. "If you're planning on walking past the gates, Sledge, I'd watch out for the raptors out there. I understand this is their feeding time."

Shame pushed Drgastin aside as she leaned toward the Grannywagon with death in her eyes. "Take that Cuban, Meads, and jam it where the sun don't shine."

"Just trying to be helpful, Madame," Meads told her.

The gutter language continued as she grabbed Drgastin by the arm and yanked him away from the wheelless car. The two continued on their way out the gate with both right-hands raised high in the air. The officers figured it was their way of saying, 'Have a nice day.'

69

Ça va. Ça va

Tinkerville Compound
Unkown World

PAPA'S HUMVEE DROVE through the heavy gates of the compound with no one knowing who he was or if he was anyone to them. Hanging high overhead, a plain metal sign read: "Welcome to Tinkerville."

BigBoard grunted his displeasure, offering up a chain of profanity. "I'll rip that kid's heart out the next time I see him."

DuckFart snorted, "Yeah, right. Did you see how easily he took down Leader and that Southern banker? Consider yourself lucky to still be alive, suckwad."

Papa ignored their conversation. He heard nothing beyond his own personal space. He had been silent as death since his plan to seize the alien ship had turned into a catastrophic failure. He should have known better. Looking back, the warnings were clear. When President Sanborne failed years ago to capture Caesar with the full might of the United States military behind him, that should have been the end of it. But the chance to possess the most powerful weapon ever known to man had been too great a prize to pass up. After many centuries of power the Zmaji were finished. There was no going back, no second chance, no do overs. The Du Bear banking cartel would join the trash dumpsters of history along with the other fallen empires of Rome, the Ottomans, Mongols, Troy, and Alexander.

Papa cupped his head in his hands in disbelief at how the kid had played him. He had sucked them in like a giant vacuum. Pylott was beyond a mere player. He was a grand master. Unbeatable. He lifted his head and looked out at the light blue and white flying fortress. Even Shame had lost. No member of the cartel was spared. The greed for power, the "one ring to rule them all," was their downfall. In a single day, what his family had spent hundreds of years to amass had ended on a planet light-years from Earth. Who could have seen that coming?

He was so incensed by the helplessness he felt, that death seemed his only way out. He tried to believe it was all a dream. But as his vehicle drove through the compound, the manufactured huts and the people mingling around in an almost zombie state, it was shatteringly obvious that Tinkerville was not a dream, but a stark and ugly reality. The thought of spending the rest of his life exiled on an unknown speck in the middle of the galaxy without the power he had known all his life, was too much to accept. The luxuries, the privileged existence, the making of kings, emperors, presidents, prime ministers, oligarchs, and despots, were all behind him. Waging war, manipulating stock markets, currencies, commodities, was gone forever. He had no control over anything but his own pitiful life, and now all he wanted to do was end it with a bullet.

A silver-haired man in his late sixties stepped to the car and opened the door. "Hello, Papa." The man's voice, as was his eyes, was filled with the fear of the unknown. His eyes darted from side to side, shaking with hopelessness. He was unable to focus on anything for longer than a brief moment. Papa finally recognized the overweight man in his dirty bathrobe, baggy shorts, and bedroom slippers. He was Lawrence Circosta, the senior United States Senator from New York. He had been on Papa's payroll since he entered politics thirty-seven years ago. But without his toupee, his $10,000 William Fioravanti Super 220 merino wool suit, his entourage of yes-men and Secret Service agents, and the slew of handpicked reporters with their cameras and mics, he was nothing more than a street bum.

"Who else is here, Senator?" Papa asked.

The Senator's voice trembled. "Who else?"

"Yes, Larry, who else was taken?"

The Senator pinched at his lower lip. "Why everyone, Sir. Nearly the entire United States Congress. The British King and Queen are here, the Prime Minister, and much of the parliament arrived yesterday. In C, D, and E huts are the French and German parliaments, the entire European Commission, IMF in total, the FED, all here, all eight districts, and all the central bankers from around the globe. The Church..." He coughed as he wiped the drool from his chin. "So are many clergy of all denominations. Middle Eastern royalty, princes and princesses, and their whole line of succession are all in B hut. How did this happen, Papa?"

He knew the answer, but what difference did it make? He stepped away from the politician and watched Father Espinosi shuffle past him without looking up. Everyone inside the compound had the same look, that of a crowd of lost refugees after the apocalypse. He saw associates, allies, and puppets, his yes-men, and CEOs of his banking empires. They were all exiled like him. A beautiful dark-haired woman in her forties pressed her way through the crowd coming toward him. Her blue eyes were full of tears. "Papa!" she cried out, reaching for him. It was his daughter, and the person he loved most in his life. He had groomed her since childhood to take over when he was gone. But sadly, her place at the Zmaji table would never be.

"Andressa," he said as she fell, trembling into his arms. "Cher Dieu. You as well?"

"Oui, Papa," his daughter replied, sobbing.

"And my sons? Jacque and Jean Luc?"

"Yes, they are here," she sobbed.

Papa didn't know whether to be happy or sad that his sons and his family were part of the outcasts.

Through her sniffling Andressa added, "The Cercle came last night, Papa."

The *Cercle* was Du Bear's family of central bankers. A dear friend of Du Bear's great, great grandfather once said, if he "controlled the nation's money, he cared not who wrote the laws." Because Du Bear and his *Cercle* controlled the money, they had controlled the world.

"Will we ever see home again, Papa?" she asked.

A squad of olive dressed soldiers interrupted his reply. Not one soldier was from his team. The look on each face left no room for kindness. They were not here to greet him. They had come to escort him. "Monsieur Du Bear?"

"Yes," Papa replied. "What do you want?" he inquired with his daughter still in his arms.

"I'm not at liberty to say, Sir, only that you are to come with us, immediately," the soldier replied.

"And if I refuse?"

"Come with us under your own power or ours. The choice is yours, Sir, but you are coming with us, Sir."

"Papa…" Andressa said fearful.

BigBoard and DuckFart marched forward ready to assist Papa, but he held them back. "No. I will go. But thank you," he told them, and then added, "You have served me well. But now you are free to follow your own paths."

"But Sir…"

"No, you must not interfere."

Andressa would not leave his side. "Papa…"

"*Ça va…*" Papa said quietly in her ear. "*Ça va. Ça va.* It's okay, my sweet." He gently gave her to BigBoard. He then straightened himself up, brushed his sleeves, and faced the guards proudly, chin held high. "Messieurs, I am ready."

70

Like Arguing with a Zabit

A Nameless Lake
Unknown World

TWO MILES FROM the ship, Harlowe and Leucadia let the ceffyls run flat out. No earthly horses could have matched their speed. As they splashed along the shore, kicking up sand, feeling the spray and wind in their faces, they headed back to the ship. Leucadia pointed at her wrist first then at the ship, reminding Harlowe his mother wanted him back to Earth as soon as possible for the meeting with Mr. Cross. "That's horse hockey!" Harlowe protested. Didn't their parents realize their current vocation didn't require a degree? "A million degrees from Harvard or Yale couldn't replace what he had experienced as a Gamadin," he would try to argue.

Harlowe might as well have been arguing with a zabit. Tinker had arranged for a private graduation ceremony with his Principal, Jim Cross for the three of them, Harlowe, Riverstone, and Ian, and there were no ifs, ands, or "but Moms." "You're to be on this planet, in Mr. Cross's office by noon tomorrow, or there will be problems bigger than star systems, young man."

Harlowe threw up his hands. He was captain of the most powerful ship in the galaxy, and his mom was still telling him he had to be home by a certain time. "How much longer do I have to put up with this?"

"Until you're ninety should about do it," Leucadia replied, kissing him on the cheek.

The smooch didn't help at all, but he would do it for his mom and consider it an early Mother's Day present for his trouble. "Wiz won't be back for another week. He's taking the long way home to show Chee the sights. Can you tell her that? She won't believe me."

"Coward."

Harlowe agreed wholeheartedly. "Yup, ya got that right. A coward through and through. I would kiss a grogan any day." Harlowe looked up and pointed between Delamo's two massive horns. It was the Grannywagon racing along the top of the lake, kicking up a big roostertail behind it.

"Sheila wouldn't drive that fast!" Harlowe shouted out.

Even from this distance, Leucadia's alien eyes picked up on the telltale physical attributes of the individual driving. "It's Admiral Meads!" she laughed out loud. "General Van Dyke is next to him, holding his drink, and Sheila's in the back seat with General Branch."

"I think they've had one to many umbrella drinks," Harlowe said, then directed her to tell them to be back in twenty minutes, or he was taking away the keys.

* * *

"Captain on the bridge!" Monday announced. Harlowe stepped away from the blinker and went directly to the command chairs still in his off-the-clock clothes. Simon relinquished the center command chair and moved to his station, leaving the left chair vacant for the person he knew would be arriving shortly. Jewels had a fresh uniform of the day ready for Harlowe, who immediately began barking orders, as he slid into his pants. "Everyone accounted for?"

"Everyone but Riverstone, Captain" Monday replied. "He's checking in on one of our guests. Do you want me to call him?"

The entire crew knew who Riverstone's guest was.

"No, let him be," Harlowe replied, fixing his pants. "Have our joy-riding officers returned, Mr. Prigg?"

"Yes, Your Majesty," Prigg replied. "They are being lifted into the utility room now."

"Cool." Harlowe held his hand up. "Hold on, Mr. Platter. What about Molly and Rhud?"

Simon answered: "Poolside, Skipper. Leucadia says that Molly brought in a half-eaten raptor still kicking and put it down in front of her as a gift."

Harlowe rolled his eyes, "Well, she is a cat." He cinched his waistband and sat down in his command chair. "Millie ready, Mr. Platter?"

"Aye, Captain, She's good to go," Monday affirmed.

Harlowe turned to Prigg and ordered, "Set course for home, Mr. Prigg, but at a casual pace. We have some time to kill before Mr. Wizzixs returns."

Outside the forward observation window the lush green prairie grass and the calm lake with the white sand beaches dropped away as *Millawanda* rose toward the green sky and set course between the distant moons.

71

Good-bye Forever

Tinkerville Compound
Unknown World

DU BEAR HAD LITTLE doubt where his escorts were taking him. What did it matter, he thought? Their abduction was complete. There was no going back. The only way off the planet was the saucer. And when it left… Well, when it left, it was goodbye forever. Adieu pour toujours!

He supposed someone believed that he was useful because he was their leader, the ultimate kingmaker. He would have a leadership role here, of course. From the way the colony looked, most of the people, like the Senator, dressed in his bathrobe and slippers, were still in the clothes they wore the moment they were captured. The colony needed some kind of direction, if they were to survive. If not, then…well…they would die.

For the time being, everyone inside the colony had a numbness about them. They stood around in small packs, still in shock, their predicament too unbelievable to face. Without someone in charge to show them the way, their numbers would dwindle. Soon they would cease to exist. They were all equal now. All stripped of their power. Nothing to live for really, other than the remote possibility they could find a way off the planet.

Adieu pour toujours, he told himself. "Good-bye forever."

His escort guided him between two long Quonset huts to a path they followed past more huts and more lost souls. Finally, they rounded a large metal building, where more guards stood around safeguarding the supply huts. Food and water were the only things of value left. Money, diamonds, gold, and silver had no place in a community of banished souls.

Curiously, the guards did not stop there either. He was running out of structures. They kept escorting him on toward what looked like the outer fence line of the colony.

"What is this?" Du Bear asked indignant. "I am very tired. I want to go to my quarters," he insisted.

A middle-aged man stepped forward dressed in olive green. He was tall and fit, like Chance, with short, gray hair around the temples. He said nothing, only nodded toward the guards standing beside a small gate in the fence.

Two soldiers took Du Bear by the arms and led him through the gate. He tried to protest, but no one answered his shouts to stop this madness. Behind him, he heard protests and screams of a woman. He looked back and Andressa was being led toward the gate along with his three sons.

"No, she did nothing. My daughter is innocent!" Du Bear cried out.

"No Du Bear is innocent," a gruff voice said from behind.

Du Bear's sons, his two brothers, his sister, his cousins, and all their wives and husbands from the inner Cercle were forced through the gate as well, fifty-seven humans in all, but no children. It seemed those below the age of sixteen had not made the trip from Earth.

"Why?" asked Jacque, Papa's middle-aged son.

"You're not welcome here," the soldier directing the expulsion told them all.

"Where will we go?" Jean Luc, his youngest son asked.

The soldier spread his arms. "You have a whole planet out there. Good luck…"

The gate was locked, and the escort guards turned away, leaving the

Du Bear clan to fend for themselves outside the compound.

* * *

A short time later, the clan made their way to the road that led to the saucer. They carried nothing but the clothes they wore. They now believed their only hope of survival was to plead for mercy to Pylott. At the very least, he could transport them to a new location on the planet where they could begin a second colony. Along the way, they heard strange sounds. Some were terrifying animal outcries. When several young men, including his son, ventured off the road in search of water, two enormous beasts suddenly appeared out of the tall grass. The creatures snatched his son and another man in their jaws and they were never seen again. Horrified, the others ran toward the rising saucer shouting, "Help us! Help us, please!" But their outcries went unheard. The ship retracted its long spindly legs, turned slightly on its axis, shot between two small moons above the horizon, and winked away.

Adieu pour toujours!

72

Knock, Knock

Millawanda

THE KNOCK AT the door gave Phoebe a start. Tap, tap, tap, it repeated. Was it the soldiers coming for her again? She was confused. Where was she? How did she get here? This was no cell. She wasn't tied up and gagged. Her room was a thousand times nicer than the dirt floor the kidnappers had thrown her in. Twice she had ventured outside her room. There were no guards at her door, either, or anywhere else she could see, for that matter. The corridor was completely deserted. With only a blue robe on, she would go no farther without makeup. Whether they be soldiers or hotel employees, she didn't want to be caught inappropriately dressed. Not yet anyway. During her brief foray, she found no references that would indicate her new location. She wasn't hungry or thirsty. The croissants and coffee she found at her bedside were tasty and satisfying, so there was no point to leaving. Eventually, she knew whoever brought her here, would be by to check on her.

Tap, tap, tap.

So there they are now, she mused.

The knocking was a little louder this time.

"Phoebs! It's me, Matthew," the voice called to her.

She quickly slapped the activator at the side of the doorway, and instantly the door slid back into its pocket.

"MATTHEW!" she screamed, and ran into Riverstone's arms, nearly knocking him over. "You're alive! The last time I saw you, you were being beaten and tortured. I thought you were dead."

"I know."

Phoebe pushed him away at arms length. "You're okay. You don't appear like you've been hurt at all. How is that possible?"

"I know."

"Who were they? Why did they want to harm us?"

"Some bad guys, Phoebs. Nootzy's Hoods, I don't know. But you're safe here," Riverstone told her, holding her in his arms.

"Where's here, Matthew? Where are we? I don't recognize this hotel."

Riverstone smiled thinly. "It's my ship, Phoebs. And this is your cabin."

"Your ship? My cabin? You're losing me, Matthew," she said, shaking the fog of suffering from her mind.

"Yeah, my ship."

She looked around in silence and wondered, "How come I don't feel anything like swaying or hums, that sort of thing?" She pointed a finger at his nose. "And don't say, I know."

"It's complicated..." Riverstone tried to explain, but before he could say anything, her attention went to his uniform.

"Look at you. You're so nicely dressed. Are we on a movie set, Matthew? Is that what we're doing here?" She touched his sleeve. "Nice. That doesn't look like a Distant Galaxy uniform, mister," she joked.

"It's not, Phoebs. It's my ship's uniform."

"You look so...so military."

"I am."

Phoebe was surprised by the answer. "Really? This is a military ship?"

"Yes and no. I guess it once was."

"Refurbished? How cool."

"This is *Millawanda*, Phoebs."

"*Millawanda*? Love the name. What's it mean?"

Riverstone's face wrinkled up. Now he was at a loss for an answer.

"Don't know. Really cool ship, I think."

Phoebe cocked her head sideways and added a demurring smile. "Yeah, right Matthew. Destroyer? Cruiser? Aircraft carrier? What? "

"Bigger," Riverstone replied, holding his tiny smile so as to not appear like he was teasing her.

"Bigger? What bigger than an aircraft carrier?"

"This ship."

She laughed, hugging him. "You're so full of it. I guess I'll know when I see it." He nodded. "So how did we escape?" she asked, "I don't remember a thing."

Riverstone turned more serious. "After the toads knocked you out, we were rescued, and they brought us here."

She touched her chin. "Simy, too? Tell me he's okay."

He kissed her. "He's fine, Phoebs."

She thought a moment. "I remember that...sort of. My face is still a little sore." She looked back at her room and her eyes turned playful. "Did you undress me?"

He shook, defensively. "Noooo."

She smiled at his innocent face. "Don't fret, Matthew, it's the bad girl in me."

Riverstone raised his right hand. "It wasn't me, I swear, Phoebs. It was Lu."

"A girl?"

"One of our crew."

Phoebe's lower lip stuck out like she was pouting. "I'm crushed." She turned and went back into her cabin. "Oh well, where are my clothes? A girl needs something to wear if she's going to go touring *Millawanda*."

Riverstone watched her toss the robe aside, revealing her shapely figure in all its glory. There was not one tattoo, one scar, not one line or flaw, on her entire California tanned body. It was as if her skin had been airbrushed to perfection.

"Okay, Matthew, find me something to wear or the crew will get an eyeful." She was not the least bit shy.

Riverstone called his girlbob, Alice, who Phoebe already knew from their backyard dinner. The droid led her into the nearby closet, and after a few giggles and bursts of laughter, Phoebe emerged wearing a turquoise and blue jump suit that looked as if it had been sprayed on. Walking to the middle of the room, Phoebe turned to Riverstone, in a New York model pose, and asked, "Does this make my legs look fat?"

Riverstone tried to swallow. "No way."

Phoebe admired Alice standing by the closet door. "I never thought such technology was possible. It was like she knew exactly what I needed to wear. I didn't turn down one thing she picked out. My suit, my shoes, everything fits perfectly."

Riverstone admired his girlbob with a father-like pride. "She is remarkable."

Phoebe tapped the girlbob on the shoulder. "Thank you, Alice."

Alice's lighted brim glowed slightly brighter as she tipped her triangular head toward the couple. Phoebe looked briefly away to admire the sleeve of her jumpsuit, and when she looked back again, Alice had vanished.

Phoebe was startled. "Oh, my, where did she go?"

Riverstone smiled. "She's still around. Just call her name and she'll be there for you."

"That's it? She'll know when I need her? No buttons to press? No bells to ring? Just say her name?"

They left her room and started walking down the corridor together. "You got it. It just takes some getting used to."

Phoebe grabbed Riverstone's arm. "So where are we off to first, my handsome young man?"

As much as they had been together the last few weeks, Riverstone was still a little anxious around the famous star. "Your hands are cold. Do I make you nervous, Matthew?"

Riverstone didn't know how to answer her and stay cool about it. "Kinda…"

She stopped him and kinked her head up. He was so tall and striking in his uniform. She had never been with anyone so physically attractive. It almost took her breath away to stand next to him. "I'm sorry. It comes with the territory. I think I'm okay, but my relationships never last long. Two weeks, a month. That's it. Poof, they're gone. My therapist thinks I need to date someone outside the business." She sighed looking briefly away before she asked a bomb. "You're not really an actor are you?"

"No, not even close."

She clapped. "Perfect! Can we make a go of it then?"

Riverstone leaned down and kissed her long and passionately. "That answer your question?"

Phoebe took his hands again. "Totally. And you're hands are warming up, too," she said with a coy smirk, as they continued walking. "How tall are you?"

"Six-seven the last I checked."

"You're still growing?"

"Not so much now."

"Hollywood guys are always short. I'm always patting them on the head. But you... You're way up there."

"You want me to pat your head?" Riverstone kidded.

Phoebe giggled. "That would be a change."

As they went along, Phoebe asked more questions, and, when he got the chance, he asked her about life as a famous actress. Along the way he showed her the medical room with long tables she found hard to believe would hold her purse, much less a body. But when he grabbed her by the waist and lifted her up like she weighed nothing at all, she was amazed at how solid and sturdy the table was.

"Are we going to play doctor?" she asked, bringing him closer.

Riverstone pointed at the wall that was now blazing with glowing screens of internal organs. It was as if someone had taken a miniature x-ray GoPro and was videotaping her insides in real time.

"Whoa! Is that me?" Phoebe asked with her mouth agape. For the first time she was silent for more than twenty seconds.

"Wave your hand at the screen," Riverstone directed.

And when she did, the hand on the screen, the muscles, the tendons, bones, and blood vessels all moved with her.

She turned to Riverstone. "Will our dream end soon?" she asked almost ready to cry.

Riverstone studied every holograph with care. What he saw gave him great concern, the yellow and red discoloration of her infection should have shown up clearly on the screen. Had Millie already stepped in when she was unconscious and removed her tumors from her body? He shut his eyes, thanking his wonderful ship. Prigg and Leucadia could tell him more. They understood the readouts and what they were telling him. But even he, with his limited knowledge of the medical room, could see Phoebe appeared disease free. He gave her a confident hug and kiss, "You're going to be all right, Phoebs."

She twisted around to the screens. "What do you mean, I'll be all right?"

"My ship has the latest technology, and while you were resting, she repaired what was wrong with you."

Phoebe slid off the table without Riverstone's help. "Can we go now?" She appeared to have lost some of her cheerfulness.

For months she had been living with the idea that she was about to die, and to suddenly be told by someone who wasn't a doctor that she was cured, was hardly a laughing matter to her. They continued walking, not saying a word until Phoebe asked, "How big is this ship, anyway?"

"Big," Riverstone replied.

"You said that." Phoebe said with an edge. "I thought we would be there by now. I could use some air."

Riverstone stopped in the middle of an intersection of two corridors. There was no easy way around it. He had to risk telling her knowing he would be an instant toad in her eyes. That was a risk he had to take if they were to survive this together. When she found out later, and she would, he would be a bigger toad. Either way, he was toast. There would never be a walk along the corridors again. No holding hands, no kissing, no tiramisu by the pool. Their relationship would end before it got off the ground if he didn't come completely clean. It was like a bandage over a wound. His dad used to say; "Better to rip it off quick and get the pain overwith, son than to suffer slowly." In this case it felt like thousand cuts to his heart was more like it.

Phoebe saw the angst in Riverstone's face. "You saw it back there in that medical place, didn't you?"

"I'm not sure—"

She wouldn't let him finish. "You know about my heart."

"I saw something, yeah, but—"

"Listen, you have to promise me, you're not going to tell anyone. You can't, Matthew—"

He covered her mouth with his hand. "Would you stop talking for just one lousy minute?"

She had never been told that before, ever! She was someone of privilege. She told people what to do and when to speak. No one had ever told her to shut up like that. She tried to break free of his hold, but nothing she did could release her. Finally, she relaxed her shoulders and nodded.

"Good." Riverstone removed his hand and said, "Your heart is fine. I told you the truth. You have no more disease in you. Understand? You're not going to die. At least not now."

"When?"

"A hundred years, I hope."

"That's not possible. I've seen my MRI scans. I'm going to die!"

"No you're not, and I'll prove it to you."

"How?"

"By showing you something that will blow your socks off."

"Now you're scaring me," Phoebe said.

"I'm trying not to, but that thick head of yours has to listen for once."

Phoebe pushed his arms aside and came next to him, snuggling next to him with her sprayed on jumpsuit. It was like they were touching skin. "I'm a big girl. Tell me what I'm not going to believe…" Her bright blue-green eyes gazed sensually into his. As strong as he was, he was suffering what Harlowe often called a "weak moment." If she told him to swim through shark-infested water to get her lemonade, he would do it in a heartbeat.

"We're on a ship," he gutted out.

"I got that. We've docked, everything's cool, and soon we'll be in a limo to take me home. What's the big deal? Why so glum?"

"It's not that kind of a ship, Phoebs, not a cruise ship, Millie…I mean *Millawanda* is a starship, and we're traveling back to Earth from another planet, where we dropped off some swampdaks."

She stared at him without blinking, trying to digest what he was trying to tell to her. Swampdaks were not part of her vocabulary, but she did have questions about a spaceship. "Can I talk now?" she asked.

Riverstone nodded. "Yeah… Your turn."

"We're on a spaceship, correct?"

"A really big one."

"You sound like someone out of Simy's movies," Phoebe stated.

"Well, did you see Bolt's last movie…*Distant Galaxy?*"

"Three times. It was the coolest sci-fi flick I've ever seen. His crew was soooo hot."

"The movie was about us . . . and this ship. We're the real deal, Phoebs. Those guys in the movie are us. Simon, too, and the lives we lead every day."

Phoebe hardly breathed. She began to back away and bumped into something huge and furry. When she turned around, two giant blue eyes were staring at her, nose-to-nose. She leaped into Riverstone's arms, screaming at the top of her lungs, "ARE YOU KIDDING ME!!!"

"It's okay. It's okay, Phoebs."

"IT'S DEFINITELY NOT OKAY!"

"Molly meet Phoebs. She's a friend of mine."

Molly sauntered over and rubbed her head against Riverstone and Phoebe with her motor running full tilt.

"See. She's just a lovable little puddy tat," Riverstone said, caressing the fluffy white mane that was as high at his shoulder.

"There's nothing little about her!"

With Phoebe still in his arms, Riverstone carried her to a large, arched doorway. He touched an activator with her foot, and the door slid gracefully away. As they entered the large room of overstuffed chairs, lounges, cool coffee tables made of a blue crystalline stone, and the most incredible blue-wood piano Phoebe had ever seen, Molly remained outside, giving them their privacy.

Phoebe said, awed by the furnishings, "This room is so beautiful, Matthew."

Riverstone turned her toward the immense observation window where a heaven full of a billion, billion points of light looked down upon them. *Millawanda* was sliding between two moons of the unknown planet on her way to another yellow star a short, four light-years away.

"As beautiful as this, Phoebs?" he asked.

"OH…MY…GODDDDD!"

73

Dinner for Two

Aztec, New Mexico

ANN SAW THE long blue limousine pull into the parking lot. It was almost quitting time. A red sunset appeared like fire on the horizon. All she had to do was restock some items on the shelves, lock up, and she could go home. She was in no hurry, though, so whatever the limo wanted she would remain open until they were done shopping. She turned back to her restocking as the little dinger bell went off, indicating that someone had entered the store.

"Welcome to Kare Drug Store," Ann said to the shopper. She turned around to the customer to add, "How may I help…" But those were the last words she was able to say before she collided with the tall hunk standing over her.

"Is this a bad time," he asked.

"Dodge?"

"I could come back later."

She slammed a fist into his shoulder then grabbed him by the shirt and kissed him hard. "You're not going anywhere, Mister. I didn't think I would ever see you again."

"I've had an interesting few weeks. If that dinner date is still on…"

"Ya dang straight it is! Wait right there. Don't move . . . not one inch," she ordered. She ran to the back of the store, turned out the lights, set the alarm, ran over to the register, checked out, grabbed her purse, and waved at Dodge to follow her out the door. She stuck the key in the lock and forgot something. "Wait!" She popped back in and turned the "We're Open" sign around to "Sorry, We're Closed" and rushed back out to finish closing up.

Dodge laughed. "I've never seen anyone move that fast."

Ann giggled innocently. "I was afraid you would disappear if I took too long."

He kissed her this time. "Not a chance," and led her to the limo.

"Is this yours?" she asked.

"My brother's."

She pointed at the robob driver. "Who's that?"

"Clicker."

Ann waved. "Hi Clicker." The robob politely nodded and waved back.

"How cute. Where should we go? There's no place in town that I know of, and I'm certainly not dressed for anything in Aztec."

Dodge opened the door to the limo. "I've got us covered, and you're beautiful just the way you are."

Ann was about to climb in when she stopped, eyeballing the small, white linen table, crystal glasses, silverware, and beautiful blue and gold plates. A single candle burned in the middle of the table with two long stem red roses lying next to it.

"For us?" Ann asked, holding her chest.

"I hope you like grilled sea bass, sautéed vegetables, and brown rice."

"Do I!"

They sat down. Dodge, because of his size, had to put his legs to one side, but there was plenty of room for her.

"Where would you like to go?" Dodge asked.

"I don't care. If we ate here, I would be perfectly happy," Ann replied.

"Well, we can do better than that. Clicker," he called to the robob in front, "take the long way home for the lady, if you please."

74

Walk with Me

THE SMALL CROWD sat quietly as Harlowe completed a flawless performance of Chopin's Nocturne in E-flat major, Op. 9, No. 2. on the blue-wood piano. Beneath the massive window in the forward observation room, his mother, Tinker, and the former President of the United States, Peter Delmonte, Generals Branch and Van Dyke, and Admiral Meads, remained quiet, not one word of "well-played" salutations. Harlowe traded puzzled looks with Leucadia. Had he missed a note? Was he off-key? What? She gave him a small shrug. She didn't understand either. He had played the piece as well as she had ever heard him. Why they were seemingly unappreciative was baffling, until they saw that their faces were full of admiration, and they were unable to move, much less clap. Slowly, the audience surrounded him at the piano. President Delmonte spoke first, "I've never heard Chopin performed so beautifully, Harlowe."

"Thank you, Mr. President," Harlowe said.

"Your mom never told me you played."

Tinker put her arms around him. "That's because I've never seen him play anything but sports," she said, teary-eyed and proud. "You are amazing, son."

Harlowe stood. "Thank you, Mom." He then addressed his guests and apologized for making it an early evening, giving, "I need to check in with the bridge before I go to my cabin," as an excuse. The small crowd thanked him again for a wonderful performance. On his way out, Harlowe took Van Dyke aside and said, "Walk with me, General." Harlowe's grip on his shoulder implied it was not a request. They stepped into the corridor and walked a short distance before Harlowe stopped and faced Van Dyke.

"If this is about us joy-riding in the Granny—" Van Dyke tried to say, before Harlowe cut him off with a wave of his hand.

"What do you know about the Crodo Quadrant and the Dawash group of planets, General?" Harlowe knew the answer. He forced an all-knowing grin, and added with a smirk, and a wink, "Captain Sextonis gives his regards."

Van Dyke turned rigid, his mouth dropped, mouthing something but speaking nothing.

Harlowe pointed at a framed sign on the wall, and stated, "This is the Gamacode. Study it. Memorize it. Know every word, for you will be enforcing it on this planet . . . and yours. " He kept walking, not looking back, stepped on a blinker, and winked away.

Gamacode

PREAMBLE: THE GAMACODE IS LAW. ALL GOVERNING BODIES (GB) WILL OBEY THE GAMACODE. A GOVERNING BODY IS ANY INDIVIDUAL (*ie*. DICTATOR, PRESIDENT, OR MONARCH *et al*) OR GROUP OF REPRESENTATIVES THAT HAVE AUTHORITY OVER SENTIENT BEINGS.

1. NO GB CAN INTERFERE WITH A BEING'S INHERENT AND INALIENABLE RIGHT TO ENJOY A LIFE FREE OF OPPRESSION.
2. A GB CANNOT INTERFERE WITH A BEING'S ABSOLUTE RIGHT TO ARM, PROTECT, AND DEFEND ONE'S PERSON, FAMILY, COMMUNITY, OR PROPERTY.
3. THE GB WILL BE LOCAL, ACCOUNTABLE, FULLY OPEN AND TRANSPARENT WHERE THE RIGHT OF PUBLIC SCRUTINY SHALL NOT BE DENIED.
4. NO GB CAN INTERFERE WITH A BEING'S RIGHT TO ACQUIRE, SELL, POSSESS, AND ENJOY PRIVATE PROPERTY.
5. IT IS GB'S DUTY TO ENSURE A BEING'S RIGHT TO DUE PROCESS.
6. THE GB CANNOT PASS ANY LAW FORBIDDING FREEDOM OF SPEECH OR TO CONGREGATE "PEACEFULLY."
7. THE GB CANNOT SUPPRESS A BEING'S RIGHT TO FREEDOM OF WORSHIP.
8. NO GB HAS THE POWER TO CREATE MONEY.
9. NO GB HAS THE POWER TO ESTABLISH A CENTRAL BANK.
10. NO GB HAS THE POWER TO TAX OR LEVY A PERSON, PROPERTY, OR BUSINESS.
11. NO GB AND ITS WORKFORCE CAN BE GREATER THAN ONE, ONE-THOUSANDTH (.001) PERCENT OF THE POPULATION.
12. NO GB ELECTED OFFICIAL OR REPRESENTATIVE MAY SERVE MORE THAN ONE, THREE-YEAR TERM IN THEIR LIFETIME.
13. GBs DO NOT HAVE RIGHTS, THEY HAVE A DUTY TO THE BEINGS THEY REPRESENT, AND THE GAMACODE.
14. GBs ARE SUBJECT TO THE LAWS THEY PASS.
15. NO GB HAS THE POWER TO CREATE A WELFARE STATE.
16. NO GB HAS THE POWER TO PROSECUTE.
17. NO GB CAN ISSUE DEBT OR OPERATE IN A DEFICIT.
18. NO GB HAS THE RIGHT TO OWN LAND.
19. NO GB HAS THE POWER TO CREATE A SECRET, CLANDESTINE ORGANIZATION OR MILITARY FORCE.
20. NO GB CAN REVOKE THE GAMACODE.
21. WHAT THE GAMACODE DOES NOT COVER IS LEFT TO THE GB OF THE PARTICULAR SOCIETY, COUNTRY, OR STATE THEY REPRESENT, TO RUN AS THEY CHOOSE, AS LONG AS THE GAMACODE IS NOT VIOLATED.

CONCLUSION: THE GAMACODE IS ABSOLUTE AND UNEQUIVOCAL. THE GAMACODE DOES NOT REQUIRE TRUST OR ACCEPTANCE. NO ENTITY, BEING, OR GOVERNING BODY IS EXEMPT. THE GAMACODE IS NOT AMENDABLE. THE GAMACODE IS NOT LIVING, TRANSITIONAL, OR TEMPORARY. THE GAMACODE IS ENDURING AND FOREVER. GOVERNING BODIES AND/OR INDIVIDUALS VIOLATING THE GAMACODE WILL BE IMMEDIATELY EXCOMMUNICATED TO A WORLD OTHER THAN THEIR OWN WITH NO RECOURSE OF RETURN.

HARLOWE PYLOTT, CAPTAIN
GAMADIN STARSHIP, *Millawanda*
EFFECTIVE IMMEDIATELY

Coming in 2018 . . .
the Prequil

Author, **Tom Kirkbride**, grewup in Southern California and has a degree in Economics from San Diego State University. When Tom is not working on the next sci-fi adventure, he enjoys touring the country, speaking with students and meeting with Gamadin fans. Tom presently lives on a northwest ranch with his wife, their dog Jack, two horses, Baily and Andy, and "still" too many cats.

www.ingramcontent.com/pod-product-compliance
Lightning Source LLC
Chambersburg PA
CBHW021845010726
47493CB00005B/1567

* 9 7 8 0 9 8 8 3 6 3 3 3 5 *